WHILE JUSTICE SLEEPS

ALSO BY STACEY ABRAMS

Our Time Is Now

Lead from the Outside

WHILE JUSTICE SLEEPS

A Novel

STACEY ABRAMS

DOUBLEDAY · NEW YORK

Copyright © 2021 by Stacey Y. Abrams

All rights reserved. Published in the United States by Doubleday,
a division of Penguin Random House LLC, New York, and distributed in Canada
by Penguin Random House Canada Limited, Toronto.

www.doubleday.com

DOUBLEDAY and the portrayal of an anchor with a dolphin
are registered trademarks of Penguin Random House LLC.

Jacket photograph by cmcderm1 / iStock / Getty Images; background from Shutterstock
Jacket design by Emily Mahon
Book design by Maggie Hinders

Library of Congress Cataloging-in-Publication Data
Names: Abrams, Stacey, author.
Title: While justice sleeps : a novel / Stacey Y. Abrams.
Description: First edition. | New York : Doubleday, [2021]
Identifiers: LCCN 2020046349 (print) | LCCN 2020046350 (ebook) |
ISBN 9780385546577 (hardcover) | ISBN 9780385546584 (ebook)
Subjects: LCSH: Law clerks—Fiction. | United States. Supreme Court—Fiction. |
Washington (D.C.)—Fiction. | GSAFD: Suspense fiction. | LCGFT: Political fiction.
Classification: LCC PS3601.B746 W45 2021 (print) | LCC PS3601.B746 (ebook) |
DDC 813/.6—dc23
LC record available at https://lccn.loc.gov/2020046349
LC ebook record available at https://lccn.loc.gov/2020046350

MANUFACTURED IN THE UNITED STATES OF AMERICA

5 7 9 10 8 6 4

First Edition

To the ones who taught me to love a good story, my parents, Carolyn and Robert Abrams. To those who help me tell the new stories, my siblings, Andrea, Leslie, Richard, Walter, and Jeanine. And to my nephews and nieces, Jorden, Faith, Cameron, Riyan, Ayren, and Devin, whose stories are yet to be told.

Chess grips its exponent, shackling the mind and brain so that the inner freedom and independence of even the strongest character cannot remain unaffected.

—attributed to ALBERT EINSTEIN

WHILE JUSTICE SLEEPS

PROLOGUE

His brain died at 11:47 p.m.

At nine o'clock on Sunday night, Supreme Court justice Howard Wynn shifted testily in his favorite leather chair, the high-backed Chesterfield purportedly commissioned by Chief Justice William Howard Taft. The wide seat resembled a settee more than a chair, but the latter Howard appreciated the capacious width. Unlike the robust former president, Justice Wynn was built along trimmer lines, a sleek sloop to the fearsome cargo ship of a man who preceded him on the bench. But he enjoyed the chair for its unexpected utility. Extra space at his hip for the books he habitually tucked to his side, on the off chance the chosen tome for his nightly read bored him.

Howard Wynn did not suffer boredom or mediocrity well.

He felt equally dismissive of willful ignorance—his description of the modern press—and smug stupidity, his bon mot for politicians. To his mind, they were a gang of vapid and arrogant thugs all, who greedily snatched their information from one another like disappearing crumbs as society spiraled merrily toward hell. With the current crop of pundits, bureaucrats, and hired guns in charge, America was destined to repeat the cycles of intellectual torpor that toppled Rome and Greece and Mali and the Incas and every empire that stumbled into short-lived, debauched existence. Show man ignoble work and easy sex, and there went civilization.

"A righteous flood, that's what we need," he muttered into the dimly lit study. "Drown the bastards out."

Behind him, a chessboard stood in mid-play, the antique wooden pieces beginning to attract particles of dust from disuse. Once, he'd played the game with a ferocity that rivaled that of grandmasters, a prodigy in his youth. Careful maneuvers and contemplations of end-games had been sufficient until he learned that he could do the same in real life, when his mind became destined for the law. The game in progress was with a man he'd never met, who lived half a world away. But even his new friend had deserted him to this last room of refuge.

The door to the study had been shut tight for hours, leaving him alone in his sanctuary. Beyond the study, an early summer storm rattled the windows. White flashed in the distance, and then came the inevitable bark of thunder. Wynn nodded in weary recognition of the tumult. To drown the thunder, he turned on the small television he kept in the room. As a rule, he despised the idiot box, but now he reluctantly acknowledged its utility. Tonight, it would tell him if he'd destroyed his life's mission or saved it.

A commercial offered discount car insurance, followed by the opening graphics for a popular evening talk show of comedic and political invective. Wynn watched with hawkish eyes as the host wasted no time before launching his shtick. "And earlier today . . . the epic meltdown at American University by Justice Howard Wynn . . . or, perhaps he should be called Justice 'Where the Hell Am I?'"

The studio audience roared with laughter as the screen flickered to a shot of Wynn speaking that afternoon at the university's commencement ceremony. He'd done this countless times, offering pithy lies about the promise of the next generation. The clip caught him as he leaned over the podium, clad in his academic regalia—simply another meaningless black robe. A tight shot of his face flashed on-screen, mouth sneering.

"Science is the greatest trick the Devil ever played on man!" he pronounced to the undergraduates squirming uncomfortably in their metal chairs. The man he watched on-screen lifted his fist in anger. "He let us believe we could control our destiny, but we've only built our demise. Breaking the laws of nature to construct a shrine to Satan's handiwork. We must be stopped!"

The television screen filled to frame a shot of a stone-faced Brandon Stokes, the president of the United States, staring stoically ahead as Justice Wynn raged on. The graduation of the president's youngest daughter had brought him to the festivities, and he'd graciously agreed to share the podium with the jurist who reveled in swatting down his initiatives and eviscerating the laws signed by his administration. The animus between the men had been the source of great debate at the college—one brought to a head by Zoe Stokes's unexpected early graduation, fulfilled by a recalculation of her study-abroad hours. With the invitation to the Supreme Court justice already accepted, the college had no graceful way to rescind his speaking engagement.

Wynn stared at the crowd, his face frozen in irascibility. In the next image, clearly realizing her grave error, the college's president warily approached from the side of the podium, extending her hand in the universal gesture of *nice doggy*. Her voice was faint but clearly heard by the cameraman. "Justice Wynn? Are you okay?"

Wynn spun around and swatted at the proffered hand, his voice dismissive. "Of course I'm not. I'm trying to warn you of the coming apocalypse, and you want me to tell these children that the world awaits them. What waits is death. It will come for the others first, but the Devil will have his due."

At that point, uncomfortable murmurs spread through the crowd, peppered with chuckles of derision, and Wynn turned back once more. "Laugh if you will, you carrion of society. But mark my words—hell has come to earth, and your parents have elected its offspring."

With that, he shoved his hand into his pocket and glared at President Stokes, then marched toward him. Yanking his hand free from his pocket, Justice Wynn stopped in front of Stokes and extended his right hand. The president came awkwardly to his feet and accepted the gesture, and the justice muttered something near his ear.

The video played the strained handshake before the justice stalked offstage, trailed by the clearly distraught college president.

"Not sure what Justice Wynn whispered there, but I think it's safe to say he won't be endorsing the president for reelection," deadpanned the late-night host, to raucous applause. "They call Justice Wynn the 'Voice of the People,' but now everyone is wondering if he's the one hearing voices. He's known for riding the subway in DC, but this makes me wonder if he'll be living in the tunnels soon. Scary that he's the swing vote on some big decisions the Court will make this month. And even scarier is that he's probably not the worst one. I wonder if they'll give him his own reality show, *Crazy Justice*." Laughter followed, and Wynn flicked off the television.

"Funny man," he muttered to himself, staring again at the storm raging beyond the windows. "Thoreau had it right about nature versus man. Nature always wins." As he spoke in the empty room, his voice held no venom, only resignation. Nature, he knew, was a crafty adversary. While a man slept peacefully in his bed, Nature rummaged through tissue and cell down to chromosomes so slight as to be invisible. With a capricious flick, it switched on the time bomb that would explode a man's life. A man's brain.

"Leaving me a mewling, puking shadow of myself for others to feed upon like viscera," he acknowledged morosely. No one replied. Too often, these days, his conversations spun out to meet no response.

They'd all left him. One wife dead, another deserted. His only son despised him.

The Court was no better. A collection of sycophants and despisers, plotting against him. Pretending to care about him. But he'd discovered the way to do what must be done, and the few to whom he could entrust the tasks ahead.

Wynn struggled from the chair and crossed to a bookshelf. He shifted the books to the carpet. The task was harder than it should have been. With a glance over his shoulder, he checked that the door was still closed.

"Don't want that sneaky viper to creep up on me and steal more of my secrets," he muttered. Wynn entered the combination to the safe. The lock popped quietly and flashed its green entry signal. He tugged at the handle.

Inside, the contents were exactly as he'd left them. Soon, though, he'd forget what lay inside. Worse, he'd forget that he even had a safe and the other hiding places he'd set across the whorish town. Places that might betray him by refusing to be found. Such was his fated end. From brilliant jurist to a hollowed-out shell of a man chased by shadows, betrayed by memory.

Time had winnowed itself down to nothingness. At some point, his enemies would attempt to rush him toward death, but he knew a secret. Between the end and now lay uncharted territory that he alone had begun to map. His enemies would try to follow him, but they would fail. All except the ones who could follow the breadcrumbs.

Each term, the U.S. Supreme Court held its hearings and issued its edicts like gods from Olympus. By law, they commenced their deliberations on the first Monday in October, parceling out times for lawyers and the wretched they represented to beg the indulgence of him and his fellow jurists. But the clock struck midnight at the end of June, shutting the door on deliverance or condemnation. By tradition, they parceled out their weightiest decisions in those final weeks, occasionally eking into July, but never during his tenure. No, June 30 was his D-Day, his Waterloo, his checkmate.

He slammed the safe door shut and leaned heavily against the cold metal, his forehead pressed against his lifted arm. What if she couldn't finish it? If they too got lost, like he had. Perhaps if he told the Chief what he'd done, what he'd learned, she'd be able to help him. But if she knew, she'd be honor-bound to stop him. Deny him this last act of penance.

Part of him recognized the argument swirling in his head. A vicious tug-of-war he scarcely recalled from day to day. The neurologist had warned him that the symptoms would worsen. That the shadows in his once-clear mind would grow fangs and horns. That he would see enemies.

No, he reminded himself. There were enemies. Enemies he had to fight. Because if he told the truth, they might not believe him. Worse, they would destroy the truth. Too many doctors whispering about his deteriorating health, about paranoia and anxiety and conspiracy brought on by neurological disease.

It was better this way, to wait and see if his opponents accepted his King's Gambit. An opening sacrifice to strengthen his game. The White House thought itself so clever. Use his body's own betrayal against him. Send in a spy to watch his moves and figure out what he'd learned. Executive privilege versus the great jurist Howard Wynn? *Pah!*

Filled with adrenaline, Wynn replaced the books, opened the study door, and returned to his chair. His mind was made up. *Again.* He would play the labyrinthine game the law demanded, and he would win. They wouldn't stop him.

Abruptly, the anxiety sharpened, its razor claws slicing through reason in his suddenly clouded thoughts. Wynn jerked upright and hissed into the empty room, "You want to kill me, don't you? Silence me?" He punched the air with an angry, shaking fist. "I know what you've done. How you've lied to us! Soon enough, I'll prove it, and even your guard dogs won't be able to save you!"

"Justice Wynn? Who are you talking to?" At the doorway to the study, his nurse appeared and frowned at the outburst. "Are you on the phone?"

The clouds receded, and he snarled, "I am conversing with Nature, woman. Smartest companion I am likely to encounter in this house."

Unconvinced, his nurse, Jamie Lewis, crossed the threshold. She plastered on a smile. "It's time for your medication and for bed, Justice. You need your rest. You had a long day today, and I don't want you too tuckered to go to work tomorrow. Busy week."

Wynn slapped the arm of the Chesterfield chair with a satisfying crack. "I'm not a goddamned child, Nurse Lewis. I don't need to be coaxed into bed like a whelp in diapers. I sit on the bench of the United States Supreme Court."

"Yes, you do." Jamie edged closer, her crepe-soled shoes silent on the hardwood. Only her pale yellow skirt made a whisper of sound as she closed the distance between them. With the dulcet smile that she knew would irritate, she cooed, "You're a fine lawyer, Justice Wynn. God knows, I've met enough of them, thanks to Thomas." She gave a false laugh. "Perhaps I should have married a doctor, not a salesman."

"A doctor? Scoundrels!" This time, the smack of his hand echoed for an instant. "Damned charlatans . . . refusing to do an honest day's labor. Off golfing and finding diseases that were never lost."

"Doctors are important, Justice. As important as lawyers, I'd wager. They're keeping you here, aren't they?"

"There's no comparison," he barked. "Jurisprudence is one of the last pure métiers of Western creation, like the blues or bid whist. I find modern physicians only slightly more capable than leeches and witches' cauldrons. Eight years of training, and still they only barely practice at their craft!"

"Don't lawyers practice the law?"

"When we stumble, no one dies." His hand trembled as he flipped defiantly through the musty pages of *Faust* and knew he had lied. "Doctors are nothing but cranks and convicts roaming the earth, telling lies to the healthy. Gathering corpses for their experiments."

Bushy eyebrows, twin shocks of alabaster against bronzed skin, lifted and lowered in rage. "But then, that's not much better than this new crop of lawyers roaming the Court. A generation laid to waste by the putrescence of their own thoughts. Not an incisive mind among them. Computer-addled miscreants who'd rather be told the answer than investigate. Can barely find one smart enough to fetch my coffee."

"I thought you liked Mr. Brewer and Ms. Keene," Jamie reminded him, standing at his elbow. His rant slid into a cough, and soon would warble off into mutterings. To urge the sequence along, she poked: "Just yesterday, you told me Ms. Keene was a bright young scholar worth watching."

"I said no such thing!" He levered himself into a fighting stance and spat, "Don't tell me I've said things I didn't say. Especially about persons whom you are ill-equipped to hold small talk with, let alone discuss their relative cerebral merit, *Nurse* Lewis." He sneered her title and clutched her arm, desperately afraid that he had indeed paid the glowing compliment about one of his clerks.

Too often, these days, he could not remember his own words from moment to moment. Or from afternoon to night.

Wynn glanced up to find the nurse watching him, checking him for signs of dementia or the coming of death. *Had he finished his sentence? How long had he been silent?* "Stop staring at me!" he snapped and tightened his hold on her muscular arm.

Jamie obliged and looked away before he could see her worry. His lapses were coming more frequently now. One day, the lapse would freeze in time. She'd seen it once before. Boursin's syndrome was the name of the disease, and she could read its trek in Justice Wynn's panicked eyes. Gently, she probed, "What were we discussing, Justice?"

"Why? So you can report me to the president or whatever goon sent you to spy on me?" He snorted derisively. "Did I go too far at the graduation? Have they told you to kill me?"

The nurse blanched. "Sir?"

"Of course you're spying on me," he told her gruffly. "I may be paranoid and dying, but I am not stupid."

"You believe I would kill you?"

"Nothing so bold and direct. You simply write down your observations and pass them along, in violation of medical privilege, building their case against me."

"Sir—"

"I assume they make you report on my impending demise on a regular basis. Probably have you reading my papers at night, snapping photos so they know what I'm doing. Would love to have you tape me, but their surveillance can't get inside. That interloper in the White House is afraid I'm going to crush his dreams, and they sent you to keep tabs on me. My speech today must have him cursing my name."

Her eyes widened. "I don't know what—"

"Don't lie to me!" he barked. "For God's sake, be the last exemplar of honesty left in this house." A cough rattled through him, and he bowed his head as his lungs struggled for air. "How did they turn you? A bribe or a threat? Did they use your husband?"

The flush turned pale and the nurse's head hung slightly. "Thomas is in trouble again. They're considering arresting him for some scam. He swears he didn't do it," she whispered. "I didn't have a choice."

"You had a choice, Nurse Lewis," he corrected tersely. "You simply chose the living over the dead."

"They want to know if you can do your job, sir. If you still have the capacity to function. That tantrum at the commencement didn't help."

"That was no tantrum, you silly cow! It was strategy. It's all strategy. Opening move of the King's Gambit! Every breath is a movement toward the endgame." His eyes widened, and he shook his fist. "Did you tell them about my research? That I know what happened?"

Jamie frowned in genuine confusion. "Research? For the Court?"

"Of course for the Court! Why else would they have you here? I am a threat to national security, but one they can't prove without admitting what they've done. So the White House trespasser sends in his carrier pigeons to watch me like a hawk. I know their secret!"

"Justice, you're not making sense. Please, sit down."

"I won't sit, and I won't be silenced!" The bellow carried an edge of hysteria. He thought again about his estranged son. "They can't kill my boy with their lies!"

"No one is trying to kill Jared," Jamie soothed, her hand stroking his stiffened back. "Please, Justice, calm down."

"It's a prisoner's dilemma," he whispered as his voice shook. "My son's life for their defeat. But I've outsmarted them. Lasker-Bauer, which they will never suspect."

"Lask Bauer? Who is he?"

"Not he, you simpleton. In the middle game, both bishops will die to save him. To save the endgame."

"Who are the bishops?" Jamie frowned in confusion and gripped his shoulder. "Justice Wynn, who am I?"

"Leave me be!"

Jamie leaned closer and demanded, "Who am I?"

His eyes snapped to hers, his mind clearing. He snarled, "Someone I cannot trust. I can't trust anyone anymore."

"I'm here to help you."

"Liar. You're telling them I'm crazy. That I'm infirm. I am still strong, madam. Stronger than he is." Still, agitation knotted his belly. If the call came on the right day, a day when he'd forgotten his plan, he might accept their demands and ruin everything he'd so carefully plotted.

Not yet. By God, not yet. Forcing his once-agile mind to focus, Justice Wynn summoned the thread of his conversation with Nurse Lewis. "Stop staring at me."

"What were we talking about?"

"Before you admitted your perfidy, we were discussing the intellectual capacity of my law clerks, and I made a reference to a strategy beyond your grasp. And for the record, Ms. Keene is no better and no worse than the rest of her kind. Her sole differentiation is the glimmer of *potential* she tries to hide. Otherwise, she is as bright as one can expect given the utter absence of scholarship among her tutors."

Jamie closed plump, steady fingers around Justice Wynn's upper arm and steered him to the open door. "I thought she went to Yale? Isn't that a good school?"

"A cesspool, just like Harvard, Stanford, or any other bastion of education in this end of days. A sea of sloppy thinking posing as legal education." He stumbled and caught himself on the hallway wall. "No wonder lawyers want strict construction of the Constitution. Hell, that way, it's already written down for their feeble minds."

At the staircase, Jamie nudged him to the left. Wynn halted beneath a framed photo displaying a sweep of glacier, the blue vibrant and grand. Remembering their earlier exchange, he shook his head. "Knowing the law isn't about the school. It's about the mind. The heart. About understanding what the law intends as much as reading beneath what it says. Knowing how to find one's way to the truth." He breathed deep, resting more of his weight on Jamie's sturdy frame, confident she'd hold.

He lifted his eyes to meet hers. Staring intently, he demanded, "Do you like Avery?"

She nodded hesitantly. "She's impressive. Well-spoken."

"That's all you can say?"

With a shrug, Jamie countered, "Well, she has a bit of an attitude, if you ask me. Tough. Not like that charming Mr. Brewer. He's going places. I can tell."

"Brewer will build shallow empires," Wynn snorted. "But Ms. Keene is a smart girl. Very smart. A bit preoccupied with proving herself, but she's got a brain that she occasionally puts to use. Could be brilliant if she were a more precise thinker."

"More precise?"

"Precise, Nurse. A condition you have yet to stumble into." Forcing his spine erect, he yanked his hand free. "I'm not an invalid. I can take myself to bed. Get me those pills of poison they've told you to foist upon me."

"Yes, sir." She propped open the bedroom door and waited as he lumbered through. "Why don't you slip into your pajamas, and I'll bring your medication in two shakes?"

"Don't condescend to me, woman. I'm dying, not senile. I can hear your feeble attempts at patronization before they pass your lips."

"I've laid the black pajamas on the bed. Do you need any help?"

"Only if it means I get a replacement for you." Wynn glared at her retreating form. "Bring me a goddamned whiskey with my death pills."

.   .   .

Eleven o'clock arrived before the private nurse crept into his room and discovered the open, vacant gaze, felt the reedy pulse that slouched through veins constricted by disease. She knelt beside him and winced as something bit into her flesh. Shifting her knee, she reached for the lamp with one hand and for the foreign object with the other. Her fingers closed over a pill bottle top that had fallen to the carpet. Raising it to the light, she saw the colored stripe she'd placed there herself and gasped. She reached under the bed, searching frantically for the bottle she knew she'd find.

The plastic bottle knocked against her hand and she drew it out, the label confirming her worst fears. He'd taken pills prescribed for the seizures that occasionally convulsed his limbs. Alone, the medication was dangerous, but when combined with his other meds and alcohol, the dose could be lethal. She groped under the bed, scooping up fallen pills, but she wouldn't know how many were missing until she checked her charts.

But the evidence was clear. Justice Wynn had tried to kill himself.

Guilt clutched at her throat, forcing her eyes to the man she'd come to respect, even like, despite his fiery temperament. The promise of freedom and stability for her husband, Thomas, funded by the U.S. government, had seemed adequate justification for betrayal when she had accepted the post and her instructions. Become caretaker for a powerful but sick old man whose illness was slowly rendering him a security risk. Monitor his writings, report on his status weekly, and act when instructed. But that had been before she knew Howard Wynn.

Now her hands clenched around the disposable cell phone.

The number she was supposed to call, once she had confirmation that he was near death, had been drilled into her. A call, once made, that would guarantee he never awoke. She hesitated, unwilling to be the one to betray him as he suspected, but she told herself it was done now. Too late to undo the bargain she'd made. First, though, she'd check and be sure.

Pressing her stethoscope to his lungs, she heard labored breath sounds. The plastic cuff around his leaden arm registered a low blood pressure. She flicked the pen light with practiced care. Minimal response to light. In short order, she ran each test that would confirm his imminent death.

The whispered words caught her by surprise.

"She has to finish it. For him."

Instruments tumbled to the carpet, and she knelt again, this time in shock. "Justice Wynn?"

A feeble hand jerked up and seized her sleeve. "I'm not dead. Though you can try."

"I didn't want to—" Her fingers closed over the cold, trembling ones on her arm. "You took pills—"

"No time for excuses." A hacking cough shook through him. "Avery has to save us. Swear it!"

"Let me call the ambulance," she whispered, fumbling. "I'm so sorry!"

"It's too late for apologies," he wheezed as his eyes flickered. "Promise me. You'll deliver a message. Just in case. Swear it."

Too shocked to object, she responded, "I swear."

"Tell her . . . tell her to look to the East for answers. Look to the river. In between. Look in the square. Lask. Bauer. *Forgive me.*"

"Justice? I don't understand." Frantically, Jamie leaned closer. "Who is Mr. Bauer?"

"Tell Avery. East. River." He gasped then, choking on a bitter gulp of air. "Between. Square. *Forgive me.*"

Jamie shook his shoulders, trying to rouse him once more, to make sense of what she'd heard. But the irises stared out blankly into the tepid light, unresponsive. She moved his hand back to the bed.

"No. No," she muttered aloud. "They won't make me kill you." She lifted the bedside phone and punched the speed dial assigned for such a moment.

"U.S. Marshals. What's your emergency?"

"Justice Howard Wynn is unconscious. He needs immediate medical attention."

"Identify yourself."

"Nurse Jamie Lewis," she answered tersely. "Now send an ambulance. He's dying."

"Please stay on the line."

Once she was sure the ambulance was en route, she reached for the other phone and dialed the man she'd never met. She waited mere seconds for a connection.

"Is it done?"

"I think he took an overdose."

"On purpose?"

"Maybe." She hesitated. "Pulse is weak, and he's in and out of consciousness. He's near death."

"Do nothing. I will arrive in twenty minutes."

Her eyes squeezed shut. "I can't."

"You can't do what?"

"I can't do nothing. It's not right."

A long silence, then: "Leave the house, Nurse Lewis. At once."

"I said I can't. An ambulance is on the way," Jamie confessed. "I had no choice."

"This is a national security matter. You were told not to contact anyone except for me. Not to take heroic measures to prolong his life. Did you misunderstand?"

"No. But I had to help him. He needs a doctor."

The admission of the former Army nurse told the man on the line that her usefulness was at an end. "Understood."

Nonplussed by the response, she asked, "What happens now?"

"Take him to the hospital, and then you are relieved of duty. You'll receive your payment tomorrow." The line disconnected.

Jamie stared at the phone. She was free? Relief snaked through her, and her knees gave way. She sank onto the bed, her hip against the limp hand that had grabbed her only minutes ago.

A dying man had made a request of her. A last request. Her eyes fell on Justice Wynn, a man who'd served his country well. All he'd asked in his last moments of lucidity was for her to deliver a message. *Save us.*

Smoothing down the wrinkles in her uniform, Jamie dialed the cell phone again. *In for a penny . . .*

This time, it was the number she'd learned after months in his office. The rings gave way to a short greeting and then a tone. Jamie repeated the message the dying man had offered. She spoke quickly, her eyes on his. Then she finished: "Avery, his last words were *Forgive me.*"

ONE

Sirens shrilled outside the dingy casement window. The high whines seeped in, piercing sleep with pinpricks of sound. Avery Keene rolled to her side and tugged the lumpy pillow over her head. She continued to drift along the Danube, serenaded by the lead singer of some innocuous boy band clad only in his Calvin Klein finest. The sounds jangled louder, transforming into the insistent chime of a phone ring. Avery flung out a searching hand and fumbled blindly for the cell phone. Green eyes shut tight, she grabbed the device.

"What?"

"Avery, baby." A rasping cough. A sullen giggle. "It's Momma."

The sirens dropped away, leaving a more jarring reality. Wearily, Avery slid up to lean against the wall, braced against a raft of pillows. She hadn't been able to justify the expense of a headboard yet. *One more year.* Peeling open tired lids, she tracked the neon flickers against rain-spattered glass. "Rita. Where are you?"

Another giggle. "Adams Monathalan."

"Adams Morgan?" With her free hand, she shoved the heavy fall of black away from a smooth, caramel-toned forehead, the kinky-curly mass tumbling down bare shoulders squared with tension. Sleep cleared quickly, and she checked the bedside clock. Nearly three on Sunday, no, Monday morning. Figured. Nothing good would be happening for her mother in the Adams Morgan neighborhood at this time of night. After the well-to-do retired to their neat row houses, the clubs spewed out partyers looking for hotter action. "Are you in Adams Morgan, Rita?"

Rita Keene harrumphed. "Absolutely. I said so. Adams Morahan."

Recognizing the rise of belligerence, Avery spoke quickly, tightly. "Are you in jail?"

"Won't be if you come and give this cutie pie some money."

Cutie pie? Brows furrowed, Avery puzzled over the statement. If Rita was in jail, arraignment wouldn't come until morning. Sunday-night busts had to wait until the judges arrived for Monday-morning calls. But just in case, she asked, "They've set your bail? Already?"

A sudden shout forced Rita to raise her voice. "No bail, baby. No jail. Friend's house. He's a good friend. I just need to settle up. Can you come by?"

"I've told you before, Rita. No more." *For God's sake, no more.*

There was momentary silence. "I'm not getting wasted. I promise. But I have to be good for my word," her mother wheedled. "I know you can spare a hundred dollars for your mother? That's all I'm asking. If not, he might get mad."

"I can't."

"Won't," Rita corrected. "Stuck-up bitch. Too good to help your mother out of a jam." The cajoling tone slid into a string of expletives.

"Rita." Avery had heard it all before, and she silently recited the Al-Anon mantra, but serenity was a slippery commodity when your mother was holed up in a crack house cursing your birth like a drunken sailor. Hearing a break in the rant, she asked quietly, "Give me an address, and I'll pick you up." Hell, she was going to get only four more hours of sleep anyway. Might as well kick off the week with the great whirligig of fun that was her mother. "Momma, where are you?"

"Not gonna tell."

"Why not?"

"I'm not going to another goddamned rehab. All I need is a hundred. That's it. Maybe if you took the stick out your ass, you would help your mother out. Just this once." In the background, a man asked if the daughter was pretty. "Not ugly," came Rita's stage-whisper reply. "But you want the original, honey, not a secondhand copy. Especially when I can trade you—" The rest ended on a high, desperate laugh.

Heat snapped through Avery's veins, seared her cheeks. She wanted to disconnect the call, but the shaky laughter signaled that her mother was nearing a crash and worse. Years of training had her tamping down the riot of emotion she swore each time would not return. For an instant, she wondered how different life would be if her father were alive. With his deep brown eyes that crinkled at the corners and his hickory skin stretched tight over a square jawline. His ready patience and easy smile—she'd inherited neither of those traits. Who would Rita have been if he'd survived?

Cutting off the useless musing, she swung her legs over the side of the bed. Dad was dead. Rita was high. And she lived stubbornly in reality. In the dark, she felt around for her tennis shoes and a baseball cap. Luckily, she'd chosen to sleep in running shorts and a tank, a vain attempt to stave off the coming DC summer heat. "Rita—Momma, tell me where you are."

"No. Stuck-up little bitch . . ." Just as quickly as the venom poured, sugar followed. "Baby, I didn't mean that. I love you. My one and only . . . I'm so proud of you. My brilliant lawyer baby. She works at the Supreme Court," she told the dealer.

"Momma." Avery bit off the word, her eyes desert dry. She'd grown accustomed to the balancing act, keeping her mother's demons partitioned away from the world she lived in by day. Bail and rehab versus drafting memos and hunting for precedents. Fighting for patience, she swigged from a bottle of water that sat on her nightstand. The taste of sleep swished for seconds, then disappeared.

"Momma, you there?"

"Where else can I go?" A tiny sob hitched on the line. "Don't have anywhere else to go."

"You can go back to the rehab, Momma. I'll ask them to let you come back." *Again.* She'd spent her last chunk of savings on the in-patient facility in February. Rita had lasted twelve weeks, a personal best. But the fee had cleaned out her accounts and maxed out her cards. She'd gotten the meager balances down, as was her habit, but until she hit pay dirt with a job at a fancy law firm, she'd be living very frugally—especially if Rita wanted to return to rehab. And Avery's boss forbade interviews until the close of the session, so she had only the illusion of employment to tide her over. "Do you want to try again?"

"At that shithole? No way in hell." More brittle laughter. "I don't need to get clean, and I don't want your fucking charity."

Which defied the call for money, but Avery knew better than to attempt reason. At this stage, placating worked best. Slipping her feet into the shoes she carried, she squatted to tie the laces tight. No telling if tonight's excursion would include a flight from danger. Always best to be prepared. "Tell me where you are, Momma."

"So you can come and preach to me? No way."

"You have to." Rising, Avery's hand slipped into the drawer of her nightstand and pulled out a small knife. It was illegal to carry a switch-blade in DC, but old habits had died hard. She didn't like guns, but she couldn't afford to go to her mom's preferred haunts without it. One of the few precious inheritances from her dad that her mom hadn't pawned along the way. Mother-of-pearl handle and their initials engraved on the hilt. Her father's cosmic joke—Avery Olivia and Arthur Oliver—*AOK*.

The palm-sized knife wouldn't stop a drug fiend, but it might slow one down if she ever had to use it. The weapon went into the pocket of her shorts. "If you don't tell me where you are, I can't bring you any money."

"Really?" Hungry to believe, Rita hissed into the phone, "Gotta come soon, though. Real soon."

Avery headed for the living room, grabbed her keys, and yanked open the front door. *Keys. Cell phone. Wallet!* She'd forgotten it. Twist-ing, she kicked at the closing door and rushed back inside. She juggled the cell, hoping Rita wouldn't hang up before she could get better direc-tions. The signal would die as soon as she entered the stairwell. "I need an address, Rita. Now."

"You'll really come?" The wheedling tone begged for a lie. A promise. "You'll come for real? Bring me some cash?"

Avery stared at the threadbare wallet on the table and contemplated bringing her last fifty to the addict who'd grudgingly given birth to her twenty-six years ago. Screw that. She slipped a ten into her pocket and tossed the wallet onto the table. "Sure, Momma. Just tell me where I'm going."

TWO

The hollow sound of the ebony cane striking ceramic tiles echoed along the deserted hallway. Dr. Indira Srinivasan enjoyed the eerie thuds, the reverberations signaling her presence in this isolated wing of Advar Biogenetics, Ltd. This was her dominion. Midday here in Bangalore, a city teeming with high-tech industry, her technicians, analysts, and staff filled the building, but no other soul would be in these corridors, save the security guards whose gratitude for their positions was owed to her. The tortuous path to her offices intentionally discouraged all visitors except the most urgent.

She limped along the wide, vacant length of the hallway, heading for her ground-floor suite. Western tradition dictated a corner office in the penthouse of a towering modern facility in one of the city's ubiquitous biotech parks. It galled that with her advanced rheumatoid arthritis, she could not risk such a journey should the sleek elevators fail. In concession, she inhabited a spacious, sun-drenched suite walled off from the metropolis of Bangalore by thick layers of tempered glass and steel. She could see out, but no prying eyes peered inside.

Indira stumbled and grabbed at the nearest wall to steady herself. She waited for the tremble of palsy that shook her limb to cease. More and more, the arthritis competed with nerve damage to topple the body she religiously disciplined into fighting form. Ropes of muscle snaked along arms that today wore sapphire silk crepe.

Her weight never fluctuated, never crept above or below the physician-recommended standard. The thirty-eight-year-old face and soul of genetic engineering—the engine of India's emergence into the next wave of technological advancement—could not risk distractions. No silly gossip about bulimia or a fascination with samosas when the *Wall Street Journal* featured her penned likeness above the fold as the next Bill Gates.

The intricate knot she had twisted into her hair that morning bobbed cunningly as she neared her office. She calculated the opening share price Advar would need to reach on the stock exchange to soothe the shareholder anxiety that peppered her emails. A grimace twisted the long, dark mouth as the office door swung on mute hinges. As she passed through, the door shut behind her, locking out every thought but the one that had occupied her for too long.

The U.S. Supreme Court continued to fritter away time as her destiny hung in the balance. Her company's acquisition of GenWorks, a closely held biotech company in Chapel Hill, North Carolina, now relied entirely on the whims of nine men and women who knew little of genomics, epistasis, or bioinformatics. While she awaited their decision, her stock price continued to drift toward junk status. If the Advar share price fell too low, the collection of chauvinists and harbingers who populated the board of directors would also be plotting her demise.

The merger of a century and a cunning masterstroke of economic and biogenetic genius—felled by a vindictive American president facing a tough reelection. He'd called the denial of their merger an act of national security, but she knew his actions for what they were. Revenge and self-preservation.

Fear.

The same fear gripped her. She'd taken another risk before this, a favor to another president at Chairman Krishnakamur's urging. Take over a rival and absorb its secrets, and she'd reclaim her full life. She'd own the world and all of its sins.

Now Advar stood at risk, and she had no way to redeem herself without telling the truth. A truth as damning as the lies she told now.

Moving to the slab of desk that consumed the center of the office, she lowered her trembling body gently down to sit. Spasms jerked muscle into tight knots. She closed her eyes, breathing deeply. Too much to accomplish. Too much in motion to cavil with a broken body. She had mere days until triumph or defeat. Her body would damned well hold until then.

As the microprocessors whirred through their exercises, booting up her computer, her private line jangled imperiously. She yanked it to her ear, impatient with the interruption.

"Srinivasan."

"Good morning, sunshine."

Indira relaxed her scowl into a mild frown. "Nigel, it is the afternoon here, as you well know. However, it is barely dawn there. What do you want?"

On the other end of the line, Nigel Cooper, founder and president of GenWorks Labs, jogged lightly on a treadmill, his breathing even and steady. He was in his last year before forty pushed him into a new demographic, but he refused to age like the pale wunderkinds he'd studied with in grad school. The early-morning runs kept his body toned and fit, perfect for candid shots of him frolicking on beaches or entering movie premieres with his latest starlet. A thick shock of dark blond hair draped charmingly over his forehead, and he pushed it away.

Nigel was renowned as much for his financial expertise as for his model-perfect looks—which made him equally popular with CNBC and E! But this morning's call had more to do with what would be broadcast on PoliticsNOW. "Thanks for the warm greeting. I can't imagine why we stopped seeing one another."

"You proved to have a singular inability to grasp the concept of fidelity," she reminded him blandly. She slid a stack of contracts across the desk. "But a rehash of our wasted youth is not the point. Why are you calling me? We're scheduled for a conference call in a few hours."

"Because I have news now." News that would soon whisper along the tangled channels of medicine, money, and power, made juicier because of how hard someone had tried to bury the story. There were armed guards at a private room at the Bethesda Naval Hospital, and a patient brought in by military chopper. The arrival of a premier neurologist and a medical team that could revive Lazarus had only ginned up the rumor mill.

"The story will break across the international wires as soon as one network gets confirmation, but I've got my intel on good authority." He paused dramatically. "Supreme Court justice Howard Wynn has been hospitalized."

Indira hissed out a breath, her stomach clutching. "I saw headlines about a rant at a university commencement, but I did not hear details. When did this happen? What is wrong with him?"

"There was an incident last night. The word is that he's fallen into a coma. Conveniently, right after he accused President Stokes of being in league with the Devil and of trying to kill everyone. Sound familiar?"

"Tigris." The revelation ricocheted through her, sent curses flying through her mind. Though she didn't believe in any of the Hindu gods, she felt certain several conspired against her. "Are you sure?"

"He didn't say the words, but I'm willing to bet that he knows more than we realized." Nigel's soft southern drawl did little to soften the blow. "The swing vote on the Supreme Court went batshit crazy and then fell into a coma. Assuming he was our ace in the hole, we are now potentially fucked."

Indira forced her mind to play through the odds. "Was it a stroke? An aneurysm?"

"What does it matter?"

"We need to know if he'll wake up and how soon."

"I'll find out."

"Good. My board is becoming restless."

Nigel cautioned, "Tell them to hold still. The end of the term is in a few days, but he could be in the hospital for months. The Court doesn't have to rule this term. If they wait until the fall, we buy ourselves more time to ratchet up the pressure on President Stokes. Every month there's a poor jobs report, I put out some statement about the number of jobs that could have been created with our merger. November is a long time to survive Chinese water torture."

"My board has no faith in your judicial system at this point," Indira retorted bitterly. "Tigris is not going away, Nigel. The board wants their money out of this fiasco as quickly as possible. Besides, your bankers are getting worried, too."

"Yes, but I've kept them calm. We would make a mountain of billionaires with this deal. Do whatever you have to, but we can't fold yet."

"My board reads *Bloomberg News* too. Only you and I continue to believe this merger will happen."

"Money men always think the sky is falling."

"Perhaps this time, they're not wrong." She shut her eyes, her head leaning against leather. "They've told me to break the agreement if we do not have an answer when the Court adjourns."

"You pull out, and we won't get another shot! GenWorks is ruined if I don't get access to your tech, Indira. Not to mention what it could mean for you personally."

"GenWorks has nothing that will help my medical condition."

"Not yet, but in time." Nigel punched the emergency stop button on the treadmill. "We can't give in now. Maybe we go to President Stokes. Threaten to expose him if he doesn't change his mind."

"Are you mad? We will do no such thing!"

"Think about it. He's got to be as worried as we are. His four votes are no more certain than ours. Justice Wynn living or dying is no guarantee. Either way, President Stokes could still lose and cost himself the election." Leaning heavily against the rails, he reasoned, "If Americans learned the truth about this, they'd crucify him."

"And us along with him." She rubbed at a knot of tension forming at her nape. "It is too great a risk, Nigel. They would say I am as culpable."

"Not by a long shot. No actual harm done."

Her hesitation was brief, imperceptible. Personal. "We've had this discussion before. If we admit we know the truth, the president will destroy us. Right now, he can only suspect what we know, and we have no proof."

"We know it's out there. We simply have to find it."

"We've tried," she reminded him, frustration growing in her voice. "The records show what was invested, not the source. And the officials who know the truth will never admit it."

"Then we force his hand."

"Or let the case play out. It would help if you didn't insist on antagonizing him at every opportunity." Despite years in American schools, she still barely understood the deep divisions between the Left and the Right in a country with so little to argue over. "This merger should not have required an international incident."

"Money and power make people irrational. You know that better than most."

She stared out the window, wondering if Tigris would ever stop punishing her. "What do you want me to do?"

"Nothing for now."

"What are you planning?" A woman didn't sleep with a man for as long as she had without learning the nuance to his voice. Cunning, shot through with guile. "No secrets."

"I'll keep my ears and my options open. There's always an angle, Indira. You keep your board in line. Fortunes and principalities are at stake, my dear."

"I am well aware of the consequences." Indira's hand trembled, reminding her of why she'd allowed Tigris to live and die. "Keep me informed."

Nigel Cooper disconnected and pulled up the next number. When the call connected, he said, "Sorry to wake you, Mr. Leader, but we've got a situation. I'll be in DC in five hours. Have the Speaker join you and meet me at the St. Regis. Be discreet."

THREE

In an apartment tucked into Tacoma Park, Maryland, early-morning sunlight filtered through blinds she'd drawn weeks ago. Jamie Lewis was curled on the sofa watching an old black-and-white movie, hoping it would lull her to sleep. A cup of chamomile tea cooled on the coffee table in front of the couch, beside the boarding pass for her flight to New Mexico. In eight hours, she'd be on her way, leaving behind Justice Wynn and the last few months.

Exhaustion dragged at her, but sleep remained elusive. Soon, she'd see her husband and tell him of their plans. He could stop hiding at his cousin's place and meet her at the airport.

If she left today, perhaps her secret employers would forgive her. Perhaps Justice Wynn would as well.

The knock on the door startled her, and she belted her robe tight. The clock told her it was nearly six in the morning.

Jamie hurried to the door, quickly smoothing her faded brown hair into a semblance of order. She peered out the keyhole and frowned at the man standing outside. Her voice croaked out, "Can I help you?"

A badge flashed in the keyhole. "Mrs. Lewis? It's about your husband. May I come in?"

Distressed, resigned, she fumbled with the locks and chain. "What's happened this time?" she asked wearily as she shifted to admit him. "What has he done?"

"Thomas is in trouble." He tucked his badge away, then gestured toward the room.

Jamie obediently moved into the living room, leaving the officer to shut the door. "Is he under arrest?"

"He's not in custody." The officer followed her into the barren living room, scanning an array of boxes stacked against the faux fireplace. "Planning to move?"

"Yes," she answered, waving the question aside. She frowned. "Your badge said DC Police. If he's not in custody, why are you here?"

"Because he is in trouble, Mrs. Lewis." He laid a hand on a box. "Do you already have a place, Jamie?"

Fear for her husband morphed into personal terror. She abruptly recognized the voice if not the face. This was the man who'd engaged her to work for Justice Wynn. "I don't . . . ," she stammered, her hand rising to her throat. "You're not with the police."

"No, I'm not." He folded his hands behind him as his legs braced apart, subtly but effectively blocking her route to the front door. "You disappointed us. You had a very simple task, and you failed."

She took a small step back. "I tried."

"He's still alive."

"I panicked, sir."

"No, Mrs. Lewis. You didn't panic. In fact, we engaged you because you don't panic. You were a field medic with two tours in the Gulf." He shook his head. "No, you chose to disobey orders. Why?"

"Because it wasn't right," she blurted out. "He's a good man. I couldn't sit there and watch him die."

"According to you, he tried to kill himself. You simply could have allowed it to happen." Another thirty minutes without care, and Howard Wynn would have been a corpse. "He's a threat to national security. You know that. You were with him at the graduation."

"He's a terrified old man who sees shadows. Now he's a threat to no one."

"Not your decision to make."

"He's in a coma and probably won't wake up. That should be enough."

The man watched her steadily. "Nurse Lewis, did you make a call after we spoke last night? To the Supreme Court?"

Jamie started to formulate a lie, then nodded haltingly. He wouldn't ask if he didn't already know the answer. "He woke up for a couple of seconds. He asked about his law clerk, Avery Keene, and I thought she should know what he said."

"What did he say?"

"That Avery has to save us. Look to the East and the river," she recited. "He was adamant. And someone named Lask Bauer. It was gibberish."

"Then why make the call?"

"Because I swore I would tell her."

"You were hired for your discretion, not for heroics. I thought you understood this."

"I did. I do," she stammered. "I haven't told anyone else about you or what you asked me to do. I doubt Avery will understand his message. There's no harm done."

"How can I believe you, Nurse Lewis, when you've just admitted you broke protocol? You called the U.S. Marshals rather than follow orders. You called his clerk." He took a step closer, his eyes cold on hers. "I must know the truth. Did anyone else know that you'd been asked to report on Justice Wynn?"

"No!" The protest squeaked out; then she flushed in memory. "I mean—no one else, besides the judge." When his cold blue eyes flattened, she sputtered, "You must have heard him yesterday. He figured it out; but now, with the coma, he's the only other one who knows." She held up her hands, pleading. "I haven't told anyone about you, God's truth."

"Thank you, Nurse Lewis." He turned away and walked over to the single stretch of windows. The blinds were closed. *Good.* "I believe you."

Jamie watched him in silence. The man in her apartment looked perfectly pleasant, which failed to explain the knots tying themselves in her stomach. Her hands fluttered nervously to her throat, and, eager to have him gone, she asked, "Is there anything else?"

"Yes." He slipped his hand into his jacket. "May I trouble you for a glass of water?"

"Of course." She smiled in relief and turned.

The shot was silent and accurate, exploding through her brain with ruthless efficiency. The bullet lodged in the drywall.

Jamie's body crumpled soundlessly to the ground, the yellow flowers of the carpet darkening with blood. Snapping latex onto both hands, he leaned over the body and pressed two gloved fingers to her throat. Like any good officer, he regretted the necessity of killing; but sometimes, options were limited. With her betrayal, she'd become a liability.

He pulled out a set of needle-nose pliers, removed the bullet, and collected the casing. Removal of the body was possible, but an unnecessary risk. Her husband would keep hiding until he got a signal from her, and no one expected them in Santa Fe. By the time she was discovered, the authorities would chalk the death up to home invasion. He considered violating her, but he hadn't come adequately prepared for that scenario.

With efficient motions, he replaced his tools, then crossed to the thermostat on the window unit. After adjusting the knob to its lowest setting to keep the stench of death at bay, he collected his bag and walked out the front door. Satisfied, he returned to his vehicle, though no evidence showed in his stiff expression. The resolution to his mission had been sloppy, but the objective had been achieved.

The swing justice of the Supreme Court was on the verge of death, and the only person who knew of this operation had been terminated. The hospital's doctors would try to save Justice Wynn. If they succeeded, Wynn could still be terminated.

The man opened the door to the car he'd parked blocks away, a nondescript Ford that would be found abandoned in the coming days, and started the ignition. Traffic had begun to creep onto the quiet streets of the city, and he merged into the stream of cars advancing toward Washington, DC.

Jamie Lewis's confession had revealed a loose thread: Ms. Avery Keene. Though the man recognized it was more of a formality, he dialed his aide.

"Sir?"

"We have a new project."

FOUR

Y ou're late." Matt Brewer offered the indictment as Avery trudged into the conference room that adjoined the offices of Associate Justice Howard Wynn. "Really late."

"Shhh." She pressed past her fellow clerk and weaved toward the oblong table where they would begin the week. Tiny jackhammers wielded by spiteful elves threatened to split her skull, and the Egg McMuffin she'd scarfed down on the Metro seemed determined to force its way back up and out. Despite the muted light of most government buildings, this morning the fluorescent glare seemed obscenely intense to her sleep-deprived eyes. She lifted an unsteady hand to shield against both the death ray above and the unholy smirk that twisted Matt's aristocratic mouth. "Long night."

"Should have gotten your rest. The chief justice's office called for you, but you weren't here. I'd have covered for you, but I hate to lie."

Avery felt her stomach cartwheel. She'd missed her accidental coffee with the Chief, a chance meeting she'd been plotting for months. The stiletto sounds of Matt's amusement were quickly joined by frantic tap dancers without rhythm kicking at her roiling gut. *How could I have forgotten?*

Chief Justice Teresa Roseborough maintained a careful distance from the clerk staff, including her own. Polite greetings and head nods comprised her communication with the lower beings who inhabited the chambers. In Roseborough's two decades on the bench, she'd been known to hold a handful of personal conversations with clerks. A private audience with her carried more weight than a tête-à-tête with the pope and much better benefits.

It took a year and a half for Avery to pick her strategy. The multi-pronged attack included sucking up to the Chief's two secretaries. Adoring coos over the prized basset hound of Debi Starnes and the cockeyed three-year-old grandniece claimed by Mary Gonzalez had opened a sliver of a window in January. By March, Debi was offering Avery scotch oatmeal cookies and dating tips.

But it was Mary, the harridan who guarded the Chief's calendar like the nuclear football, who mattered most. The Great Thaw occurred on April 7. That morning, during her six a.m. sweep of the chambers, Mary uncovered a nest of water bugs who'd somehow penetrated the layers of concrete and steel of the U.S. Supreme Court. Avery woke up from her overnight slumber in camera to the woman's frenetic screams and rushed into the common room, where Mary perched on a rickety ladderback chair.

Avery sprang into action. Armed with a dustpan and a memorable summer in southern Mississippi, she cornered and crushed the vermin, to Mary's amazed delight. By May, she'd been invited to meet the blessed grandniece. Then last Friday, Mary and Debi casually dropped the forbidden intel about the Chief's plan to come in extra early on Monday.

"Last few weeks of term brings out the tiger in her," Mary had offered. "Likes to be here by the break of day."

"Yep," echoed Debi. "I remember that time Serena came in early to get a jump on her cases. She and the Chief grabbed some coffee and gabbed for hours."

"Isn't she managing partner at Wachtell now?" Mary cut her eyes to Avery, to make sure she was listening.

"Serena Sparks?" Avery widened her eyes, as they would have expected. "I didn't realize she'd clerked for the Chief."

"Didn't. Old Justice Fiss. But smart as a whip, she was. Could pump out pool memos in half the time of the others."

"Cute little thing too. Just as polite as you'd please," Debi added. "From the South, like you. Virginia, I believe."

"No, Debi. She was from Arkansas. You always get that wrong."

"I do not—"

Avery reeled with triumph. The gatekeepers had told her to be at the Court by six on Monday, and she'd be able to talk to the Chief over coffee.

And she'd missed it. *Shit.* Throat closing over the return of the McMuffin, she sank into a conference chair that leaned drunkenly when she collapsed into its embrace. Trying to breathe, Avery contemplated the relative merits of matricide and suicide.

When Matt propped a bony hip on the polished surface at her hand, the scales tipped toward clerkicide.

"What do you want?" she mumbled, trying vainly to keep her voice from wavering.

"Did you see our boss's performance yesterday? Wow."

"He didn't say anything he hasn't expressed before," Avery retorted. "They should lay off him."

Matt smirked. In a tone designed to reach the rafters, he responded, "And you might want to lay off yourself. Too much fun this weekend? We're not in law school anymore, babe. Save the binges for the recess, 'kay?"

Fun? That's not how she would describe hours spent creeping along Sixteenth Street and into neighborhoods usually featured on *Cops*. Hours when she'd discarded her future. Hot tears burned against her lowered lids, stunning her with their appearance.

She didn't cry. *Ever.*

Certainly not over an eternity spent looking for a woman who didn't really want to be found and could have been in Dupont Circle or down in Shaw for all she knew. She'd spent the early morning pub-crawling and visiting heroin dens in search of the last person she wanted to see, while she had missed the one she'd wanted to speak with desperately.

Now Avery faced a long week of writing legal opinions for a man who seemed to consider her only a step up from the merry monkeys that could type Shakespeare. In cooperation with a raving asshole like Matt Brewer who made her life miserable. One of these indignities she could take—but not all of them.

She reached into her oversized bag for the Advil she was sure lay at the very bottom. Finding the bottle, she dry-swallowed one and then another.

Matt watched her and taunted, "Hungover? Hope Justice Wynn doesn't find out." They both knew he planned to tell him.

"Bite me." Avery would have said more, but her head refused to sit still long enough to feed her the pithy insults she kept on hand for Matt "I Kiss All Ass" Brewer of the Boston Brewers. But the old standby was good in a pinch.

"You're slipping, Keene. Need some hair of the dog? Or does that explain your appearance?"

"Screw you."

Stroking a long, soft finger along her wan cheek, Matt replied, "I've offered. Happy to take a spin. After you shower."

The slick rise of OTC pain meds and eerily round fast-food egg sandwich warned Avery to turn her head. She didn't. Instead, she bent at the waist, opened wide, and let revenge run free.

"Goddamn it, Avery!" Matt leaped up and barely resisted the urge to kick her face with his ruined shoe. "These are John Lobbs. Three thousand a pair, for Christ's sake! What the hell?"

Wiping vainly at her mouth, she mumbled, "Sorry . . . rough morning."

"It'll get rougher when you get my bill." He spun toward the door and stormed awkwardly away.

Avery turned away to find something to mop up the mess. Grabbing a handful of Kleenex, she also retrieved her water bottle. She took a hasty swallow, then crouched down to clean as the justice's phone rang. Several rings later, she noticed that neither of his secretaries had answered. With a curse, Avery snatched the receiver up. "Justice Wynn's chambers. Avery Keene speaking."

"Chief Justice Roseborough wants you in her chambers. Now." Mary spoke quickly, her voice oddly muffled.

A second chance? Stunned by her good fortune, Avery quickly agreed. "I'll be right there. Thanks, Ms. Gonzalez."

In response, Avery heard a soft hiccup before the line disconnected. She stumbled to her feet and quickly swished more water, wishing she had time to make herself more presentable. As she tried to gauge how long she could delay, a new thought occurred.

Opportunity didn't knock twice. How likely was it that her accidental meeting would be replaced by a real one for good reasons? Slim to none. The disquieting alternative occurred as she circled the table. She froze.

Rita.

Panic abruptly dislodged nausea. Somehow, Rita had managed to find her stoned way to the Great Hall and was downstairs, demanding to see her supplier. Or she'd been arrested and told the DC cops that her daughter worked for the Supreme Court. In Washington, that would either be laughed off or readily believed, depending on what Rita was wearing in lockup and who was taking her statement.

For the first decade of Avery's life, Rita's femme fatale skills, accented by wild red hair and emerald-green eyes, had kept her daughter in diapers and jeans and school. The following decade hadn't proven as successful, which often left Avery to her own devices, a state Avery preferred. Left alone, she could occasionally provide for trips to rehab and nights at hourly motels when Rita crashed. The model worked—as long as Rita remembered the rules.

Avery took a slow, measured breath. She'd been at the Court for two terms now. She did good work. Too good for the sudden appearance of her strung-out mother to derail everything. *Right?*

With careful steps, she left the conference room and wound her way through the anteroom. Down the hallways and through the warren of spaces that lay between the associate offices and the sanctuary of the chief justice.

Avery smoothed her hair with her fingertips and took a final deep breath as she approached the Chief's offices. Flanking her inner sanctum doors were the desks of Debi and Mary. "Ms. Gonzalez? Mrs. Starnes?" Avery approached Mary's desk. The taller woman, her burnished black hair pulled into a severe bun at her nape, lifted her head.

"Ms. Keene. The Chief said you should go right in." Mary pressed a button on her phone, and the faint buzz echoed and lingered.

"I'm so sorry," murmured Debi as Avery passed between them.

Avery looked back, wondering fatalistically what waited on the other side. She'd never rapped lightly on the door to announce her presence. Never turned the brass knob before.

"Come in, Ms. Keene." Teresa Roseborough, the most powerful judge in the world, stood in front of a broad partners desk that even Avery's untutored eye knew was a Chippendale. Out of her robes, the Chief looked almost diminutive in a dove-gray suit piped at the lapels in black brocade. Barely five-four, she often wore three-inch heels that added height, but not stature.

Feigned stature was unnecessary. One listen to the famous voice provided all the authority she needed. The crisp tones had been marinated in a smoky voice that edged on husky. With a sharp face that boasted a pointed chin and almost beaked nose, the Chief was a study in angles and planes. Observers of the Court called her striking. Political foes preferred haughty.

The Court family simply recognized the power.

"Please come in." The Chief stepped away from the doorway and ushered Avery inside. When she pushed the door closed, it shut with a click of the lock. "Have a seat."

Avery chose the creamy taupe leather sofa closest to her knee. Unsteady, she lowered herself, trying not to gape at the supple fabric. Instead, she focused on the man standing across the room at the windows, nearly hidden.

Following her gaze, the Chief nodded. "This is Major William Vance, the president's liaison from the Department of Homeland Security."

"Major Vance." Avery turned back to the Chief. "Ma'am?"

"I have some troubling news, Avery." The Chief crossed to Avery and sat on the sofa, angled toward her. "How close are you and Justice Wynn?"

Puzzled, Avery responded, "I'm his clerk, ma'am. He gives me instructions, and I follow them."

"Nothing more?"

"No, ma'am. I work for him. That's all." Wondering where the question had come from, Avery glanced at the tall, hulking figure at the window. Built like a defensive lineman, Vance stood stiffly and said nothing, simply looked back at her. The hooded blue gaze carried no expression. Turning back to the Chief, she asked, "Why? Is there something wrong?"

"Yes." The Chief reached out, covered Avery's hands with tapered fingers bare of polish.

"What happened?"

"It is imperative that you tell me the truth, Avery."

"Of course." *What in the hell is going on? Did something happen to Justice Wynn after his speech?* Avery nodded sharply. "You can trust me."

Major Vance sent a look to the Chief, who ignored the warning glare. It was her office, her court. Her choice. "Last night, Justice Wynn fell into a coma."

"Oh, God." Avery whipped her head around to the agent, then turned back to the Chief. "He wasn't sick. He's never sick."

"His nurse found him early this morning. Unconscious. It may explain his recent outbursts." She gave Avery's hand a gentle squeeze. "Howard has been ill for some time, Avery. He has a degenerative brain disorder known as Boursin's syndrome."

"A brain disorder? Why—what—" Avery fumbled through the questions. "He's been moody lately, and short-tempered, but that's not really out of character." She didn't mention the odd instructions he'd given her several weeks ago to rewrite an order to nullify a contract between two milk producers, using the Dutch Defense as a metaphor. No one else would care about an obscure chess opening move. Avery loved the game, but even she barely understood Wynn's point. Besides, it didn't prove anything.

"He wasn't erratic," Avery stressed. "Just more—himself. I never guessed he was ill."

"Howard is a stubborn man. I know about his condition only because I had to authorize his private nurse care."

Several months ago, her judge had added a third secretary who didn't know how to type. This was the same man who refused to hire the three clerks to whom he was entitled because he "didn't like being surrounded by too many fools at once when he wasn't on Capitol Hill." Putting it together, Avery asked, "Mrs. Lewis?"

"Yes. Jamie Lewis is a registered nurse."

"Matt thought she was his girlfriend," Avery mumbled, still processing the news. "But I thought she seemed too—" Remembering where she was, and with whom, she closed her teeth on a snap. "Sorry."

"Too what?" the Chief Justice prompted, fingers tightening slightly. "What did you think?"

Avery replied slowly, "That she was too sharp. I mean, insightful. She didn't think like a lawyer or someone who worked for lawyers, but she had a good ear for politics. And she was always nice, but never too friendly."

"Why didn't you think she was Justice Wynn's companion?" The question came from Major Vance, the first time he'd broken his silence.

She shrugged. "He wouldn't do that. Bring in his girlfriend as an employee. It's unseemly."

"Unseemly."

The statement, intended as a question, bore no tone of query. Still, Avery understood the man meant to ask for explanation. Too shaken to resist, she explained, "He despises nepotism, favoritism, and poor utility. Unless his girlfriend was the best legal secretary in the country, he wouldn't give her a job. Plus, he'd probably break up with her first."

With an impenetrable look at the agent, the Chief agreed. "Very discerning."

"He's an honorable man. That's why everyone got so angry. You can argue with him, but you can never question his logic or his values." Not the man she knew. The man who now lay in a netherworld, unable to do what he loved most.

When the silence dragged on, she ventured, "Ma'am, is there something I can do for you? For the Court?"

Another look passed between the Chief and Major Vance. Avery waited.

"I know this is a lot to take in at once." The Chief focused on her, eyes narrowing in decision. "Howard has a special fondness for you."

Avery drew her hands free. "What do you mean?"

A smile curved the Chief's mouth. "He thinks quite highly of you. Finds you 'bearably brilliant.' High praise, indeed, from Howard."

"Yes, ma'am." Avery swallowed the lump that rose in her throat. Ducking her head, she blinked back unexpected tears. Twice in one day, she thought dismally. Keep this up, and she'd be a fountain by lunch.

Justice Wynn would ream her out if he caught— It struck her then. The oddity of it all. "I appreciate you calling me in here, Chief. But why tell me alone? Why not me and Matt together?"

"Because this concerns you directly." Major Vance came from the window and stood in front of them, before it ever registered with Avery that he'd moved. He loomed over the two women on the sofa, his hard blue eyes boring into them.

She'd seen men like him around DC, usually where important people gathered. But his type didn't frighten her. Massive and deadly existed in darker places than the military. She cocked her head. "What else is there?"

"Justice Wynn left this for you." From behind him, he proffered a slim white envelope whose seal had been slit. Major Vance spoke before Avery could protest the breach. "A precaution, Ms. Keene. We had to verify the contents."

Knowing how Wynn valued privacy and hated the intrusion of government, Avery was tempted to argue, but curiosity pulled at her. She tipped over the envelope and caught the folded sheets of white in her lap. Lifting the first, she scanned the contents, eyes growing wide with disbelief.

After a third read-through, she let the pages fall to her lap, and one slithered off to land on the thick red carpet beneath her feet. She turned to the Chief Justice. "You can't be serious."

"It was his wish. Is his wish."

Avery struggled to comprehend the contents. "He has a child. A wife. A family. I'm just a clerk. I don't understand."

"Neither do we, Ms. Keene. Which is why we wanted to speak with you," Major Vance explained. "Did you have any knowledge of these documents?"

Scooping up the fallen pages, she forced her voice to be polite. "No, I've never seen them before." This had to be a mistake. A colossal misunderstanding. But her legal eye told her the pages were authentic, the decision real. She pivoted back to the Chief. "I didn't know he was going to do this, I swear."

Vance continued, "And you have never had a conversation with Justice Howard Wynn about this? Not even in passing?"

His incredulity bit at her temper, and she twisted her head to glare at him. "For the last time, no."

Avery got to her feet, annoyance supplanting the shock that still trembled her knees. She'd never been more or less than Justice Wynn's clerk, and she'd be damned if she'd let some Homeland Security thug imply otherwise. In elementary school, she'd beaten up kids for lesser insults.

She pushed past the agent and crossed to the mahogany-paneled door. Pages clutched tightly, she turned to the Chief, ignoring Vance. "I swear to you, I had no idea that Justice Wynn had given me his power of attorney and named me his legal guardian. Now, if you'll excuse me, I'd like to get back to work."

FIVE

I'm not finished," Vance commanded. "Sit down."

Remaining stubbornly upright, Avery countered, "I've got a memo to write."

"This isn't a request, Ms. Keene."

Sensing the rising mutiny, layered over shock, Chief Justice Roseborough intervened. "Avery, Major Vance is doing his job—investigating the circumstances of Justice Wynn assigning you his power of attorney. He intended no insult. Please, sit."

Vance restrained a sneer. *Intended no insult?* Clearly, he'd intended that and more. This girl had complicated what seemed like a godsend to the president—his nemesis on the Supreme Court in a coma. "I have a few more questions, Ms. Keene."

Avery held her ground. "I don't know anything else."

"I will decide that."

Moving closer, Vance focused on Avery. The girl was taller than he'd expected, nearly six feet tall in the absurd heels women her age wore. More attractive too. Ripe for seduction by a powerful man like Wynn. If sex was at the core of this decision, she could be dealt with fairly quickly in the age of social media. "When did you last speak to Justice Wynn?"

Avery folded her arms obstinately. "Homeland Security has a broad mandate, but I didn't know it reached inside the Supreme Court."

"We go where the questions are. We can continue this conversation here, or I will find more suitable surroundings."

Hearing the threat, the Chief said to Avery, "You've been given a grave responsibility. Surely you understand why there'd be questions."

"Questions, yes. Accusations, no. I've done nothing wrong."

Saying nothing, Vance simply watched Avery. The file he'd pulled on her from the National Counterterrorism Center had created more questions than it answered. A useful system, the NCTC retained data about U.S. citizens, drawn from DMV records, flight data, local law enforcement, and even dragnets from cell phone records, casino employee lists, and any information source that could not justify denying Homeland Security access. Under the rubric of antiterrorism, the NCTC analyzed their findings for suspicious patterns of behavior.

Justice Wynn's choice of guardian had not been explained by a review of her NCTC file. The records indicated a dead father, a drug-addicted mother, and the hint of a gambling habit. How she'd made it into the Supreme Court after a background check baffled him, but not everyone in government leveraged NCTC to its fullest potential. No doubt Justice Wynn, a libertarian hippie, refused to access the system he'd publicly criticized.

More than likely, the cursory background check he'd allowed had homed in only on her peripatetic if exemplary educational history and her previous stint as a clerk at the DC Court of Appeals. To Vance, though, her predilections coupled with her new authority moved her high on his list of problems to eliminate.

"If you've done nothing wrong, then you shouldn't mind answering my questions. Honestly."

"Major Vance," the Chief interjected before Avery could. "Howard's decision is a shock to everyone, especially Avery. There is no need for this to become hostile." She turned to her. "Help us figure out what Howard intended."

"I don't know what else to tell you. In two years, the most personal conversation we've ever had was about my preference for steak versus shrimp at some boring function. Justice Wynn barely tolerated me. I haven't a clue why he'd give me his power of attorney."

Vance asked, "Do you know his son? His wife?"

"I've met Mrs. Turner-Wynn." Avery recalled her as a sharp-faced, pencil-thin woman swathed from head to toe in the fashion last decreed to be au courant. A pit viper of a human who'd spent much of the evening abrading her husband, flirting with Matt, and needling Avery. "She and I didn't have much in common. But I thought they were getting a divorce?"

"Did he tell you that?" Vance pressed.

"Justice Wynn told me nothing about his personal life. I read it in the *Washington Gazette*." She declined to mention the gossip hotline that ran through the Court. In a cloistered place like this, few secrets were kept, and almost none were kept well. "He never discussed his marriage with me."

"What about his son, Jared?"

"No." According to the grist, Justice Wynn hadn't spoken to his son since the death of his first wife. Then-ten-year-old Jared Wynn had been sent to live with his aunt and uncle a week after his mother died. Suddenly a thought occurred, and her head whipped toward the Chief. "Do they know about Justice Wynn?"

The Chief nodded. "Jared and Celeste will have been notified of Howard's condition by the doctors."

"I should go to the hospital." Perhaps the doctors could tell her when he'd regain consciousness. She scooted forward, intending to rise, but Vance shifted to block her.

"Not until we understand exactly what's going on with this POA. If you head over now, there will be questions."

"Like how long I will be his guardian." Before Vance could respond, she held up a hand. "I know comas are not predictable; but given his condition, they must have some idea of when he'll be better. When is he expected to wake up?"

"Avery, right now he's at Bethesda Naval Hospital, where they are running tests on him. A coma is often the final stage of the disease." She drew in a breath. "He may not wake up again."

"Oh, God."

"So you can understand our concern that his law clerk holds his power of attorney." Vance gave her a steady, cold look. "This would be easier for everyone if you would relinquish your position. Allow his wife to perform her duty."

The Chief responded before she could: "According to Howard's wishes, Avery is his guardian. Not Celeste."

"For reasons we cannot verify. Unless Ms. Keene can give us a clearer explanation, we have every reason to suspect this document is a forgery."

The Chief stiffened, her chin lifted imperiously. "His reasons should be fairly obvious. Howard is estranged from his son and in the process of divorcing his wife. Clearly, he decided that he required an alternative solution."

"Yes, but—"

She spoke over him, continuing: "As to your suspicion about the validity of this document, Howard Wynn gave this envelope into my keeping on February 11. It has been in my office safe since that time, as per his instructions. You were present when the seal was broken." She smoothed her unwrinkled skirt with a slow motion, her expression stony. "Are you suggesting I tampered with the document?"

Vance refused the bait. "No, ma'am. But I would request further clarification before we reveal too much more about Justice Wynn's condition or she goes to the hospital."

"Certainly." She turned back to Avery. "Think carefully," the Chief ordered quietly. "Did Howard ever mention his illness to you?"

"Never." Ashamed, she admitted, "I didn't realize he was sick. He's been the same for the past two years."

"Which is?" asked Vance.

"Smart. Brusque. Caustic."

"A jerk," the Chief interpreted.

"Yes." Instantly contrite, she amended, "But he's also very considerate of his clerks. He's fair about assignments. Even though he won't participate in the cert pool, he takes a portion of the cases himself."

"You mentioned meeting his wife," Vance interjected. "Have you spent much time with him out of the office?"

"At functions, mainly. Like every other clerk in the Court, I go where the free food is. Typically, we glom on to the justices' invitations. We're not special enough to rate our own."

"What about in smaller groups? Has it ever been the two of you outside the office?"

"I've been to his home three times," she answered, the white lie coming easily. "And to dinner at a restaurant once."

"That's it?" Vance prodded, hearing something in her response. "Why were you at his house?"

"Once to drop off a brief he'd left at the office. The second and third times for dinner."

"Were you alone?"

"To drop off the brief, yes. The other times, no. Last year, my fellow clerk Amanda Reyes attended the first dinner party. His wife was absent."

"How long were you there? Each event."

"I didn't clock it, but when I dropped off the brief at his house, he stuck his hand out the door, took the folder, and grunted something at me. The second time, for dinner, I'd guess a couple of hours. And dinner this term was only an hour."

"Who attended the dinner parties?"

"He invites both clerks to dinner twice a year. Like I said, it was me and Amanda my first term. No one else. I suppose *party* is a strong term—he fed us, chatted, and sent us home."

"The second one?"

"Matt Brewer and I attended."

"It was shorter?"

Avery bit her lip, then shrugged. "It was a disaster. When he kicked us out, Justice Wynn said that he found Matt's conversation cloying and fawning and that I had the conversational skills of a scullery maid let upstairs."

"And no other personal encounters?"

"When the session starts, we have dinner at his house; and at the end, he swings for a fancy dinner in a restaurant we can't possibly afford. His secretary made reservations at Vieux Marché for June thirtieth, the end of term this year." Avery turned to the Chief as a new thought occurred. "What happens if he doesn't wake up?"

"We can discuss that later," the Chief cautioned. "Major Vance, do you have any more questions for her?"

"You've never been alone with Justice Wynn outside the office? For more than a brief visit?"

"Ask me straight out, Major Vance. You want to know if I've slept with him."

"Yes, Ms. Keene. I'd like to know if you've had a sexual relationship with Justice Wynn. Prior to joining the Court or since."

Rising again, Avery carefully folded the pages in her hand and crossed to the door. This time, when her hand closed on the brass handle, the rage was steady and cool. She'd been a lot of things in her life, some legal, some questionable, most of the latter courtesy of Rita Keene. But never in her life had she been a whore.

When she was sure she could, she turned to speak to both of the room's occupants.

"I am a piece of furniture to Howard Wynn. A very handy typewriter with the ability to read. I come into the office at seven a.m., read cert petitions that will never be heard, draft legal memoranda on obscure points of law no one really cares about. I draft opinions he tears to shreds, and then I write them again and again. When invited, I go to dinner. When I'm not here, I go to sleep.

"This job doesn't allow for a social life or much else. Howard Wynn has been the bane of my existence and my constant critic. He has been my boss and my mentor. But I am not his friend or his confidante or his lover. I am his clerk."

"And now, according to those papers, you're his guardian." Chief Roseborough stood as well. "Go back to your office, Avery. Major Vance and I need to clear up a few more things; then we'll discuss you going over to the hospital."

After Avery left the office with a curt nod, the Chief returned to her desk, forcing Major Vance to come around to the opposite side. Vance's phone buzzed, demanding his attention. As the Chief watched, he lifted the phone to his ear, the volume too low for intrusion. The stolid face held its marble flatness, the jaw too rigid by nature to offer clues. Instead, the Chief listened to a one-sided conversation peppered with three quiet "yes, sir" responses to unheard questions. After ninety seconds, Vance disconnected the phone call.

Anticipating her question, he said without preamble, "This is not news one delivers over the phone, ma'am."

"True," the Chief allowed. "What exactly do you intend to tell him?"

"The truth."

"Which is?"

"Howard Wynn delivered a sealed document to your office for safe-keeping. In my presence, upon learning of his incapacity, you opened said envelope and learned of his intent to appoint his law clerk Avery

Keene to serve as his guardian. I raised questions as to her appropriateness, which you and Ms. Keene have dismissed."

The Chief suspected his actual report would contain a more colorful description of their encounter. "Do you intend to investigate Ms. Keene?"

"I had my team pull her NCTC file while we awaited her arrival. When I have additional information, I will review it as well. This is a matter of national security, and I intend to do my job."

"Come now, Major Vance." The Chief relaxed against the padded leather chair and lifted her lukewarm tea. "In my two decades on the bench, I am not aware of anyone serving in quite the same role that you currently occupy. Even with the creation of Homeland Security, I find it interesting that you retain military title and weaponry, as well as occupying a civilian office. What exactly does a liaison from the"—she lifted his card from the desk—"Science and Technology Directorate do, and why would you be assigned to the Supreme Court?"

"My duties are fluid, Chief Roseborough."

"And vague. So what do you want, Major Vance?"

"For now, your silence. The president believes Justice Wynn's condition to be a matter of grave importance. Until otherwise determined, information about him and his choice of a guardian is considered highly classified."

"Is this about a specific case?"

"The president is concerned about the operations of the Court," he responded. "Unless you believe a specific case should be of concern?"

"You know I can't tell you that."

Vance leaned forward. "You should reconsider that posture."

The Chief stood. "I will pretend you didn't ask me to do something unethical, Major."

"This is simply a request from a grateful president," he temporized. "The Court has important decisions to make in the next ten days, and neither of us wants the validity of your work compromised, Chief."

"It won't be."

"Both the president and I would consider it a personal favor if you would limit discussion of the power of attorney to necessary personnel until we have had time to vet Ms. Keene."

"You won't find anything."

The absurdity of the statement startled him, until he realized the Chief was serious. "Everyone has secrets. Avery Keene's might provide an ulterior motive for securing guardianship."

From behind her desk, Chief Roseborough scoffed. "An ulterior motive? My God, the child barely has a direct one. I will not have you destroying her reputation over an old man's decision."

Vance stood then too, his hands coming together behind his back. The military pose was lost on neither of them. "Justice Wynn's life is a matter of great importance to many people, Chief Roseborough. There are those who will see his illness as an opportunity to strike at America, to aim for her heart—the rule of law. Surely you understand why we must be vigilant?"

"As long as vigilance doesn't stray too far afield," the Chief retorted.

"Good day, Chief Roseborough." Vance turned and strode across the room to the door.

Once her office cleared, she summoned Mary. "Are the justices assembled?"

"As you requested, Chief. They're waiting for you."

"Notify the clerks that I'll meet with them at nine. I need to see Gary Stewart briefly now." The press hits would come fast, and no one was better equipped to parry them than the Court's press secretary.

"Yes, ma'am."

"For the next hour, tell the switchboard to route all calls coming into the building to either you or him. No one else is to answer a phone or dial out. Understood?"

Mary knew better than to ask why. "Yes, ma'am."

SIX

A hemisphere away from DC, Indira sat at the oblong table with its teak surface, chopped from an ancient forest that had long disappeared beneath the advance of civilization. Around the gleaming length, eight men and one other woman waited for the hastily called meeting to come to order. A wide television screen hung suspended at the foot of the table, where a distinguished gentleman with burnished copper skin and alabaster hair watched from a compound in Davos.

"Lady and gentlemen, I thank you all for agreeing to this emergency caucus," she began, her voice clear and steady. "As we are all now aware, there have been some major developments in America that will impact our upcoming merger with GenWorks. Justice Wynn, who represents a key vote on the U.S. Supreme Court, is in a coma."

"Do we have an update on his condition?" inquired the woman, a budding mogul who operated one of the nation's most profitable call centers. She'd devised a system that kept young Indians glued to telephones for twenty-four hours a day, all of whom spoke pitch-perfect flat Midwestern American English. Rumors claimed that her company would add Microsoft and Verizon to its clientele in less than a month, increasing her wealth exponentially.

Indira responded cautiously. "My intelligence reports that Justice Wynn's condition is unchanged. The cause and likely length of his coma are unknown. That information is highly guarded, but I should know more by tomorrow."

A wiry, middle-aged financier with a receding hairline and a skier's tan pressed: "Explain what this will mean for the lawsuit. I understood from our last briefing that we were hopeful Justice Wynn would lean in our favor."

"We were. We are," she corrected smoothly. "His incapacity may have no bearing on the outcome."

A man who had begun his rise to wealth by running rickshaws through the streets of Mumbai grumbled, "Or it may spell the end of this foolhardy endeavor. I objected to the acquisition of that accursed company and to our participation in this imprudent venture."

"I heard no such objections to the rapid rise in our share price, Vinod." The murmurs around the table whispered over Indira, who fixed her eyes on the man in Switzerland. "Indeed, the lovely yacht you purchased when the news of our 'endeavor' spiked the market is set to sail in a few weeks, no?"

Vinod huffed out a breath. "No one denies the economic benefits of the merger. Yet rather than the simple matter it was held out to be—"

"It has become more complicated," Indira finished. A flicker passed between her and the man on-screen, and she continued: "Chairman Krishnakamur, we appreciate you joining us."

The man nodded. "The news from Washington is quite disturbing. I too remain concerned about the wisdom of our merger with Gen-Works. Our government's refusal of his trade agreement did not sit well with President Stokes, and now we mock him by joining with a rival. He may prove volatile."

"GenWorks is the only partner that has the patents and technology able to effectively market what we have developed in-house or acquired from Tigris. Moreover, it is precisely Nigel Cooper's relationship with President Stokes that allows us leverage." Indira inclined her head in acknowledgment of the assembled group. "We are not politicians. We are visionaries. I firmly believe that by combining our technological superiority with GenWorks' pharmaceutical expertise, Advar will emerge as the most significant and substantial biotechnical corporation in the world. In economic terms, this could yield trillions when fully activated. While I share your caution, Chairman, I am loath to forfeit our position due to a shrill xenophobe of a president who is losing his own political support daily."

"A xenophobe, perhaps, but still the most powerful politician on the earth," he cautioned. "I would not underestimate President Stokes or his willingness to halt this merger. If this fails, his cronies will steal GenWorks, and we become a forgotten enterprise. Do not overestimate your brilliant maneuvers."

She allowed herself a small wrinkle of annoyance, a visible but controlled reaction to admonishment. "I understand the stakes, Mr. Chairman."

The man on-screen bent forward until his face filled the monitor, filled the room. "We do not have time for contemplative action. If Advar loses this fight, we lose our edge in the marketplace, and the consequences to our share price will be catastrophic. I expect you to take every necessary precaution against such a loss. Including resolving the unfinished business of Tigris."

Quiet choruses of agreement surrounded Indira, who merely nodded once. Krishnakamur had performed as expected. As directed. "I appreciate your concern, Mr. Chairman, board members. As the founder of Advar, I have a vested interest in not only its current success but its future prosperity. Thus, I have convened you to ask for your permission to take the following actions." She met the somber eyes that surrounded her at the table. "There will be no recording of these minutes."

SEVEN

Avery sat in her office, the door shut tight, the lights off. Her phone blinked with urgent messages, but she ignored the summons. Instead, she read again the bombshell spread across the surface of her desk. Justice Wynn's notarized signature stared up from a declarations page. The final page in a terse document that conferred upon the bearer the ability to make all legal, financial, and health decisions for Howard Wynn.

The signature was authentic. She recognized the barely legible scrawl with its cramped *H* and miserly *W*. The letters in between jumbled together in a morass that left the actual words to the reader's imagination.

January 28. The date he'd sat before a witness and signed over control to a woman he barely knew. Nearly five months ago. Avery clicked open her computer calendar for that day, but she knew what she'd find. Nothing out of the ordinary.

However, the Monday before it was a different matter. As had been that Sunday. The other time she'd been alone with Justice Wynn outside the office. Or nearly so, despite what she'd told Major Vance.

"Come on, Rita," Avery had pleaded as she half carried, half dragged her drunken mother along the Metro platform.

"Just one more dance," giggled Rita, her head lolling on shoulders covered by a ratty fake fur. "The man just wanted one more dance. A last dance." She lifted her chin and began singing, "Last dance. Last chance, for Rita. Yes, it's my last chance, for romance, tonight!" The butchered Donna Summer number caught the attention of others disembarking the train. Realizing she had an audience, she shoved away from Avery and gave a quick shimmy. "'Cause when I'm bad, I'm so, so bad. So let's dance!"

"Rita!" Avery reached for her mother, only to have her spin around and bump into a man who clutched at her mother's satin-covered hip.

"If the lady wants to dance," he said as he swung her around. Rita giggled again and tossed thin, track-marked arms around his shoulders, as the oversized sleeves bunched around her elbows. Her dance partner wore the uniform of the downtrodden: unwashed jeans, a stained over-coat likely donated to a Salvation Army years after it had gone out of style. A baseball cap shadowed his forehead, but dull brown hair curled against his neck.

Avery hurried toward them. The scent of marijuana was pungent on the man's tattered clothes, and she clutched at Rita's brittle shoulder. "Let her go, please."

He jerked Rita closer, grinding against her. "She said she wants to dance."

"She's high. She wants whatever she can dig out of your pocket," Avery corrected. Rita's hands had inched toward his pockets, and her eyes glazed, signaling her impending crash from whatever she'd ingested. If her mother passed out before they got aboveground, she'd be screwed. Even a 120-pound woman was hard to carry as deadweight. "Fun's over. Let my mother go."

The stoner wrapped his arm more tightly around Rita's waist, pulled her against him; in response, she tucked her head against his shoulder. "See, she likes me."

Avery yanked at Rita, and the man used his free hand to shove her away hard. "You can back off, bitch." Riders sidled away from them along the platform, ignoring the exchange. Even early in the evening, most decided to mind their own business or hope someone else would intervene.

Not wanting a fight or an audience, Avery pleaded quietly, "Rita, come on. We have to go." She advanced again, her fingers closing around the small knife she carried in her pocket for Rita-rescue duty.

Rita slumped half-conscious against the man, who rudely palmed and squeezed her breast as he leered at Avery and glanced down the platform. "Me and Rita here are going to the corner for some fun. Stay right where you are, and I'll have her back to you in a few minutes. Come at me again, and I'll drop you."

The threat of rape failed to penetrate Rita's haze, but it clarified Avery's choices. Behind her back, the blade popped from its sheath. Hopefully, the Metro cameras would capture her attempts at negotiation as well as the assault to come. "Let her go—now. Last chance."

"Kiss my ass, bitch."

Avery took a step forward, the knife at the ready behind her back.

"The young lady asked you to unhand her mother, sir. I would advise you to do so."

The voice behind Avery made her spine stiffen. Unwilling to believe it, she took another step toward her mom. "Give her to me."

"Don't make me call the authorities or force the young woman to demonstrate if she can use the unlawful knife in her hand," Justice Wynn chided gently. "I might even be compelled to assist her."

The stoner stared over Avery's shoulder, then roughly shoved Rita away. "She smells like piss. Take her."

Avery awkwardly caught her mother as he ran down the platform. With a practiced move, she closed the knife with one hand, holding Rita with the other. She then turned reluctantly toward her rescuer. As she'd guessed, Justice Wynn stood behind her. Brandishing a thick ebony cane that would have caused serious damage to a human body. "Sir."

He lowered the cane and leaned on it lightly. "Ms. Keene."

"Thank you." Wrapping her arm around Rita's waist, as she still hummed brokenly, Avery said, "I can explain."

"I don't recall asking. Good evening." With that, he turned away and headed up the escalator.

A mortified Avery bundled Rita onto the next train and dropped her off at her latest flop. When summoned to Justice Wynn's office the next morning, she knocked on the door, prepared to be fired.

"What?"

From the half-open door, she answered, "It's Avery, sir. You asked to see me."

"Then don't hover in the corridor." He waved her inside with an imperious flick of the wrist. "Do you have the *Holley* opinion?"

"Yes, sir. I took the approach you used in *Morton.*" She entered the room quickly. "Mr. Brewer has the lead on the *Hugley Inc.* decision. We should have a draft in the morning." Setting the tabbed stack of notes and rulings on the leather blotter, Avery added, "I've also emailed a copy to your account."

"Fine, fine." Justice Wynn lifted the folder and thumbed the pages, watching Avery beneath hooded lids. "Ms. Keene, you have worked for me for nearly two years now."

Recalling their evening encounter, Avery nodded warily. "Yes, sir."

"You don't exhibit the typical signs of incompetence that I'm used to seeing."

Allowing herself a small smile, flashing a single dimple, she responded dryly, "Thank you, sir. I try to keep my incompetence to a minimum."

"Though not your sarcasm." Before she could stammer an apology, he continued: "Did you enjoy your time at Yale?"

" 'Enjoy' is a strong word, sir. I appreciated the opportunity for a stellar education."

"And before that, you were a student at Spelman College. And at Oberlin. And Centre College. Where you had several different majors. Chemistry, French literature, history, and political science."

"I have a variety of interests."

"Including history."

She nodded. "Yes, sir."

"History. An overly broad endeavor unless you intend to learn the entire biography of man."

Avery said, "I only studied history for a few semesters."

"A biochemical lack of focus? Did you require special aids for your erratic attention span?"

Avery barely avoided gritting her teeth and said, "I preferred American history, but as a freshman or sophomore, it is difficult to specialize."

"Why American history? Other nations have achieved greatness with less hubris and narcissism."

"Agreed. But America is a contradictory and precocious country, sir. We have, in a very short period of time, managed to commit venal sins against our own people and offer the world repeat examples of exceptionalism. Americans are greedy, brilliant, ambitious, and compassionate. We like to remind everyone about our genius, and yet our leaders make fun of smart people. In less than two centuries, we took over more than half a continent, placed a man on the moon, and invented the Clapper. I enjoyed the contrasts."

Wynn continued to watch her, with what Avery perceived as an ounce of amusement on his face. "A nation of favor and folly, one might say. Where justice is known but rarely seen. Which begs why you would also be enamored of studying the French. Not many tales of derring-do outside a Dumas novel."

"French literature seemed romantic, if not terribly practical. That's why I dropped it later."

"I am a student of the French writers myself. They possess a singular ability to make the barbaric elegant. Who did you prefer during your brief acquaintance?"

"I was partial to Corneille and Voltaire."

"Voltaire's tendency to jump from subject to subject would appeal to you, I suppose."

They'd covered this territory in her interviews, but she played along. "It did."

"And traipsing from school to school?"

"Family circumstances." Which he'd gotten a firsthand example of last night.

"A paltry phrase," scoffed Justice Wynn. "Did 'family circumstances' impact your education?"

"No. At all three schools, I maintained a 4.0 GPA."

"Your eidetic memory is responsible for most of your success in that, I'd wager."

Avery avoided the instinct to wince. "My memory, sir?"

"Think I didn't notice, young lady? No one naturally retains cases as you do. Then there is your tendency to gaze up when recalling details. You're reading the pages in the air, aren't you?"

Caught, Avery nodded again, tightly. "My memory is an asset, Your Honor. Not a crutch. I know what I'm doing, and I know what I know."

"Got your dander up now, I see. No questioning your family or your ability to cheat on learning by using a parlor trick."

Avery wanted to react, but she held her tongue. He'd caught her off guard, and he wanted her to react. But she'd learned from the best to hold still. To wait for it.

When she said nothing, Justice Wynn grinned, a twist of the mouth that held little humor. "Nicely done. You even know how to keep your eyes cool."

"Excuse me?"

"Your eyes don't give you away. When I served in district court, I could always tell. Lawyer or defendant, same reaction. Dilated pupils, gritted teeth. Do you play chess?"

Bemused by the changing subjects, she nodded. "I'm okay at it."

"Liar."

"Excuse me?"

"You're lying. Probably, you're an excellent player who lies out of habit. Don't want folks knowing how good you are."

Avery shrugged and conceded, "I can hold my own, sir."

"Hmm." He studied her until she wanted to squirm. "Liars are all alike, aren't they?"

Holding her temper with effort, Avery reminded herself of the prestige of her current position and the penalty for being fired for insubordination. She'd worked too hard to get here. The wrong words, and she'd be out on her unemployable butt. He was looking for something, goading her. She wouldn't fail whatever test he was giving. In a low, controlled voice, she queried, "If that's all—"

"I will dismiss you when I'm done, Ms. Keene. Not before." He pinned her with a level look. "I asked you a question. Do you believe liars are all alike?"

"No, sir."

"Why not?"

With a shrug, she explained, "Some lie for gain, others for protection. The lie matters."

"You're saying there are good lies?"

"Lies and truth aren't good or bad. A bad person can tell the truth, and an honest person can lie."

"That's an evasion."

"Yes."

"Hmm." He nodded once. "Do you still gamble?"

"On what, sir?"

The explosion of gruff laughter filled the room. "Excellent question. What would you gamble on? Theoretically."

Avery paused, considering her answer carefully. This was the longest personal conversation she'd ever shared with him, other than her interviews. That one had been equally difficult, but he hadn't been as intrusive. He wanted to know something; she just didn't know what. Or why.

She replied, "Games of chance are entertaining, but ultimately, they're only worth it if you know when to cut your losses. A good gambler knows how to balance risk and reward. For example, telling your boss that you made the rent during college by fleecing other students reveals a penchant for nonlegal behavior but also shows ingenuity and a flair for the unconventional."

"Indeed. And a flouting of the law, if the South is as I remember it."

"Not much has changed."

"What's your game?"

"Poker. Blackjack at casinos if the pit boss isn't watching too closely. Chess in the park if I'm in the right town."

"How often do you gamble now?"

"I don't."

"Why not?"

"My salary meets my current needs. I never wagered for extravagance, sir. Only for necessity."

"How do you gauge the difference?"

Avery's mouth curved. "I've got a lot of experience with need, sir. It's not hard to tell them apart."

He bent forward, lifting a Montblanc LeGrand that could feed a small family for a week. Balancing the pen on his palm, he pressed: "Others would disagree. Need and want look identical to most. What makes you better at seeing the difference? The nobility of poverty?"

"I'm not noble, Your Honor. Just practical."

"Practical?"

"Yes, sir. Gambling for want is a risk. I don't believe in jeopardizing what I've got for a negligible chance at something better, not unless I can't make what I've got work somehow."

"Poker is a risky game for most. I prefer chess. A noble game. Not one that should be denigrated by speed matches in a park."

She winced. "It can be fun. Racing against the clock and your opponent."

"I do not believe that the maharajahs of ancient India would agree. When first invented, the game was known as chaturaṅga. The Moors brought it to Europe, and it became the game we call chess. That's when the queen became the most powerful piece, but still in service to a king. What do you think of that?"

"Of what, sir?"

"Of the queen being responsible for saving the king, but that only his life is sacred. Should offend your feminist sensibilities, no?"

Avery grinned. "My feminist sensibilities are not offended. In a game of strategy, the king is a figurehead, unable to save his own life without the aid of others. The queen is powerful and dynamic. She will protect the king, but not because of weakness. It's because that's what she's supposed to do." She added, "It was in the tenth century that the queen replaced the vizier on the chessboard. *Vizier* meant leader, and in the next five hundred years, she became the most powerful piece on the board. A nice evolution."

"Because I find most people too pedestrian to engage in person, I play online. A hardy game without the chatter."

"I'm surprised." She'd never taken the justice for a gamer.

He tapped his computer screen. "Chessdynamo.com."

"Oh." Unsure of what to say, she looked at the screen. "I'll check it out."

"You should." A finger tapped his chin thoughtfully. "And what of loyalty?"

Confused by the shifting conversation, Avery tightened her fingers on the folder in her hands. "What do you mean?"

"Loyalty, Ms. Keene. How does that factor into your decision-making?"

"I keep my promises and repay my debts. Is that what you're asking?"

"In part." He reclined and steepled his fingers in contemplation. "Do you stand by those you promise loyalty to, even when what they ask seems absurd or even perilous?"

Avery met his eyes with a level gaze. "I choose my friends carefully, Your Honor. Friendship carries obligations; and, as I said, I keep my promises and repay my debts."

Justice Wynn continued to watch her, his expression inscrutable. She refused to fidget. Instead, she stood there, her arms hanging loosely at her sides. A few moments later, he asked, "What about me, Ms. Keene? Where do I fall in this hierarchy of loyalty?"

"Your Honor?"

"A simple question. Are you loyal to me?"

"I'm loyal to this Court," she began cautiously. "I swore to uphold the law and support the Constitution. As your clerk, it is my obligation to do everything in my power to achieve that and to assist you in doing so."

A bushy white eyebrow rose. "Ah, then it is the job that holds your respect. Not me."

"I didn't say that, sir. You asked about my loyalty. I work for you, so I will do my best to support you and the decisions you make, as long as they are constitutional and legal."

"And if what I assert as legal is not squarely within the four walls of the Constitution? What then?"

"Then we look for a way to make it fit, if we can," she replied. "If not, though, I won't break the law for you or anyone, Justice Wynn. I respect and admire you, but the law comes first. Always."

"Carry knives, notwithstanding." Justice Wynn grunted and lifted the folder again. He replaced it and picked up a blue folder with a yellow tab and uncapped the pen. "You do not, however, pay careful attention to all your paperwork. Personnel sent up a form that requires your signature."

Chagrined, Avery approached the desk and accepted the proffered pen. She opened the folder and saw the signature block. She reached for the next page, asking, "What did I forget to sign?"

"I'm not your administrative assistant, Ms. Keene. Sign the papers, and please return to the tasks for which I am certain you are overcompensated."

The curmudgeon's back, she thought, as she ignored the other pages. She scrawled her name across the dark line and added the date in a hurried rush. Share time and Justice Wynn's version of the Inquisition obviously ended, she returned the pen and quickly left the office.

.   .   .

As she stared down at the papers now, a chill shivered through her. The guardianship papers were signed by Justice Wynn the following Monday and witnessed by a Noah Fox. None of them had her signature. Had she really signed personnel papers that day? Avery lifted the phone and dialed the person who might know.

"Clerk's Office, Lisa Borders speaking."

"Hi, this is Avery Keene."

The voice softened. "Yes, Ms. Keene. How can I help you?"

Avery heard the unasked query about Justice Wynn but ignored the request. Lisa would get her information like everyone else—from the news. "In January, Justice Wynn had me sign some personnel papers. I was wondering if I could get a copy from you."

"Personnel documents? Hold on a second for me." The line went silent, and Avery scanned her emails. A couple of minutes elapsed before Lisa returned to the phone. "I'm sorry, Ms. Keene, but you haven't signed any new documents since you were hired, except for your updated W-4. Did you need to see that?"

Surprise clashed with foreboding, but Avery managed to respond, "No, thank you. I must have been mistaken."

"Well, let me know if you need anything else."

The line disconnected, and Avery returned the phone to its cradle. If she hadn't signed a personnel document, what had she signed?

EIGHT

How the hell did we miss this?!" The smash of the ceramic cup against a priceless urn from a now-deposed head of state punctuated the question. As the pieces scattered on the plush carpet, the Oval Office returned to silence. "You were supposed to be watching the Court, Will! Homeland Security, my ass. Why give you a cushy job over there with military-grade clearance if you're going to disappoint me?"

President Brandon Stokes glared across the room, fuming. The daily sweeps and high-tech antisurveillance technology provided by his liaison from the Science and Technology Directorate guaranteed he wouldn't be overheard. Post-Watergate and the LBJ tapes, no president ran the risk of eavesdropping. The Oval Office was one of the most secure rooms on the planet.

Will Vance watched his old friend in silence, knowing the hot temper would soon cool. A crystal ashtray was swept off the desk and a volley of pens sailed through the air, and then the president dropped into his chair and folded his hands beneath his chin. "Pick those up for me, will you? We have a photo op in here in an hour. Brownies or Webelos or street urchins. Who the hell remembers?"

The urn had broken in clean pieces, which Vance dutifully recovered. As he dropped them into the wastebasket, he explained, "The chief justice kept the letter to herself. Swears she didn't know what was inside. I find it hard to believe that he gave her no hint of what the contents were."

"Justice Wynn is a crafty bastard," President Stokes acknowledged. "That performance at the graduation was a warning. But if he'd known exactly what happened, that son of a bitch would have shouted it from the steps of the Court. No, this anointing of the girl is all about self-preservation. Mortality is a strong motivator, and there's nothing like a young woman to keep the depression at bay."

"I don't believe this was an office romance. He had something worth sending coded messages for."

"What are you talking about?"

"Surveillance picked up a call from Wynn's house. The message said, 'Look to the East and to the river' for starters."

The president's eyes narrowed. "He couldn't know."

"We cannot dismiss the possibility. A vague clue about a river in the Middle East isn't much to go on." Vance scooped up the scattered pens and dropped them into the holder on the desk. "As for how we missed this, our surveillance was only a few weeks old. My team tracked his inquiry to the High Court judge in India, but we couldn't find any other communications. Just the reference to the Tigris Project, which even the Indians believe is just urban legend." Laying the ashtray on the corner of the wide mahogany surface, he asked, "Do you know anyone named Lask Bauer?"

The president's head jerked up. "Who?"

"Lask Bauer. Maybe one name or two surnames. That was also in the message we picked up. I haven't had a chance to run the IDs through NCTC yet."

"Are you certain that's what he said?"

"Yes."

President Stokes leaned forward, slowly shaking his head. Then he gave a brief laugh. "Son of a bitch."

"Do you know them? Lask or Bauer?"

"I never had the pleasure," President Stokes said. "Justice Wynn didn't either. He's referring to a chess strategy known as the Lasker-Bauer sacrifice. In 1889, Emanuel Lasker defeated Johann Bauer at a tournament in Amsterdam. Lasker used his bishops on the board to lure Bauer into taking them. But in the process, Bauer left his queen vulnerable, and Lasker used that failure to win the match. Damn, that crafty bastard is still playing a game, even in a coma."

"I am not a chess player, Mr. President."

"I keep forgetting. Seems right up your alley." The president turned to stare at his own chessboard that sat atop a credenza. The pieces had been hand-carved by an artisan in Nepal. "The bishops are interesting pieces. They stand next to the king and queen—the third most important pieces on the board. One might call them the guardians."

"So Avery Keene is one of the bishops." Vance folded his hands behind himself.

The president nodded. "Wynn is using her as bait to force us to make a careless move.

"If he's being literal, we need to identify the second bishop in play." He lifted the two pieces and set them side by side. "Whoever it is led Wynn to India. The project was so secure, not even their government knew about it until we had to shut it down."

"Tigris was buried until Srinivasan tried to take GenWorks. It might be her," Vance said.

President Stokes shook his head. "Nigel Cooper is more likely. He's already convinced Wall Street that I'm the second coming of Herbert Hoover. I let this merger happen, and Cooper becomes a billionaire, while I get marched off to prison." The president recognized the greedy reach that propelled the man, an avarice that should have been useful to him. But the ultraliberal entrepreneur despised him, and he hated Cooper right back. "We find out who tipped off Wynn, we find the second bishop."

"I've pored over the intel. Justice Wynn served on an international commission on the rule of law with Arun Mohan, the High Court chief justice for Karnataka. Mohan's wife sits on an NGO board tasked with securing foreign aid for medical research. Apparently, at a dinner party, Mrs. Mohan chattered to her husband and his American colleague about a biogenetics company called Hygeia that has collapsed. Banal dinner conversation, except that Justice Wynn had already begun his research into possible cures for Boursin's."

"When?"

"The encounter was right before the start of term last October. By then, Advar had dismantled and absorbed Hygeia. The Tigris Project and the tech were buried, but Mohan gave Justice Wynn a place to start."

"And he thought he had sufficient reason to keep digging." President Stokes pushed away from the desk and circled around to the shelves lined with tchotchkes collected over nearly two centuries by his predecessors. "A dinner conversation leads him to Tigris."

"A dinner conversation and the research capacity of the U.S. Supreme Court, sir," Vance corrected. "Knowing about Hygeia did not lead him to Tigris. Someone else did. However, we're tying off the ends, Mr. President, and this will be one of them."

"Faster, Will. I'm too close. Do you remember what happened in Darra Adam Khel?"

"You don't need to ask me about Pakistan."

Vance's reaction was almost undetectable, but Stokes had known him too long not to see. Vance revealed too little to allow any expression to go unnoticed. Satisfied, the president said, "I have not gone a day without remembering. Not in more than a decade. We've masterminded a solution for the greatest threat facing America in the twenty-first century."

He clenched a miniaturized ceremonial mace from the Philippines and turned to Vance. "Nigel Cooper and those West Coast snobs mock me for believing in God. For believing in freedom and patriotism. We will not be brought down by him or a comatose judicial tyrant."

"No, sir," Vance replied.

That night in Pakistan, though years past, had bonded Vance with the man who'd become president and given him his life's mission. Tigris was more than a stealth military project. It was a revolution, one he'd help birth. "Our contact assures me that their end is taken care of, and you've stopped the merger between Advar and GenWorks. Justice Wynn is lying in a coma instead of leading the efforts on a faulty judicial opinion. All the intelligence we've gathered says the Court is otherwise split. Wynn is the swing vote, and for all practical purposes, he is dead to the world."

Not placated, Stokes countered: "Bullshit. Being in a coma does not take him off the Court. And now some girl with a law degree is in charge."

"Sir, we have no reason to believe the Court won't deadlock with Justice Wynn incapacitated and near death. Justice Wynn can't sign a majority opinion from a coma, nor can he empower his clerk to vote for him. I have already asked White House counsel to provide a detailed memo on the options. As you've rightly pointed out, he stays on the Court until he resigns or dies. A guardian may be able to proffer his resignation, but this situation is unprecedented, Mr. President."

The president stopped beside a low blue brocade sofa with an end table. He opened a ceramic bowl, a gift from the Ghanaian prime minister, and popped a square of licorice into his mouth. The bitter tang matched his mood. He stopped in front of his old friend and consigliere. "Wynn put the law clerk in play as the first bishop. We need to figure out who the second bishop is. Wynn anticipated that we'd try to stop him, and he has set up a separate path to victory. They may not even know they both exist."

"We'll figure it out, sir."

The president said nothing. He counted Vance as one of his few friends, a term he used very carefully these days. Stokes had been surrounded by fair-weather allies during his first year in office as President Warren Cadres's young and vigorous vice president. They'd heralded Stokes as a military hero turned political rock star. A Purple Heart and Bronze Star had boosted his campaign for the U.S. Senate, which he'd launched after his last tour of duty. He raised record-breaking sums of money and trounced his opponents. Appointed to serve on the Armed Services Committee, he became the telegenic attack dog who destroyed a shaky Democratic president. They'd tapped him in committee hearings to disembowel the hapless Navy secretary whose wife had divested millions in stock in an insider trading scandal. Two years later, he got elected as President Cadres's chief lieutenant at the age of forty-eight. In a landslide campaign, he'd been the toast of the Republican Party and the model for all politicians, of any political stripe, seemingly more popular than the president himself. Heir apparent to the throne.

And helpmate to a doddering old man too incompetent to be an effective president. As vice president, he had assumed the mantle of leadership, calling upon his years in military service to calm the nerves of a nation in the grips of buyer's remorse. It had been he, not President Cadres, who had traveled to meet foreign dignitaries and address the

United Nations. He was the one who had negotiated treaties and run the government. He who'd summoned his boot camp bunkmate Will Vance, who'd created a brilliant plan that would dwarf the Manhattan Project.

Two years into his term, President Cadres stumbled onto their work, a discovery solved by a precipitate heart attack that vaulted Vice President Brandon Stokes into the presidency; his reputation soared. He'd been expected to cruise to reelection, but that was before a plummeting stock market, an ill-fated rescue mission into Antananarivo, and a private conversation caught by a hot mike.

Worse, on the eve of his resurgence, the nation of India—his unwitting partner in their great act of patriotism—decided to grow a backbone and deny his signature trade deal. The timing couldn't have been worse.

The very next week, he'd had to sign an order stopping a merger that would destroy him. The financials on GenWorks would show clandestine U.S. funding for a covert military project. American tolerance for such behavior had eroded during Vietnam and ended altogether after Iran-Contra.

And that was without knowing what the Tigris Project could do.

So he'd issued the order, let Nigel Cooper's investors yell bloody murder, and watched, stunned, as Silicon Valley took out hate ads across the country.

His once-glowing poll numbers now lingered inches above electoral death. All because he and Vance had tried to protect the nation they revered. "I don't have to remind you how critical this operation is. What we've done is something those lightweights in Congress will never understand."

"Tigris was imperative, Mr. President. We had no choice."

"How will you deal with the law clerk?"

"She seems as baffled as anyone about Justice Wynn's intentions. I have her under surveillance, and I will know what she knows."

"Why not bring her in for questioning?"

"The chief justice has warned me that we have no grounds." Anticipating the protest, he held up a hand. "Yet."

"Can we check Justice Wynn's computer now that he's down?"

"The Court is a fortress. The justices will not accept Secret Service security, and they run on a network that is impenetrable from the outside. I have not found a vulnerability we can effectively exploit. Until I know more about the clerk, we have to move cautiously."

Lifting one of the ergonomic stress balls he kept on his desk, Stokes completed the thought: "Can't we get a friendly judge to replace the clerk with Celeste Wynn? She's still his wife."

"Possibly. I've reviewed Keene's NCTC file and am having one compiled on her mother and roommate. We'll know why he chose her by this afternoon, and I'll try to put this to rest."

"See that you do." Stokes motioned to Vance to join him at the French doors overlooking the lawn. "I appreciate your loyalty and your efficiency, Will."

"Thank you, sir."

"To maintain the peace, I cater to the Far Right and cavil to the farther Right and pretend to have patience with the weak-willed Left. I've denounced what I know to be true, all in the name of patriotism and bipartisanship."

"You've made tough choices, sir."

"I made the only choices I could, given the threats we face. Tigris could stop terrorism in its tracks." He faced Vance. "We are patriots, Vance. Men committed to the common good. A common good that will have dire consequences if the Advar and GenWorks merger is allowed to proceed. The world won't understand the knowledge we've gained. You know what's been done—and what must be done."

"I can handle Avery Keene. We'll find a loophole."

"I want a vacant seat by recess, Will." The president looked through the glass again. "Did you know that Eisenhower put William Brennan on the Supreme Court through a recess appointment?"

Because they'd had this conversation a dozen times in the last three weeks, Vance did know, but he answered, "Sir?"

"Eisenhower waited until Congress scattered back to their homes and put Brennan right on the Court." The president watched as armed men changed shifts beyond the Oval Office. They each had only one mission, one objective. Protect him, and by doing so, protect the country. "With Justice Wynn off the bench, I can make history. *History.* And none of the damned Democrats on Capitol Hill will be able to stop me. Not with a split vote and an empty chair. Empty until I fill it. But the chair needs to be empty first. Make that happen, Will. Then this whole mess is behind us."

"I understand, sir."

NINE

What did Justice Wynn trick me into signing? Avery stared at the neat tower of files on her desk, contemplating the myriad possibilities. Realizing the answer was probably in his office, she quickly jumped up and peeked outside her door, but no one waited. Matt was likely in another justice's chambers, trying to get hired on for next year. Justice Wynn's overwrought secretaries had been sent home for the day, which left her free to look around.

Quietly, she unlocked Justice Wynn's office, pushed the heavy door shut behind her, and turned the latch. Papers stood in careful stacks, and legal tomes lined the walls and tables. Although Justice Wynn was computer literate, he preferred the touch and utility of bound volumes to the efficient speed of Westlaw or Lexis. Avery methodically checked each of the files, hunting for one that she might have signed. Most of the documents were categorized by topic, including requests for certiorari, opinions to be read, and items that had caught his eye. None included a form with her handwriting.

Frustrated, Avery crossed to his desk and sat gingerly in the leather swivel chair, which had taken the shape of its owner. Unlike the tables, the desktop was clear except for a jar of pens, a stack of legal pads, and his computer. With one hand, she jabbed the power button on the computer. While it booted up, she reached for the closest pull. The drawer didn't move.

"Come on," she muttered as she yanked again, harder, to no avail.

"Of course he locked it." Thinking of her own government desk, Avery reached into the center console where Post-it notes and other office debris collected. Beneath a slab of pink messages, she found a letter opener. Lifting the slim silver piece, she ran her thumb over the surface and pushed back to study the lock. Basic bolt style, she realized, as she inserted the tip and maneuvered the letter opener. The metal rod slid, and she yanked on the drawer, which opened beneath her tug.

Files lined in dark green folders had been tabbed by content. Most tabs corresponded to an appeal the Court had agreed to hear that term. In her first year as Justice Wynn's clerk, it had been her responsibility to organize the files, from request for certiorari to amicus briefs and attendant research. Brewer had done the honors this year. When Matt had complained, Justice Wynn had dismissed the work as beneath the dignity of his secretaries.

Smiling slightly, Avery riffled through and read the names in a whisper: *"Arnoste. Cavanaugh. DeLeCroix. Evans Wholesale. Frontage Street Development."* The files continued to the drawer below. She closed the top drawer and opened the bottom. *"Fulton, et al. GenWorks."*

Her hand froze. The *GenWorks* folder, which should have held volumes, sat empty. Nothing inside except the tab that indicated its former contents. Eleven files with *GenWorks* on the hanging tab, all empty. She'd been assigned to *GenWorks,* an assignment she'd regretted when Justice Wynn had gone beyond his usual meticulous detail into obsessive data gathering. She had been required to write several memos analyzing case law and chasing down information about executive privilege and presidential overreach.

Hundreds of pages of work product, and none of it was in the desk. After the empty *GenWorks* folder, the next tab read *Human Resources.* Pulling the file out, she found two slim folders, one with *Brewer, Matthew* in neat type, the second with *Keene, Avery.* She glanced up at the door, then opened her file first. Inside, she found her application for the clerkship, law school transcripts, letters of recommendation, and a note scrawled on top in Justice Wynn's handwriting. *Adequate.* She shuffled the pages again in search of the document she'd signed, to no avail. Whatever she'd agreed to, it wasn't in his office.

Avery started to close the file, then decided to peek inside Matt's compendium. She snorted when she saw that the note attached to his application read *Bearable.*

Stymied, Avery shoved the drawer closed and jerked open the third compartment, which sat on her right. *International Coastal Alliance,* a water wars case, began the files. A quick review showed the rest of the folders filled to capacity. All except the empty *GenWorks* drawer.

"Where's all our research, Justice Wynn?" She began to search the office, methodically quartering the room, knowing it was futile. Unlike some lawyers, Justice Wynn despised clutter. No leftover documents or unread journal articles rested on tables beyond the unfiled information on active cases. As she thumbed through, she couldn't find any of her work or Matt's on the case. The office was nearly as empty as it had been when he'd inherited the space decades ago. Wherever the *GenWorks* file had gone, the answer was not there.

Her eyes returned to the computer, and Avery sat down again. The screen requested a password from her, the icon blinking helpfully. She typed the first name that came to mind: C-E-L-E-S-T-E. The response was *invalid password.* A second attempt used his title. *J-U-S-T-I-C-E.* Again, the computer rejected the command.

Slouching against the chair, she chewed on her bottom lip. Justice Wynn didn't have a pet or hobby or anything she could think of. The most personal information she knew about him was his favorite sandwich, pastrami on rye with mustard, and his estrangement from his family. Indeed, the single personal item in the office was a framed photo of him and a young boy with a fishing rod, who she assumed to be his son.

Giving a wild guess, she leaned forward again and typed in *J-A-R-E-D.* When the computer warned that another try would result in a lockout, Avery froze. She stared at the photo again, recalling the article she'd once read about him. He was only a few years older than her. Avery typed his name once more and added his birth year.

The computer whirred to life. Elated, she waited for the system to load. As soon as it did, she made her way to his computer directory. "Where would you hide whatever you're hiding, sir?"

Her search revealed nothing more than notes on all the Court's current cases and opinions he'd agreed to write. As with the desk files, the folder that should have contained *GenWorks* information was empty. "You don't want anyone to know what you think," she whispered into the room. "So you clear out the files and erase them from your hard drive."

Avery considered the implications. Justice Wynn was notoriously obstinate and rarely shared his thoughts with his colleagues outside conference, when a stated opinion was eventually mandatory. "Given the rumors, I'm the only other person who knows what you were thinking." She gave a rueful laugh. "And I don't know what you were thinking."

The research in her office had focused exclusively on executive privilege and the legislative intent of the Exon-Florio Amendment. No mysterious assignments.

But, she thought suddenly, what about emails? She opened his Outlook and began to skim through the folders. He organized his messages by sender and subject. A folder marked *Chief* sat at the top of the food chain, followed by each of his fellow justices and then a folder labeled *Clerks*.

She clicked on the plus sign and found three folders. The first bore her name, the second Matt's. But the third folder bore another name she recognized. *Chessdynamo.*

Avery clicked on the folder. The first message in the box was from Justice Wynn to himself. It was the subject line that caught her attention. *Ani Is in the River.*

Perplexed because Ani was neither a case name nor an employee, she opened the message, only to confront more confusion. *Dumas Find Ani.* WHTW5730.

Dumas. Wynn had told her that he was the only French writer with any sense of adventure. *Like breaking into your boss's office and into his computer files.* Yet, except for a strange message and the code of numbers and letters, the email was empty. No direction or clear indication that this wasn't a moment of confusion for an increasingly ill man.

She closed the email and scanned the contents of the folder. Several messages had been sent to different phone numbers, each ending with @comcel.co.in. These were SMS texts transmitted via email to India. Nearly twenty in all. Each message was short and on different days and times that spanned nearly a year. The message for each was the same: *In the square.*

Interspersed, Avery found additional items that were equally opaque, including a link to a YouTube video. She clicked on the link. The noto-riously slow connection spun its warning circle as the browser searched for the video. Eventually, the site announced that the video was no longer available. Frowning, she printed the page and quickly scrolled through the remaining messages. More broken links and terse messages filled the folder. Realizing she might not be allowed to log on to his computer again, she scanned the messages once more, committing the contents to memory.

Frustrated, Avery shoved away from the desk and spun the chair toward the windows. Who was Ani and what did Dumas mean? Who or what was in the square? Avery reached for the drawer handle, won-dering if perhaps she'd overlooked something, but her phone's vibration caught her attention.

While she answered, she decided to print the folder contents, just in case. Her memory was excellent, but not infallible. "This is Avery Keene."

"Ms. Keene, this is Dr. Michael Toca, Justice Wynn's neurologist. I understand you are the woman in charge right now."

Warily, she replied, "How can I help you?"

"I've got a bit of a situation on my hands, Ms. Keene. I need you to come to Bethesda Naval Hospital immediately."

Avery asked quietly, "Has Justice Wynn's condition changed?"

"No, Ms. Keene, but his condition isn't the issue." With a sigh, Dr. Toca explained, "His wife and son are. Please get down here as soon as possible before I have a new patient."

"I'm in DC, but I'll be there as quickly as possible."

"Hurry."

The doctor disconnected, and Avery closed the folder she'd reviewed and collected the papers from the printer. As she prepared to power down the computer, she hesitated. The Court files were notoriously impenetrable from the outside, but anyone on the Court's team could locate what she'd discovered. She didn't know what that was, but instinct told her to get rid of what was there. Sitting back down, she deleted the *Chessdynamo* folder and its contents, tucked the papers into an enve-lope, and left the office.

TEN

Avery entered the wide, white hallways of Bethesda Naval Hospital and found her way to the information desk. Around her, families milled with friends, many in uniform. She despised hospitals and waiting rooms, the medicinal scent of death's arrival. Impatient to be done with her visit, she waited in a short line to explain her business to the receptionist and present her ID. "I'm here to see Dr. Toca. He's in neurology."

A lanky frame ensconced in a white lab coat approached her post near the desk. "Ms. Keene," he greeted her, extending a long-fingered hand that could have played Mozart. "Dr. Michael Toca. I appreciate you coming so quickly."

"You said it was urgent," she responded as he ushered her along a tiled corridor. "His wife is here?"

Dr. Toca led her through a maze of halls and into an elevator. As they rode up, he explained, "Not just Mrs. Turner-Wynn, but his son, Jared, too."

This surprised Avery. Jared Wynn bore the distinction of being the only child of Howard Wynn, a status he apparently did not covet. In her time at the Court, she'd met Mrs. Turner-Wynn a number of times, but Jared had never put in an appearance. Though his photo was the only one in the justice's office, the man never spoke of his son or the marriage that had produced him.

However, the secretaries of the Court provided all the salient details. The first Mrs. Wynn had been a fellow law student with Howard, one of a handful of women in her class. They'd fallen in love and married right after graduation. The union produced one son, and, ten years later, the first Mrs. Wynn died in their tony Georgetown home. Young Jared went to live with his aunt and uncle, and Howard Wynn sold the house. He bought another one two blocks away and never lived with his son again. For the next fifteen years, he lived as a bachelor, until he married socialite Celeste Turner.

Avery had never asked about his son; nor had she inquired about the very public estrangement of his second wife, Celeste. Six months ago, under Celeste's orders, according to the gossip, movers had parked on Reservoir Road and bundled suitcases and boxes into a truck. The next morning, she'd become a resident of the St. Regis, and Justice Wynn had once again become a bachelor. But the oft-rumored divorce from Celeste had never materialized.

Which explained the tableau that greeted Avery in Dr. Toca's office.

Celeste Turner-Wynn clung to youth with a fighter's tenacity. At forty-one, she claimed thirty-five and looked twenty-five. Ruthlessly pampered sable brown hair flowed from a high widow's peak down to perfectly sloped shoulders. Haughty brows hovered over liquid brown eyes framed with a thick fringe of lash.

She stood near a tall window, where sunlight cunningly gilded her hair, firing strands into gold. For today's meeting, she'd worn widow's weeds, as interpreted by Versace. Severe black, unrelieved by the black seed pearls at her neck and ears, befitted the mourning wife. The look of annoyance directed at Avery wasn't a sharp departure from Celeste's usual expression of haughty dismissal.

Avery glanced at the room's other occupant. The man she assumed to be Jared Wynn lounged on the single sofa in the capacious office, long legs clad in jeans frayed at the hem. Black work boots that had never seen a construction site bore the casual scuff marks of pedestrian wear. In deference to the solemnity of the occasion, he'd tossed a blue polo shirt over his white tee, the buttons half undone. The angular face with its square jaw and hollowed cheeks replicated photos of Justice Wynn from his younger days.

She took a quick step back, surprised by the painful resemblance, only to bump into Dr. Toca. "Sorry."

"Wait until you talk to them," he whispered behind her, not unkindly.

Toca guided her inside and shut the door firmly, not eager to have an audience. "Avery Keene, this is Celeste Turner-Wynn and Jared Wynn," he explained as he ushered her into a chair by his desk.

Avery sat on the edge of the cushion, ready to spring up at any moment. Reaching for her manners, she began, "Hello. I'm sorry to be here under such difficult circumstances. Justice Wynn means a great deal to me, and I'm praying for his recovery."

Celeste waved imperially and spoke to Dr. Toca. "I still don't understand why she's here. I am his wife."

"Estranged," corrected Jared, who did not move from his insolent repose. "I'm his legal next of kin, Doctor. And with all due respect to Ms. Keene here, I'm the only child he's got."

Dr. Toca shot a look of apology to Avery. "As I told you both, Ms. Keene has information relating to Justice Wynn that must be taken into consideration before any actions can be taken on his behalf."

"She's his clerk, Doctor. Not his attorney," Celeste scoffed. "A cute little thing, right up Howard's alley, and her concern is touching but irrelevant. Until I sign the divorce decree, he's still my husband."

"I am as shocked by his decision as you both must have been." Avery clutched her bag in her lap, a copy of the POA folded inside. The original had been locked away in her office right after Toca's call. "I didn't know until today."

For the first time, Jared moved, shifting forward to stare at her. "Didn't know what?"

With a confused look at Dr. Toca, Avery's pulse spiked. "Didn't you tell them?"

He shook his head. "On advice of the hospital counsel—they thought you should be the one to do it. I'm sorry, Ms. Keene."

"Sorry about what?" Celeste lost her hauteur and crossed briskly from the window to slap her hands on the doctor's desk. A diamond winked below the lights. "What exactly is this woman doing here?" She straightened and folded her arms. "I've expressed Howard's wishes about this matter. He told me several times he wants no heroic measures taken on his behalf. I demand he be removed from life support today. As he has said, if God wants him to live, he'll be able to breathe on his own."

"Like God gives a damn." Jared's muttered epithet came as he rose and advanced to the desk. His tall, lanky frame had the athletic build of a runner, and his close-cropped hair echoed the paler brown of his eyes. "I didn't know him too well myself, but from what I recall, the judge is too self-involved to have a death wish, Doctor. But regardless, no one in this room has the right to speak for him but me."

"You?" Celeste challenged as she whipped her head toward Jared, lips curled into a snarl. Color streaked along razor-edged cheekbones. "You admit you haven't bothered to speak to him in years. Now you know what he wants? What about when he wanted your forgiveness? Where were you then?"

"What happened between me and him is none of your business, Celeste. I don't ask why you're living in a hotel and who visits you there, do I?" The warning was cool, direct. Anger was palpable in his voice, as was a tone that nearly sounded like sorrow. Turning from Celeste, Jared pointed to Avery. "It's not your concern either. I'm the judge's next of kin. I decide."

"Ms. Keene?" Dr. Toca gave her a look of chagrin. "I think you should explain what's happened."

She'd rather feed raw meat to a den of ravenous lions with a toothpick as her weapon, Avery realized. They'd probably be less vicious.

Trapped, Avery got to her feet, bag in hand. She looked at everyone in the room, took a deep breath, and then plunged in: "Mr. Wynn, Mrs. Turner-Wynn, there is something you should know."

"Unless you suddenly received a medical degree, I have no interest in hearing from you." Celeste skewered her with a withering glance. "Unlike Jared, I know who you are, Ms. Keene. An opportunist and a glorified legal secretary. Neither of which qualifies you to be in this room. This is a family matter, and whatever you were to my husband, you are certainly not family."

Jared shrugged in agreement. "With all due respect to Dr. Toca, you have no business here. If you'll give us some privacy." Turning his back to her, Jared shifted and cut off her view of Dr. Toca.

Avery had never cared for Justice Wynn's wife, and his son apparently had inherited his father's social skills. Dr. Toca gave her a desperate look.

Steeling herself, Avery explained without preamble, "Justice Wynn has named me his legal guardian. I hold his power of attorney." Silence fell as Avery reached into her bag to produce the pages. "I have the notarized document right here."

"What?" Celeste lunged for the pages, certain there was a mistake. The White House had promised her—

With claws tipped in carmine, she snatched the offending sheets from Avery. "No. No." She flipped through to the last page, where Justice Wynn's distinctive signature glared up at her. "This is a fake! It's a forgery! He wouldn't do this to me."

"But he would do it to me," Jared said slowly. "Even at the end, he'd push me away." He didn't argue, didn't reach for the papers. Instead, he moved away from the unfolding scene. "So be it."

"This isn't real," Celeste whispered, her eyes still frozen on the POA. "I'm his wife. I decide."

"I'm sorry, Mrs. Turner-Wynn," Avery managed.

"Sorry? You will be." The elegant mouth thinned into a razor's edge, blindingly white teeth barely visible. "I know your kind, Ms. Keene. I won't let you do this to me."

"I didn't do this," Avery protested. "Justice Wynn did."

"Why would he do such a thing? Unless you seduced him."

"Mrs. Turner-Wynn—"

"More likely, he was senile. Which makes this invalid." She waved the documents and then began to rip at the pages.

Jared stepped between them and caught Celeste's wrist, forcing her to open her hand. Avery snatched the papers back. They weren't the original, but Celeste didn't know that.

"Cut it out, Celeste. This isn't her fault. The judge did exactly what he wanted—like always—and damn everyone else." He walked to the sofa and bent to retrieve a black canvas satchel, reaching inside the front pocket, then slinging the strap across his broad shoulders. He returned to the desk and extended his hand to Avery. As she placed hers inside, he closed his fingers tight. "Take care of him, Ms. Keene."

He dropped her hand and strode out of the doctor's office. Celeste, teeth still bared, shoved past Avery and snatched up her purse.

She tossed her head and declared, "Jared may be willing to let you steal his birthright, but I won't. You will hear from my lawyers."

In outraged splendor, she sailed from the room, leaving the office door ajar. The doctor sank back into his chair and ran his fingers through the remaining thatch of graying brown hair on his scalp. "I'm sorry about that, Ms. Keene." He looked up and caught her eyes. "May I call you Avery?"

"Yes," she responded absently, her fist shut hard. "I'd like to see him. Justice Wynn."

"He's in testing right now. You can visit him soon."

"Okay. Is there anything I need to know right now, Dr. Toca? Any decisions to be made?"

He shook his head. "No decisions, but we'd like to brief you on his condition and the prognosis."

"Thank you, I'd appreciate that." She returned to her abandoned seat and set her bag on the carpeted floor beside the chair. "The Chief told me he has Boursin's syndrome. I did some research on the Web, but I don't know much else."

"Justice Wynn is stable for now, but we have no idea whether he'll regain consciousness. I'm sorry."

"Can I meet with his other physicians? And the hospital's general counsel?"

"Certainly. I let them know you've arrived. They are eager to speak with you. I'll get them and find you something to drink."

"Water would be fine."

"Just a moment," Dr. Toca said as he stood, eager to gather reinforcements. He'd dealt with angry families, but nothing like today's melodrama. And, given his meeting before calling Avery, Act II was about to begin. Rising, he headed for the door with undue haste. "I'll be back soon."

He left the office, and Avery rose to check the door, which he'd pulled shut behind him. No one stood on the other side. Which left her free to open her clenched fist. And read the note Jared Wynn had pressed into her palm.

ELEVEN

Kramers Books—the patio. Midnight. Please. JW

Then, scrawled below, in smaller, cramped letters,

Be careful.

Crumpling the note, Avery raced to the door and yanked it open. She bolted down the long white corridor. Nurses and white-coated physicians gave her a wide berth, matched by annoyed glares. Oblivious, she jogged toward an exit sign and shoved through the swinging doors. Seeing a tall, jeans-clad man in a blue shirt, she yelled, "Jared! Mr. Wynn! Wait!"

As she darted forward, she caught the man's arm, swinging him to face her. "Jared, I—"

"Excuse me?" The man was older, the face craggier, his eyes a puzzled dark brown rather than the whiskey brown Jared had inherited from his father. "Can I help you?"

Embarrassed, Avery released his elbow and shook her head quickly. "I'm sorry. I thought you were someone else." She frantically scanned the other occupants. To no avail. Jared wasn't there.

Giving up, she swung around, only to bump into another man. She stumbled back and realized that she'd collided with Scott Curlee, one of the daytime anchors for PoliticsNOW. He stood beside a smug Celeste Turner-Wynn. Avery turned away into a blinding light perched atop a video camera, and she lifted her arm across her face. "Leave me alone."

"Ms. Keene, can you tell me why you're at the hospital?" Curlee demanded, pushing a microphone forward. "Is it true you've stolen custody of Justice Wynn from his wife?"

Avery backed away. "Of course not."

Undeterred, Scott shoved the microphone closer. "Why were you chasing Jared Wynn? What was your relationship with Howard Wynn?"

"This is neither the time nor the place, Mrs. Turner-Wynn," she urged.

"You won't get away with stealing my husband," Celeste announced, angling to catch the camera's eye. "I've told Mr. Curlee what I told you. I'm his wife and his guardian. You have no right to take him from me."

"I had nothing—" Avery halted, the Court press secretary's admonishment to the staff ringing in her ears. "No comment." She hurried toward the doors leading to Dr. Toca's office, with Scott Curlee on her heels. The *Authorized Personnel Only* sign stopped the cameraman, but not the reporter.

"Americans deserve to know your intentions, Ms. Keene." The reporter jogged along beside her. "Did you have an affair with Justice Wynn?"

"Ms. Keene?" Dr. Toca met her halfway along the corridor, accompanied by a pumpkin-shaped man on spindly legs whose overgrown mustache served as the only hair on his head. He cast a squinted look at her that appeared to assess and dismiss in a single motion.

The doctor closed the distance between them and touched Avery's shoulder, placing himself between Avery and the reporter. "This area is off-limits, sir."

"I don't see any postings."

The portly man stepped forward. "Big red sign on the other side of this door says *Authorized Personnel Only.* If you have a complaint, I'm happy to summon the security staff. They've been well trained by the U.S. military."

Curlee held up his hands. "No need," he said. "I'll see you later, Ms. Keene."

He walked away, and Avery slipped the wrinkled note into her suitjacket pocket. "Thank you both."

"Thought you told her to wait in your office, Toca?"

"No harm done, Robert. Did you need something, Ms. Keene?"

Avery fibbed, "I was hunting for the bathroom. Must have gotten turned around."

"We can wait."

"That's okay." Avery gave a nod. "Your office?"

"This way." Inside, a woman waited. Dr. Toca introduced them. "Dr. Michelle Knox, and you've met Robert Mumford, the hospital's general counsel."

"Hello." Avery turned to Dr. Toca. "When can I see him?"

"As I said, he's still undergoing tests that will take some time. But I will make arrangements for you to visit as soon as possible."

Before she could respond, the lawyer spoke: "Ms. Keene, why did Justice Wynn give you his power of attorney?"

"I have no idea," she replied in stark honesty. "I didn't know anything about it until this morning."

"Don't you find that odd?"

"Of course I do."

"And?"

"And nothing. All I can do now is what he asked." Dismissing the attorney, she focused on the physicians. "Beginning with understanding more about what's wrong with him. What is Boursin's syndrome? I read a bit on the Internet, but—"

"It's a rare degenerative neurological disorder. It mimics both Parkinson's and brain cancer." Dr. Knox leaned forward from her perch on the couch. "Boursin's is aggressive and mutable. For months, it's been attacking his nervous system. He would have been erratic at times, anxious. Short-tempered and hostile, perhaps."

"He's rarely anxious, but he's not known for his patience," Avery protested.

"Hmm. Justice Wynn developed a brain tumor that has been sitting on his cerebral cortex. In some patients, they display signs of paranoia and irrational fears of others."

"Like his tirade at American University," she supplied, but silently considered the strange emails on his computer. *Ani Is in the River. Find Ani.* Perhaps not a real message at all. "Would he be prone to less public displays?"

"Yes," Dr. Knox answered. "A number of patients develop fairly elaborate hallucinations, grounded in their realities. Do you remember something?"

Caution made her respond, "No, I don't."

Clearly skeptical, the doctor continued: "Boursin's affects the emotional centers of the brain, but it does not harm the patient's intellectual capacity at first. Most of the time, he would appear unaffected."

"What happens now? How long will he be in a coma?"

Dr. Knox exchanged a solemn look with Dr. Toca, who gave a slight nod. "Avery, Justice Wynn is unlikely to ever wake up. When he developed the tumor, his best option was to undergo radiation therapy to slow the metastases. He refused."

"Because of the time it would take away from the Court," Avery guessed.

"He was immovable on that point," Dr. Knox confirmed. "Justice Wynn's sense of self-importance is"—she searched for a polite phrase—"formidable—even to doctors. He claimed his absence would set the course of jurisprudence back a century."

Avery could well imagine the argument, and she cracked a smile. "Maybe not that far, but he did author some critical opinions this term."

"He allowed the tumor to go untreated," Dr. Knox retorted. "Against our very strong recommendations."

Avery nodded. "He's stubborn."

"This coma, coupled with the size of the tumor, makes an operation ill-advised. Radiation therapy will not reduce or reverse the damage already caused. Dr. Toca and I believe that at this stage, Justice Wynn's illness is cutting off oxygen to his brain."

"Celeste said she wants to disconnect him from life support." Avery leaned forward. "But based on what you've told me, he's in serious condition, but Justice Wynn isn't dead yet. Brain-dead, I mean."

"No, he's not," Dr. Toca said quickly. "According to our tests, though, his brain wave patterns are markedly reduced. The tumor is now pressing against his spinal column and reducing the flow of blood throughout his body. He's on a respirator, and most of his bodily functions are being assisted."

"Will he recover? Even temporarily?"

"I don't know," Dr. Knox answered. "But the prognosis is not positive. He's in a deep coma."

"Other people have come out of comas." Even as she made the arguments, Avery reeled from the implications. Those people had been in car accidents or plane crashes. They hadn't ignored a massive growth laying siege to their brains like invading armies. They hadn't been stubborn old men who imagined themselves to be gods of jurisprudence, invaluable to the progress of humankind and the virility of democracy. The traitorous thoughts shamed her. So much for loyalty.

Looking at the physicians, Avery pleaded, "You have to do something to help him. People do wake up."

Dr. Toca answered gently, "It is unlikely, Avery."

Pressing the point home, Dr. Knox added, "For all the progress of medical science, we cannot reverse his condition. He is barely alive."

"But I just saw him last week. Did he know it would be this sudden?"

Both physicians looked at Mumford, who shook his head. Avery caught the exchange and demanded, "What is it? What aren't you telling me?"

"We don't have sufficient information—" Mumford began.

"Tell me."

Dr. Toca placed a hand on her shoulder. "When Justice Wynn was brought in last night, he showed signs of a drug overdose. Nurse Lewis brought in a pill bottle she found at his bedside. It appears he may have attempted suicide."

"No." Avery jerked away from Dr. Toca. "Justice Wynn wouldn't do something like that."

"He was getting worse, Avery." Dr. Knox moved to her other side, but did not touch her. "Howard might have wanted to accelerate the end."

As though waiting for his cue, Mumford spoke: "The question of the hour is how long he stays in this netherworld, Ms. Keene." He folded his arms, examining her closely. "Assuming you are his legal guardian, it appears you have the power to decide how long he remains on the machines keeping his body operating."

Avery caught the intentional note of doubt. "'Assuming'? 'It appears'?" she repeated, her back stiffening. "Do you have something to say to me, Mr. Mumford?"

"Appropriate questions have been raised by Justice Wynn's next of kin about the validity of his power of attorney. As you know, Mrs.

Turner-Wynn is planning to contest the document. I've already received calls from her attorneys."

"The power of attorney is valid, and your concerns are noted," Avery replied stiffly.

"My concern is family squabbles being played out on the grounds of this hospital," he huffed. "It is highly unusual for the next of kin to be passed over in this manner."

"Justice Wynn has the right to choose whomever he wants to speak for him."

"Ms. Keene, this hospital has never had to wage a public relations battle about one of its patients, despite the caliber of clientele we receive. I have never before had occasion to dispel the media from the lobby."

"I'm sorry for the inconvenience."

"As you should be." His chest puffed out as he continued: "I must admit that I am dubious about why a venerable justice of our nation's highest court would select his law clerk to make life-or-death decisions for him. He could do better."

"Robert!" Dr. Toca glared at the attorney as Avery stood. The chair toppled behind her, while Dr. Toca chastised, "We discussed this. For now, this is our patient's chosen representative. You will show her due respect."

"Forgive me, Michael, but I'm the only one in this room responsible for the reputation of this facility. Your job is to treat the patients, even suicidal ones, but I am charged with keeping the hospital out of the courts. And allowing this woman to decide the fate of one of this country's leaders who clearly suffered from mental distress is absurd." He crossed to a stack of files and jerked a sheaf of pages free. "A power of attorney conferring unlimited authority on a child. This is either an act of senility or an act of romantic stupidity. Either way, this hospital will not be the pawn in her melodrama."

"I'm twenty-six," Avery corrected coolly, her hands hanging loosely at her sides, lest she lunge for the squat attorney's throat. "And I, for the moment, am his guardian. Justice Wynn was many things, but never senile and never stupid."

"Was he suicidal?" Dr. Knox broached the question quietly, holding up a hand to forestall Avery's angry response. "Ms. Keene—Avery—if you did have a more personal relationship with him, you might have better insight into his behavior. Why he refused treatment and why he chose to vest control with you rather than his wife or son. Why he took an overdose last night. If you had a—deeper—relationship with him, we should know. It might help us."

"I have never had any relationship with Justice Wynn other than that of mentor and employer, nor have I ever considered any other. He's married, and despite your colleague's insinuations, he held those vows to be very sacred."

"How do you know?" snapped Mumford.

"Because he took every oath as sacred. Especially his oath as a judge." Avery couldn't explain the pills, but she could explain what she knew of the man. "Justice Wynn has been the swing vote on most major decisions in recent years on the Court. Without him present to vote, decades of his work would have been lost. He'd hold that responsibility to be graver than any medical crisis. I know this because it is my job to know," she added, anticipating Mumford's reaction. "I wrote his opinions, vetted his decisions. I know Howard Wynn."

"Then do you know if he wants to remain on life support indefinitely?" Dr. Toca asked quietly. "If removing him from life support becomes a viable question, what were his wishes?"

Avery focused on the kindly face and the suspicious eyes. And answered honestly: "I have no idea."

TWELVE

Sitting in her darkened office in the late afternoon lull, Avery struggled to make sense of her day. She wouldn't meet with Jared Wynn until midnight, and focusing on work seemed impossible. She wanted to return to Justice Wynn's office, but now the Court vultures were starting to circle. Avery tipped her chair back on protesting springs and stared at the ceiling. In the corner of her eye, her message light flashed insistently. Sighing, she reached across the desk and punched the button.

Messages played from latest to earliest—a preference she'd developed after discovering Justice Wynn's penchant for long diatribes that resulted in an edict by the tenth pronouncement. Better to cut to the chase.

Calls had come from friends who knew she worked for Justice Wynn, and those who had a passing awareness of her existence. Interspersed among them were requests for comment by news organizations that usually ignored the field of law clerks. Absently, she noted the names and numbers, her eyes reading through the onslaught of emails that filled her in-box.

As soon as she'd met with the Chief and Justice Wynn's lawyers, she'd start making return calls and replying. The mechanical voice announced a message, received at minutes past midnight. Avery looked at the phone, wondering if Rita had called her here before waking her at home last night.

But the woman's voice was not her mother's.

"Ms. Keene, this is Jamie Lewis. Justice Wynn's nurse. He asked me to call." The voice halted, and Avery heard the tightness of a swallow.

"He said that you have to save us. Then he said, 'Look to the East for answers. Look to the river. In the square.' He said it a couple of times, like it was very important. He also mentioned someone named Las Bauer. Said you should remember him." The message paused again; then Jamie added, "Avery, he said, *Forgive me.*"

Avery heard the voicemail announcement reminding her to save or erase, and, out of habit, she deleted the message. She knew she wouldn't forget. *Save us.* And the last. *Forgive me.*

The same message she'd found in his emails. *Dumas.* But she had no idea who Ani was. She pulled out the pages she'd printed from his computer. *Ani Is in the River. Dumas Find Ani.* And Jamie's message: *Look to the East for answers. Look to the river. In the square.*

But staring at what she'd found so far did not make his message any clearer.

Maybe Nurse Lewis could tell her what all this meant. Avery grabbed her purse and keys. Outside her office, Matt and a handful of clerks hovered around the main area, talking. As soon as she emerged, the conversation ceased. They watched her as she crossed to the secretary's desk. "Does anyone know where Ms. Hallberg is?"

Chelsey, one of Justice Lawrence-Hardy's clerks, offered, "I saw her with the other support staff a few minutes ago. She was still pretty upset."

"That's putting it mildly," Matt said. "What's going on, Avery?"

She glanced at Matt and the others. Scott Curlee's report of her new status had clearly made it back to the Court. "What do you mean?"

"Where are you going?" Matt replied with a pointed look at her bag. "Running back to Justice Wynn's bedside?"

She tightened her fingers. "Actually, I was about to look for a phone number."

"For whom? His banker or his broker?" The snide comment came from one of Justice Bringman's clerks. "How'd you manage to pull this one off, Keene?"

"Shut up, Caryn." The mild rebuke was offered by Justice Lawrence-Hardy's clerk. "Anything we can help with?"

"No, thank you, Chelsey." Avery moved behind the secretary's desk, where an old-fashioned Rolodex sat on the far corner. Justice Wynn embraced technology, but he rarely trusted it, so his secretaries kept a paper file of everything. While the group watched, she found the card she sought.

Jamie Lewis's name and address had been carefully written in her handwriting. Her cell phone number had been outlined in a red box. She quickly committed the card to memory, then flipped through to another name, and a third, in case anyone tried to determine whose name she sought. Boursin's syndrome may have been the cause of Justice Wynn's hyper-secrecy; but, Avery conceded as she glanced over her shoulder, paranoia was contagious.

For the second time that day, she headed downstairs. Evading reporters came more easily this time. Instead of a cab, she made her way to her car. Parking at the Court was difficult, which meant few managed the feat. She'd head to Jamie's home in Tacoma Park first and then go over to see the attorney who'd drafted Justice Wynn's guardianship papers.

Half an hour later, she pulled up in front of a squat brown apartment building with a stingy lawn struggling against weeds. Dark patches showed where foot traffic ignored the broken flagstones leading to the main walk. Some hopeful neighbor had hung a pot filled with irises from the overhang. Shabby fought with desperate and managed to stay in the fight. Jamie Lewis had found one of those buildings where the middle class clung by its fingernails, unable to afford a house but too proud to move deeper into Maryland.

The open apartment style offered no protective call box or secured gate. Avery rushed along the interior walkway, then up the stairs to the second level. At the nurse's door, she knocked in quick staccato bursts. No response. She tried again, but the apartment remained silent.

Undaunted, Avery removed her phone and called the cell number from the card. The jazzy summons echoed in the apartment and out to where Avery waited. Despite the sound, no one answered.

Maybe she's sleeping, Avery thought as the call rolled into voicemail. Normally she'd leave a message, but she needed answers now. She disconnected and dialed again. Once more, the ringtone warbled out into the corridor.

Thinking Nurse Lewis might have left her phone at home, Avery dialed her employer's number at Covenant House.

When the operator answered, Avery asked, "Is Jamie Lewis in today?"

"No, she isn't."

"Can you tell me when she'll be back?"

The operator hesitated. "May I ask who's calling?"

"I work for Justice Wynn. I really need to find her."

"I'm sorry, miss, but Jamie resigned. We got a message this morning. Can I help you?"

"No, thank you." Disappointed, Avery ended the call and turned toward the steps to leave, then stopped.

Jamie Lewis had called and left her a strange message, and now she wasn't at work or answering her phone or her door. She could leave, or she could find answers. Checking around, but seeing no one, Avery tried the knob to the apartment. The door was locked. She looked around again, then, making a quick decision, knelt low.

Rummaging in her bag, she found a manicure kit. One of Rita's ex-boyfriends had entertained a ten-year-old Avery with lock-picking tricks. He'd also taught her about fingerprints and how they could land you in jail on a B-and-E charge. With a few practiced motions, the lock on the door gave way. She removed a tissue and hand sanitizer from her bag, spritzed the metal, wiped, and turned the knob.

Avery waited for the sound of an alarm, and, hearing nothing, she eased inside. A blast of frigid air hit her in a solid wall, and she shivered in the doorway. Stepping fully into the apartment, she noted the boxes leaning against the wall and the muted murmur of the television. "Nurse Lewis?"

She moved into the living room slowly, calling out a second time: "Hello? Nurse Lewis?" Rounding the couch, she saw a low table and a mug sitting on top. Her gaze slipped over the top and toward the wall leading to the open kitchen. A single hole stood in stark relief. Then she saw the blood.

"Oh, God." Avery dashed around the table toward the kitchen. On the flowered carpet, a woman sprawled facedown. Dropping to her knees, Avery knew instantly that the woman was dead from the blood that haloed her prone form. Bile rose and lodged in Avery's throat, and she clapped her hand over her mouth. She braced her free hand on the carpet. The wet, sticky surface had her recoiling, and she scrabbled back along the carpet, streaking blood across faded yellow flowers.

Terror drove Avery to her feet, and she stumbled out the open door.

She dragged the tail of her shirt out to jerk the door closed behind her. Avery hurried to her car, and her wet fingers slipped against the metal handle. She snatched it back, cursing. With her other hand, she managed to unlock the door and scramble inside. She plucked the hand sanitizer from her purse, saw a discarded napkin on the floor. Quickly, she doused the napkin and wiped at the blood.

Avery forced herself to calm. She pushed the key into the ignition and stared out the car window at the apartment building. She needed to report that she'd found Jamie Lewis's body.

In the next instant, she balked. What would Major Vance make of her discovery? What would the Chief think? *First Wynn goes into a coma, and then the last person to speak with him is dead.*

She had to leave. Now. Once she was away, she'd go to a pay phone, call the police, and report the body, anonymously. *The murder.* Because she'd seen gunshot victims before.

"Oh, God. Justice Wynn." He could be next, she realized.

Avery revved the engine and headed for Bethesda, never noticing the dark blue sedan that followed her onto the street.

THIRTEEN

The hospital ward housing Justice Wynn had been cordoned off years before for the high-profile clientele whom Bethesda served. Gone were the impersonal bays of nurses who ignored the distraught families who wandered through, checking for their loved one's name on a dry-erase board beyond the room. Instead, a single attendant monitored the elevator that opened onto the ninth floor. Before being allowed beyond the sentinel, a guest was required to provide identification, a thumbprint, and have a photo taken.

The man checked his phone, noting that he still had no signal in this blacked-out area of the hospital, which had left him dark for nearly thirty minutes as he waited for the attendants to return Wynn to his room. The woman he had assigned to track Avery had last reported her heading out to lunch from the Court. Sufficient time to accomplish his task.

He approached the desk and folded his hands behind his back. If asked to describe him later, the nurse would recall a man with dark brown hair, muddy brown eyes, a ruddy, almost sunburned complexion, a tick in his upper lip, and a paunch that belied the military insignia on his jacket.

"May I help you, sir?"

"Corporal Randall?" he read from the placard on the desk. "I am here to see Senator Wayne Stafford, please."

"I'll need to scan your identification and verify that you are an authorized visitor."

"Of course," he said. He reached inside his jacket and proffered a billfold with a photo and the appropriate credentials. The name on this badge read *Ethan James,* and if pressed, he could produce a matching passport and credit cards. As well as a handful of other fully vetted identities.

"Thank you, sir." She returned the billfold. "Now I'll need to take your photo and thumbprint."

He gave a slight frown. "I believe I have been cleared."

She typed his assumed name into the database. A green stripe indicated that he'd been given permission to bypass their security protocols. Looking up, she said, "Yes, sir. Room 9112."

"Thank you."

He entered Stafford's room, where the U.S. senator lay sedated. He'd been diagnosed with a rabid strain of venereal disease contracted on a trade mission to Thailand that required routine hospitalization and intensive treatments. The male prostitute who had transmitted the disease had died a year earlier, unable to access the care available to the legislator. Stafford would remain hospitalized for another week before discharge.

Stafford's misfortune had earned him a rare moment of utility. His well-appointed hospice shared a wall with Room 9113. According to the rotation, no one would be checking on Stafford for another twenty-three minutes. Working quickly, he locked the door as a precaution. He removed his jacket, button-down shirt, and pants, revealing a fitted tactical suit beneath, and tucked his clothes into a drawer. Then he quietly positioned the dresser to give him access to the subceiling, opened the panel, and levered himself up and into the crawl space.

On the other side, he lowered himself down, landing lightly on the floor. Like his neighbor, Justice Wynn had an IV dripping fluids into his arm, while a monitor beeped his vitals in a steady pattern. Advancing on the bed, the man removed a needle and vial from his pocket. With the ease of repetition, he prepped the needle with the synthesized dose of saxitoxin. A paralytic, the injection would result in respiratory failure, a not uncommon side effect of Boursin's syndrome. At Justice Wynn's bedside, he reached for the tube that snaked its way down to the comatose man's arm. The raised voices came through an instant before the door began to open.

"Ms. Keene, Dr. Knox does not want him to have visitors."

"I'm not a visitor. I'm his guardian, as I explained to Lance Corporal Randall. That's why she let me into the ward. Now I'm going inside to see him. If you have a problem with that, please call Dr. Toca."

Dropping the tube, the intruder swiftly crossed the room and slipped into the bathroom seconds before the visitors entered.

"If you insist on violating doctor's orders, I will contact security, Ms. Keene."

Avery walked over to the bed where Justice Wynn lay pale and still. "Please do. In fact, please ask the head of the security staff to meet me up here."

The nurse remained in the open doorway and glanced over her shoulder at the desk attendant, who lifted the phone and shrugged. "Lance Corporal Randall has already contacted them."

"Good." Avery turned away from the nurse and back to Justice Wynn. "I'll be here."

Hidden in the bathroom, he cataloged the space. In a ward designed for long stays, the bathroom came equipped with a shower and tub, as well as a shallow linen closet. With no real options, he entered the shower stall and drew the curtain.

The pneumatic door to the bathroom opened. Avery entered, flipped on the faucet, and began to wash her hands. She leaned her forehead against the mirror and whispered, "What have you pulled me into, Justice Wynn?"

"Ms. Keene?"

Avery shut off the water and shakily dried her hands. She opened the door and let it swing wide. Behind her, the man moved from the shower and caught the door before it fully closed.

Dr. Knox and Dr. Toca stood together at the foot of Justice Wynn's bed. Avery approached them and said, "Thank you for coming so quickly."

Dr. Toca nodded. "The nurse was quite anxious about your visit. However, I was going to contact you. We've run additional tests on Justice Wynn."

"What's wrong?"

"We're not sure what Justice Wynn took or if he intended to commit suicide," Dr. Knox answered. "The pills he took may have caused his coma, but they were not the ones in the bottle brought in with him."

"I don't understand. He didn't overdose?"

"We're not sure. Several of the pills from his seizure medication are missing, but that's not what's in his system."

Dr. Toca added, "As soon as Justice Wynn was admitted, we conducted a toxicology screening based on Nurse Lewis's report. From the bottle that was brought in with him, the effect should have been a cardiac episode preceding death. A coma was possible, but not likely. But there's no evidence of a heart attack or stroke, so he couldn't have taken the seizure medication."

"Then what did he take?"

"The initial findings were inconclusive. Apparently, the lab found an anomaly in the blood analysis and ordered another round of tests. We're still waiting for the results."

"How soon will you know what he took?"

"Hopefully by the end of the day. Tomorrow at the latest." Dr. Toca hesitated. "I asked that a second sample be sent out to Quantico for analysis. Our techs are good, but they raised concerns. In addition, we've contacted Nurse Lewis, but we haven't heard from her."

Avery barely flinched. "Anything else?"

Dr. Toca pointed to the papers he held. "The chemicals he ingested would have mimicked the effect of a slow-motion aneurysm."

"What would do that?"

The doctors looked at each other before shaking their heads. Dr. Knox answered, "No one here can identify the drug. It has recognizable markers, but there's no manufactured medication that has this effect."

Dr. Knox studied her patient, adding, "Avery, based on our initial analysis, he has put himself in a coma, but he's not at risk of death."

Avery considered the new information, her eyes fixed on the man in the hospital bed. "He faked a suicide attempt?"

"We simply don't know."

Crazy bastard. Avery cleared her throat. "Until you know exactly what happened, I would like a twenty-four-hour guard placed on his room. I also want to restrict access. For now, other than medical personnel, I am his only visitor."

Nodding, Dr. Toca reached out a hand to take her elbow. "I'll take you to the security office myself and alert the U.S. Marshals. I've asked one of our officers to stay outside his door until the marshals set up their rotation. He won't be alone."

"I will wait with him. Someone must be in here with him at all times."

Dr. Toca hesitated, then nodded again. "Dr. Knox will be in touch with you as soon as we have the full toxicology report. Take as much time as you like. We'll make sure he's kept safe."

When the physicians exited the room, Avery reached for the bedside phone. After the first ring, Mary Gonzalez answered.

"It's Avery. I need to speak with the Chief."

A few seconds later, she was connected. "Avery, is everything okay?"

"No, ma'am. It's not." Avery paused, then said in a rush, "I went to see his nurse this afternoon. Someone shot Jamie Lewis, and my DNA is at the scene. I fled because I'm afraid that Justice Wynn might be in danger. Right now, I'm at the hospital, but I don't know what to do next."

"Where are you? Exactly."

"I'm in Justice Wynn's room."

"I'll alert the marshals to join you there immediately, and one of them will bring you to the Court."

"I have my car."

"Leave it. I'll take care of the rest."

Inside the bathroom, the man cursed silently and considered the syringe in his hand. He could kill Justice Wynn now and execute a hit on the girl, but with the marshals inbound, his likelihood of escape was slim. Not impossible, but an unnecessary risk.

He eased the door closed and climbed onto the toilet tank. Soundlessly, he opened the ceiling access and levered himself up through the opening. Using the crawl space above, he returned to Senator Stafford's room.

Dressed again in his suit, he exited the room just as the U.S. marshals got off the elevator. He passed by them and headed to his car. Once he had a clear signal, a series of messages swarmed onto his screen, including several warning him of Avery's discovery and approach. Local police

investigating Nurse Lewis's death would mean local press and a swarm
of reporters misreading every scrap of evidence uncovered, not to mention overzealous cops looking to make a name.

He keyed in a terse response. Perhaps he wouldn't have to go back to
his boss empty-handed.

FOURTEEN

FBI Special Agent Robert Lee wore the plain dark gray suit and polished black shoes endemic to his kind. His mahogany cheeks tended toward jowls, saved only by the strong chin that added definition to an otherwise hangdog face.

His expressions matched his rather dour appearance as they ranged typically between mild irritation and patent disbelief. In his line of work, which required the taking of statements and the parsing of truth, these reactions were customary. The Office of Law Enforcement Coordination, or OLEC, to which he was loosely attached, often had this range of response not only to civilians but to the other law enforcement agencies with which they reluctantly coordinated. A product of the FBI's Criminal Investigative Division himself, Agent Lee found the coordination a bit of a hair shirt for all involved—a sacrifice of expertise for the illusion of cooperation.

Time in the Bureau, especially at OLEC, had taught him to suspend his native predisposition for efficiency and honesty. He no longer expected either when he left FBI headquarters, and he had even lower expectations when he entered another government building. When Homeland Security was the other dancer in the pas de deux, he assumed everything told to him was a lie or a cover-up for a bigger lie. Still, he was unprepared for the unusual interview he was now conducting. Dinner plans with his wife would have to wait, but she'd never believe where his job had taken him today, assuming he could tell her.

Dusk hovered over the city as he sat in the well-appointed offices of the chief justice of the United States Supreme Court. It was his first time this deep inside the Court, and he had been granted entry only to interview the young woman whose grisly discovery had freed him from prepping a seminar on interagency data mining. Instead, a summons to the FBI via OLEC, necessitated by the unusual addition of Homeland Security, had allowed him to hand off the honors. En route to the Supreme Court, he had also quashed the aspirations of a homicide detective in the Tacoma Park PD by seizing jurisdiction over their case and the related files, such as they were.

Seated at an antique table that had the high gloss of disuse, he held his pen over a notepad with precious few details to show for an hour of interrogation, despite the presence of the Homeland Security liaison, Major William Vance, who stood impassively as Agent Lee repeated his questions.

"Let's try it this way, Ms. Keene. Why were you at Mrs. Lewis's apartment in the middle of the day?"

"To visit."

"How'd you get inside?"

"Door was open."

"I'm running out of patience, Ms. Keene. I know you picked the lock on her door."

She repeated flatly, "The door was open."

"Why did you go to her house?"

Avery dutifully responded, "I've explained this several times. Jamie Lewis was Justice Wynn's nurse. The last person to see him. I went to visit to ask her some questions."

"The lock on the door was clearly jimmied open," Agent Lee insisted. "Did you do that? Will your hand match the bloody print we found next to her body?"

"I knocked. The door was open. I found her body and checked to see if she was alive. Then I panicked and left."

Agent Lee capped his useless pen. "You're lying to me, Avery. I know it, and so does everyone in this room. If you don't tell me the truth, then I intend to book you on murder charges and let the judge figure it out."

"Enough." Chief Justice Roseborough glared at the FBI agent. "She's explained herself. Move on."

"We're in your office as a courtesy," Major Vance interjected. "Ms. Keene has committed a crime. She will answer his questions."

"I appreciate the help, Major Vance, but I've got it," Agent Lee said, rebuking his Homeland Security counterpart. "Ms. Keene is afraid that if she admits how she got inside, she'll hurt herself. She's a smart young lawyer who's watched a lot of cop shows, I bet."

A buzz sounded on his phone, and he glanced at the information that had come in from the coroner. Scowling, he tried a different tack. "Where were you at five this morning?"

Knowing her answer would only lead to more questions, Avery said nothing.

Agent Lee's scowl deepened. "Silence isn't your friend, Ms. Keene. Why can't you tell me where you were at dawn?"

A lie rose to her lips, but then she thought of the cameras installed in the Metro and along high-crime streets in DC. Streets that likely included the shooting gallery she'd pulled her mother from that morning. "I was out. But not in Maryland."

"Can you prove it?"

"No."

The Chief gave Avery an appraising look. Standing, she waited for Agent Lee to rise as well. "Thank you, Agent."

"I'm not done, Madam Chief," Agent Lee said as he remained seated, ignoring the dismissal. "I've been more than cooperative. I agreed to interview her here, and she isn't currently under arrest. Both situations can change."

Unused to the lack of deference, the Chief gave a narrow smile. "It's been a very long day, and I'm sure you can understand that Avery is exhausted. She has told you what she can."

"Which is nothing. If this is about her having the power of attorney for the justice in a coma, I don't care. What I do care about is why she's not down at the Hoover Building being questioned in less cushy surroundings instead of being cosseted here. So what am I missing?" The last he directed at Major Vance.

"I share your frustration, Agent Lee, but this is a delicate situation. The privacy of this investigation must be sacrosanct," Vance replied.

"I'm a delicate kind of man, Major, and if either of you want my help, I need to know more than her name, rank, and serial number." He lifted his pen. "The one forensic staffer I was allowed to bring to the crime scene indicated that the bullet that killed Jamie Lewis had been dug out of the wall, and the casing was missing. Apparently, she was shot at close range, in the back. Do you own a gun, Ms. Keene?"

"No."

He looked at Vance. "Is Ms. Keene under investigation by your office? Whatever the hell office that is. I'm still not quite clear on your jurisdiction."

"Ms. Keene is a person of interest to Homeland Security."

Agent Lee cocked his head. "A person of interest because someone might draw a conclusion from the fact that the private nurse for a comatose Supreme Court justice was shot to death hours after she accompanied him to the hospital? Or the fact that the dead woman seemed prepared to flee the jurisdiction, given the boxes in her living room and the plane ticket in her name at BWI? And the primary beneficiary of his demise is the one who conveniently discovered the body? Yeah, I consider her of interest too, Major. I recognize a hit when I see one. Do you?"

Vance merely inclined his head in acknowledgment. "Our expectation is that you will pursue your investigation with all deliberate speed, Agent Lee, and that you will keep me apprised of your findings. Thank you for your time and discretion."

Lee shook his head. "This farce of an interview was a waste of my time and a bit of an insult to the dead woman, too. But until I'm told by the director himself that I need to back off, I intend to treat Ms. Keene as a suspect."

"Am I under arrest?" Avery asked.

"Not yet." He finally rose and shoved a hand into his jacket pocket. "But don't plan on going anywhere."

The Chief led him to the outer office and passed him off to Debi, who would not leave until the Chief did. Avery remained in the chambers, waiting with Major Vance.

He took a step closer to her chair. "The FBI is gone. So why were you at the nurse's house, Ms. Keene?"

The lie was easy. "I thought she'd want to know his prognosis. When she didn't answer, I went inside."

"By picking the lock?"

Avery shrugged. "The door was open."

The Chief reentered the office. "Avery, I'm sorry you had to be the one to find her." With a warning look at Major Vance, she instructed the law clerk: "I'm sending you home. As I expressed to Agent Lee, this has been a traumatic day."

Avery's head came up. Inside the Court, she was safe. More importantly, Justice Wynn's desk was here—and possibly some answers. She let her eyes well with tears, not entirely an act. "I'd rather not go home just yet," she told her. "If you don't mind."

"I have more questions for her," Vance interjected. "Agent Lee's inquiries do require a response."

"I've told you, I don't know what happened to Mrs. Lewis." Avery thought again of the moment she discovered the body. "I found her. I panicked. I ran. I'm not proud of myself, but she was already dead."

"We're done for today, Major Vance," the Chief said firmly. She slid a hand under Avery's elbow, bringing the younger woman to her feet. "Return to your office until you're ready to go. Mrs. Turner-Wynn has been busy granting interviews since your unfortunate meeting at the hospital. As the public is now aware that you hold Justice Wynn's power of attorney, all calls are being directly routed to the communications team. If the doctors need you—"

"They have my cell phone number."

"Good." She patted Avery's shoulder. "A car will be ready when you are. I've also arranged for a detail at your house."

"A detail?" Which meant a federal agent following her to her meeting with Jared Wynn. "I don't want one."

The Chief gave her a stern look that echoed the one from Major Vance. "It was part of my compromise with the FBI. Until we learn what happened to Nurse Lewis, there will be a car stationed outside your apartment, and you will be chauffeured to and from the Court. Yours has been impounded. This isn't negotiable."

Avery started to argue, then stopped. It wouldn't be the first time she'd been sent to her room and told to stay there. With a short nod, she said, "Yes, ma'am," and left the office. She avoided the other clerks, whose late hours weren't unusual for the end of term. Still, more clerks than usual had found reason to hang out near Justice Wynn's chambers, rather than huddling in their offices over the latest queries from their judges. Collapsing into her desk chair, Avery allowed her head to loll against the seat, the morning's nausea returning, accompanied by a piercing headache.

When her cell phone rang, she answered it primarily to stop the noise. "Yes?"

"Avery Keene?"

A man spoke on the other end of the call, his voice distorted and unrecognizable. Her gut clenched, but she kept her voice steady. "Yes, this is Avery Keene. May I ask who's calling?"

"You must protect Justice Wynn. Don't let him die."

Suspicion hardened her tone. "Who is this?"

"A friend."

Common sense told her to hang up and alert Major Vance or the FBI, but instinct kept her on the line. Perhaps he could shed light onto whatever rabbit hole she'd fallen through. "What do you want?"

"To assist you with your new job as guardian."

"How?"

"I want to help you protect Justice Wynn."

"Protect him from whom?"

"From anyone who tries to harm him."

"A threat on the life of a Supreme Court justice is a serious matter." Avery stood slowly, moving toward the door. As her hand touched the knob, she probed, "Who wants to hurt him?"

"Get him to the end of the term alive, Avery."

"Why? What do you want?"

"We're counting on you." The phone crackled for a millisecond. "I will help. Watch for it."

FIFTEEN

A very's apartment felt like an isolation chamber. For the fifth time in as many minutes, she checked her phone. The time read 11:18 p.m., and according to her plan, she still had twelve more minutes before she needed to head out. She paced in front of the mirror, checking her outfit—again. She'd chosen slim-fitting black jeans and a black tank top, both a nod to the swelter of DC nights and a bit of vanity. She'd inherited her father's swimmer's frame. Strong shoulders, long limbs, and excellent muscle tone. Rita had passed along her narrow waist and green eyes, but the dense fringe of lashes were definitely her dad's. It was her light-brown skin and the naturally corkscrew hair that blended her parents' tones and textures, and her complicated features—high cheekbones that arrowed toward a wide, strong nose; full lips with a cupid's bow set in a narrow face.

Seeing too much, she instead looked down at the crumpled note from Jared Wynn. An hour ago, when she'd decided she'd had enough drama for the day, she'd crushed it into a ball and thrown it into the trash. But then her latest round of second thoughts had her fishing it out of the wastebasket.

Jamie Lewis was dead, and Jared might know why. And she'd learn nothing by hiding out in her apartment. Cursing, she pulled on a dark cap and tugged it low on her brow. She tucked her wallet into her back pocket and tied a black shirt around her waist. The black sneakers she wore made no sound as she locked her front door. She turned onto the main corridor and walked faster.

After striding past the row of front doors, she opened the egress window at the end of the third-floor hallway, which led out to a rickety fire escape. Avery climbed out and made her way down the steps. Taking the short leap to the pavement, she waited for a few breaths. When no one moved, she walked quickly to the front of the alley and checked her surroundings. The patrol car sat in front of her building, as promised. Head down, she rounded the corner and started down the street. On the next block, she found a cabdriver dropping off a fare.

"Time for one more?"

The cabbie shook his head. "I'm off the clock, miss."

Avery slid into the backseat, then passed him a bill she'd pulled from her pocket. "Fifty bucks to take me to Kramers Books. I'll be your best fare all night." She glanced out the window, but she was alone.

Taking the fifty, the cabbie grinned. "Sure. What's one more?"

Situated in the heart of Dupont Circle, Kramers bookstore boasted twenty-four-hour service for bibliophiles, politicos, and food junkies addicted to a tart key lime pie. Avery stood outside on the still-busy sidewalk, as nerves coursed through her. Her adrenaline had been pumping ever since she'd arrived, rethinking her decision to show up.

This wasn't the life she'd planned. Justice Wynn had snatched away her future and left her holding his fate in her clumsy hands. Agitated, Avery turned in the direction of the Metro stop, ready to leave and deal with the guilt. Justice Wynn wasn't Rita. His life wasn't her responsibility.

She stepped off the curb, and a strong hand clasped her shoulder.

"Ms. Keene?"

Spinning, Avery slid the knife from her pocket, and her thumb rested on the release. The streetlights cast Jared Wynn's face into shadows, giving a saturnine appearance to the machete nose and prominent brow. Whatever of his features came from his mother, she decided, they had to be more subtle.

"Mr. Wynn." She drew her shoulder from beneath his hand and inclined her head toward the bookstore. Returning the knife to her pocket before he noticed, she covered: "I thought I was supposed to meet you out on the patio."

"Call me Jared." He gave a dismissive shrug coupled with a quirk of lips that seemed reluctant to smile. "You looked like you were leaving."

"I'm here."

"Thanks for not stabbing me."

Avery glanced at him, startled. "You saw that?"

"Old habit. I spent a little time in the military—naval intelligence. I'm trained to look for people trying to kill me."

"I'm not." Avery tucked balled fists into the pockets of her jeans, her fingers numb despite the warm summer evening. Her window of escape had vanished, so she might as well learn what she could. "Care to explain your note?"

"Let's go inside first." Jared pulled open the door, and the chattering inside enveloped them. With a touch to her elbow, he guided her through the teeming store. They went up a shallow set of stairs and out to the patio, where a server dressed in a T-shirt and khakis led them to a squat wooden table.

The table tilted slightly beneath the weight of the silverware and slim menus, and the waiter efficiently shoved a coaster beneath the errant leg. "Do you know what you want to drink?" he queried with polite disinterest.

"Diet Coke," Avery answered.

"Chamomile tea," requested Jared.

"Sure."

The refined order seemed to Avery at odds with the unsmiling, almost stern face. He struck her as a guy more likely to carry a flask than to drain herbal tea from a china cup. Jared was dressed as he'd been earlier. Dark jeans molded to a lean frame. The white shirt had been exchanged for blue, but the dark work boots and the scowl on a face that could have been beautiful remained. Somehow, more years than he'd earned had etched themselves into the wheat-colored skin. Jared Wynn had maybe five years on her, but she could have sworn it was more. He sat stiffly, alertly, as though poised to run at the first cause.

Avery was determined to wait in silence until Jared revealed the purpose of this meeting, but before she could settle in the waiter reappeared with their drinks and took their order. "I'll have your meals up shortly."

Jared stirred the tea, seemingly lost in thought.

"This is your show," Avery said. "What do you want?"

"I didn't mean to alarm you."

She gave a mirthless chuckle. "Then I'd advise you not to include dire warnings in your secret notes to strangers."

"Sorry." Jared lifted his knife and skillfully flipped the thin metal over and under scarred knuckles. After another pass of the knife, a habit he'd picked up in the Navy, he caught Avery's impatient look. He began, clearly reluctant: "I hadn't spoken to the judge in more than twenty years."

"Since your mother died?"

"Since he sent me away and refused to see me." Bitterness, long since submerged by resignation, surfaced briefly. Talking about his family had never come easy. "My mother died a few years after he was appointed to the Supreme Court. The day after the funeral, the judge took me to live with her sister in Maryland. He never came back."

"Do you know why?"

"No, but there are dozens of theories. My aunt has always romanticized that I reminded him too much of my mom, his one great love."

"But you don't believe that."

His laugh was short. "I think one has to be capable of love to pine away like that. My theory? The judge is a selfish, cold man who didn't want the responsibility of raising a child. After he was appointed to the Court, he had the perfect life. Then my mom dies. With her gone, I served no practical purpose."

"Did you ever try to make contact?"

"Every day for a year. I was quite insistent and pathetic as a child."

"But nothing happened?"

"Every summer, I snuck down to the Court for the last day of the term, hoping to see him. Did it every year until I turned eighteen." Before she could ask about how he gained access, he explained, "The clerk of court had been fond of my mother. So he always saved me a place."

"What happened when you turned eighteen?"

"I begged my way over to his chambers. I saw him. He was arguing with someone, and I saw him look at me. He never even paused. I didn't wait around after that. But I finally realized that I was eighteen years old, and I would never be a part of his life." Jared rolled his shoulders once, a jerky movement quickly controlled. "The next morning, I joined the Navy and went off to see the world."

When Justice Wynn was in the throes of a good fight, he barely paid attention to anything else. She didn't know if he had even noticed Jared, let alone recognized him, but Avery still found herself appalled. She stopped herself from offering sympathy, asking instead, "How long were you in?"

"Long enough."

"Care to be more specific?"

"Not really."

"Why not? What? Were you a SEAL or something?"

"Or something. I was a boring analyst. Then I came home and put my training to use. I run a consulting firm doing computer and electronic security."

"An analyst in naval intelligence? That's not boring."

He shrugged. "Not exactly."

"What, exactly?" Nothing in the trim, hard man before her suggested physical weakness. "What was wrong?"

"I was up for a fairly special promotion. They ran blood tests and a DNA panel. The doctors told me I'd tested positive for a congenital defect I inherited from my father. A sleeping killer in my brain that will render me as useless as the judge one day."

"Boursin's syndrome."

"Yes." When he saw the look of pity, Jared shook his head. "Don't feel sorry for me," he commanded. "Listen, we're all going to die sometime. I just happen to have a good idea of what will kill me, if not when."

Avery wiped all expression from her face, exorcised it from her voice. "I talked to Justice Wynn's doctors. There's no cure."

He stretched an arm across the table, his fingers splayed close to her. "Not yet."

Avery's eyes widened. "What do you mean?"

This was his opening. Jared leaned forward and lowered his already raspy whisper. "The judge believes there is a gene therapy under development that could cure me."

Avery frowned. "Dr. Toca didn't mention a protocol."

"Because it's not on the market. According to the judge, there's a company that has figured out which genes are killing my brain, but they need access to a certain technology to continue trials. The potential delivery system is proprietary and in the hands of an overseas company. It's called a restriction enzyme sequence. And it's manufactured by—"

"Advar. The GenWorks merger."

Jared visibly stiffened. "So you know about it. Advar's biogenetic technology, if coupled with GenWorks' pharmaceutical research, could save my life." Jared took a quick glance around the room and leaned toward her. "President Stokes is trying to kill the last hope I've got."

A cure, she thought dazedly. "Could the merger save your father?"

Jared hesitated over the lie, then shook his head. "No. It's too late for him. But he does know about what's happening to me. He told me about GenWorks and Advar. About you."

"What? He was in contact with you?"

The waiter materialized beside them and set a plate of French fries in front of Avery, with a hamburger for Jared.

When they were once again alone, Jared explained, "Yes, he told me that if anything were to happen to him, I should find you."

"But . . . why?" The question had been hovering in her mind for hours. "If he reached out to you about his illness, why give me his POA and not you?"

"I don't know." Jared bit into his burger and chewed on it thoughtfully. "I hadn't been in contact with the judge since that day at the Court. Then, one evening, about four months ago, he appears at my apartment. Tells me he needs to talk to me."

"Did you?"

"No. I slammed the door in his face. An hour later, I left my apartment on my way to a bar or something. Anything. And he's just standing in the hallway. Waiting."

"You talked to him, then."

"No. He followed me to a bar on the corner. Just waiting for me to acknowledge him. Three hours later, when he wouldn't go away, I cursed him. Still he didn't say a word." His voice softened as he spoke. "Finally, I told him to sit down. He looked like he could fall over. We shared a scotch, and I asked him what he wanted after all these years. I assumed he'd come to say he was sorry."

"He apologized?"

"The judge? Of course not."

That didn't surprise her. "What did he say?"

"He told me he was dying." Jared pushed his plate aside. "Said he was trying to help me, but that it was complicated."

Complicated? Rigging a Supreme Court verdict to allow a merger was more than complicated, Avery thought edgily. It was grounds for impeachment and damned near impossible. As was telling anyone about the status of a Supreme Court decision. "He told you he planned to vote in favor of the merger?"

"At first, he didn't tell me much at all. But we've stayed in touch. Turns out he'd followed my career from the minute I enlisted. He wanted me to understand the course of the disease. Then, over the past few weeks, he started hinting at more, rambling on about international problems and 'the tiny minds of tiny men.' I did do intelligence work, and I'm not bad with research. A few searches and the right questions, and finally, I confronted him. Asked if his solution had anything to do with the president's block on the GenWorks merger."

"He told you about the case?"

"Not fully. He still played coy. All he'd say was that he was working on a solution. But he dropped enough hints to know I'd go looking. I found the cases, and I know about GenWorks' biogenetics work, but not much else. I'm guessing that's where you come in."

"I'm not sure what you want. What he thinks I can do."

"I don't know either." He lifted his tea. "This court decision about GenWorks. Is it final?"

The fact that it wasn't was the source of gossip in the Court. Rumor had it that Justice Wynn held the deciding vote, but he'd refused to sign on to the Chief's opinion yet. No one knew why not, and Avery knew better than to ask. Instead, she shook her head. "The Court will continue to issue rulings until the end of the month. But I can't reveal the status of court proceedings. Don't ask me."

His jaw tightened. "I have to ask you. We're talking about my life. About my father's life."

"You said he can't be helped."

"He can't, but he thinks you can help me."

"How can I? The workings of the Court are confidential until the justices issue a final decision. I couldn't tell you anything, even if I thought I knew it." But the GenWorks case was a black box, and if Justice Wynn could have resolved it, why hadn't he? Instead of putting himself into a coma, like his doctors suspected. Avery's mind swirled with possibilities, but none of them made sense. If all it would take to save his son was one vote on the Court, surely Justice Wynn would have done that himself. No reason to bring her into this.

"Avery? Where'd you go?"

"What? I'm sorry, Jared. I really don't know how I can help you."

Impatient, he leaned across the table. "You have to, Avery. The judge said you'd know how to put the pieces together. What pieces?"

Jamie's warning played shrilly in her head. *Save us. Forgive me.* Why would saving their lives require forgiveness? And who was she to be in the middle of this?

Avery shoved her chair back and stood. "I'm not sure what your father thought I knew or told you I could do, Jared, but I don't know anything. I'm sorry about your illness, but I can't fix this for you. For either of you."

SIXTEEN

Jared quickly rose, stepping toward Avery and placing his hand on her arm. The gravelly voice lost its anger in a plea. "Avery, you know something. I saw it."

"You're imagining things," she whispered, unwilling to attract attention.

"I'm sorry." Jared dropped his hand. "Please, don't leave. Look, my father has asked me for one thing in the last twenty years. To come to you if he got too sick to do it himself."

"This isn't about him," she argued, sitting again. Jared sat again as well. "It's about you. Justice Wynn isn't coming out of his coma. Anything I do saves your life, not his."

Jared lowered his voice and locked eyes with Avery. "You're right. But I'm not sure that's all there is to this."

Save us. "What do you mean? Why?"

"Because I don't think the judge loved me that much." He exhaled sharply. "He was anxious when he talked to me. Frightened. Kept looking over his shoulder as we talked. There's more to it. This is about more than me and some disease that's killing us both."

"The doctors said he might have shown signs of paranoia."

"Paranoia—or knowledge? He kept telling me that it was too dangerous to tell me the truth, but that this was a matter of national security."

"Jared, he could have been having delusions. And he knew what you did in the Navy. Maybe guilt was creating a fantasy scenario where he could save your life."

"Perhaps. I don't know. He never gave me details, but he would rant about the president. He truly hated President Stokes, and he didn't like his doctors. But he said that if he ran out of time, he had a backup plan."

"Which is?"

"You." Jared held her gaze. "That's why he told me to come to you if anything happened to him. That the fate of the world would be at stake. It sounds like hyperbole, but he was dead serious."

"And you don't think he was delusional and paranoid?" she protested.

"I don't know what to think. He broke a twenty-year silence to come and warn me. That has to mean something. His mind was crystal clear on that, Avery."

She thought about the folder she'd found on Wynn's computer. Of Jamie Lewis's dead body. Of the caller's cryptic warning. "Did he tell you anything else?"

"He was insistent—he said if he didn't make it to the end of term, you'd have to finish it for him." Jared scrubbed at his face. "No, I don't know what 'it' is. I'm not a lawyer, so I didn't question what he meant."

"I don't know either," Avery replied honestly. "This could be the last stages of his disease, Jared. Seeing threats where none exist."

"Or maybe seeing something no one else could." Jared leaned back in his chair, lost in thought. "What can you tell me about the GenWorks case? Legally."

Avery had been assigned to help with the research on GenWorks, which made her more privy to the workings of the conference committee than others. "Only what's already known. An American genetics company wants to merge with an Indian biotech firm and share technology. The president objected and stopped the merger—first time in history."

"Why?"

"Depends on who you ask." Recalling the day of the oral arguments, Avery frowned. "There's the moral issue of genetic research. These companies are manipulating the basic elements of our humanity. Cloning sheep and mapping the human genome was simply the beginning. The hyperbole about ordering a genetically perfect child or manufacturing new limbs isn't science fiction. Stem cell lines are producing more and more data, and what used to take years can now be done in weeks with CRISPR. It's a new frontier, but no one is in charge."

"You agree with President Stokes?"

"I didn't say that. Critics say that President Stokes expanded the limits of executive power beyond the Constitution. As dangerous as biogenetics may be, so is a president who has authoritarian leanings."

"So who is right?"

"I don't know. I'm not on the Court."

Hearing her annoyance, Jared asked, "What else can you tell me about the case?"

"That none of the normal ideologies held up. Justices were all over the place during the questioning. The core issue is the Exon-Florio Amendment. It's supposed to balance national security interests against America's interest in foreign investment."

Warming to her topic, Avery leaned forward. "Nigel Cooper, the head of GenWorks, is claiming that the president does not have any valid national security concerns, but is simply being a protectionist in retaliation against India since they shot down his signature trade deal last year. India agrees with China on a few trade routes, and six months later, Stokes blocks the biggest tech deal in India's history. Because of the national security angle, the case gets fast-tracked, and here we are."

"You agree there are national security implications of sharing that kind of technology with a foreign country. President Stokes may be a prick, but he's not wrong."

"Neither is Nigel Cooper, but his public feud with the president doesn't help either one of them with credibility. GenWorks might be his baby, but Nigel Cooper poured millions into a super PAC in the last election to defeat the GOP, and he's at it again. Billionaires will be made overnight if the merger goes through. He could be a trillionaire if their technologies actually work."

"Or we weaken our national security by putting dangerous technology in enemy hands."

"India isn't our enemy," Avery cautioned.

Jared's expression offered little comfort. "No, but India is now friendly with other countries who are definitely not our allies. Add to the geopolitical mix the kind of technology that can change DNA, put it in the wrong hands, and it could become weaponized—for profit. Or it could save my life."

"It could save a lot of lives," Avery agreed. "This isn't a clear-cut issue, which is why folks are so at odds."

"So do you think the merger should proceed or not?"

Remembering her role, Avery responded carefully: "I don't have an opinion."

"Okay. For the sake of argument, what happens in a split decision?"

"In the event the Court is equally divided and declines to issue a decision, then the lower court ruling would stand."

"And if that case is GenWorks?"

"Because the lower court agreed with the president, the merger fails."

"With the judge out of the way, the odds are in the president's favor, right?"

"You'd think so, but it's not so cut-and-dried. The president wins if there is a split decision *or* if they decline to issue a decision, which is an option. But the Court can also continue the case and not issue a ruling until the next session. If they want, the justices can hold a rehearing and start the process all over again. There are a number of options. It's a chess match." As the words left her lips, her thoughts raced. *Las Bauer.* How had she missed it?

"That's just like the judge," Jared murmured. "I just wish I knew which piece I was and which square I was on."

In the square. Lasker Bauer. Her mind continuing to swirl, Avery stood abruptly. "I have to go."

"What's wrong?"

"Nothing. Just, I have to go." Watching him closely, she said, "Lasker Bauer."

"What?"

Other than confusion, she saw no other reaction. She leaned in closer. "Lasker Bauer?"

"Avery, what are you talking about?" Concern replaced confusion.

"You play chess?"

He shook his head. "Not since I was a kid. The judge taught me, but I only played to make him happy. I never wanted to look at a chessboard again after he sent me away."

"But you were just talking about pieces and squares."

"Something the judge said to me that last night. He told me to watch which square I was in and to keep my eyes on all the pieces."

"And the names Lasker and Bauer?"

"No one I know." Jared paused. "Avery, you've had a rough day, and I'm not helping. It's almost one in the morning—you should get home." He tossed some bills onto the table. "Come on—I can give you a ride."

Her instinct to protest was overwhelmed by a wave of bone-weary exhaustion, and she accepted. They navigated out of the restaurant, and he guided her to a black '67 Corvette parked down the block. Avery slid across the butter-soft seat and felt her body relax. Jared climbed into the driver's side, and she gave him the address.

"Nice ride."

"Belonged to my aunt and uncle. We used to work on it every weekend. They gave it to me for my twenty-fifth birthday. Beat the hell out of my used Honda Accord."

"I once got to drive a '68 Charger," she said sleepily. "Best joyride ever."

" 'Joyride'?"

"Forget I said that."

The streets were empty this time of night, and the desolate blocks clicked by in silence. Suddenly Avery thought about the security detail she'd evaded back at her apartment. If she arrived in a car at the front door, they'd certainly report her to the Chief.

Her building occupied a corner of Fifteenth and Q. As they neared the apartment block, she asked, "Would you mind circling and then driving down the alley? I don't want to go in the front." Jamie Lewis's pale corpse flashed before her, and Avery felt a chill.

Jared gave her a knowing look, but instead of asking questions, he turned the corner, cut off his headlights, and drove down the narrow alley. In the shadows, he put his car in park and got out to open her door. Despite her protest, Jared escorted her to the fire escape. "I assume this stealthy approach has something to do with the police detail out front."

"How did you—?"

"Military intelligence, Avery."

"Yes. Thank you." She fumbled in her bag for her key. "I'm sorry I couldn't tell you more."

"Not yet. But you may remember something." He held up his hand before she could reply. "I don't know him the way you do. But he was afraid—and so are you. I want to help."

Avery hesitated, then reached back into her bag. "Here's my card."

"Thanks." He squeezed her hand once and turned toward his car.

"Wait." On impulse, Avery rummaged in her bag for a pen. She plucked the card from his grasp and scrawled a number across the back. "That's my cell."

"Good. I thought I was going to have to hack the phone company to find you again."

She grinned. "You can do that?"

"Sure."

Avery hesitated, then scribbled a second number on the card. "I received a call today from an unknown number. It came in around four thirty p.m. to my cell—not the Court's line. Do you have a way to track it? Figure out who called?"

Jared nodded in the lamplight. "I'll see what I can do."

Grateful, she smiled at him. "Thanks, Jared. And let me know you made it home safely, okay?"

Jared returned the grin, a slow, slightly crooked curve that skittered her pulse. "Will do. Take care, Avery . . . thanks for meeting with me tonight." He gave her a polite kiss on the cheek and pointed up at the fire escape with another smile. "I'll wait until you're inside."

"Thank you." Before she could do something foolish, Avery climbed the three flights of the fire escape and entered the apartment building through the unlocked window in the hall.

As she rounded the corner, she stopped. "Rita. What are you doing here?"

"Hey, baby." Her mother scrambled up from the floor, dark red hair hanging in greasy hanks over her pale, mottled face, the green eyes she shared with her daughter glassy and red-rimmed. "Waiting for you. I've been knocking for an hour. Where were you?"

"None of your business." Avery pocketed her key and blocked the door. Rita had never been inside this apartment, had never had occasion to case it for movable objects easily sold. Avery planned to keep it that way. Legs braced, she asked flatly, "How did you find me?"

The coquettish smile slipped a fraction. "I didn't know you were hiding."

"How?"

"I don't have to tell you."

Avery could read the signs of a recent high and knew she'd get no good answers anyway.

"What do you want? If it's money, I'm all tapped out right now."

"I don't always come around for money, honey." She giggled at her rhyme.

Avery inched away, but Rita closed the distance between them, her eyes battling with thick layers of mascara. The once bright green had been dulled to a drab olive of unremarkable hue. Feeling abruptly weary, Avery lifted a hand to ward off her advance. "Rita. What is it?"

Teetering on heels too spindly for wear, Rita pouted, "I just wanted to talk to my baby. I've been waiting all night." She ran black-tipped nails through her disheveled hair. "Can't we go inside and sit? This floor is hard, and I could use a quick shower. Maybe dinner, if you've got it?"

Avery saw the gleam of avarice. If she opened the door, she'd be cleaned out by the weekend. Steeling herself to reject the pitiable woman who had given her life, she sighed. "It's very late, and I've got work tomorrow. Go away, Rita."

"Go away? Is that any way to speak to your momma?"

"If she's you, absolutely." The sharp retort escaped before Avery could bite it off.

Rita responded with a quick slap across Avery's cheek, followed by a moan of regret. She tried to hug her daughter, who froze. "Oh, honey, I'm sorry. I just lost my temper. Baby, I'm so sorry."

Then, on cue, came the weeping. Tears ran down poorly rouged cheeks, dripping their sincerity on Avery's throbbing skin. Wrapped in the emaciated arms, her nose buried in the rancid scent of unwashed hair, Avery felt despair creep through her heart. A lifetime of carefully plotted escape from this woman, this mother, and she'd never been able to shake her.

Oh, she thought spitefully, *to be Jared Wynn.* Both shared the death of one parent, but he'd been blessed with the disinterest of another. Why hadn't the bus accident claimed the woman instead of the man who'd given her life? She remembered a broad-shouldered, handsome man with rich brown skin and a booming laugh. He was the one who quietly soothed away the taunts about her having a white mom and a black dad. Who explained Rita's mercurial nature and sudden streaks of mean over fast games of chess. Who celebrated her strange memory when others called her a freak. Even her faintest memories of her father glinted more brightly than the best day she could recall with Rita.

She raised her arms and untwined Rita's serpentine grip. Plastic bangles clacked with the motion. "I don't have anything for you. Please go, Rita. Just go."

"Well, I have something for you!" Gone was any pretense of maternal affection. The threat slid out smooth and practiced, serrated by jealousy. "I might not get inside your apartment, but I know where you work. You want me to come and visit tomorrow? Maybe say hello to your boss. Tell them all about the real Avery Keene."

"They wouldn't let you in," Avery retorted, ignoring the first trill of fear.

Rita heard it anyway. "It's a public building, baby. And when I tell them it's an emergency, they'll have to show me right into your fancy office. How do you think the big law firms will feel when they find out how you abandoned your mother? Or maybe I'll tell them how you used to help me score? Remember that, Avery?"

Memories, burning, freezing, coursed through her. No one would wait for an explanation, not the white-shoe firms. They had no need for a tainted black lawyer with her druggie mom, not with so many pristine candidates vying for their attention. One whiff of scandal and her Yale Law degree wouldn't be worth the paper or the student loans. All they'd see was a darker-skinned version of Rita—a potential drug addict, not a rising star.

Exhausted, Avery asked, "Will twenty dollars make you disappear?"

"If I could have slept on your sofa. But I'm probably gonna have to find a shelter this late at night. A hundred ought to do."

"I don't have a hundred on me."

"You also said you had no cash," Rita reminded her slyly. "You've got it in your apartment. Probably stuck inside a book."

Which she would move to a safer place the instant she made it inside. Avery opened her purse and grabbed her wallet, keeping it hidden inside. "I've got eighty dollars, Rita. That's the best I can do." She held up the cash and waited.

Rita pinched the bills out of Avery's fingers and turned toward the elevator. She teetered on her stilettos, and she glanced over her shoulder. "I hope you get a daughter just like you one day. A frigid bitch who thinks she's too good for you."

Avery said nothing, simply stood in the hallway, eyes fixed on the glowing light of the elevator arrow. She resisted the urge to wipe at a slowly forming tear. When the doors opened, she watched Rita wobble inside. Under her breath, as the doors closed, she prayed futilely, "Goodbye, Rita."

SEVENTEEN

Pushing open the door to her apartment, Avery entered, then kicked the door shut behind her. She flicked on the light, dropped her keys on the table, and turned to flip the dead bolts into place. Ling had the graveyard shift this rotation, which meant she'd crawl into the apartment hours after Avery left in the morning.

Avery considered paging her to give her an update on the day's events, but even the thought was exhausting. In silent confirmation, the telephone flickered with blinking message lights.

"What now?" she muttered. Avery opened her bag and removed the envelope with the pages she'd printed out from Justice Wynn's computer, tossing it on the coffee table. She sank onto the futon that doubled as a sofa, propped her feet on the table, and picked up her memo pad to write down the messages.

Beep. "Ms. Keene. Rebecca DeHart, Channel Nine. I'd like to speak with you about your recent appointment to serve as guardian for Justice Howard Wynn. Please call my cell at your earliest convenience. (202) 555-0105."

Beep. "Avery Keene, this is Wendy Kavanaugh with Talk 1280. We'd like to have you join us on air tomorrow to discuss the ethics of euthanasia. Our special guests will include Dr. Azzie Preston and Dr. Barb Marston. We go on air at seven for morning rush hour. I'll call this number then."

"Crap." Dropping the pen to her lap, she rubbed her eyes.

Beep. "Avery, honey. Ayanay Ferguson from Spelman. I don't know if you know this, but I'm now a producer with *The Harris Hour*. It would be a big favor to me if you'd agree to a one-on-one exclusive with our anchor, Michael Holloman. He'd like to discuss your friendship with Justice Wynn and why he selected you to make the final decisions about his life. I know we haven't talked much since college, but I hope I can count on you. I'll give you a call in the morning—will see if I can get your cell. Ciao!"

On and on, messages begged her to come on every radio, television, and Internet broadcast in the greater DC area, and all four national morning shows. When she reached the death threats, she threw the pen across the room. Avery snatched the phone from its cradle and jabbed the familiar sequence of digits, not pausing to consider the time.

A drowsy voice answered, "Avery, I'm on my first break following an eighteen-car pileup and a double rotation. The house had better be on fire."

"Have you seen the news?"

"I've seen a punctured spleen, a severed thumb, a man who tried to perform plastic surgery on himself to resemble Jimi Hendrix, and I've seen dawn twice, but no, I haven't been watching television today."

"I'm sorry. My stuff can wait. I'll call back—"

Ling cut her off: "I'm awake now. Tell me what's going on."

Avery tucked her legs beneath her, the story spilling out. "Justice Wynn is in a coma and he appointed me his legal guardian and his son thinks I'm supposed to save both their lives and his wife wants him taken off life support. His nurse is dead and a thousand reporters have our home number. Plus, Rita found the apartment and—"

To stop the torrent, Ling latched on to the last revelation. "Rita found us? Did she take anything?"

"No, she didn't make it past the front door." Avery shut her eyes, shame warring with experience. "She's strung out. I gave her some cash and made her leave."

"Good. Now, tell me what's going on again—slowly."

Settling back, Avery launched into a description of her day. From the early hunt for Rita to the strange dinner with Jared Wynn. "Then I check my messages and the entire press corps has the story. It's insane." Her eyes fell shut, and she rested her head against the wall. "I'm just—"

"Overwhelmed," Ling supplied. "Rightfully so. Plus, you're stupid."

Her eyes shot open. "What?"

"I said you're stupid."

"Did you hear what I've just told you? Exactly what part of this is my fault?"

"You're stupid because you waited until two in the morning to call me."

"I thought I could handle it."

"Which is also why you're an idiot."

"Thanks for the support."

"That's what I'm here for." On a narrow hospital cot, Ling flipped onto her stomach, phone propped against her ear. Friendship with Avery Keene had never been dull. Avery had left their school in second semester, but Ling had stubbornly stayed in touch, tracking her wherever she landed. Unlike everyone else, she wouldn't allow herself to be shunted aside. Avery needed her. "What's the bottom line?"

"I was with Jared when I realized what 'Las Bauer' was—from Nurse Lewis's message. It's a chess reference. I think Justice Wynn was saying that I'm one of the key pieces in the game, and he's telling me that I have to find the other one."

"Okay. Well, if you're important, that's good news, right?"

Avery waited a beat. "The novelty of Lasker Bauer was the death of the bishops. He sacrificed those pieces to win the game."

"Meaning you?"

"Possibly."

"Then you're going to have to refuse the power of attorney."

"Don't be ridiculous. I'm not refusing it."

"Someone killed a nurse and is making secret calls to you. Your boss thinks you're a chess piece that's disposable. This isn't your fight. Get away from the Wynns."

"Justice Wynn asked for my help," she replied firmly, ignoring the twist in her gut. "He said he needed me to finish this. Whatever this is. I can't walk away. Not yet."

"He's as good as told you that you're expendable, Avery. Be smart." Ling paused, searching for the right words. "Justice Wynn is using you. Just like Rita. He knows you'll put his welfare before your own, because that's what you do. Between your martyr syndrome, the years of maternal guilt, and transference of affection to a father figure, you're a doormat."

"Spare me the psych rotation bullshit," Avery shot back. "If I decide to help Justice Wynn, it will be because I think it's the right thing to do. Not some daddy complex."

"Even if you put yourself in danger? And me?" Ling reminded her. "If a crack addict could find you, Avery, whoever killed that woman can too."

She had no answer for that. Taking a deep breath, she said, "Then it might be better if you didn't stay here for a while."

"You're kicking me out of my own house?"

"It's a temporary solution." Avery dipped her head, the heel of her hand pressed tight against her forehead. "U.S. marshals are circling the building. I'll ask the Chief to station one right outside the door."

"And you won't go outside?"

"I could be misunderstanding his message. We don't know that I'm in danger."

"You don't misunderstand puzzles, Avery," Ling countered.

"Then I'm going to help him because he asked me. He didn't trust anyone else."

"Apparently, he trusted you so much, he left you a handful of unintelligible clues and a crazy man pulling the fire alarm." The sarcasm traveled clearly into the apartment, but before Avery could respond, Ling warned, "He's not your responsibility. You don't owe him your loyalty."

Avery thought of the subway platform and the moment of chivalry. Her eyes closed, and her head fell against the sofa. "You're wrong. I owe him. I just don't know what he wants."

Nigel Cooper studied the dossier on Avery Keene. Like most in DC, her vulnerabilities were easily discerned and exploited. His meetings with the congressional leaders had gone well, but she had to do her part. Hopefully, his gift would help her make the right choice.

As confirmation pinged on his computer screen, Nigel dialed his partner in crime.

"Nigel."

"Did you get the information I sent?"

"I did." In Bangalore, moonlight drifted across dark water, trailing alabaster beams in still waves. She sat on a marble bench along the footpath. At that hour, the few to wander the path were young, employees of call centers and laboratories chasing American ingenuity. Smog hung low over the city, swathing her in heat and the detritus of progress. "The restriction enzyme sequence GenWorks has been perfecting uses a disease similar to Boursin's as a model for its sequencing." Nigel's lack of response forced Indira to bite off a sigh of disgust. "I forget you are not a scientist."

"I'm a financier and a miracle worker," he replied. "I got you Wynn's medical records so you could explain the situation to me in terms I'll understand."

"Then I will be plain. Combine the work of Advar and GenWorks, and we can cure the disease." On the bench, Indira's fingers curled against the smooth stone. "The potential gene therapies would be based on use of haplogroups."

"Tigris?"

"One and the same."

"Fuck."

"Precisely. Our Achilles' heel is also a source of hope for Justice Wynn."

"Could we save him?"

"No, even with our combined technology and resources, his case is far too advanced. However, Boursin's is a hereditary neurological disease passed from father to son. Jared Wynn is thirty-one. He would not yet have begun to manifest symptoms, but the markers are there."

"Wynn knew about Hygeia," Nigel said. "But he couldn't possibly have found out about Tigris. You've assured me that your team has dealt with that."

"We did." Indira stared across the pond. "All Justice Wynn would need to know is that we had a potential way to cure his son. His contact on the High Court gave him that already."

"Hell of a lot of good that does us now. Unless we can keep his guardian from doing something stupid and taking him completely out of play."

"That is your domain. I've transferred the funds authorized by the board. They should suffice."

"We're all set."

"One more item, Nigel. Can you secure a blood sample from him?"

"You have his complete medical records."

"I require a recent blood sample for my own tests."

"Why?"

"I do not want to anticipate a new problem, but if I am correct, we have another issue." Indira paused. "Secure the blood sample. I will keep looking."

EIGHTEEN

Avery woke at half past six, one phrase echoing in her mind. *Lasker Bauer.* True chess aficionados knew about the match, and how foolhardy the gambit seemed. If the man who'd called her was connected to Justice Wynn, perhaps he'd know who or what an Ani was.

Until she heard from him, she'd try to decipher the rest of Justice Wynn's message. Bleary-eyed, she wove her way into the kitchen and made her daily breakfast of cereal and milk. She retrieved a can of Diet Coke and climbed onto a stool at the breakfast bar. Absent motions added cereal and milk to the bowl, and she gulped deep, grateful for the hit of caffeine. Ready for her dose of news, she clicked on the television. And dropped her can on the Formica surface.

LAW CLERK AND JUSTICE'S SON'S SECRET ROMANCE, screamed the bolded headline below a grainy photo of her and Jared at the fire escape. His lips against her cheek, his hand on her shoulder. Her smiling profile clear to the hidden photographer.

On the screen, Scott Curlee spoke into the camera: "I attempted to interview Ms. Keene for this story yesterday, but she refused to answer questions." Footage rolled of their encounter at the hospital. "Sources report that Avery Keene has been romantically linked to both Justice Wynn and his son. This photo raises serious questions of her fitness to serve as guardian for the gravely ill jurist."

Avery choked as Matt Brewer appeared in front of a microphone. The words KEENE'S COURT COLLEAGUE ran under his image.

"Avery is really ambitious. She keeps to herself and rarely fraternizes with her fellow clerks. I wish she understood that friendship and competition aren't mutually exclusive. I pity her. She's missed out on making dear friends here at the Court. It's a tragedy."

Curlee continued, "Ms. Keene is remembered by her classmates at Yale as distant. Admired for her legal acumen, few contacted for this story could recount a single personal anecdote about her, though she served on the *Law Journal* for two years. Attempts to locate family members were also unsuccessful. The Court's press secretary had no comment."

The story switched to a death row inmate's plea for a new trial. As if on cue, the shrill of the phone filled the apartment. Numbly, Avery lifted the receiver she kept on the counter.

"Hello?"

"Avery, it's Debi from the Chief's office. She wants to see you in her office right away." The tone was brisk and distant. Near the end of term, the Chief usually arrived at six thirty a.m. and left long after the others. But a seven a.m. summons had never happened to Avery before.

"Is there a change in Justice Wynn's condition?"

Ignoring her query, Debi asked, "How soon can you be here?"

"I've got to shower and get ready. The driver said yesterday he planned to pick me up at eight."

Debi whispered her response to someone, the words muffled. Avery waited, certain the impetus for the call was the same story she could now see on other channels as she flicked the remote.

"Avery?"

She focused on the voice in her ear. "Yes, ma'am?"

"The Chief is sending a car for you. Please be outside in twenty minutes." Without waiting for confirmation, the call disconnected.

Avery abandoned her now-soggy cereal and rushed through her shower. With seconds to spare, she snapped on her watch and smoothed her skirt. She headed down the stairs, unwilling to chance an elevator malfunction.

Head down, she emerged from the stairwell and pushed through the front door. A phalanx of cameras flashed lights, capturing her frozen image a dozen times. Shouted questions pummeled her from the knot of reporters, and she scanned the street desperately for the promised car.

A long black sedan was parked at the curb, and Avery began to push her way through the throng.

"Is it true you're having an affair with Jared Wynn?"

"What will you inherit from Justice Wynn upon his death?"

"Are you conspiring with Jared Wynn to disinherit his stepmother, Celeste Turner-Wynn?"

The shouted questions came from every direction. Avery reached the car and jerked open the door, tossing her bag inside. Behind her, a microphone grazed her cheek and a reporter queried, "Can you compare sex with Justice Wynn and Jared? What is it like being with father and son?"

She shoved the tanned wrist and mike away, slid inside the car, and jerked the door shut. Gunning the quiet engine, the driver pulled away from the curb. Reporters gave chase, and Avery watched in amazement as they faded from view. The car and its silent driver wound through the early-morning traffic of Washington. On the radio, NPR recounted the story, leaving out the more salacious accusations.

Fatigue returned with a vengeance. She gazed wearily at the driver's closely cropped head, noticing for the first time the military cut. "Excuse me."

The driver's eyes met hers in the mirror. "Yes?"

She caught a fuller look at him in the rearview mirror. "Agent Lee?" Her driver was the FBI agent who'd grilled her the day before. Avery sank back into the seat. "What are you doing here?"

When he said nothing, she demanded, "Am I under arrest?"

Cynical eyes met hers in the mirror. "Not yet."

They traveled in silence to the Court. Once they'd cleared security, Agent Lee opened the sedan door, took her arm in a firm grip, and guided her inside the Court. Avery tugged once at her captivity, to no avail. She was getting sick of being handled.

In record time, the FBI agent whisked her past security and into the Chief's office. At his usual post, Major Vance watched her silently, a living stanchion by the same window he'd glared from yesterday. Sunlight poured through the windows, but Vance was caught in the slash of shadows left in the corners.

Chief Roseborough looked up as Agent Lee guided her to the desk, but did not rise from her seat. A quick glance at the Chief's desk revealed a copy of the damning photo of Avery with Jared.

With an imperious nod, the Chief indicated that she should sit. "Avery."

"Chief." Avery shot a quick look at Agent Lee. "This isn't what it looks like."

The Chief lifted an elegant hand to smooth ebony tendrils into place. "It looks like you do know Jared Wynn, contrary to what you indicated yesterday."

"I didn't know him before yesterday." The protest sounded feeble even to her. She tried again: "I mean, I met Jared at the hospital yesterday afternoon, and he asked me to meet with him last night. Nothing else happened."

"A meeting request that you failed to mention. According to the marshals, you must have snuck out through the fire escape. At least that's what the photos show."

Avery winced. "I'm sorry. I won't do it again, I promise."

"We'll get to that." With a look at Agent Lee, the Chief asked, "What is your financial status, Avery? Are you in any trouble?"

"I've got what I need, Chief. The Court is very generous."

"Do you gamble?" asked Agent Lee.

Avery almost laughed, but realized Agent Lee probably wouldn't appreciate her sense of humor. "I played cards in college and bet on a few basketball pools during March Madness."

"What about the four trips to Las Vegas where you won nearly fifty-six thousand dollars all told?"

"It wasn't illegal. I played well and won. I reported it as income on my taxes."

"How did you spend your winnings?"

Bailing my mother out of jail. Paying for rehab numbers five, seven, and eight. "I splurged on my friends, paid some debts."

"You didn't have any debts, Ms. Keene," Vance corrected from the corner of the office.

"Exactly," agreed Avery. "I paid them."

"No, I mean you've never had any debt except for student loans." Vance emerged from the shadows, brandishing a file. "According to your credit reports, you have never failed to pay your credit cards off within thirty days. So, exactly what debts did you settle with your winnings?"

Avery jutted out her chin. "With all due respect, Chief, my financial affairs are not germane to my employment. Can you tell me what's going on here?"

Chief Roseborough shook her head. "Answer the questions, Avery."

"There's nothing to answer." She glared at Vance, then at Lee. "I gambled in college, made some money, and spent it. I went to Vegas during law school and got lucky. I pay my taxes and come to work on time. What else do you want to know?"

"What is your relationship with Jared Wynn?" asked Agent Lee.

"As I just said, I met him yesterday at the hospital. He subsequently asked me to meet him to discuss his father's condition and the power-of-attorney decision. We talked for an hour or two, then he drove me home."

"And this photo?" The elegant finger of the Chief tapped at the damning image.

"It is of a polite kiss on my cheek in gratitude."

"For what?" The potentially lewd question came from Vance, whom she had quickly learned to hate. "Why would Jared Wynn be grateful that you stole his birthright and his father?"

"I did nothing of the sort," she ground out, her grip on her temper slippery. Her stomach, a new barometer of mood, began to tighten with anxiety. This morning's command performance had a purpose. Looking to the Chief for support, she reminded her of the situation: "Justice Wynn asked me to do this, and I've done my best to figure out why. Jared understands that now, and he was appreciative of my willingness to speak with him. End of story."

"Not quite." The Chief stood then and circled the desk. "The FBI has received inquiries about the validity of Justice Wynn's decision and your role. I asked you here this morning to allay their suspicions. But eluding their security detail didn't help; nor does this photo." She perched on the mahogany edge and leaned forward, bringing her gaze level with Avery. "There are legitimate questions about what happened yesterday."

Vance chimed in: "You must admit, Ms. Keene, your sudden rise in power and liaison with Justice Wynn's son are cause for concern. Not to mention your convenient discovery of his nurse's body after she was executed."

Avery turned in his direction, exasperated. "Rise in power?" she stammered. "You really think I killed Nurse Lewis?"

"Everyone in this room knows what hangs in the balance." Vance closed in, flanking her.

"I have nothing to gain by hurting Nurse Lewis or Justice Wynn."

"Nothing?" Vance's query held more than a note of doubt. It reeked of a trap, steel-jawed and menacing.

Unable to avoid it, Avery responded severely, "I'm just doing as Justice Wynn asked."

"Then perhaps you can explain why you received a wire transfer into your bank account at four this morning, in the amount of five hundred thousand dollars?"

The steel jaws clanged shut.

NINETEEN

Five hundred thousand dollars?" she sputtered. "I have no idea what you're talking about." Which wouldn't matter. Whether she'd seen it or not, obviously, she had received the money. From someone, somewhere. "I know nothing about a transfer."

Vance flipped open the folder and removed a thin sheet. The page floated down onto the desk's surface, beside the Chief. The bank name at the top was a familiar one. "This is a transaction record from your bank, received this morning. An electronic transfer of five hundred thousand dollars from an offshore account, posted right after your rendezvous with Jared Wynn."

She lifted stricken eyes to the Chief. "I've never seen this before," she whispered. "I swear to you, I don't know where this came from." Suspicions weren't the same, she reasoned.

"Have you traced the origin of the transfer?" inquired the Chief.

"Not yet. Whoever made the deposit took great pains to disguise their identity." Special Agent Lee shifted closer, surrounding her in a triumvirate of suspicion and disbelief. "If you will cooperate, Ms. Keene, we can try to keep the press to a minimum. Maybe avoid revoking your law license."

Anxiety became terror. "Revoke my license? On what grounds?"

"Fraud, to start." Vance spoke from above her head, the dark baritone carrying the ring of inevitability. "If you conspired with Jared Wynn to defraud his father or to thwart the justice's intentions . . ."

"And if you had anything to do with the death of Jamie Lewis, we'll seek to add a charge of murder," finished Agent Lee.

"The FBI has asked me to place you on administrative leave, pending an investigation," Chief Roseborough added. "As of now, I see no reason why I should not comply."

Beneath the cool delivery, Avery heard the opening for explanation. An explanation she would dearly love to offer, but could not. She shouldn't have a thousand dollars in her account, let alone half a million.

The agent's threats spun in a maelstrom. *Revocation of her license. Administrative leave. Fraud. Murder.* Head swirling, Avery reached for slippery control, forcing her mind to focus.

Any charges would mean an end to her career. Even if exonerated, she'd be fortunate to get a gig defending jaywalkers and flashers. Reputation was all you had when you'd been born without the relationships.

Avery got to her feet and planted her hands on the desk, pleading, "Chief Roseborough, please. You can't believe I killed anyone. I went to her apartment to find out what she knew about Justice Wynn. And I snuck out to meet with Jared because he asked me to, and I was worried and confused."

"Explain the deposit," barked Lee. "Tell us where the money came from and who it's for. Was this payment for a hit?"

"God, no!" Avery stumbled back. "I didn't kill anyone, and I didn't accept a bribe."

"I don't believe you." Agent Lee snatched up the sheet and waved it once. "No jury will believe you either."

The Chief rose as well. "Avery, give us some explanation. Anything."

"I would—if I knew. Chief, I haven't done anything wrong," she repeated shakily. Yet she—as much as the others in the room—understood the tenuous connection between crime and punishment. The allegation was often more than sufficient. Innocent until proven guilty was an urban myth. Terrified, she mumbled, "Yesterday morning, I was a law clerk."

"Avery, I'm sorry. But my hands are tied." The Chief paused, her face imperturbable. "You are on administrative leave, effective immediately."

Agent Lee added, "Until you can explain your newfound wealth, Ms. Keene, we have no choice but to restrict your access to governmental property. You will surrender your badge, and your access to the Court's systems will be suspended."

He recited the restrictions in the flat affect she assumed they'd been taught in FBI school. Avery tried to listen, but the words swirled in a blur of sound. *Save us. Finish it. Protect Justice Wynn. In the square.* She couldn't do any of that from behind bars.

It was then that she realized no one had placed her under arrest. A clerkship on the district court had taught her the rules of the game in federal court. She took a step toward Agent Lee, cutting off the dry recital from the FBI. "Am I being detained?"

"Not yet."

"Indicted?"

"No." Agent Lee cast a look at Major Vance. "Until we have more information, we're willing to hold off."

Vance added, "However, we expect you to relinquish your power of attorney to Mrs. Turner-Wynn. If you do so, neither Agent Lee nor I will pursue this matter any further."

She studied both men. "No."

"This is not a request, Ms. Keene," said Agent Lee, taking a step toward her. "You are under investigation, and it would be improper for you to exercise authority in this matter. Take the offer."

Avery shook her head. "Unless you can prove I'm a danger to Justice Wynn or that I coerced him into appointing me, you have no jurisdiction over my guardianship. Either arrest me or leave me alone."

"Chief Roseborough?" Agent Lee spun toward the justice, looking for assistance. "Mrs. Turner-Wynn should have her husband's power of attorney."

"I am very aware of Howard's relationship with his wife," the Chief demurred. "It would not be in his best interests or consistent with his wishes to give her control over his legal or health affairs."

Obviously surprised by the response, the FBI agent argued, "Then what do you recommend?"

"I recommend you do as Avery suggests. Either arrest her or leave her alone."

"Then you leave us no choice." Vance waved a hand at the FBI agent. "Agent Lee, place Ms. Keene under arrest."

Lee folded his arms, not moving toward Avery. "Hold on, Major, we've got—"

"No grounds," Chief Roseborough interrupted. "Which is why you will do no such thing. I have agreed to place Avery on administrative leave pending your investigation and proof of malfeasance."

"I agree we don't have cause to arrest . . . yet. But with all due respect, this isn't what we asked for either. I requested immediate termination. Administrative leave was a compromise. I've only known her a couple of days, and I have a difficult time placing any trust in her veracity or judgment."

"What do you suggest?" the Chief asked.

"That Agent Lee detain her as a material witness, at least," Vance suggested. "And that she relinquish guardianship to a third party, if Mrs. Turner-Wynn isn't the right person. She is a flight risk."

"I'm standing right here," Avery reminded them sharply. "I don't plan to go anywhere."

Major Vance jabbed a finger at the damning report. "In a matter of days, you've amassed quite a bit of power and a small fortune. I don't think we can afford to wait for the hat trick."

Avery turned to plead with the Chief. "I promise you, I have no reason to run. I didn't want any of this, but I want to do what he asked of me. Please."

The Chief studied her, then stood, forcing everyone to step back as she rendered her verdict. "I will certainly cooperate with the FBI in this matter, but the management of the Court's employees is not your domain. Avery will be on administrative leave, but she holds Howard's power of attorney. I would urge against a material witness warrant, Agent Lee."

When Vance moved to protest, Lee shook his head once. "We appreciate the Court's cooperation in this matter, Madam Chief." He turned to Avery. "I will need you to go to the Hoover Building with me."

"No."

"Excuse me?"

"I said no." Avery bent and collected her bag. She plucked out her badge, having neglected to put it on that morning. Special Agent Lee had made wearing it unnecessary as he'd bundled her past security. She slapped the badge on the desk.

"Chief Roseborough, I will accept the forced leave of absence. There's nothing much I can do about the restricted access. But until they have any evidence that I've committed a crime, I will not be going anywhere other than home."

"We can make your life very difficult," Agent Lee warned.

"Because I've been having such an easy time so far this week?" Avery spoke past the knot in her throat, the tremors of nerves that expected handcuffs in an instant, finding instead the bolster of righteous indignation. She turned away from the FBI agent. "Chief, I am Justice Wynn's clerk. I know the bounds of civil liberties, and I won't be pushed past them. He wouldn't want it, and you shouldn't ask me to."

Chief Roseborough watched her silently, then released a low chuckle. "I won't. He trained you well, Avery. You're dismissed."

Clawing for dignity, Avery made her way out of the office and past the inquisitive eyes of the Chief's secretaries. Her composure held as she entered the elevator and rode down to the lobby. A stream of clerks waited in line near the metal detectors.

A brunette with a piquant face and the soul of an archconservative called out, "Hey, Avery! Going the wrong way, aren't you?"

Her life was ruined. Whether they found anything to condemn her or not, a forced administrative leave and the publicity from Jared would end her life in DC. But no one had to know that yet. "I'm taking some leave to deal with this stuff for Justice Wynn."

"Hope he's going to be okay," offered a short, burly man whose IQ had been recorded in *The Guinness Book of World Records*. "We'll be pulling for him."

"Thanks." Avery began to push at the heavy glass doors, but the brunette stopped her.

"Wait," she told Avery. "The vultures are camped outside with their cameras. See if they'll let you use the other exit."

With her badge, she could have, but she was no longer one of the Court. She was an outcast. Still, she'd learned a few tricks from Rita. Always be kind to the folks who make the world run, including security guards and secretaries. After the clerks had clambered into the elevator, she found her favorite security guard.

"What can I do you for, Ms. Keene?"

"Vince, the press is outside waiting for me. They want to talk about Justice Wynn."

"So you need another way out."

"And a taxi," she added on a plea.

"Let me see what I can do." Vince signaled to his colleague to take over the metal detector and motioned for her to follow him. Five minutes later, he helped her into a cab.

"I really appreciate this."

He flushed with pleasure. "You just take care of the judge. He's good people."

"Yes, he is."

The guard smacked the top of the cab, which pulled into traffic on Pennsylvania Avenue and began to travel north. "Where to, miss?"

She gave her home address to the driver. In a rush, the adrenaline left her, and she sagged against the broken vinyl of the seat. Her hand came to her mouth as she caught back a sob.

It was over for her. Her life's work, gone in an instant. All for a man who'd barely acknowledged her existence.

With the FBI and Homeland Security working together, she'd be in custody in a matter of days, if not hours. Scott Curlee would trumpet the story across cable, and she'd be finished. She didn't have a firm lined up, thanks to Justice Wynn's stupid ethical rules. No job, no money.

Except for half a million she wouldn't and couldn't spend.

Ling's admonition from the night before came screaming back: *Refuse the power of attorney . . . Your boss thinks you're a chess piece that's disposable. This isn't your fight. Get away from the Wynns.*

Howard Wynn had set her up and put her entire life in jeopardy without the courtesy of a simple explanation. Her roommate was afraid to come home, and strange men were manipulating her exactly like a chess piece on a board. Like an ill-fated bishop—filled with useless power and limited moves.

She'd been an excellent clerk and a loyal worker for Howard Wynn.

She owed him nothing more.

As the driver wound his way through morning rush hour, Avery removed her cell phone and dialed the law firm that represented Justice Wynn.

"Noah Fox."

"Mr. Fox, this is Avery Keene."

"Yes, Ms. Keene. We were sorry you couldn't meet with us yesterday to review Justice Wynn's estate information."

Ice coated Avery's stomach, but she ignored the sense of betrayal. She had to take care of herself. Hadn't Rita taught her years ago that no one else would? "Mr. Fox, do you have time now to discuss Justice Wynn?"

"Sure."

"Good. I'm on my way over."

Ten minutes later, Avery reached the glossy office building and rode the elevator upstairs. She met Noah Fox in the lobby. He extended a hand and welcomed her. "Nice to finally meet you, though I wish it were under different circumstances."

"As do I."

He pointed to a hallway and they began to walk. "While we're all very hopeful, you have a significant responsibility."

"I know," Avery acknowledged brusquely.

If she hadn't realized it before, she certainly understood that now. Problem was, she didn't want the responsibility. She'd spent a lifetime taking care of one lost soul; she wouldn't risk her future on another one. A bribery or fraud charge from the FBI wouldn't simply disappear. A murder charge would guarantee she couldn't sit for the bar anywhere, assuming she wasn't rotting away in a federal supermax.

Anything that happened with the justice, any decision she made, would be evidence of a conspiracy. The perfect snare. Keep him alive or kill him, either action would evidence a guilty mind. Worse, she'd have a red flag on every background check, a redacted document in every file. Her legal career lay in ruins—unless she made a grand gesture that exonerated her.

They wound through a corridor, and Avery glanced at the attorney. "Mr. Fox, I need your help."

"Of course." He nodded solemnly. "Justice Wynn left careful instructions, and I'm sure we can figure out what needs to be done as his guardian."

Avery stopped, turned. "That's just it," she said bluntly. "I don't want to be in charge."

"Excuse me?"

"It's simple, Mr. Fox. I quit."

TWENTY

Noah Fox ushered Avery into a small conference room. The table had been stacked with the compendium of Justice Wynn's estate planning. "Ms. Keene, are you sure this is what you want?"

"It's what I intend to do," she corrected, wandering to the opposite side of the table. A bottle of water had been put on a blotter, along with a pen. "I want to relinquish my authority and assign it to Chief Justice Teresa Roseborough, effective immediately. She's known Justice Wynn for a long time, and she is better suited to make his medical decisions."

Her first thought had been to give it to Jared, but the FBI already suspected the two of them of conspiring together. The Chief was above reproach. A perfect solution. "Can you draft the appropriate documents today? I can wait here to sign them."

"You truly want to refuse guardianship?"

"Yes," she insisted, starting to believe it herself. What he'd asked cost too much. "I am rejecting his power of attorney."

Across the glass-topped table, the silence lengthened. Finally, Noah replied, "I'm sorry, Ms. Keene. You can't transfer guardianship to Chief Roseborough."

Avery frowned. "Why not?"

"Justice Wynn made strict provisions for his care. In the event you fail to serve as his legal guardian, Mrs. Turner-Wynn takes control."

"Celeste? No, he couldn't have intended to do that. She can't have guardianship."

"She can if you refuse to accept the power of attorney."

"She'll kill him."

"If Mrs. Turner-Wynn chooses to remove Justice Wynn from life support, unless the doctors offer a medical reason to stop her, it's her choice."

But if I don't do something to allay the suspicions of the FBI and Homeland Security, I'll lose everything, Avery reminded herself. All to save a dead man. "There's got to be a way, Mr. Fox. Some loophole."

"There isn't. One of the papers I was planning to review with you is the conditional addendum to his power of attorney. The addendum clearly states that if you refuse to accept power of attorney, Celeste Turner-Wynn controls."

"Why would he do this? He didn't trust her." Even as she spoke, she knew why. Choosing Celeste was intentional, the bastard. Serve or be damned.

"He was very insistent about these provisions. Tore up a dozen drafts." Noah hadn't understood what Justice Wynn's endgame was, but he'd speculated—as had the other attorneys privy to the rash of documents Justice Wynn had signed in the past six months. A labyrinth of codicils and durable powers of attorney, each with a different name, a different objective. Until late January, when a new name appeared. Avery Keene.

Justice Wynn wasn't Noah's favorite client, not with his penchant for biting remarks. Assigned to Wynn as a third-year in the firm's trust and estates group, Noah had been thrilled about the coup. Until their first encounter. The memory of Wynn suggesting Noah had won his law degree at a county fair still grated. He'd discovered then that serving Howard Wynn was the T&E group's version of hazing. Survive him, and you'd be on your way to partnership.

Noah recalled their last meeting, which had taken place in a conference room down the hall. Already prepared for the occasion, he'd removed a sheaf of papers the size of a halved encyclopedia. Only forty of the pages belonged to Justice Wynn's original will. The rest had been built of numerous codicils, taunts, and jeers to be delivered from beyond the grave. Today's revision would become the latest codicil to the last will and testament of Mr. Howard Wynn.

"Shall we start at the beginning?"

"No time for that," Wynn barked. "The nosy witch will return soon to ferry me home. I don't trust her."

"Your wife, sir?" Noah hadn't expected her at the office and would need to give her name to security. A driver had deposited him and waited outside. "When will she be arriving, sir?"

"I said witch, not harlot," Justice Wynn corrected acidly. "I don't know if she works for me or not."

Noah felt a tendril of unease. Legally, Justice Wynn could not change his will again if he showed signs of dementia. "Sir, does who work for you?" he inquired gently.

"Nurse Lewis, you brass-plated charlatan. The harridan that nips at my heels until I send her off to fetch something or other," he explained angrily. "The blasted woman sneaks about my house, prying into my every closet and secret. It's not right that a man be reduced to hiding his secrets from himself."

"From yourself?"

Justice Wynn's eyes flashed with impatience. "Will you continue to repeat everything I say? If so, you might as well return to your cubby-hole. I'm not paying usury rates for a parrot."

"I'm just trying to make sure I understand what you want, Mr. Justice."

"I haven't asked for your understanding," he retorted. Shifting in the conference room chair, he thumped padded leather with his balled fist. "You can't possibly comprehend the machinery of justice and the lengths to which others will go to thwart it. Therefore, you'd do well to keep your puerile mind focused on the small tasks I assign to you. Take my dictation, fancy it up with the words that will earn your five hundred and twenty an hour, and then bring the documents to me for signature."

Noah repressed the urge to snipe back. As much as he wanted to tell Justice Wynn to go to hell, the man had upped his billable hours by a quarter in the last six months. Gnawing on the inside of his cheek, he probed, "What exactly do you want to change?"

"First of all, I need to execute a durable power of attorney. And I will require a backup, in case she refuses to act."

They'd spent three hours in conference, changing the will and setting up contingencies for contingencies. During that time, Noah had learned more about trust and estates law than he'd ever gained in the classroom or on the job. By the end of the night, the documents produced had been presented to Justice Wynn for signature and witness. Later, Noah had speculated with his best friend in corporate about the relationship the justice had with his clerk.

Now, sitting with the woman in question, he felt he possibly understood the justice's choice. Avery Keene wasn't magazine beautiful, but with her wildly curling hair, lush mouth, and sharp green eyes, she had the striking looks that men of any age fell prey to upon sight.

"Ms. Keene, Justice Wynn gave me specific instructions to provide for only two options. Either you agree to serve as his guardian in all matters or the privilege goes to his estranged wife. I asked about using his son or a close friend, but he refused."

"His son hates him, and he has few close friends."

"So he said."

"What about Jared? Can he sue for guardianship, if I support his claim?"

"No. I'm sorry, Ms. Keene, but—"

"Avery."

"Avery," he repeated dutifully. "Jared Wynn can sue, but if he does and you fail to object, guardianship is awarded to Celeste."

"There has to be a way around it," Avery argued stubbornly. "The courts can certainly consider whether Jared is fit, and they can stay any action by Celeste."

"It's not that simple. My obligation is to abide by the judge's wishes. He didn't ask for his son or the chief justice. He asked for you. Even if you refuse or Jared sues and you don't protest, then I am obliged to represent Mrs. Turner-Wynn." He paused, then added, "We're quite good at this, Ms. Keene, and so is Justice Wynn."

Frustrated, Avery stared at the papers arrayed across the table. He couldn't have thought of everything. "Exactly what is in here? What documents did Justice Wynn ask you to draft?"

He reached for a labeled stack. "Here's the durable power of attorney. The one he signed in January."

Avery barely glanced at the now-familiar document. "I've seen it. What else?"

"His last will and testament. Basically, he names Jared as the primary beneficiary."

"That's all?" She placed her hand on the tall stack of pages. "It doesn't take this much paper to give his estate to his son. What else does it say?"

Noah sighed. "The justice had done several versions of his will during his lifetime. The original one designated his first wife as the beneficiary. Then he added a codicil after Jared was born. When he wrote his auto-biography, he placed the proceeds in trust." He lifted a set of papers and put them in the growing pile. "Next, he gave his wife's fortune to Jared after she died. According to our files, he disclaimed his portion, and the entire estate passed to Jared." He'd read the woman's will a dozen times himself. "The first Mrs. Wynn left her family more than ten million dollars and several pieces of property. Justice Wynn gave everything to Jared, except for a house in Georgia."

He cut his son off at the age of eleven, leaving him to be raised by his aunt, using his mother's money, Avery realized grimly. "When did Jared become his beneficiary?"

Pulling up the next codicil, Noah responded, "Five years ago."

Avery quickly did the math. That would have been around the time Jared received his medical discharge from the Navy. "Which codicil was this?"

"Number thirteen. In between, he periodically would select a random charity as his new recipient." He flipped through the pages. "The ACLU. La Raza. The NAACP. The United Farm Workers of America. The Boys and Girls Clubs. You name a charity, and it has found itself inside one of these codicils."

Avery skimmed the list. "He's kept you busy."

"I could make partner on his hours alone," Noah muttered. He looked up at Avery and felt a moment's chagrin. "Anyway, once he named Jared as primary beneficiary, he continued to add charities to his list."

"Any discernible pattern?"

Noah admitted, "I did a chart once, when I first got his file. Every group that lost a case in a decision where he dissented—he's placed them in his will."

"Really?"

"Each year, he creates a new codicil adding those organizations he thinks were robbed by the Court. Fifteen codicils."

"What about Mrs. Turner-Wynn? Is she in one of the codicils?"

"No." Noah shuffled the documents together. "If Jared predeceases his father, the entire estate is equally divided among the organizations in his will, with a substantial stipend to his executor, which is you. His wife inherits nothing."

One more nail, Avery thought despondently. "Does she know?"

"I doubt it." He explained, "She came storming in here yesterday, after you met at the hospital. Demanded to see his estate papers. When I refused, she threatened to have me fired."

"Has she ever been in the will?"

"No." Noah folded his hands on the table, coming at last to his final revelation. "But there is a problem, Avery."

"What is it?"

Sliding codicil number twenty-eight across the table, he turned to the page that had troubled him and a senior T&E partner. "I've got his original will and testament and twenty-seven codicils, including this last one."

"Twenty-seven? This says number twenty-eight."

"Number twenty-seven is missing. Although he had us refer to it in number twenty-eight, I didn't draft it, and I've never seen it." He indicated the paragraph that had caused an uproar when he'd shown the partners Justice Wynn's latest revisions. "He references a codicil that directs the actions of his attorneys in case of a catastrophic event. When I inquired about what he meant, he told me to mind my own damned business and do as he dictated."

"Did he give you any clue about where the codicil was located?"

"Yes. One." Noah caught her quizzical look and held it steadily. "He told me that you'd know where it was. And when the time was right, you'd give it to us."

TWENTY-ONE

While Avery absorbed the news, her cell phone beeped. "Excuse me." She glanced at the screen but did not recognize the number. "Hello?"

"Did you get my present?" Nigel asked. "I thought you might need a little incentive to stay in the game. Hope the funds help."

Avery hurried to the far end of the conference room. "What in the hell were you thinking?"

"I thought your reluctance might be mitigated by financial incentive."

"Whoever you are—because of your 'gift,' I'm under investigation by the FBI," she explained harshly, her voice barely above a whisper. "Now they think I'm conspiring with someone to do harm to Justice Wynn."

"You didn't seem gung ho about your assignment, Avery. Keeping Howard Wynn alive is of critical importance to a great many people. We simply require assurance that you will hold the line until we determine the best course of action. I may also require some intelligence gathering."

"I don't work for you."

"According to what I've heard, you don't work for the Court anymore either. Let's be clear. Administrative leave is the least of your worries."

"I have no control over his vote," she insisted. "I can't help you."

"You don't know what I want yet."

"And I don't care. I'm relinquishing the power of attorney. His wife will have guardianship."

"You won't do that."

"Why not? Because of you, I've lost my job and possibly my reputation."

"No, I've merely put them in jeopardy," he corrected smoothly. "If you cooperate, you'll emerge from this period with a shiny halo and a healthy bank account."

"All I want is to practice law, which you've now made all but impossible."

"You protect Justice Wynn and tell me what I want to know, and I'll make sure you never have to work another day in your life."

"No."

"Don't you owe him your loyalty?"

The echo of her conversation with Justice Wynn tightened her hand on the phone. "What I decide to do is between me and Justice Wynn. Take your money back and leave me the hell alone."

"Keep Justice Wynn alive and stay out of trouble, and we'll all be happy."

"Go to hell." She cut off the call and pressed a hand to her throat.

"Everything okay?" Noah asked as she returned to his side of the room.

Avery waved the question off. "Did he have any other instructions?"

Noah reached into the pile of items. A beige envelope had been clasped and taped, and the seal carried Wynn's scrawl to certify that nothing had been tampered with during its stay at the offices of Lowry Kihneman. "This should have the keys to his town house. Codes for the door and the safe should be inside as well. Perhaps the codicil is in the safe."

"Maybe," she replied noncommittally. She had no idea what Justice Wynn meant or what he thought she knew. But apparently, he enjoyed having her operate in the dark with her hands tied behind her back. "Is there anything else?"

"I have made copies of the wills and other documents for you." He pointed to a small blue-and-white box on the carpeted floor. "It also has miscellaneous contracts and agreements he's executed through the firm. I'd planned to go over them with you as well."

"Another time, maybe." She reached for the envelope. If the contents got her inside Wynn's house, she could look for answers. Nothing prevented her from reneging tomorrow. One more day. "I appreciate you meeting me today, Noah. My apologies for the melodrama."

"You've had a shock. We had no idea he hadn't told you." He stood and shifted a sheet across the blotter. "I'll need you to sign this form indicating that you've agreed to accept the responsibility for holding his power of attorney subject to the terms and conditions I've laid out. Take your time."

Without a word, Avery read the simple form and scribbled her signature above the words *Legal Guardian.*

As she signed, she reminded herself that she wasn't lying to him. Any good lawyer understood that a signature could be undone. Once she saw what was inside Wynn's safe, she'd make her choice.

She laid the pen on the conference table. "Can you hold the box here until later? I have some errands to run, and I'm traveling by cab."

"Sure." Noah fished in his pocket and removed a business card. "Avery, I know this must be very difficult to absorb all at once. I hope you'll call me if you have any questions."

Avery accepted the card with a short nod. "Thanks."

"Of course." He rounded the table and led her out of the conference room to the elevator.

The car dinged, and Avery stepped inside and pressed the button. "I appreciate your help. I'll talk to you soon." When the car reached the lobby, she walked out to the street to hail a taxi. "Georgetown, please. R and Wisconsin."

The cab pulled into traffic, and Avery tore open the envelope. A key ring fell into her lap, and she tugged out a single sheet of paper. The sheet had three sets of numbers scrawled across in Justice Wynn's handwriting.

Alarm: 9-1-8-7-4
Safe: 2-5-7-1-1-6-3-8-2 (behind the Caro compendium)
VGC: 3-1-0-7-7-4

Avery folded the sheet and tucked it into her purse, then hefted the keys, toying with them. The cab deposited her in front of Justice Wynn's town house. Avery entered and disengaged the alarm. Remembering her prior visits, she headed to the study. Books lined built-in shelves and rested on every flat surface. Intent on her task, she walked to the far west wall and scanned the titles there. Carefully, she removed Robert Caro's weighty biographies and laid them on the hardwood floor.

Soon, the steel frame of the safe came into view. She glanced around herself, then typed in the numbers, reached for the handle, and lifted it to release the lock. Inside, a thick black binder leaned against the safe wall, propped up by a stack of cash. A silver velvet box peeked out from behind the currency, and a slimmer file had been slipped in between the binder and the wall.

Avery reached for the folder first. As she pulled it free, she saw that a black lighter had been taped to the folder's front. She opened the file, which contained a single sheet of paper with black script. The sheet was flimsy, almost transparent, and she recognized the consistency immediately. Nitrocellulose.

"Very clever, Justice Wynn." Nitrocellulose, a mixture of nitric acid and sulfuric acid, could be applied to ordinary paper for a simple vanishing trick. Any chemistry student worth her salt had tried the experiment.

She read the note he'd written on what was also known as magician's flash paper. Scratched across the top were the words *BURN UPON REVIEW*. Below, a series of letters, numbers, and symbols marched across the page. She stared, committing the garbled text to memory, then, out of an abundance of caution, captured the image with her phone.

e4c5Gf3d6Ob5+Od7Oxd7+Vxd7c4Gc6Gc3Gf6oog6d4cxd4Gx
d4Og7Gde2Ve6!?Gd5Vxe4Gc7+Rd7Gxa8Vxc4Gb6+axb6Gc3H
a8a4Ge4Gxe4Vxe4Vb3f5Og5Vb4Vf7Oe5h3Hxa4Hxa4Vxa4Vxh
7Oxb2Vxg6Ve4Vf7Od4Vb3f4Vf7Oe5h4b5h5Vc4Vf5+Ve6Vxe6+
Rxe6g3fxg3fxg3b4Of4Od4+Rh1!b3g4Rd5g5e6h6Ge7Hd1e5Oe3R
c4Oxd4exd4Rg2b2Rf3Rc3h7Gg6Re4Rc2Hh1Rf5b1=VHxb1Rxb1
Rxg6d2h8=Vd1=VVh7b5?!Rf6+Rb2Vh2+Ra1Vf4b4?Vxb4Vf3+Rg
7d5Vd4+Rb1g6Ve4Vg1+Rb2Vf2+Rc1Rf6d4g71–o

Justice Wynn had typed gibberish onto a piece of paper that he'd demanded be burned upon reading, as though he'd escaped from a John le Carré novel. She held the paper in one hand and pried the lighter free with the other.

The paranoia of his instructions fit the absurdity of the last twenty-four hours. Then the image of Jamie Lewis's body flashed, and she crumpled the page and flicked the lighter into a flame. She turned and set the paper on the edge of a nearby table and touched it with the fire. In an instant, the code flashed and disappeared.

"First task, done." Wondering what came next, Avery returned the folder and lighter to the safe, reached for the binder, and opened the plastic cover. Curious, she flipped to the table of contents. A series of company names marched down the page. *Hygeia. GenWorks. Advar. Remar Pharmaceuticals. Genei Bioservices.* She counted nine names in all. The documents inside had been tabbed and filed first by company name, with plastic tabs for each topic. *Financial Statements. Products. Patents.* And a last category: *Source of Funding.* She recognized several of the companies from her research for Justice Wynn, but not all. In the binder, certain files had only one or two pages; others had many more.

Scanning the contents, she cataloged details from habit. Country of origin had been of note to Justice Wynn, and she noted that the companies were American, British, Chinese, and Indian in origin, which explained the disparity in information, she realized. Chinese companies were nearly impenetrable; and despite its open economy, India hadn't become an open corporate book quite yet.

As she skimmed the dense details, Avery wondered who'd collected the information. Justice Wynn rarely researched for himself. Unless he'd tasked Matt with this, which she doubted, he'd compiled all the information himself. Hundreds of pages, she realized in astonishment as she riffled through pages of dates and numbers.

The sudden swish of air came too quickly for her to react. Before she could utter a sound, her head exploded in a kaleidoscope of colored pains. She felt her knees give way as she collapsed, vaguely aware of being caught by her attacker as she sank into unconsciousness.

Faint words: "Sir, she's down."

Minutes later, he entered through the back, out of the sight lines of other homes. Nevertheless, the rest of his team quickly made their way inside, all attired as moving company personnel. He barked out orders to men used to instant compliance: "Continue to monitor the perimeter. Dispatch Castillo to the mother. No mistakes."

"Yes, sir." The stocky adjutant replaced his gun.

The man, who had spent his career cleaning up after politicians, reluctantly stepped over Avery's body and reached for the open safe. The public attention she'd drawn made permanent disposal more difficult. Instead of killing her, he'd decided to follow and observe.

Inside the safe, he found a woman's diamond ring and matching wedding band in a velvet box, along with a pair of sapphire earrings dripping stones from a platinum setting and a pearl choker gleaming with the luster of authenticity. He shoved the jewelry and the cash into a rucksack brought along for this purpose. An empty folder and lighter rested inside, but a cheap one that seemed to have no value.

Tucking the binder into the satchel, he shifted and scooped up the purse lying beside Avery. A single page had been stuffed inside, and he took out his phone to snap a photo, recording the codes for the alarm, the safe, and the cryptic VGC.

Checking his watch, he calculated that the girl would rouse soon. He reached inside the purse again and removed her phone. "Seven minutes, then I want us out of here," he said to Phillips as he closed the safe, stuffing the crib sheet into the sack. "She's going to wonder what happened. Make it look like a robbery, and I'll meet you back at the site."

"We'll take care of it."

He passed over her cell phone. "While she's down, clone this. They want to know everything she does, where she goes, who she talks to."

"Yes, sir."

He left the team, certain his directions would be followed. His car waited in an adjacent parking lot. As he drove away, he made his encrypted call.

A voice answered promptly. "What do you have for me?"

"A full binder and files on the matter. He had the right river."

"How much do they know?"

"More than we thought. But he is not going to tell anyone, sir. By the end of the day, we'll know what she knows. We should have the ability to bring this to a close shortly."

"You'd better. Time is running out."

TWENTY-TWO

A very came to abruptly. She jackknifed up, her hand reaching for her throbbing skull. The room spun dizzily around her as she struggled to regain her bearings. *Where am I?*

Panic surged, but she forced the twist of angst and terror aside. In panting breaths, she sucked in oxygen and willed her heartbeat to slow and her memory to return. *Focus,* she demanded. *Remember where you are.*

Fragments of memory scattered, refusing proper arrangement. Meeting with the attorney. Watching the news. Opening the safe. Standing in the Chief's office. Then a disturbance of the air and a loud, deafening crack. Her fingertips probed the knot swelling on the back of her skull.

Someone had hit her. *Hard.* Avery drew her knees up and rested her chin on them. The thought that she should run flashed through her mind, but she remained still. At this point, she reasoned, if anyone wanted to do more harm, they'd have already done it. No, she decided, better to sit still and figure out what happened.

Books surrounded her. Justice Wynn's study. They'd had cocktails in this room twice, at the start of each term. On the floor, various biographies lay scattered across the carpet. She'd stacked them before she opened the safe.

Swiftly, Avery scrambled to her feet, ignoring the rise of nausea that accompanied her motions. She crossed to the safe, the door now firmly shut. With trembling fingers, she typed in the code again. The chamber was empty. Avery's stomach sank. The cash, the jeweler's box, gone. Worse, the binder and the clues to her mission had vanished too.

Justice Wynn had been robbed.

Moving fast, she snatched up her purse and fumbled for the codes. The paper was missing. Burglars had tracked her into Justice Wynn's home and stolen from him, from her. It was her fault, she thought, sinking down to the carpet again, her hand still inside her purse.

If she'd locked the door, rearmed the alarm, they wouldn't have come in, wouldn't have taken everything. Her battered head dipped low, eyes closed in remorse as much as pain. Day two of failure. Another day without knowing what he wanted and why she was there.

If she had any sense, she'd take her one credit card and hop a flight to Antigua. Lie low until the session ended. Her fingers caressed her wallet longingly. She could be wearing a bikini on a beach in seven hours.

Her wallet!

Avery clenched her fingers around the nubby leather and jerked it free. Inside, her credit card, debit card, and painfully small collection of bills were exactly where she'd left them. What kind of thief stole a piece of paper filled with numbers but left the wallet?

She looked at the room again, more carefully. The contents of the safe were gone, but the antique clock on Justice Wynn's desk was untouched. Just like the expensive-looking oil painting on the far wall. The burglar had done a good job of staging the scene, but the missing paper didn't fit. Not unless the burglar was the kind not looking to make money on the job.

Avery clambered to her feet, grabbed her phone, and dialed.

"Jared, I need to see you right away." She slung her purse over her shoulder and rushed to the front door, where she reset the alarm and engaged the lock. Whoever had the codes might return before she reprogrammed the system, but she'd bet the contents of the house that they had what they came for.

"Meet me at the Starbucks on Wisconsin and Thirty-Fourth." Without waiting for an answer, she disconnected the phone as she jogged down the street, oblivious to the high-heeled shoes and the constricting skirt.

Before someone had struck her, she had scanned several of the binder's pages. Not for terribly long, but sufficient time to recall what she'd seen. Companies from around the world. Usernames on an email account: justicewon@ariesworld.com and tigrislost@gmail.com. And a jumbled code that she'd burned.

As she raced along the busy street, she dialed a second number. "Noah, this is Avery Keene. Are you busy?"

"Avery, is everything all right? What do you need?"

"Can you meet me in Georgetown right away?" She gave him the location, checking over her shoulder for signs of pursuit. Her breath stuttered as she bodily pushed past the knots of tourists and neighbors crowding the streets. "If you can come as soon as possible, I'd really appreciate it."

"Sure . . . yes. Are you okay?"

"No, I'm not." She shouldered past a phalanx of walkers, avoiding a collision with a nanny and a stroller. "Noah, don't tell anyone where you're going, please."

"Should I call the police?"

"Don't talk to anyone. Just come." Disconnecting the line, she entered the teeming coffee shop and scanned the area for a table. A corner nook with a settee and a chair had been abandoned by its previous occupants, who'd left behind a familiar brown pastry bag and a wad of discarded napkins. Her legs gave way, and she sank onto the sofa.

Calling Jared and Noah posed risks, but she saw no alternative. Both men had information she desperately required. Trust cost more than self-reliance, but she'd been boxed into a corner. Justice Wynn had left her with no clear allies except for his son and his lawyer.

She barely knew Jared Wynn, but he possessed computer skills she might be able to use. For his part, Noah understood Justice Wynn's machinations as well as anyone. At the very least, he might be useful in keeping her out of federal prison before she figured out Justice Wynn's strategy.

Too nervous to sit, Avery made her way to the counter. "Iced white chocolate mocha Frappuccino. Grande." The drilling at the base of her skull sharpened, and she amended, "Actually, make it a venti. With extra whip."

As a barista rang up her order, she wondered who else might have had access to the house. Perhaps they hadn't followed her. Maybe they were already inside. Waiting.

"Can I have your name, please?"

"Celeste," she whispered as the name popped into her head.

"Ma'am?"

Avery blinked. "What?"

"I asked for your name, but I didn't hear what you said." He held up a cardboard cup and a marker. "Can you spell Selst for me?"

"Selst? Oh—no. It's Avery. Sorry about that."

The teenager stared at her oddly, then scribbled the name on the cardboard and passed her the receipt. "She'll call when your order's up. Have a good day."

Avery moved out of the way and rubbed at the lump on her head. "Too late," she muttered.

Chimes tinkled to admit a new patron. She glanced up, and her eyes widened in dismay. Special Agent Robert Lee stood in the entrance, looking around.

She considered ducking into the women's bathroom until he left. But she refused to run. Puffing out a breath, she crossed the store. She stopped in front of him and cocked her chin. "Agent Lee."

"Ms. Keene, are you alone?"

"You probably already know the answer."

"I assume you came here to meet someone." Shaded eyes scanned the Starbucks. "He stand you up?"

"Who?"

"Jared Wynn."

"Iced white mocha!" yelled the barista.

"That's my order. Excuse me." Avery turned, only to have Lee take her arm. She looked down at his grip, then lifted her eyes to meet his. "Am I under arrest?"

Lee shook his head, but his hold remained firm. "I must speak with you."

"If you want to ask me about more than the weather, I'd advise you to get a warrant." With disdain, she peeled his fingers away. For a second, she considered whether he could be her assailant, but dismissed the idea. The FBI wouldn't have needed to bash her over the head. They'd simply give themselves a warrant to go inside.

As she turned away, she stopped. Agent Lee might know who did. "How long have you been following me?"

He flicked his gaze over her shoulder. "I have no obligation to disclose that information, Ms. Keene. As you well know."

"That's right, you don't. However, if you expect me to be even the slightest bit cooperative, it wouldn't hurt to answer." She heard her order called a second time. "Take that table over there."

She walked slowly to the counter, found her drink, and took a deep draft. The first shot of caffeine hit her veins with the precision of an IV. She returned to Agent Lee, his stolid face unchanged. "I assume you tracked me from the Court to Lowry Kihneman and from there to the justice's house."

"I'm not following you, Ms. Keene." He extended his hand, indicating the seat she'd staked out. "We had an alert placed on the alarm system at Justice Wynn's house. The security company called as soon as you logged in."

"But you didn't have a unit there?"

"No. Why?"

That meant no one to identify her assailants. He had no idea about the burglary. She shifted to watch him. "What do you want?"

"You left the house in a big hurry . . . almost a panic." He waited for a reaction. "What's going on?"

Her headache flared painfully at the mention, but she said, "I came, I saw, I left."

He sighed. "Let's try this another way. Tell me what you found inside the house."

"I was just looking around," she countered.

"Okay, if you don't want to answer questions, then just listen." He slowly glanced around, running his eyes over every face in the café. "Ms. Keene, I have every reason to believe you could be in danger."

Avery smirked, her mouth drawn. "Now I'm in danger? This morning, I was a tramp who'd accepted a bribe and possibly killed a woman. I think you need to get your theory straight."

"I still believe you've been improperly influenced," he retorted. "But that does not preclude the possibility that you could be in danger. If you had nothing to do with Mrs. Lewis's death, that puts you on the wrong side of the equation. I'm afraid you might be the next target."

"Of whom?"

"Of anyone who has a case before the U.S. Supreme Court," he answered simply. "You hold an enormous amount of power, Ms. Keene. One person close to Justice Wynn is already dead. You have the ability to terminate his life and open a spot on the Court. People have died for less."

"I am not killing Justice Wynn," she protested. "I didn't hurt Jamie Lewis. All I want to do is figure out what he wanted."

"And the money? A coincidence?"

"Yes," Avery lied. Neither of them believed it.

Realizing he'd made no headway, Agent Lee stood. "I don't have a side in this. My job is to protect the justice system—including the Supreme Court."

"Based on whose direction?"

"Attorney General Walters himself." Returning his notebook to his pocket, he removed a business card. "Call me when you realize you need my help."

"Right now, it would help if you got me the LUDs for Justice Wynn's house for the past six months."

"You've been watching cop shows, Avery?"

"No, I clerked for a district court judge in Baltimore. We had a number of cases where the defendants challenged the legality of call detail records and local usage data. LUDs."

"Okay, then you know I need a court order."

"I'm asking as his guardian. There's no issue of privacy or need for a warrant. If you want to be helpful."

"I don't know."

"Fine," Avery said with a dismissive glance. "I don't think I need help from the man who is trying to get me fired—if not arrested."

"Then take it from the man who will also try to keep you alive." He dropped the card onto the table. "I can't do this, but I'm not your enemy. However, you might want to ask yourself who is." He began to walk away, then turned back to her. "And you should have someone take a look at your head."

Avery sat very still until he left.

About twenty minutes later, Noah entered the Starbucks. "Avery? I came right over. You all right?"

"For now." She glanced past him out the window.

"Expecting someone else?"

"Jared Wynn."

"Jared? Okay."

Because she needed to tell someone, she added quietly, "While I was at Justice Wynn's house, I was attacked. Someone struck me on the back of the head and emptied out his safe."

"Someone attacked you? Are you okay? Did you call the police?" Noah looked aghast. "You think Wynn's son was involved?"

Avery gave a wan smile. "I'm okay except for a raging headache. No, I didn't call the cops. And I don't think Jared had anything to do with it, but he might have information to help me figure out who does."

"They have people who do that—figure out crimes. They're called the police."

"I don't want the police involved." When he started to argue, she gave a shake of her head and almost moaned. "Nonnegotiable."

"Then at least go see a doctor."

She dismissed the suggestion. "For a bump on the head?" Unless her head actually split open, she had no intention of going anywhere near a hospital as a patient. "I'd spend hours in an emergency room only to get a nurse practitioner who tells me to take aspirin and get a good night's sleep."

"Or she'll tell you that you have a concussion and require observation." Moving closer, he studied her pupils. "Have you been dizzy or experiencing blurred vision?"

"No, Dr. Fox," she said with a grimace. "Nor am I sleepy or dopey."

"But you've got grumpy down pat." Without asking permission, he slipped a hand behind her neck and tilted her head forward. "I worked as an EMT in college; let me take a look at the wound."

Avery allowed her head to fall forward, hair swinging down to cloak her face. "Knock yourself out."

"You appear to have done that quite well," he retorted. Gently, he probed the swelled area with careful fingers. Blood had caked to the split skin. "Looks like someone hit you with a narrow, hard object—maybe the butt of a gun."

"Felt like they used the whole thing," she muttered, her voice muffled. "Any permanent damage?"

"Not that I can tell." Noah eased her head back and again checked her eyes, the focus improving. He sat deeper into the sofa. "What's going on, Avery?"

"Did Justice Wynn ever let you see inside the safe?"

Noah looked at her incredulously. "I was allowed inside the house once, and even then, I was confined to the foyer. What did they steal?"

"Jewelry, cash, and some files full of notes." She shook her head and immediately regretted the motion. "I'm trying to figure out who compiled all the information for him. It's more than what I put together."

"Maybe one of your fellow clerks?"

"I doubt it." She massaged the nape of her neck, her mind playing through options. "The files contained information relating to several companies. We've been working on the GenWorks case against President Stokes, but the files included companies that aren't part of the suit. You ever do any research for him? Off the books?"

"Justice Wynn barely trusted me to rewrite the wills he drafted." He scooted forward, his voice dropping to a whisper. "Look, I've got to ask again. I've been a trust and estates lawyer for the absurdly wealthy for six years, Avery. The possibility of inheriting millions of dollars makes people do crazy things. According to the papers, Jared Wynn has become your newest friend, right?"

Avery's expression hardened. "Which would give him a reason to attack Justice Wynn, not me."

"Except that you're all that stands between him and his inheritance. It's all over the news, Avery. Jared knows if you take Justice Wynn off life support, he inherits everything."

"Jared got ten million from his mother, according to you. I can't imagine he'd risk jail simply to get me out of the way."

A figure suddenly pulled up a chair and sat across from the cozy sofa. "I appreciate the vote of confidence," Jared said dryly, eyeing Avery. He flicked a glance at Noah. "Who's he?"

"Your father's attorney," Avery replied. "I asked him to come."

Jared felt a tendril of relief that she hadn't said *boyfriend*. But the relief quickly died. "You didn't need the judge's lawyer to speak to me, Avery. Should I have brought my own?"

Avery waved the question away. "Of course not. Listen, I asked you both to come because I need information. Fast. Jared, I went to your father's house, and while I was inside, someone knocked me out. Whoever it was removed all the items in his safe." She took a sip from her cup. "Who had a reason to steal from him?"

"Celeste," both men said in unison.

Noah looked at Jared suspiciously. "If Jared here didn't jump you, Celeste has the next-best reason. She's desperate to learn what's in his will."

"I thought of her too," Avery said. "But she strikes me as the kind of woman who'd have a lawyer attack me, not a thug. Plus, she'd likely have access to the alarm codes and the safe. Celeste could have taken that material at any time."

Avery aimed her next question at Jared: "Justice Wynn had a binder filled with notes on various companies. Based on the names I saw, some of them seem to be related to biogenetics. Companies other than Gen-Works and Advar. Was he carrying something like a binder the night he came to see you?"

The question pricked a memory, and Jared nodded slowly. "Now that you ask, yes. He had a thick black binder with him." The recollection was followed by a curse.

"What's wrong?" asked Avery.

"He told me he wanted to show me something, but I refused."

"Did he tell you what was inside?" Noah interjected.

"It was that first night at the bar. After a while, he didn't bring it up again." Jared paused, then muttered a fresh curse. "I didn't even look."

TWENTY-THREE

That's okay, Jared. We have a place to start." Not much of one, but she'd take crumbs. "There was a second file in the safe," she continued.

Noah held up a hand. "Before we get to the safe, can I take this meeting to mean you're keeping guardianship? You didn't seem so sure when you left my office."

Avery bit at her lip. "I signed the papers."

"Agreements get broken, Avery. We both know that."

Jared frowned at her. "Why would you give up guardianship? You didn't mention that last night."

"Last night, I didn't have reporters camped out on my doorstep and a thousand messages on my phone," she defended. "Or a stranger offering me half a million to be at his beck and call."

"What?" Jared demanded.

Avery quickly recounted the call and her meeting in the Chief's office. "So you'll forgive me for not being sure of what I want to do. Noah and I discussed my alternatives today, and I raised the possibility of placing the chief justice in charge."

"Why not me?"

"She couldn't," Noah answered. "Your father made it Avery or Mrs. Turner-Wynn. No one else."

"You're saying he refused to allow me to take care of him?" When no one responded, he muttered, "Of course."

"Your father is trying to force my hand, Jared. That's all."

He gave her a long, shadowed look. "You'll do this for him? Deal with being attacked by strangers and harassed by the press?"

"Yes."

"Why?"

"Because he asked me to." Refusing to elaborate, she shifted gears. "Do either of you know what VGC is?"

"VGC?" Noah repeated. "Never heard of it."

Avery glanced over at Jared. "VGC? Ever hear about it from your father?"

He mulled over the initials, but shook his head. "No, it's not familiar. What does it stand for?"

"I was hoping you could tell me." Stymied, she sank against the couch. "The initials were on the list of access codes in the envelope Noah gave me for the house," she explained, her mind clicking through possibilities. "One set controlled the alarm. I used the second set to open the safe. But the third line of numbers just referred to VGC. There's nothing at the Court with those initials, and it doesn't sound like any bank I've heard of. We need to figure out what it leads to."

"Can I see the paper, Avery?" Jared asked quietly.

"No."

"Come on." His mouth tightened. "I swear I didn't attack you, and I don't plan to steal the codes." He leaned forward, bringing his face closer, his eyes direct. "I have absolutely no interest in going inside his house, now or ever."

"I meant no, you can't see the paper because whoever hit me stole it from my purse."

"So we have no codes and no idea what the codes opened," Jared summarized. "Or any way to figure out what VGC is."

"Actually, I do have the codes." When both men looked at her expectantly, Avery explained vaguely: "Look, I have a very good memory. If we can figure out what VGC stands for, I can get us in."

"Do you have a place for us to start?" Jared wondered, his skepticism obvious. "Or are we shooting in the dark?"

"I'd say it's a bit of both," she confessed, the plan forming as she spoke. Junkies liked to hide their stash and their tools. Part paranoia, part selfishness. She'd learned how to scope out niches and ferret out the contraband. Locating a dying man's hiding place shouldn't be any different. "Jared, who has your mother's belongings?"

"Why?"

"VGC is either a personal reference or a professional one. If it's personal, the best place to start is the beginning. Photos, letters, anything that can give us a hint."

The haunted look came and went almost unnoticed. "My aunt Laurette kept most of the boxes the judge sent over. She stored them in the attic at her house in Arlington." He nodded once. "I'll head over now."

"Noah, I'll need you to comb through the will and codicils. Look for any beneficiary with those initials. Also, verify that he didn't have a safe-deposit box at a bank in Virginia. Hell, while you're at it, try Vancouver or"—she paused, recalling the images of national parks in the corridor—"or any state or federal park with those initials. Look for nearby banks or any property he owned."

"You're talking about hours of work, Avery. Several days of work, really."

She raised a brow. "Lowry Kihneman has half a dozen summer associates who are doing sophisticated filing jobs. Assign them to a case that will actually generate billable hours." Knowing how the process worked, she said the magic words: "I'm authorizing this as Justice Wynn's guardian. Figuring out VGC has to be our priority. Work fast."

Avery stepped off the curb outside the coffee shop and lifted her hand for a taxi. A car pulled up, and she climbed inside and gave her destination. Once the cab merged into traffic, she reached for her phone and dialed. "Mrs. Starnes?"

"Avery?" Debi Starnes snapped her fingers to get Mary's attention. "Avery, honey, we heard you decided to take a leave of absence while you help Justice Wynn."

"Yes, ma'am," Avery confirmed. "My new responsibilities will require most of my time, and with the end of term so near, the Chief agreed that I wouldn't be missed."

"Of course you'll be missed," Debi argued loyally. "Why, I was just telling Mary how valuable you were to Justice Wynn. It's no wonder he asked you to look out for him."

No wonder? It's a complete mystery, Avery thought derisively. "I appreciate the vote of confidence. Please let me know if you hear anything I should worry about."

"Will do." Mary lifted a sheet of paper and jabbed at the words she'd scribbled across it. Debi pursed her lips, deciding if she should tell. When Mary looked close to exploding, Debi caved. "Um, Avery, honey?"

"Ma'am?"

She hated delivering bad news. Gossip felt different on the tongue than disaster. "A woman showed up here around lunchtime. Sorta pretty, with dark red hair. Real disheveled though and, uh, a bit hungover, if you get my meaning."

Avery braced for the news, her headache reaching a crescendo. "Who was she?"

"Well, honey, she said she was your mother." Debi glanced furtively at the Chief's closed door. "I got the call and told the Chief. They were about to send her away, but with all that's going on right now, I figured better run it up the chain. The Chief agreed, and they're in her office chatting up a storm."

"Oh, God." She whispered the oath, too low to carry over the line. Rita and the chief justice of the U.S. Supreme Court. She'd had this nightmare before, but she'd always woken up. "How long—how long have they been talking?"

"Maybe fifteen minutes," Debi replied. "She told the Chief she was worried about you. We all are."

The bump on her head began to throb. Her breath hitched, and she forced herself to hold off panic. "Can you put me through?"

"Interrupt them?"

"Yes. Right now." Avery spun through the collection of excuses she'd been building since grade school. Allergies for the glassy eyes. Pneumonia for the waxen face. "Please, Mrs. Starnes."

Another hesitation; then: "Hold, please."

Avery lined up her stories, checking them for holes. Yes, she had given money to a drug addict last night, but Rita hadn't given her much of a choice. No, she still had no idea where the $500,000 had come from, except from a man who had called and threatened to ruin her life.

Before she completed the list, the Chief spoke: "Hello."

"Chief."

"I believe you know I'm in conference." The Chief smiled kindly at the bedraggled woman in stained gold satin pants and an oversized shirt buttoned at the wrists. The pallid skin of the once-lovely face showed the ravages of neglect. "How can I help you?"

"Let me explain anything she's told you." Depending on whether she was flying or falling, Rita's stories either set Avery as a saint or as the ungrateful spawn who threw her away. "She's a very sick woman, and she's often confused."

"She seems quite lucid to me. I think you should hear what she has to say." Without waiting for her agreement, Chief Roseborough activated the speakerphone. "Avery."

"Oh, Avery!" Rita inched forward on the softly cushioned seat and pitched her voice loud enough to fill the room. The high that had carried her through the night had worn off early that morning, leaving her alert to a world attacking her daughter. She'd gone down to a shelter and showered, then put on her cleanest outfit. The part of her that remembered being normal, being a mother, forced her to board the Metro and come to the Court. One unsteady hand fiddled with the buttons on her cuff. "Were your ears burning, baby?"

Avery rasped out, "Rita. What are you doing at my job? We talked about this."

"I saw the paper and heard those nasty folks on the television." Rita reached out a shaky hand for the dainty cup the secretary had placed on the lady judge's desk. The pale amber contents, some fancy-sounding tea, had been filled with sugar at her request, but she'd been afraid to drink. Afraid she'd spill the tea all over the expensive rug beneath her feet. Afraid she'd forget the speech she'd planned on the ride over. Afraid her body would notice the absence of rum in the drink. But, because her hands needed something to do, she picked up the cup.

The china bobbled, and Rita used both hands to lift it to her mouth. She took a tentative drink to wet her tongue. "I heard what they said about you, baby, and I had to come and set the record straight."

"That's okay," Avery pleaded. "I've taken care of things."

Rita shook her head. "You never could brag about yourself. No, it's a mother's job to protect her child."

"Rita."

The Chief interjected: "Your mother has been quite helpful, Avery."

Rita scooted closer to the phone. "I've been telling your boss about how smart you are. How honest." She gulped more of the tea, pleased by the sweet taste, wishing vainly for more of a bite. "Remember when you won that writing award in Tucson? They accidentally gave you a hundred dollars, but you'd only won fifty. You sent them a letter and gave the money back, even though we were about to be evicted."

Avery remembered the episode clearly. The raging argument between a tweaked-up cokehead and an eleven-year-old. "It wasn't my money."

"That's right," Rita replied proudly, forgetting how she'd threatened and cajoled Avery, trying to keep the cash. "You did what was right." She focused hard green eyes on the Chief. "My baby always does what's right, no matter what. Even when folks disappoint her or hurt her. No way she's whoring around or trying to hurt that sick man. She's a good girl, my Avery."

Chief Roseborough reached out a hand to cover the trembling one on the desk. Tracks jagged along clammy skin that seemed unable to hold warmth. Aloud, she said, "I agree with you, Mrs. Keene. Avery has never given me any cause to doubt her honesty. And, regardless, I make my own judgments." The Chief lightly squeezed the fragile bones beneath her fingers. "I've been around long enough to know not to believe everything I read or hear."

"Good. Good." Rita released an anxious breath. Her desire for a drink faded for one of the rare instants, and she turned her hand over to grip the Chief's. "Avery has worked hard all her life. I don't know what I'd do if she lost everything because of a lie."

"I won't let that happen," Chief Roseborough assured Rita, whose eyes gleamed with a mix of pride and contrition. "Avery, do you understand?"

"Yes—yes, ma'am." Sitting in the rear of the taxi, she felt gratitude lodge in her chest like a boulder.

"Rita—" Her throat tightened with words she'd forgotten how to say to this almost forgotten version of her mother. "Thank you." The hot whisper seared her throat. "Momma."

"It's okay, baby."

Watching the woman in her office cling futilely to control, the Chief lifted the receiver. "Was there something you needed, Avery?"

Avery forced herself to focus on the reason for her call. "Umm, when you've finished your meeting with my mother, I'd like to talk with you about my position at the Court."

"Your leave is not negotiable." The Chief examined the woman squirming in her seat, and her voice softened. "I appreciate how difficult and complicated this has made your life, but my hands are tied."

"Chief, I didn't accept a bribe, and I didn't shoot Mrs. Lewis."

"I believe you. So, perhaps, does Agent Lee."

"But Major Vance doesn't."

"No, he doesn't believe you, but until he has more evidence, I'll hold them off." She hesitated. "Watch your step, Avery. They are."

"Yes, Chief. And, Chief—"

"Yes?"

"I didn't ask her to come. I swear."

"Of that I have no doubt." She thought of the slender young woman asked to bear such heavy burdens. Then she recalled Avery's confrontation with powerful men bent on destroying her reputation. Perhaps Howard understood more than she realized. Still, she had the Court to consider. With regret, she told Avery, "I'll be in touch. It's probably best if I contact you from now on."

Avery heard the reproach and remorse, her fingers twisting at the hem of her skirt. "I understand." She was on her own.

TWENTY-FOUR

In an empty office on the twenty-third floor of the Lowry Kihneman building, Avery stared at a computer screen. On her way to the offices she had first stopped at the hospital to check in on Justice Wynn. Like before, he lay silently in his room, connected to a battery of monitors, IVs, and machines. Avery expected him to sit up and angrily demand his release from the infernal bed, but the silence endured. She sat at his bedside for half an hour, alternately listening to the rhythmic noises of machinery and asking him questions, to which she received no replies. Then, after returning home to retrieve the pages she'd printed from Justice Wynn's computer, she'd headed to the offices of Lowry Kihneman.

For the last several hours, Avery's time had been spent plugging in multiple permutations of key words, to no avail. Paper was piled up along the credenza, each stack correlated to a company listed in his binder—her attempt to re-create the files from his safe. Justice Wynn hadn't chosen those companies at random. She'd already skimmed them for references to rivers and squares and the word *Ani*.

Look to the East. Look to the river. In between. She leaned forward, rubbing at her forehead, muttering. She'd already eliminated the East River in New York, although several of the companies had bases in Manhattan. "Ani. An Indian name. A company? The East? India? China?" Then she recalled the email addresses and nearly cursed. "Damn it. It's in the email." Turning, she grabbed sheets she'd printed from his computer. On top of the pile was the email exchange with TigrisLost. How could she have missed something so obvious? "He meant the Tigris River. The Middle East."

She pulled the stacks that corresponded to the companies. "Okay, Justice Wynn. I'm looking at the Tigris River and the companies. Genei Bioservices is based in Beijing. Remar Pharmaceuticals and Hygeia are Indian. Remar is in Hyderabad, and Hygeia is in Mumbai. Advar, based in Bangalore. Nothing from the Middle East."

She paused. *Advar.* Having pored over dozens of briefs on the company that would merge with GenWorks, Avery could recite the entire corporate bio by heart. Justice Wynn would have known that. She shifted some of the files to one side. For now, she'd focus on the new guys.

Genei Bioservices had a thin résumé, but an interesting corporate management team. At least two of their members had testified on Gen-Works' behalf during the lower court proceedings. One was a Nobel laureate and the other a MacArthur genius. Both, she recalled, had argued that GenWorks sat on the cusp of revolutionizing treatment of genetic diseases like Huntington's and Parkinson's. Stopping the merger, they'd asserted, would be akin to killing off Jonas Salk.

A quick scan of Remar Pharmaceuticals, an India-based company, revealed that its lead funder was none other than Nigel Cooper of Gen-Works. Remar dealt in the dicey research domain of stem cells and cloning. As an American company, GenWorks faced prohibitions on the use of stem cell lines. "Mr. Cooper sends his money overseas and does his biotech research offshore," Avery murmured. "He doesn't even try to hide it," she realized. "No wonder President Stokes hates him."

The Chinese firms—Qian Ku and Shen Fu—benefited from copious state funding and tight controls on information. The slimness of Justice Wynn's files matched her own research. Putting the scarce pages aside, she turned to the next company on the list.

"What have you got for me, Hygeia?" Downloaded pages recited dry details of founding and acquisition for this short-lived venture into high-end research. The lab geniuses at Hygeia had specialized in a specific chromosomal objective: chromosome consortium. For the first time, Avery regretted not having added biology to her list of temporary majors.

"Maybe Ling can explain what this means." She tabbed the page and continued reading. For a few years, Hygeia produced lauded research, its innovations drawing international attention to Mumbai's latest gem. Venture funding poured in from around the world, and the founder scored invitations to Davos and the Clinton Global Initiative.

Then, abruptly, Hygeia folded. News clippings from the Indian press reported a fire sale of Hygeia's assets to Advar Biogenetics, Ltd. Avery thumbed through the articles. Every one told the same story: rising star company crashes to earth. Everything came back to the GenWorks/Advar merger.

"Avery?"

She looked up to find Jared standing in the doorway. Glancing at the computer clock, she realized how late it had gotten. "Jared . . . hi. Lost track of time."

"No worries. I talked to Noah, and he told me you were holed up in here reading. Any luck?"

"Not that I can tell." Avery massaged the juncture at her neck and shoulder where a knot had begun to form. "What about you?"

"I think VGC is in Georgia." Jared explained, "I went through all my mother's boxes and found a photo album—lots of old pictures from when my mother and father and I were actually a family." He sounded tired, looked emotionally drained as he leaned against the frame. His low voice continued: "Once a year, before she died, my parents would take a fishing trip together. After I came along, they kept up the tradition. We drove down to Black Rock Lake in the North Georgia mountains. The annual family road trip. Mom used to call the cabin her hiding place."

Avery's eyes lit up. "Your mother's name was Vivian. Vivian's Georgia Cabin." Jared nodded and confirmed her guess.

"Your father liked games," she said. "Everything is a chess match—move, countermove. To him, we're just pieces trying to get across the board."

"You want to quit playing?"

She gave a short, rueful laugh. "No—he knew I liked games too. I need to know what all this means."

"I see why he picked you." Jared stepped into the office. "Also, I pulled your phone records, like you asked. Tried to trace the unknown number."

"And?"

"Whoever called you bounced the number off several satellites. The trail was convoluted but not impossible to unravel. According to what I found, the call terminated in Raleigh, North Carolina."

"Raleigh? Are you sure?"

"That's where it landed. I had a friend in intelligence double-check my work. Someone from there went to a great deal of trouble to hide, only to leave a marker in the data trail." Jared hesitated. "But no one who could ping satellites like that would be so sloppy at the end. There's a backdoor that I'm trying to pick the lock on. Should give me an identity soon."

"That's what you do for a living? Pick electronic locks and chase satellites?"

"I have a number of special talents courtesy of Uncle Sam, and they are still willing to work with me, even though I can no longer serve."

Noah appeared behind Jared. "What's going on?"

"Jared discovered what VGC means. Vivian's Georgia Cabin." Standing, she stretched muscles that were cramped from hours of sitting. "You two up for a road trip?"

"How can you be sure that's what he meant?" Noah asked. "Georgia is a long way to go for a scavenger hunt."

"It has to be."

Jared stared at her. "Why?"

"Because otherwise, I'm stuck." She closed her eyes in exhaustion. "Justice Wynn said to look in between. I don't have anywhere else to start."

"What?" Both men asked the question in unison.

Jared added, "What are you talking about, Avery?"

In for a penny, she thought resignedly. "I got a message from his nurse on my machine at work yesterday." She quickly explained what she'd learned.

"Did you call Mrs. Lewis?" Noah asked. "He was paranoid about her eavesdropping on him. Perhaps he was right to be suspicious. She might be able to unravel his clues."

Avery repressed a shudder. "No, she won't. Yesterday afternoon, I went to see her at her apartment. I found her body. She'd been shot in the head."

"Christ," muttered Jared. "Do the police have any leads?"

"I don't know. Other than trying to arrest me this morning, neither the FBI nor Homeland Security is being very forthcoming. But if her death is linked to Justice Wynn, the reason why may be what was on my answering machine."

"Did my father leave any other clues? Other than VGC and the binder?"

"I found files on his computer that included several SMS text messages to India. He referenced the game Chessdynamo.com. There were two messages. *Ani Is in the River. Find Ani.* Another code: WHTW5730. On several of the messages, the subject was 'In the square.'"

"WHTW5730?" Jared gave a short chuckle in recognition. "When I was a kid, Dad liked to compare himself to William Howard Taft. If I were to guess, I'd assume the code uses his name and tenure. William Howard Taft Wynn, and the numbers are Taft's dates of birth and death: 1857 to 1930." He moved to Avery's desk to grab a pen. "I don't recognize the phrases about Ani, but WHTW5730 looks like a gamer's handle."

"Chessdynamo.com. In the square." Avery rushed around the desk to take her seat. Quickly, she found the online game. A three-dimensional pawn floated in midair, and a box requested the user's name. "It couldn't be this easy."

Jared and Noah circled around to watch as she typed *WHTW5730* into the username box. When asked for the password, she tried Jared and his birthdate again. The screen refused her entry. She refreshed the screen, staring as though the computer would reveal its secrets. Or Wynn's. He wanted her to find something, so he wouldn't make the clues impossible. She chewed on her lip and sifted through what he'd already revealed. Mentally crossing her fingers, she typed, *AniIsintheRiver.*

The log-in pane disappeared, offering her admittance.

"You're in!" announced Noah. "But what are you looking for?"

"He once mentioned this game to me for a reason. Perhaps if I look at the matches they played, it will tell me something. Makes as much sense as anything else he's done." An avatar asked if she wanted to return to a game already in progress. Unsure of her next move, she selected yes. A game screen opened, offering her a seat at a table.

"Play," Jared urged quietly.

"Okay." A countdown clock showed that the game had been stalled for several weeks, awaiting the next move. "I don't think his opponent is coming back."

Jared leaned closer, studying the screen. "I never cared much for the game, even though the judge tried to teach me. Can you tell which position he was playing?"

She tried to move a black pawn, but nothing happened. "He's White. His move." She moved a white pawn, and the screen darkened. *INVALID MOVE*. Avery frowned at the screen. "That move was legal." With the mouse, she tried to advance the pawn a second time, and again the screen denied her. "I don't understand. I'm trying to move my pawn to f4, but it won't allow it."

Noah asked, "F4?"

"The position on the board. Chess players keep track of moves that way. Algebraic notation—denotes the row and the space."

"Never realized chess players were so anal."

"Anal, but slow. Two days, and I'm no closer to knowing what he wanted and how I'm supposed to find it." She shut her eyes and sighed. "Justice Wynn leads me to a chess game that I can't play with clues that mean nothing. But he remembered that I liked chemistry and have an eidetic memory."

"You're getting punch-drunk, Avery," Jared warned. "Why don't we call it a night? Come at this again in the morning. We can talk about chemistry and your memory then."

A thought teased at her. She turned her chair back toward the screen, musing aloud. "He remembered that I studied chemistry. That's why I knew how to burn the flash paper."

Jared frowned. "Flash paper? What are you talking about?"

"Earlier today, before the thieves clocked me. He'd put a sheet of flammable paper in his safe and a lighter. The paper had a series of numbers and letters and punctuation, but it made no sense. It looked familiar, but not quite."

"Do you remember it?" Jared asked.

"Sure." She turned back to the computer and opened a word processing program. Typing quickly, she'd soon re-created the entire sequence:

e4c5Gf3d6Ob5+Od7Oxd7+Vxd7c4Gc6Gc3Gf6o0g6d4cxd4Gx
d4Og7Gde2Ve6!?Gd5Vxe4Gc7+Rd7Gxa8Vxc4Gb6+axb6Gc3H
a8a4Ge4Gxe4Vxe4Vb3f5Og5Vb4Vf7Oe5h3Hxa4Hxa4Vxa4Vxh
7Oxb2Vxg6Ve4Vf7Od4Vb3f4Vf7Oe5h4b5h5Vc4Vf5+Ve6Vxe6+
Rxe6g3fxg3fxg3b4Of4Od4+Rh1!b3g4Rd5g5e6h6Ge7Hd1e5Oe3R
c4Oxd4exd4Rg2b2Rf3Rc3h7Gg6Re4Rc2Hh1Rf5b1=VHxb1Rxb1
Rxg6d2h8=Vd1=VVh7b5?!Rf6+Rb2Vh2+Ra1Vf4b4?Vxb4Vf3+Rg
7d5Vd4+Rb1g6Ve4Vg1+Rb2Vf2+Rc1Rf6d4g71–0

Spinning back around, she pointed to the screen. "This is what was on the paper."

"You remembered all this? Never mind." Jared leaned in close and read the information. "This looks like it could be computer code, but not in any language I know."

Looking at it again, Avery rubbed at her forehead. "I know what you mean. When I first saw it, I thought it reminded me of chess notations, but some of the letters are wrong."

Noah laughed. "That's chess?"

"Almost." Avery smiled. "If it were really algebraic notations, this sequence records a whole game." She pointed to the first part of the message. "See, here? E4c5? It's an opening chess move, where the pawns from either side advance two squares forward. But players don't use a P for pawn, and the two moves would be separated by a space." Demonstrating, she inserted the space and then hit enter after the c5. "Each pair of moves would be numbered. This is the opening sequence."

He pointed to the second line. "Then what's the G?"

Avery shook her head. "I don't know. There is no G in chess notations. The pieces are K, Q, R, B, and N. King, queen, rook, bishop, and knight. The pawns don't get letters."

"Why is the knight an N?"

"Because the king is most important, and he gets the K. Some players use Kt for knight, but that's uncommon."

"Let me check something," Jared said, reaching around Avery for the keyboard. She slid her chair sideways, but he was already busy typing. He opened a page and scrolled down. "Avery, what do you think?"

On the screen, a chart showed the various languages and their notations for the chess pieces. Jared's finger tapped the screen beside the Hindi language. "R, V, H, O, G, P. Does that work?"

Avery flipped the screen back to her notes and began to search and replace. In silence, she added spaces and numbers, creating row upon row of moves. Sixty-two in all. "You're brilliant."

"Thanks," Jared said.

Blinking, she looked up at him. "Oh, you too, but I meant your father and his opponent. I think the other person playing was Ani."

"The one who's in the river?" asked Noah.

"And he may be my mystery caller of the five hundred thousand dollars." She tapped the lines of game notation. "This game sequence is a model game that pits Gary Kasparov against the rest of the world. They converted the pieces and the coding, but the game sequence is the highest level."

Noah hopped off the credenza and came to stand on the other side of the computer. "So what do you do with it? The suspense is killing me."

"The only thing to do is play." Avery returned to the Chessdynamo site and the game in progress. She studied the board with fresh eyes. "Let's see if this works. They're already in the game. Here. I was playing as myself. Let's follow their gameplay." Following the sequence she'd translated, Avery tried to advance a pawn. Rather than the buzz forbidding her action, the computer accepted the move and allowed the piece to be captured.

"That's it," Noah exclaimed. "But won't you need to wait for Ani?"

"I don't think Ani is coming back. Which means I should be able to move his pieces too." She quickly ran through the next moves, exactly as prescribed.

It took nineteen minutes. She matched the game Wynn had recorded move for move, while no one in the office spoke. Because she played both parts, the game proceeded quickly. The final position had Avery's pawn at g7. The screen then signaled an incoming message: *Meet me in the square.*

Jared pointed to a tiny box that hovered at the top of the screen. "That icon." Avery followed his finger to a blue box that allowed players to chat live. "Click there."

At the click of her mouse, a new box opened. Reaching around her, Jared scrolled through the chat menu. "Nothing."

"What are you looking for?" Avery asked quietly.

"I'm not sure." He drummed his fingers on the keyboard. "Gamers use the chat functions of these games to communicate."

"That sounds a bit tech-savvy for a man who used a BlackBerry," Noah offered. "But maybe the person he played with picked the method."

Jared opened a new screen and snagged the chat room's URL. "I wonder." His fingers began to fly over the keys. In less than a minute, the screen flashed blue, then white.

Then it flooded with text that had been jumbled into continuous lines.

"What is that?" Noah asked.

"Archives. Archived chats between WHTW5730 and TigrisLost." He performed another command, and a single name flashed in highlight. Satisfied, he stepped back. "Avery, meet Ani."

TWENTY-FIVE

M ajor Vance?"

Ignoring the summons, Vance flipped through the dossier spread in front of him, a condensed treatise on the lives of Avery Keene, Jared Wynn, and Noah Fox.

"Major Vance?"

Impatient, he lifted his head to check the clock above the door, which read a quarter past eight in the evening. Focusing on the woman who'd interrupted his reading, he prompted, "Yes, Johnson?"

His executive assistant entered the office. "A while ago, you asked to be notified if I received any calls about research grants authorized by the undersecretary. A staffer from Budget came to see me this afternoon."

"And?"

"He's in Betty Papaleo's shop. She's slated to deliver an S&T report to the House Budget Committee on Friday." Camille flipped through her notes. "As per the undersecretary's instructions, we redacted the mention of the CRGs for this year, and Dr. Papaleo has requested a reason for doing so."

Instructions the undersecretary had no idea he'd issued. "Tell Dr. Papaleo that her discretion is required because the undersecretary made it so," Vance said coldly.

"Yes, sir," Camille replied. "The staffer also mentioned that Justice Wynn recently requested similar information. Do you want me to contact the chief justice?"

"No. I'll take care of it."

.   .   .

Night settled lightly on Pennsylvania Avenue. In the State Dining Room, President Stokes nibbled on Brie and sipped at a glass of Château d'Yquem, a gift from an ambitious French ambassador who expected a private audience during his visit. Sequined, sculpted gowns twirled around the room, the incandescent colors interrupted only by the muted black and white of tailored tuxedos that improved even the most rotund form. In the midst of the frantic chatter about the latest scandal in DC, Major Vance held post near the president's elbow.

"Such a shame about poor Howard," offered an eggplant-attired matron of impeccable breeding and questionable chromatic theory. She hovered near President Stokes as she did at each ceremonial function where American royalty made itself present. Aware that her family ties to the White House faded with each president, she had made ingratiation her blood sport.

A beringed hand gripped a wine stem while the other fluttered to her breast. "I feel sick to my stomach about how they are treating poor Celeste. My son tells me she's been blocked from visiting her own husband's bedside."

President Stokes favored her with a look of mild interest. "Your son? That would be Garrett?"

Astonished that he remembered, she preened. "Yes, Mr. President. Dr. Garrett Forster. He's in cardiology, but word travels quickly in hospitals. Apparently, that girl has denied everyone access without her prior authorization. Celeste had to hear about it from the hospital's lawyer. Can you imagine?"

"Well, that is an outrage," offered First Lady Fontaine Stokes, a sturdy, equine woman who'd been with her husband since he'd run for student body president at Arizona State. She was well aware of how the matron Forster annoyed her husband, but she noted how his feigned interest sharpened at the mention of Celeste. Her cue to find out more. "What did the attorney tell her?"

"According to Garrett, the lawyer told her that visitation was out of his hands, and she'd have to take the issue to court."

"What about Jared?" pressed Mrs. Stokes, keeping careful track of her husband's microexpressions. "Does he have any say?"

"Not according to what I've heard." She lowered her voice to a conspiratorial whisper, pitched to carry well beyond their knot. "It's all so sordid."

Vance slipped between Mrs. Forster and President Stokes. "Mr. President, if I may interrupt?"

"If you'll excuse me." President Stokes followed Vance to a secure office, leaving Fontaine to handle the gathering. "Any news?"

"Security around Wynn at the hospital has been tightened, as we expected. The death of his nurse has everyone on edge. The FBI hasn't been willing to charge Keene with anything."

"You're with Homeland Security. Make them arrest her."

"That's outside my purview, Mr. President. And taking such an action from your position would raise unwanted questions."

"Has the girl indicated what she intends to do about the old man?" the president asked quietly. "Maybe she's one of those grandparent-killing liberals who believe in the fucking dignity of death."

"Unlikely, sir." Vance clasped his hands behind his back. "She is quite loyal to him."

"Loyalty has limits. Is she open to incentives?"

"She shares a two-bedroom apartment with a medical resident, has a negligible bank balance except for the sudden windfall, has not secured a permanent job post-clerkship, and seems to be her mother's sole legal source of financial support."

"Any leads on the source of the money?"

"Came from an account in the Grand Caymans, which our techs sourced to another account in Switzerland, with the origin account in Macao, registered to a shell corporation created in Ireland. We're in negotiations with the Irish government to secure the incorporators. We've asked for the funds to be frozen. They should be out of her reach soon."

"Be more creative, Vance. If the girl can't be persuaded to act, we may need to fully discredit her. She's already started the process for us with that stunt involving his son." President Stokes poked Vance in the shoulder with an angry finger. "With Wynn gone before the end of the month, I'll have an open seat on the Court." The president took another sip of his wine. "Release the funds and watch how she spends the money. She'll assume she's won a small victory against us, and we can use her spending as a tracking device."

"I will notify the FBI and Treasury of the decision."

"Also, it seems to me that we have a nurse who probably wrote plenty of reports on the state of mind of Justice Wynn. A road map to lunacy. Seems like a waste to keep those records hidden away."

"If we release those records, sir, Mrs. Lewis's demise becomes public knowledge. Right now, notice has been given to the marshals at the hospital, but otherwise, it's on a close hold."

"The FBI knows, so it will be public soon anyway. They've got more leaks than a sieve. The crime scene looks like a robbery gone wrong, correct?"

"Yes."

"Then it would be helpful if someone checked the nurse's home for any notes. I know a good conservative judge on the bench who will be friendly to a plea from a distraught widow who came into possession of them. Understand?"

"I'll do what I can, sir."

Downing the last of his drink, President Stokes instructed Vance: "Time to get back to the festivities. I want to be out of here by a quarter to eleven." He thrust the glass at Vance. "Make up a national emergency and yank me, okay?"

"Certainly." Together, they returned along the corridor to the State Dining Room. They entered in lockstep, Vance in position behind him so as not to crowd the leader of the free world.

President Stokes waded into the tangle of guests, satisfied with his plan. As he chatted with the prime minister of some recently overturned dictatorship, he felt a shadow fall. The president turned slightly to find Ken Neighbors at his elbow. Cursing internally, he made introductions. "Prime Minister Lamb, please meet the Senate majority leader, Ken Neighbors of Connecticut."

"Nice to meet you," Neighbors greeted as he raked back the hank of true black hair that habitually fell over his broad, tanned forehead. He extended his free hand to the president. "Mr. President, we were just talking about you."

Stokes pasted on his most insincere smile and shook his head, which gave him an opportunity to angle his neck to meet Neighbors's flat-eyed stare. The freakish giant loomed like misbegotten Gulliver at six-six, hulking over his own respectable five-eleven.

The president preferred the altitudinal equivalence of a meeting in the Oval Office to the vertical pugilism on the standing cocktail circuit. But he hadn't clawed his way to power by bending to redwoods. Coming toe to toe, he responded, "Hope you were saying good things."

"Only the best."

The prime minister drifted off in the care of one of the president's staffers, leaving him alone with the majority leader, an unwelcome intimacy. "How are you, Mr. Leader?"

"Doing well, Mr. President. Better than some."

"Is Marguerite here with you tonight?" President Stokes asked, well aware that the man's pocket-sized writer wife had booked a berth at an eating disorder clinic that treated the side effects of rabid alcoholism.

The leader's flicker of infuriation was barely visible. He replied gamely, "Marguerite is on sabbatical. You know the artistic temperament."

"Well, Mrs. Stokes and I were thinking of inviting you two up to Camp David next month. Will her respite be over by then?"

The Senate majority leader appreciated the easy thrust of the shiv into the raw wound. Brandon Stokes had never extended an invitation to him not required by federal law or the social mores of Washington society. Indeed, his presence at state functions occurred in spite of Stokes, and only out of deference to his near-absolute control of the legislative agenda—and his best friend's standing in the polls as the Democratic challenger to Stokes's absurd appeal for a second lackluster term.

Knowing that, he could afford to be generous to the tyrant. "We're leaving plans loose for now. With congressional recess coming up in a few weeks, we're thinking about heading out west to the ranch. We bought a place not too far from the one DuBose owns in Montana. Good investment property."

The only person Brandon Stokes hated more than Ken Neighbors was his counterpart in the House, Speaker DuBose Porter, Alabama-born and Yale-bred. President Stokes took a deliberate sip of wine to cleanse the acrimony. "Sounds lovely. DuBose's family joining you?"

"Of course." Neighbors ignored his drink, focused on delivering his message to the president. "He and I have been discussing this news about Wynn. We're thinking that the Fourth of July holiday should be truncated, and maybe we should reconsider August recess entirely. He is sure the House members will understand."

Stokes nearly choked. When his airway cleared, he repeated, "You both are willing to postpone recess? In an election year? How will members feel about their inability to campaign?"

"For the good of the nation, everything is on the table," Neighbors threatened politely. The possibility of a recess appointment, a procedural trick used by too many presidents to get their own way, had occupied a good six hours of his day. Stokes had strategized endlessly about sneaking in a replacement justice while Congress was in recess, thereby circumventing a nomination process—if Wynn had the grace to die in a timely fashion. "We want to be prepared to act, if the time comes."

"Have you discussed this with your caucus?"

Not yet, Neighbors conceded silently, and getting it past them would require bribery and bullying. But he and DuBose smelled blood in the water. Stokes's blood. "Things are moving so quickly with Justice Wynn's hospitalization and these rumors about his guardian. We simply intend to be cautious about sprinting out of town if work has to be done."

"Like what?"

"Oh, you know, Mr. President. None of us want to use the words, because we all wish Howard the best. Still—"

"Still?"

"A coma is usually a poor sign. And we'll want the full weight of the Congress to weigh in. It's a Senate job, but for the good of the country, we need to be unified, don't we?"

The last comment hung between them as warning and promise. "Well, Ken, I guess we'll all have to play it by ear."

Stokes turned on his heel, and, looking across the room, Ken made eye contact with Speaker Porter. Ken jerked his head toward the French doors leading out to a balmy portico.

Soon, the Speaker emerged through the glass doors. "Saw you and the president chatting," DuBose quipped. "Felt left out."

"Don't worry. There's nothing that snake will say that you can count on anyway."

DuBose reached for a cigarette before remembering he'd quit last week. His hand dropped to his side. "Did he have any news about Justice Wynn?"

"Not a word," Ken reported. "But I thought Stokes was going to choke on his own tongue when I mentioned postponing recess." The accompanying guffaw carried out into the carefully tended lawn. "Nigel Cooper was right. Joker's got a plan for that Supreme Court seat. Stokes probably thinks the geezer will kick the bucket while we're out, and then he'll shove one of his right-wing cronies up our asses while we're out begging for votes."

"Cooper may be right about his motive, but we can't stay here forever. The Senate is your baby, not mine. Confirmations are your domain," DuBose reminded him severely. "As much as I appreciate the man's help with this, he doesn't seem to get the bigger picture. My entire caucus is up for reelection, and some of these folks have tight races."

"Tight races? What the hell do you think the world will look like with a conservative neophyte in Justice Wynn's place? That jerk is difficult enough to live with. What if the Right Reverend Donaldson from the Eighth Circuit gets called up while we're off campus? Can you imagine that man with a lifetime appointment? And how excited the president's base will be in November? Tight races will be the least of your problems."

The specter chilled the Speaker into silence. With Justice Wynn gone, the fine balance of the Court would tilt dramatically to the right. His constituents would go into paroxysms of terror. "Fuck."

"Exactly." The majority leader scanned the area around them, then pitched his voice into a conspiratorial whisper: "We've got options, though."

"Options?"

"According to legal counsel, Justice Wynn can't be removed unless he dies. If Cooper is right, he's in one of those comas that go on for decades."

"My guys call it a constitutional crisis. Four and four. A split court for nearly a generation. I'm sure that's not what the Framers had in mind."

"Hell, in the Framers' day, we didn't have ventilators and artificial nutrition and living wills." Ken cast another look around, his voice even softer as he bent low. "But the Framers did vest the Congress with the ability to increase the size of the Court."

DuBose's brow soared. "Court packing? That's your solution?"

"You see a better way? Think about it. We hold hearings to rile up the public, then we offer Stokes a compromise. Expand the Court to eleven.

Until Wynn dies, that's his spot. The president gets to force Donaldson on us, and we add our own man. A thirty-five-year-old wunderkind with a clean bill of health."

"Sounds nice, but your math sucks. We're at four and four. Add two, and that leaves us right where we are."

"Until our guy wins the White House. Bringman is getting up there in years, and he's hanging on out of sheer cussedness, hoping to overturn *Roe v. Wade.* By the second year, he'll give up the ghost, and we can replace him with one of ours. Then we've got the edge. Justice Wynn can stay as long as he likes—we'll have a margin of two, and if the old man does pass away, we're up by three. It's genius, DuBose."

Intrigued, the Speaker asked, "And you've got the votes to pass this on your side?"

"Absolutely," he lied without qualm. His razor-thin margin of fifty-four included a couple of conservative Democrats elected by states sick of Republicans but not yet ready to embrace the liberal elite. But he'd make it work. "I'll have Judiciary convene hearings, and by the time we're done, every one of our people will be campaigning on a platform of saving the U.S. Supreme Court. But, DuBose, the House has to do the same and stick around in case Stokes makes a play. You in?"

"I don't know that hearings are the way to go, Ken. We've got firefights all over the map. My guys need to be on the ground campaigning, not hoping to score some points on C-SPAN." The members of the Senate loved the sound of their own voices, but the House had a different job. They had to actually talk to the people. "I need to send them home. Let them fan the flames. If Justice Wynn is down for the count, we can make this a wedge issue. Then come back early and force a compromise."

"We leave DC and that son of a bitch is going to do something," Neighbors insisted. "He'll get rid of Justice Wynn and do a recess appointment. Then we're screwed."

"I'm not sure I can keep them here, but I've got some procedural tricks that should hold Stokes off if we need to. Then we'll come back in and eat Stokes for lunch."

TWENTY-SIX

Wednesday, June 21

Crawling over the papers she'd fallen asleep reading, Avery stripped off her tank top and shorts on her way to the bathroom, where she ducked beneath the spray of the shower. Hot water sluiced through the fog around her brain, and she quickly dressed. The microwave clock read 6:23 a.m. She shook the remnants of the cereal box into a bowl, snagged milk from the refrigerator. As she ate, the door to the apartment opened, and Ling lurched inside.

A medical bag fell to the floor with a solid thump, followed by keys flopping to the coffee table. Ling kicked the door closed, rubbing wearily at her eyes. "Any chance the reporters camped outside our apartment building will leave anytime soon?"

"I'm sorry about all this. But go to sleep. We'll talk when you wake up."

"Not waking up," Ling said and yawned. "Grab me a Coke and fill me in before I crash."

Avery handed her the soda, then recounted the events of the past twenty-four hours.

Ling latched on to the story of the attack. "How's your head?"

"I don't have a concussion."

"You sure? Because the day after you're attacked in the judge's house, you still intend to serve as his guardian." Ling huffed out a breath. "I appreciate your loyalty to him, honey, but you don't owe him your life."

"I got a bump on the head, nothing more. And until I know what they wanted, I can't be sure I'm any safer dropping the POA."

"At the risk of you jumping down my throat, have you considered asking your friendly FBI agent for help? Or maybe the hulking giant from Homeland Security? Isn't this sort of intrigue their domain?"

Avery had considered doing precisely that, but caution stopped her. "Justice Wynn didn't turn to them for a reason. Until I know more, I can't risk involving either one of them. Besides, when it comes to the FBI, I don't have to. They have a tail following me around the city and a guy camped out across the street."

"And the Homeland Security guy?"

"I don't trust him." In fact, she'd decided, she'd use her time this morning to dig around about Major Will Vance. Better yet, she'd put Jared on the assignment. "I'd rather not involve the authorities yet."

"For the record," Ling announced, "I don't like this."

"Save the lecture." Steering the conversation to another topic, Avery asked, "I know you were swamped, but any progress on the names I emailed to you?"

"Yes. Let me grab a shower and a nap, then I'll print it out for you."

"I can just read it."

"Not unless you studied microbiology and genetics last night. Strange stuff."

"What did you find?"

"Sleep first, then we'll play James Bond." Ling swigged down the Coke and headed for her bedroom. "You going out?"

"Since I'm banned from the Court and have both a police and an FBI detail, I'm bringing reinforcements here." Avery hesitated. "Don't yell at me, but I'm also taking an unauthorized trip to Georgia tomorrow."

Ling halted on her way to her bedroom. "Georgia?"

"Justice Wynn owns a cabin near Atlanta. I'm hoping I'll find some answers about his motives down there."

"Is Jared Wynn going with you?"

"Yes."

"Is he as cute in person as his picture?"

Avery rolled her eyes. "Don't start. Jared is helping me help his dad. That's all. We figured out another piece of the puzzle last night. I would have gone today, but I've got another interview with Agent Lee this afternoon about Jamie Lewis and the money transfer."

"So you're planning to lie to the FBI again even though you have a good idea what's going on?"

"I don't have a choice."

Ling opened her bedroom door and shook her head. "You have a choice, Avery. I'm just afraid you're making the wrong one."

Not sure her best friend was wrong, Avery returned to her bedroom to gather the pages strewn across the bedspread. She'd spent the night trying to break the archived chats between Justice Wynn and Ani into decipherable conversations.

Thus far, she'd learned that they'd met more than a year ago, when he had been searching the Internet for more information about Boursin's syndrome. She'd also learned that they shared a common obsession with chess. Ani, apparently, was in hiding and feared for his life. In one message, he warned Justice Wynn not to reveal his knowledge of a potential cure.

The increasing hysteria in their chats spoke of a disturbing pattern of shared paranoia. She could be risking her future to help a crazy man who'd found a kindred spirit and woven a conspiracy theory so wild, the delusion had pushed him to suicide.

But the image of Jamie Lewis, dead on her living room floor, and the $500,000 in her own bank account indicated at least one shred of truth amid the insanity. She had no idea what, but she'd figure it out.

Avery gathered the papers and headed into the living room. Buried somewhere in their messages, Justice Wynn had left a clue about his plans. She gazed longingly at her briefcase, knowing that the case notes and incomplete memos inside would likely never be read by another at the Court. Then she shook her head. The best thing she could do for the Court lay hidden in the Wynn-related messages on her table.

When Ling awoke from a marathon sleep, she wandered into the living room and found Avery opening the front door. Yawning, she said, "Avery, introduce me to our guests."

"Jared Wynn, Noah Fox, this is my roommate, Dr. Ling Yin."

Ling gave a tepid wave as she wandered into the kitchen. "I'm ordering food. Thai okay?"

"Sounds good," Avery answered absently. "Jared, did you make any headway on the email address?"

He set up his laptop on the table, attaching components Avery hadn't seen before. Catching her quizzical look, he explained, "Hacking is a complicated business. I got into the judge's personal account this morning. However, I'm not sure I understood what I was reading. For the past six months, he exchanged emails with TigrisLost or Ani. Same tenor as the Chessdynamo chat room messages you've been reading. But the emails included several files they exchanged."

He brought up the screens. "Most of their communications dealt with whether it was sunny here in DC or cold where Tigris lived, but they clearly weren't discussing the weather. Bottom line, Ani believed someone was trying to kill him."

"I read the same in the chat room. Both of them were petrified about supposed assassins."

Jared tapped the screen on a particular message. "Ani thought someone had killed several of his colleagues."

"Colleagues? From which company?" Avery asked as she reached for the sheaf of papers. "I can't find an Ani at any one of the firms in the safe. Your father said to look to the river. The Tigris is in Turkey and Iraq, but Ani is an Indian name. The companies your father identified were Indian, Chinese, and American. No Turkish or Iraqi firms."

"I tried to backtrace the ISP and use traffic analysis, but this Tigris-Lost guy knew his stuff. He ran his signal through countries that don't even have electricity yet." It had been a while since Jared had been stumped. "As best I can determine, he used a series of routers, relays, satellite feeds, and encryption protocols to hide his location. He definitely hid the archives from the game too and set up that test for you."

Ling returned with drinks, and Noah reached for his legal pad. "Jared sent me notes he hacked from Nurse Lewis's cloud. According to her, Justice Wynn was fading quickly—faster than anyone expected."

"Did her notes explain what he and Ani might have been working on?"

"No. Mostly, she reports on his increasing paranoia and his obsession with President Stokes. Fairly virulent stuff, culminating, of course, with his diatribe at American University."

"Any more good news?" she asked the room.

Ling disappeared for a moment and came back with a bulging folder.

"I checked on the list of names you sent me, but I only focused on their patent research and articles." Reaching forward, she flipped through the pages, hunting. Quickly, she plucked out articles she'd tabbed for Avery's review. While Avery skimmed, Ling explained, "Mainly, I looked for any information in medical journals tying any of the companies to research into Boursin's or similar diseases."

Jared leaned forward, brows drawn together. "I didn't realize Boursin's had caught anyone's attention."

"By itself, the disease is not considered very important," Ling explained in apology. "However, the genetic markers of Boursin's syndrome have some singular properties. Like with Parkinson's and Huntington's, some biogeneticists believe that a cure exists in resequencing the DNA or in targeting the faulty chromosomes that trigger the syndromes."

Noah entreated, "A translation for those of us who didn't go to medical school?"

"Meaning," Ling responded with a smile, "that there's a theory in the field that if a gene therapy can target certain chromosomes, like Boursin's with specific signatures, techniques can be developed to apply the process across other genetic markers." She glanced at uniform expressions of confusion and expounded further: "For example, a company called Hygeia was doing some promising work."

"Justice Wynn had several pages about Hygeia," Avery recalled. "It got bought out by Advar a while ago."

"I'm not surprised," Ling responded. "They were developing cutting-edge technology in genetic research. Very controversial theories, though." She shuffled through the pages for a thick binder clip. "What I found interesting was that Hygeia did a great deal of research on Y haplogroups."

"Doesn't everyone?" Noah deadpanned.

Ling shot him a look before explaining, "Y haplogroups are genes characterized by specific geographical distributions. Basically, based on your DNA coding, there's a good chance we can determine which region of the world your ancestors came from. Hygeia specialized in focusing on these genes, and their teams secured a number of patents."

"What did they develop?" Avery asked.

"Nothing that's made it to market, but gene patents are a new field. I cross-referenced the patent holders, and the same researcher names kept coming up. Then the patents stop."

Avery skimmed the dates on the applications. "The patents stop shortly before Hygeia merged into Advar. Which takes us right back to Advar and GenWorks."

"It's not unusual for these tech firms to be acquired," Jared offered. "Usually, the brains simply produce for their new masters."

Nodding, Ling said, "Look at the most prolific inventor listed."

"Dr. A. K. Ramji." Avery flipped through the patents more slowly. "He's listed on every one. Did he go to another company to continue his work?"

"I thought about that, but no new patents have followed up on their research. The more interesting issue is the subject of the patents. Over time, Dr. Ramji focused his work on manipulating specific Y haplogroups. Groups L and H. Then a journal article questioned his focus, and he simply stopped publishing. Fell off the map."

"When?"

"About eighteen months ago, give or take." She thumbed through her documents, plucking his last article from the stack. "He did this one on applications of adenovirus vectors that published last May, but that means he probably wrote it a year or so before. I didn't have a chance to dig much deeper today."

"A. K. Ramji. It could be the mysterious Ani." Jared tapped commands onto the keyboard. "Now that we know where to look, let's see what I can dig up. What are the other names of the inventors?"

Ling plucked a page from her stack. "I've listed all the patents secured by Hygeia or any other company with a similar focus. The Chinese firms have less patience with our patent process."

"Did Ramji's research specifically focus on Boursin's?" Avery peered at the scholarly articles Ling pushed in front of her. "Justice Wynn spent a lot of time studying these companies and their research. If they weren't working on cures for Boursin's, I don't understand why he'd build such extensive files."

"Like I said, Boursin's is one of the types of diseases that gene therapies can treat. But biogenetic research isn't entirely benign. A number of bioethicists have worried about the weaponization of gene therapy."

"How?"

"It ranges. Imagine if you could target certain genes with a protein that makes a person stronger. That's basically the idea behind gene doping among athletes. Apply that to armies, and you'd have superstrong warriors who required little sleep and less equipment."

"Could you reverse that?" Avery asked quietly. "Somehow target an army and weaken them?"

"Gene therapy currently requires close-range contact with a subject. You're talking about hitting microscopic targets with the right combination of chemicals." Ling's answer was careful. "Genetic weaponization is a fringe field. Most reputable scientists would never admit to working on anything of the kind."

"Found him!" Jared announced as he turned the computer toward Avery. "A. K. Ramji is Dr. Ani Kandahar Ramji. He stopped publishing a year and a half ago, and around the same time, posts on the evils of genetic weaponization started," Jared said. "Guess who the author is?"

Avery gazed at the emails strewn across the table. *Look to the river.* "TigrisLost."

TWENTY-SEVEN

The same." Jared typed more commands into the keyboard. "The earliest posts warn about the dangers of gene patents and the direction of research. As they continue, the author contends that Hygeia was involved in unauthorized research to convert biomedical science into weapons of mass destruction. Makes accusations against Hygeia and several other companies. Claims they colluded to develop a new form of biological warfare."

"All by TigrisLost?" Avery shifted to stand behind Jared and peered over his shoulder. "Show me."

"Give me a second." He tapped in a series of commands, pages opening in quick sequence. Then, just as fast, the pages vanished. Jared typed faster, cursing beneath his breath. "What the hell?"

Avery leaned closer to the screen, reading over his shoulder. "What's wrong?"

"Damned if I know," he muttered, as the pages disappeared into the ether. Unable to stop the process, he took screenshots of several images before they were zapped. It took less than a minute to lose every document. Jared slammed his fist on the table in frustration. "I've never seen that happen before."

"How is that even possible?"

"I don't know." He got to his feet, unable to sit. "I used a cache recovery program to find all the posts using similar language or related ISPs." He pointed to the empty screen. "Once the pages started appearing, looks like a virus tripped and they vanished."

"Were you able to save anything?" Ling asked.

Jared strode back to the computer and leaned over the chair. "I managed a couple of screenshots, that's all."

"So we have nothing."

"Not yet."

Avery watched in irritated quiet as he entered commands and plugged unfamiliar technology into his computer. The silence stretched for nearly half an hour, until Jared sighed in satisfaction.

"What?" Avery asked.

"Someone went to a lot of trouble to hide references to TigrisLost. I cannot find any recent sightings of Dr. Ramji or his compatriots." Jared tilted the chair on two legs and wove his fingers behind his head. "I just plugged in several of the names from Ling's list. Every scientist listed as an inventor with Dr. Ramji as a co-inventor has died."

"How did they die?" Noah crowded close to the screen.

"This was a very accident-prone scientific team. Dr. Farooq Kuthrapali died in a car accident in Mumbai six months ago. In Bijapur, Dr. Jaya Gupta perished in a house fire. Dr. Sangeetha Malhotra was shot during a robbery in Hyderabad. And Dr. Pria Sen drowned while on vacation in Indonesia."

Avery rubbed at her arms, suddenly chilled. "Any information on Ani?"

"Other than assuming he's the judge's chess partner, Dr. Ani Ramji doesn't exist anymore. I've found an apartment he leased in Hyderabad before the merger and some stray Internet purchases from a few years ago, but otherwise, he's been wiped off the grid."

"You can check international databases that quickly?" asked Noah.

"With the right skills, yes. Money leaves a footprint. Cash is hardest to trace, but it has to come from somewhere, and I can typically locate the origin point. He may be in another country, but his Indian bank information and electronic presence have virtually disappeared."

"Then he's gone?" Ling placed a hand on Avery's shoulder as she spoke. "We've lost him?"

Jared gave a half nod. "For now. But no one can completely hide their electronic fingerprints. I've put a tag on certain search terms. We'll know if anyone else starts looking around for the same information or if he pops his head up. I've planted data mines in case he uses a credit card or tries to act online. Or, if anyone else is looking for him, you'll get a chance to chat."

Avery thought about the dead scientists and their missing partner. The trail of breadcrumbs left by Justice Wynn led directly to Ani Ramji. The rest of them were likely in a cabin in Georgia. "I think we need to look for him. Physically."

"Go to India?"

"Not yet. *In the square* must mean more than the chess game. If Ani is the key, then Justice Wynn expects us to find him. But I don't think he's still in India."

"Why not?"

"They've planned this out too well. A trip to India to find him would be unfeasible. If we're meant to find him, he's here—in the U.S."

Jared said, "I've checked passport entries and flight manifests. Ani Ramji has not entered the country in the last year. Of course, he could have traveled under an alias, and if he has, I have no way to track him."

"Why not take out an ad?"

Everyone turned to stare at Ling, who'd made the suggestion. She shrugged. "If you chased him digitally, why not hedge your bets? Take out ads and ask him to meet you. In the square."

"Because we still don't know where that is," Noah reminded her.

"Avery will figure it out. In the meantime, you use social media to make contact. Assume he is here, then post in multiple channels and let him know you've figured some of it out. Tell him to meet you in the square."

"Run digital ads to track down one guy?" Noah asked. "That'll be incredibly expensive if you want to saturate the market."

"What other choice do we have? We need something concrete, and he's our best hope." Holding up her hand to stop Noah's rebuttal, she added, "Yes, running digital ads will be expensive, but now isn't the time to be cheap. The Supreme Court session ends in less than two weeks. Which is why it's good we have half a million dollars at our disposal."

Avery turned to Noah. "I need a corporate alias to place the ads and a social media account—ChessdynamoDC. Untraceable to me. Can you do it tomorrow?"

"Sure. I'll set up a shell to place the ads and then create the profiles. That's more exciting than the research I'm working on now. What is the message?"

" 'ChessdynamoDC. In the square. Waiting for you.' "

"That's it?"

"Run digital ads that tag anyone playing chess online or who searches for chess-related info or searches for info on Justice Wynn. If he's as dedicated to the game as he seems, he'll see it. Hopefully, Dr. Ramji will understand, and he'll contact me through Wynn's game or the Chess-dynamoDC DMs."

"And if he doesn't?"

She looked around the table. "If anyone has a better idea, I'm willing to listen."

"While we go snipe hunting with digital ads," Jared said, "I'll set some pop-ups. If the person enters the right sequence of search terms on most of the engines, they'll get an invitation to connect with you."

"And what about your screenshots? What do they say?"

Opening one, he read it swiftly, getting the general gist. "TigrisLost starts off by talking about losing his job for speaking out against the advancement of evil. He calls on the Sansad to take action."

"The Indian parliament," Noah explained helpfully. "Take action on what?"

"He claims that because of his actions, the world was about to learn of Hygeia's tyranny. However, before a full investigation could be launched, Advar bought out a controlling interest in Hygeia. Got all their patents and their data. He alleges that Advar promised the government they would bury the truth."

Jared flipped to another screenshot. "This one was from a few months before. TigrisLost claims that Hygeia recruited certain subjects based on odd factors."

"Such as?"

Squinting at the screen, he read, "A tendency for L1, L3, R2, HM69."

"What are those?" Noah asked. "More algebraic notations for a phantom chess game?"

"Not quite." Ling stood near Jared. "Haplogroups. Those numbers are code for genetic and archaeogenetic mapping."

Avery leaned over, peering at Jared's screen. "Mapping what?"

"Chromosomal DNA markers. Y chromosome instead of mtDNA, which is matrilineal."

"The markers refer to specific regions of origin, based on either the mother's or the father's DNA. Researchers know that there are certain diseases that have a higher prevalence among ethnic groups. Like sickle-cell anemia among those of African descent or Sjögren-Larsson syndrome in Scandinavian countries."

"And the numbers there, what's their significance?"

The doctor reached for Jared's computer. "May I?" Jared slid the laptop over without a word. As Ling typed, she explained, "I'm not a geneticist. However, there is a human evolution project that tracks the Y haplogroups—the genetic groups—and measures their frequency in certain regions. It's part of what those DNA tests rely on to tell you about your ancestry."

"If you can get this from a twenty-dollar test, what's the big deal?" Noah scoffed.

"The ancestry tests are superficial, but they use a basic premise. The Y chromosome is transmitted from father to son largely without mutations, and it escapes recombination, so it has the best ability to show lineage."

Noah quipped, "Giving new meaning to 'like father, like son.'"

"Exactly." She broke off, reading the screen intently. "Oh. This is interesting."

Avery asked, "What is it?"

"I'm not sure. Gimme a second." Ling continued to scroll through, then shook her head. "These haplogroups. The designations he cited. In India and Pakistan, there are specific groups that have these markers."

"What parts?" Avery asked.

"The Burusho people of Pakistan. The Lodhas. The Indian states of Kashmir, Assam, and West Bengal."

"That makes sense—for an Indian scientist to be studying groups in his geographic region, right?" Noah offered. "Maybe he was developing the newest version of 23andMe for the subcontinent."

"Not if it's related to why all his colleagues are dead," Jared reminded the group. "But Pakistan and India were one country until the British partitioned it in 1947. Hindus in India and Muslims in the newly created Pakistan. Of course, nothing is that simple. Family ties, historical alliances, all of it meant that the clean division was anything but. Stands to reason that the ethnic groups would have something in common. Why would this be worth studying, Ling?"

Before Ling could answer, Avery interjected, "The partition was a geopolitical solution to a more complex issue. These groups that we're looking at have one notable characteristic that links them outside genetics."

Noah stared at the screen. "Which is?"

"Think about why the division happened—to separate ethnic and religious groups who once lived in the same nation." Avery looked at her friends, her eyes troubled. "If I'm not mistaken, all these people are part of the Muslim minority that remained in India."

TWENTY-EIGHT

A cold silence fell on the room.

"Hygeia experimented on Muslims?" Noah asked, incredulous.

Avery balked at her own discovery of the thread linking the groups. Justice Wynn could not have known about a potential for religious experimentation and said nothing. Holding up a hand, she reminded them, "Let's slow down. We have screenshots of some research, a merger stalemate, and a missing scientist. A handful of facts. One, that TigrisLost was a scientist for Hygeia. Two, that Dr. Ani Ramji is likely TigrisLost. Three, that Hygeia engaged in gene therapy experimentation, which is why the president says he objected to the merger."

"Four," Jared added, "that their subjects were selected from regions of the world with a chromosomal connection. And five, that everyone who helped Dr. Ramji is now dead."

Noah scrubbed at the back of his neck. "A biotech in the middle of India was studying genetic markers and Muslims. Sounds kind of sinister."

Ling held up her hands. "Hold on. These regions also have Christian populations, and Jews and Hindus. We don't know what the markers were used for. I warned you, I'm not a geneticist."

"Like I said, we have data but no proof. So we need more information." Avery shoved her chair free of the table and stood. "Jared and I will head to Georgia in the morning to see if Justice Wynn left more information that will help us explain this. Ling and Noah, can you keep looking into these companies? Anything you can find. I want to rebuild his notebook. And get those digital ads going. We need Dr. Ramji."

"I'll put the summers on it," Noah offered. "I'll also call our counterparts in India. See if we can track down Dr. Ramji any other way."

"No!" Avery thought of the dead nurse who'd called her. The missing scientist, his dead compatriots, and her not-so-secret admirer. "For now, it's just the four of us. No one else." She met each person's eyes in turn. "Agreed?"

The chorus was unanimous: "Agreed."

At the White House, President Stokes turned on the evening news. A blandly handsome twentysomething read from a teleprompter, joined by his preternaturally lovely, ethnically indescribable cohost.

The co-anchor gave a knowing look to the camera. "Associate Justice Wynn has been an enigma during his entire tenure on the Supreme Court. Scott, what can you tell us?"

Scott Curlee, looking equal parts somber and excited, answered from the split screen: "Davis, Justice Wynn goes into his third evening in a coma with the question of who will decide his fate still unanswered. He is known among Court watchers as the swing vote on controversial issues, and he is notoriously hard to predict."

The woman cohosting the broadcast asked, "Scott, are there cases pending where his vote might prove pivotal?"

"Well, Phoebe, Justice Wynn is widely expected to be the deciding vote in the international case of *GenWorks v. U.S.* As we have reported for months, GenWorks, an American biogenetics firm, seeks to merge with India-based Advar, a major biotech company poised for explosive growth in the next year. Advar holds a patent on a new gene therapy practice that some claim may cure deadly diseases immune to conventional treatments. But Justice Wynn's sudden illness casts a shadow over the future of both companies. The merger was expected to be a swap of cash and stock, with a heavy footprint in both countries. If the presidential objection remains, this could be a heavy blow to future international mergers."

"Why the controversy?" Davis queried.

"Because under the Exon-Florio Amendment to the American Foreign Trade Act, the president has the authority to suspend or prohibit any foreign acquisition of a company that poses a national security threat. You may recall that President George W. Bush almost used this same provision to stop the sale of a port in Florida to a Middle Eastern company."

Phoebe asked, "Does President Stokes believe an Indian company poses the same risk?"

"It's a good question. No president wants to be seen as a sticking point in commercial dealings."

Davis nodded. "And President Stokes is basically saying they should have gotten his permission. This sounds more like something President Putin would say."

Scott gave him a chiding look. "Not exactly. President Stokes asserted that biochemical and biogenetic technology shared between GenWorks and Advar would place the nation in jeopardy because the Indian company would be the surviving entity."

"But Nigel Cooper has said he intends to head up their American division."

"So he says, but anyone who has watched these mergers in the past knows that what gets promised doesn't necessarily happen. President Stokes has been consistent about his objection to genetic testing and stem cell research."

Phoebe smiled at the invisible audience. "India has become a major player in the international debate about human genetic testing, and they have been much more lenient than the U.S. Some members of Congress have introduced bills to criminalize the type of genetic research they're conducting. President Stokes may be afraid that allowing the merger will put him in a tough position about bioethics right before the election."

Davis chimed in, "There has also been a great deal of tension between the president and India since the Indian parliament refused to approve a trade deal President Stokes promoted heavily. Is the president's decision also revenge for their refusal to do a deal he'd staked his reputation on, Scott?"

"Insiders have speculated about that, but I've seen no proof."

"Do you think President Cadres would have made such a controversial decision?" prodded Phoebe.

Scott shook his head. "Conventional wisdom says no. President Cadres was a conservative, but his fatal heart attack means we'll never know. President Stokes is certainly more aggressive on foreign affairs, but what would we expect from a decorated war hero? India has been accused of aligning itself with nations angry about American trade policy. President Stokes clearly believes this is his responsibility."

Davis nodded sagely. "Thank you, Scott." A second screen popped up to replace the reporter. "We are now joined by renowned political scientist and judicial scholar Dr. Christina Greer. Thank you for joining us."

"Delighted to be here."

"The Supreme Court is expected to issue a ruling on GenWorks and Advar before ending its term on June 30, little more than a week from now, correct?"

Greer responded, "The Fourth Circuit upheld the president's decision, and GenWorks appealed. The Supreme Court took up the case and heard oral arguments in March. Wall Street is watching for this decision, but the way it will go is a toss-up."

"And what was Justice Wynn's involvement before he fell ill?"

"His line of questioning at oral arguments indicated that his sympathies lay with GenWorks. Handicapping the other justices based on their questions and prior rulings, with Justice Wynn out of commission, there are rumors of a split court. In that case, the lower court ruling stands and President Stokes wins."

Phoebe frowned into the camera. "And if, speculating only, Justice Wynn does not pull through?"

Dr. Greer gave a brief look of sadness, then offered her opinion in solemn tones: "Then President Stokes may have his decision upheld and an open seat to fill. Our prayers are with Justice Wynn and his family, but as macabre as it sounds, a vacancy dramatically improves the president's stature and the importance of this year's elections."

"What if the Court simply fails to rule?" Phoebe asked.

"Then the case remains active. This merger would create instant billionaires among a number of GenWorks' stockholders and employees. Nigel Cooper is accusing President Stokes of killing jobs in a bad economy, and his complaints are having an effect."

"Have there been any updates on the justice's condition?"

"Not to my knowledge, Phoebe," Dr. Greer replied.

"Thanks, Christina." Phoebe's face filled the screen. "We'll be watching the Court, the hospital, and the stock market closely as this saga continues to unfold. For more news on the implications of a delayed decision, let's turn to our financial analyst, Harold Faub."

Harold joined on the split screen. "Thanks, Phoebe."

President Stokes hit the mute button, already aware of what Faub would say. If the Court chose to rule in favor of GenWorks, he would face another stunning loss heading into a dicey presidential contest. If the Court ruled against GenWorks, the White House had a major victory against genetic experimentation.

A victory for him, but the markets would rebel. Chaos would reign briefly, like it always did, until he found a way to prop up the market and forced Congress to help him.

It would be a masterstroke, one where he would solve the very crisis he'd created. Just in time for November.

Dr. Elizabeth Papaleo, onetime chemist and current head of Strategy, Policy, and Budget for the Science and Technology Directorate, bent over a spreadsheet tome dense with acronyms and cost overruns her subsection would be called upon to explain to the House of Representatives on Friday for its hearing titled "Gaining Efficiencies in Science and Technology Spending in a Rapidly Changing Global Environment." Just the thought of it all made her head ache. Already, the prepared remarks had been sent up the chain of command to the undersecretary, and the redacted text sat by Betty's elbow. Duly approved budget allocations never seen by legislative eyes would get no hearing in front of the House Budget Committee.

Taxpayer funds spent under the budget function of national security enjoyed a shield of privacy, a mantle peeled away only within the confines of men and women with clearance levels well above any normal elected official. Her file contained the deeper dive of allocations, ones that rolled up into more innocuous phrases like *Research, Development, Test, and Evaluation*. Those would be the entries discussed with the House Budget Committee and its defense dollar hawks. And, according to the request from the Supreme Court of the United States, the file would be discussed with someone in their shop on Friday.

In the basement of the S&T division, she sat cross-legged on the floor of the storage room. She combed through reams of reports she'd dragged from the dust into the meager fluorescent light flickering above. In her domain, the green-and-white dot matrix printouts had not been relegated to museums. Instead, the billions they'd be called to account for found temporary homes in cramped, poorly lit closets and in musky subbasements teeming with shadows. She had lugged the boxes of reports from their hiding places, hunting for needles in a sky-high haystack.

Betty compared the printouts to budget books, each emblazoned with a prior year's date. Five in all. She carefully studied the marked pages with their highlighted rows. "Chromosomal research grants," she said to the empty room, a habit developed after decades of solitude. "Grants broken up over dozens of disbursements, none of them more than twenty-five million dollars. But I can't find any paperwork showing the grants were ever published, awarded, or reported on. No NOFAs."

In the world of government-funded scientific research, the Notice of Funding Availability was the key to the kingdom. It was the government's way of telling the world to come and get it. After the publication of a NOFA, moneys disappeared into research projects and demonstration projects—and evaluations of the evaluation protocols for research projects and demonstration projects. But rarely did a dollar leave the federal coffers without a NOFA. Certain she had missed something, she reached for her pile of procurement records. Maybe the funds went out as a payment for service.

What she found was a list of disbursements that corresponded to the funding and the grant category. But no NOFAs or service contracts or 8(a) direct awards. Nothing. Just money slipping out the back door and into accounts she couldn't locate. More than $300 million on chromosomal research in five years.

With papers scattered around her like confetti, Betty gave a cry of triumph. The transfers had gone in a dozen different directions, but she'd learned a trick or two in her time heading the division. Money could be washed by just about everyone except the federal government. Covering every track left a smudge behind—a tiny tick of information that could build a picture for the right viewer. All she had to do was look.

TWENTY-NINE

One block from Avery's apartment, a sedan parked and cut its lights and engine. The man behind the wheel watched silently, casually noticing the FBI agent stationed near the building's entrance. A short time later, a U.S. marshal on security detail arrived and swapped off with the agent. Neither was aware of the visitor whose vehicle had squeezed between cars parked along the curb for the night.

At the appointed hour, Castillo dialed the encrypted phone assigned for the day. His windows had been rolled down to accept the slightest breeze and allow cigarette smoke to filter into the still, thick air. His location was secluded, interrupted only by the skitter of night creatures. But he raised the window because precaution had been drilled into every member of this skunk works team assembled in mid-January. Former soldiers all, they had an allegiance that cut across branches of government and a battlefield loyalty to their commander. "The four targets are still inside. I assume you heard the conversation."

"Did we mirror the contents of Jared Wynn's computer?"

"No, sir. His firewalls are military grade. He didn't connect to the girl's network. But we believe we know what they know."

"Yes. They've identified Ani Ramji and Tigris." The man tipped his chair back as frustration built in a crescendo in his brain, a cacophony that threatened to drown out reason. "You'll go to Justice Wynn's cabin tonight. Phillips will assign someone to take over surveillance. Do we still have eyes on the mother? We may need to use her as leverage."

"Yes, sir."

"And the investigation into the nurse's death? I assume no movement there either."

"We are being copied on all case notes. The local police are looking for her husband, but on your orders, Wargo located and disposed of him. Agent Lee has been unwilling to share his theories, but the cops assume it's just FBI turf bullshit. If he suspects anything, he's hiding his concerns."

"Understood. Tangier on him?"

"Yes, sir. And I'll be on tonight's red-eye to Atlanta."

"No. Check for a black flight. I don't want there to be a record of you that Jared Wynn might be able to trace. Report your findings to Phillips."

"Copy that."

Disconnecting the call, Major Will Vance summoned Phillips to his office. While he waited, he skimmed his copy of the reports pulled from Homeland Security. His careful dispersal of funds had gone unnoticed for almost five years, only to be nearly undone by an overzealous bureaucrat in a DC back office.

The pages crumpled beneath his hand. When Phillips entered the room, Vance said without preamble, "Where are we on shutting down Betty Papaleo?"

"She's still here, but I've got ears on her Homeland Security phone and her personal cell."

Despite knowing how vulnerable technology can be, bureaucrats placed their faith in the myth of privacy. Their job relied on the fairy tales Americans told themselves about their government, despite ample proof to the contrary. Surveillance. Covert research. Targeted retribution. All disguised by pleasing stories told by men like Vance and President Stokes. "Any change at the hospital?"

"The blood work should be back from Quantico any moment. I have a flag on it, and we'll be notified as soon as they determine what Wynn swallowed."

"Castillo is on his way to Georgia. Send a fresh team to monitor the apartment to relieve him, and they should let him know when Avery and Jared are en route."

"Understood."

Vance left the office for his next call. The smartphone had been seized in a low-level sting against a group of college morons who thought the idea of kidnapping foreign dignitaries on U.S. soil seemed like a viable career option. Aided by an interjurisdictional task force, the young men had purchased a batch of burner phones, thoughtfully activated with a fake credit card provided by the ATF, from a counterfeit batch created by a Mexican drug cartel looking to diversify their portfolios.

His department's role in the sting had been tracking the would-be domestic terrorists using an experimental system that embedded microscopic transmitters beneath the skin. Each subject had unwittingly consented to the procedure when the ersatz ringleader, a four-year veteran of the FBI, had convinced the cell to get matching tattoos.

The Science Directorate reveled in developing the type of technology that would have made Bond's Q envious and a bit intrigued. In the quiet celebration of a successful maneuver, Vance had appropriated a handful of the smartphones for later deployment. Three of the devices had been outfitted with antihacking tech developed by the Cyber Security Division. Now the other two waited thousands of miles away, each for his call.

He drove to the Jefferson Memorial, a spot with multiple pockets of privacy and clear sky. A fitting president to overhear his latest act. The call connected on the first ring.

"Yes?"

"They've identified the scientist and the project. Have you located him yet?"

A long pause, then, "No. We have leads that tell us he remains in-country, but pinpointing a location is difficult."

"Try harder. He was your problem to solve, yet he managed covert discussions with a Supreme Court justice. Archives of their discussions have been uncovered."

"We attempted to use the discussions as bait, assuming Ramji would return for them. When they were triggered, we stopped them from downloading. Unfortunately, it was not Ramji who tripped the alarm."

"So you are no closer."

"No, but the rest of his team is gone."

"I don't give a fuck about the others. None of them embedded classified information in a chess game. Ramji did."

"We will finish it," the man replied. "When he next attempts to make contact—with friends, family, anyone we are monitoring, we'll take him."

"No, you won't. They've laid a trap for him. When he comes close, we'll take him."

"This is my problem. I will handle him."

Vance's tone was flat and controlled. "You have proven that handling Dr. Ramji is not your strong suit. Leave him to me."

Another silence, deeper and more hostile than the first. Finally: "Is that all?"

"Silence Nigel Cooper. He's attracting too much attention. Agitating Capitol Hill and the White House."

"I can do nothing permanent. Not without raising his suspicions."

"Be creative. But shut him up."

"I'll do what I can."

Across an ocean, Vance corrected, "Succeed."

Hours later, Castillo steered the rental car off the deserted highway and onto the road leading to the cabin. Houses along the lane had been set far back from the road, spearing along the mountain face in a ragged, distant swathe. The GPS beeped imperiously as he neared his destination; then the instructions went silent, out of signal range.

Using the map he'd memorized, he navigated through the pitch black. During his tours of duty, he'd gotten used to the absence of light on narrow passes—guided only by the headlamps on his vehicle. Soon, he drove up the driveway and shifted into park. Nothing stirred beyond the restive cries of cicadas and tree frogs. On the seat beside him, he assembled his tool kit. Lock pick, flashlight, and semiautomatic in case of guests. His phone had been tucked inside his pocket earlier, the signal no better than the GPS. He carried a sat phone for emergencies, but he would use it later.

With cautious steps and only moonlight to guide him, he approached the front door. Despite his attempts at stealth, the rotted boards of the steps creaked beneath his feet. Moving quickly, he leaped up to the landing and alighted with a soft thud. This close to the door, he could hear the chatter of wildlife joined by the burble of water and the scratching of mice. Castillo cupped his flashlight and circled the porch, which wound around the abandoned structure. Cobwebs clung to his skin, and the debris of neglected maintenance caked to his boots. But he was alone.

He returned to the front door and knelt. In hurried motions, he picked the lock, scraping away rust from inside the mechanism. The lock gave way. Rising, he turned the knob, prepared to enter the code he'd been given: 3-1-0-7-7-4. But the interior of the cabin didn't boast electricity, let alone an alarm.

Knowing his instructions, he activated the sat phone and placed the Bluetooth in his ear. Phillips acknowledged the call.

"No alarm code," he said in a low, hushed voice. The bud in his ear easily picked up the message and transmitted along the open cell line. "Initiating search."

In DC, Phillips ordered, "Look for a safe or a lockbox. Whatever he left is probably in there."

"Copy." Castillo quartered the open main room, searching every surface and cubbyhole, to no avail. Long-forgotten board games rested beneath layers of dust. The ancient television held no secret compartments, and the drawers in the table beneath it opened easily under his hand. "Nothing here." He swept the bathroom and found nothing of note.

"Bedroom." He moved into the second room, which was half as large as the living room. The once-cozy space had been left too long without airing. A full-sized bed sat next to a chest of drawers and opposite a closet. After fifteen minutes of fruitless exploration, he reported, "Moving into the kitchen."

In there, he checked the stove, finding only a nest of mice annoyed by the disturbance. The refrigerator held no secret safe, nor did any of the cabinets in the tiny galley. "Negative," he reported. "Checking the loft."

Upstairs, a narrow loft had been converted into a boy's bedroom. A single, heavy oak bed had been decorated with dark sheets and little else. A constellation of stars had been sketched above in blue and white paint. The floorboards failed to reveal any hidden spaces, and the area beneath the bed was empty. No box, no safe, nothing.

"House is clean."

Phillips ordered, "Check it again. The code must open something. Do another circuit and then reconnoiter outside."

"Copy." Castillo retraced his steps but stumbled over nothing new. Outside, the porch had been littered by fallen branches and mulching leaves. He spent another twenty minutes outside, including an investigation of the crawl space beneath the rotting cabin.

Grimy and damp, he scooted out from beneath the house. "I've checked everywhere, sir. There's nothing here."

Phillips exhaled slowly. Justice Wynn was sending Avery and Jared to Georgia for a reason, and Vance would expect them to find it first. "We're missing something. Return to Atlanta and track them to the cabin in the morning. They're booked on the six a.m. flight."

"Yes, sir." Castillo bounded up the porch and jammed the lock so it would appear frozen with disuse. He then circled to the rear door and did the same. The next visitors would have to expose what they knew about the cabin to get inside. "Orders?"

"Secure whatever they locate and make sure they never return to DC."

"Will do."

THIRTY

Gravel snaked up the rutted road, and the rented SUV bounced accommodatingly with each pitted groove of the unpaved stretch. Wisps of clouds hung low in the early-morning light, gauzy pale with dawn. While Jared drove, Avery used her tablet to sprinkle breadcrumbs across the Internet. Downloading every chess app she could find, she logged in as WHTW5730 and issued an invitation to play to TigrisLost. Coupled with Jared's efforts, smoking out their missing link should not take too long. If he wanted to be found.

Soon, the truck crested a rise, and a simple A-frame log cabin waited. Red flecks of dust spurted beneath the wheels as Jared maneuvered down the lane to the wooden structure. Vivian's Georgia Cabin, which to Avery's eyes resembled a dump more than a retreat, boasted a sagging wraparound porch sturdied by thick wooden beams at regular intervals. Slabs of window had been tended by nests of spiders, cobwebs shrouding the dust-caked glass. Jared brought the truck to a stop in a barren patch of hardened clay.

As the engine idled, Avery waited in silence. Jared had barely spoken once they'd landed in Atlanta and picked up their rental. His grunted responses to her attempts at conversation had dwindled into a tense stillness. His hands clenched and unclenched on the steering wheel. Gingerly, she reached out and touched the back of his hand.

"You ready?"

He stared out the windshield at the decaying cottage. "I haven't been here since Mom died. Not once." Shifting, he draped his arms across the steering wheel. "I was never closer to the judge than when we came down here. A few weeks every summer when he would stop being stern and distant. He taught me how to bait a hook. How to track. Here, he wasn't the judge." Jared gave a rueful chuckle. "I only called him *Dad* when we were here. When we were happy. Here."

"If you want, I can go inside. You can wait for me."

Shaking his head, he used one hand to rub at his forehead. "I'm fine. Just didn't expect this."

"Expect what? Nostalgia?"

"No. Loss. For the first time, I realize I'm losing my father. Again." He turned the key to kill the ignition. "Let's go."

Avery climbed out of the SUV, and beneath her feet, weeds scrambled for purchase along a flagstone path that began abruptly in the middle of the clayed ground. The stones had separated in the intervening years, like the wooden steps leading up to the porch.

She made her way gingerly up the rotted boards, wary of the strength of the cabin's foundation. Hinges rotted thick with rust hung drunkenly on their moorings. Termites had feasted on the planks of the wrap-around porch, and mice had added their expertise along the baseboards.

Jared came alongside her. Avery stepped back and handed him the key Noah had given her. He tried to insert it into the lock, but the keyhole had been jammed. After a few tries, he turned to Avery. "Step back."

Pivoting on one foot, he aimed his other heel at the knob and gave it a powerful sidekick. The decaying wood fractured, and the door swung wide. Jared crossed the threshold. "Welcome to Vivian's Georgia Cabin."

"Clearly, no door alarm," Avery muttered with a glance at the broken doorjamb. "The code must open something else."

"After you."

Dust had settled on every surface, coating the single couch, the over-sized chair, and the coffee table. Moving closer, Avery noticed streaks in the layers along an armoire. The doors swung squeakily on their hinges. Inside, the minute tracks showed movement of the puzzles and games inside. She straightened. "Someone's been here. By the looks of the dust patterns, they were here recently."

"Are you sure? Wait here for a second." Jared went through the main room and disappeared from view. When he returned, he squatted down by the front door. He removed his phone and shined the flashlight into the doorknob. "Back doorknob was jammed, just like this one. Looks like rust, but I don't know." Rising, he instructed, "Check inside the games for something that might require those numbers. I'll search the kitchen. In case we've had company, we need to move fast."

They operated in silence, opening anything with a hinge or a lid. Twenty minutes later, they regrouped in the living room.

"Nothing is down here. Certainly nothing with a code." Jared wandered across the planked floor to the stairs leading up to the second level.

"What's upstairs?"

"My parents used the one bedroom down here. I used to bunk in the loft." He took the steps quickly.

When she crested the stairs, he was standing near a single bed nestled against the wall below the slope of the ceiling. The loft space was cramped, most of it occupied by the rustic bed frame. A boy's dresser snuggled beneath a narrow window.

Overhead, a wash of dark blue had been dotted with white, the dots connected by thin, careful lines.

"What's that?"

"Dad helped me paint the constellations on the ceiling one summer when I was five," he murmured. "I had a bad cough and couldn't stay out very long. We drew the images from a book, and he would count the stars with me every night. I'd forgotten."

"Sounds like an idyllic summer."

"They always were. When I was seven, he taught me the names," Jared recalled softly. "Told me how sailors used to navigate by the stars. Clusters of them guiding the men home."

"Is that why you joined the Navy?"

He'd never made the connection before, Jared realized. "Maybe so. Counting the stars every night, knowing how many points in Aries and Orion and Monoceros . . ."

"Monoceros?"

"One of the constellations. Monoceros has four stars, but you can't see them with the naked eye in the summer. They're most visible in the winter," Jared explained, pointing up. "Next to it is Orion. Seven stars. Then there's Taurus, with seven."

Avery felt the skin on her neck tighten. "Jared, is there a constellation with three stars?"

"Triangulum. And Aries. Aries has two sets of constellations, actually. One with three stars and the second with ten."

She dropped to her knees, drawing numbers on the dirty floorboards. "That's it!" she exclaimed as she traced out the numbers: 3-1-0-7-7-4. "The code on the sheet. It wasn't for a safe or an alarm system. It's a hint. For you—to lead us right here. The constellations' stars: 3-10-7-7-4."

"A hint about what?" Jared demanded as he helped her to her feet.

"A location—your dad wanted us to come to the cabin. And he used numbers that correspond to a summer when he taught you about the stars. What else happened?"

"Not much. That summer, Mom was into foraging, recycling, and composting. Drove Dad crazy. She made us go on hikes in the woods to 'reclaim' fallen logs." He smiled at the memory. "I got in on the act and convinced Dad to help me build this bed out of the good pine timber we'd found. He complained all week, but he taught me how to hew and drill and sand."

"I can't imagine Justice Wynn making a kid's bed."

"But he knew I would." Jared crossed in front of her and went to the pine bed in which he'd spent every summer dreaming until his family fell apart. "I'm going to lift the frame." Grunting, Jared levered the heavy bed, pulling it forward, then hoisting it aloft. "See anything?"

Avery dropped down and crawled beneath the bed frame. She clawed and tapped at the boards, hoping for a space or a sound that indicated an opening. "No luck."

"Check between the springs. I used to hide cars there."

She flipped onto her back and called out. "Something's here!"

Taped below the solid frame, invisible to anyone who didn't know to look, was an envelope bearing two words in bold, black letters:

For Avery.

THIRTY-ONE

A very carefully peeled away the tape that held the padded envelope in place. She wriggled from beneath, and Jared lowered the bed and then himself beside her on the floor. Wordlessly, she extended the envelope to him, but Jared waved her off.

"He wrote your name on it."

Remnants of duct tape stripped free, and silver threads dangled from the envelope as she tipped the contents into her lap. Folded white sheets and yellow legal paper fell out, the handwriting cramped with urgency and intent. Avery lifted the yellow pages into the tepid light and began to read aloud:

Dear Avery,

I offer apologies for the cloak and dagger of this excursion; however, together, you and Jared have obviously unraveled sufficient clues to have arrived here as I'd hoped. A son's memories of a neglectful father are a thin reed on which to hang hope.

What Nature began in the weft and weave of my brain has no doubt taken its more deliberate turns. Jared has heeded my request to find you. Now it falls to the two of you to finish this. I hide this not only from myself, but those who watch, waiting to pounce and dethrone me. They will find that I controlled my last days of lucidity, not they.

I have also used my last days to hunt for answers to the disease that has ended me and threatens my son's future. In the pursuit,

I stumbled into a labyrinth of lies told by carpetbaggers and
Frankensteins and lesser kings. Revelation may seem the simpler
choice, but to tell the truth, I would have to abandon my boy to
this damnable fate. I have deserted him once. I will not do
so again. So I have left my research for your perusal, certain
you will see what I saw. I could not risk discovery and not forfeit
my honor, but what honor have I if I fail the law by serving it?
If I fail my son by betraying his only hope for survival?

My end is close, and you will be asked what I expect of
these dwindling hours. I have prepared an order, which I will
also give to the viper who lay in my bed. The enclosed pages
give you power but only until the end of term. If you have not
accomplished what I ask, then my value is at an end and so am I.

The other half is this—my directions and final proof are
hidden away, from even me. Find them. The time to untether
me from Earth's bindings will come, but not until you finish
my work. Remember this: if I had accepted absurdity and given
smallpox to my child, I would not be mourning him today and
the atrocities would not have been. You have witnessed my truth
before, and you will find it where it lies, in the space between.

Regards,
Howard Wynn

Avery passed the letter to Jared, and, tucking the manila envelope
beneath her arm, she unfolded the white sheets, reading quickly.

"What does it say?" Jared demanded as he finished rereading the letter. "What other cryptic bullshit did he leave for you?"

"When I met with Noah, he showed me the revisions your father had
made to his will. There was a missing codicil—number twenty-seven.
He told Noah that it gave directions in case of a catastrophic event. I
think this is it. Your father signed an advance medical directive. Two,
actually. In the first one, he leaves the decision to remove him from life
support to his guardian."

"And the second?"

"He explicitly gives orders to disconnect him from life support
when—" Avery paused to reread the instructions.

"When what?"

"He says when the term of the Supreme Court ends this year, he is to be removed from life support unless I proffer the document rescinding his order." She met Jared's eyes. "If I fail to solve his riddles, Celeste will be allowed to kill him."

"Then throw the second one out."

"I can't." She dropped the pages to the table. "He says he left instructions for the second one to be delivered to Celeste should I refuse to act. Lasker Bauer."

"Who?"

"The message that Jamie Lewis left for me. It references a famous chess match from the nineteenth century. Emanuel Lasker was just starting to earn a reputation in the game. When he played against Johann Bauer, they discounted him as an upstart. In the match, he used a double bishop sacrifice that had failed in a previous tournament. But Lasker knew he could give up two critical pieces and still win."

"What does that have to do with an advance directive?"

"In the game, he sacrifices one bishop to put the queen in play."

"You think that's Celeste?"

Avery replayed the game sequence in her mind's eye. "Lasker took a pawn to expose the king, and that's what set up the double sacrifice. That's also what put the queen in position to set up an intermediate check—just a few steps from taking the game."

"I'm not my father, but I do know the game a little." Jared furrowed his brow and offered, "What if you're not the bishop? What if you're Lasker? He's giving you instructions. I think Dad is one of the bishops to be sacrificed to expose the king. He knows you'll hesitate, so he's threatening you with Celeste."

"Making it impossible for me to challenge the directive. Your father would have anticipated that. It will probably go to another judge, who will enforce it. The second one is signed a month after the first. If I balk, it controls."

"Fuck."

Avery said, "Let's agree that your father is one of the bishops. If I'm not one of them, then Ani Ramji must be the other one." Recalling their discussion in his office, she bit out angrily, "He's mapped this out like speed chess in the park."

"How?"

"The Court's term . . . his coma. That's his version of a chess clock. I'm Lasker, making his moves. The murder of Jamie Lewis. The attack in his house. Countermoves."

"Okay. You're Lasker. But the question is, who is Bauer in this fucked-up game? Maybe it's your secret benefactor. Maybe Nigel Cooper, who wants his merger. Hell, maybe my dad thought it was President Stokes, for God's sake."

"His primary objective is to save your life. Who would oppose him?"

"You assume that's his objective. But, conveniently, he's in a coma," Jared said tersely. "I know he's some brilliant god of the law, but this is ridiculous. Crazy. And it's blackmail. You don't solve his riddles, and you let him die and kill me. This isn't right."

"No, but it lets me know how fast I need to move," she acknowledged quietly. "Something or someone out there will force the Court to rule in favor of GenWorks, and they can develop the treatment that will save your life. I can use the first directive if I need to, but if I fail, then the second one trumps. Plus, I will likely be disqualified for not sharing it with the Court."

"My father was ill, Avery. A paranoid man who built an elaborate fantasy to assuage his conscience." He shook the crumpled letter he held. "He's ranting about smallpox, damn it!" Standing, he ordered, "Let's go. We're not playing this game anymore."

Avery refused to budge. "This isn't a game, and he wasn't crazy. This is the only way to get the research that could help you."

"Research that may be designed to kill people for believing in Islam. Do you understand how absurd that sounds? My father and a rogue scientist are trying to rig the Court to create a cure they're not sure exists."

"He's desperate," Avery said softly. "Plus a little crazy." She peered into the envelope that had held the directives and noticed another envelope, this one slim and white. Handing it to Jared, she said, "Your turn."

He hesitated, balling his hand into a fist. When Avery continued to hold it out, he took the envelope, opened it, and removed a sheet of paper. Reading quickly, he said, "It's a copy of a letter to the Department of Homeland Security. Justice Wynn made a Freedom of Information Act request."

"For what?"

"Chromosomal research grants made by the United States government during the last five years."

"I haven't seen those. We'll have to ask again." Avery moved to the loft railing that overlooked the lower level. "Jamie Lewis is dead because of something she knew. We can't quit, Jared. Not until the end of term. One more week."

Jared didn't speak, staring at the letter. Then he looked at the constellations on the ceiling. One of the last summers before his world ended. When he'd had a real father. Tracing the grain of the wood along the bedpost, he exhaled volubly. "What do we do next?"

Grateful for his acquiescence, Avery said, "The line about smallpox. I think I remember it."

"From where?"

"I don't know."

Jared frowned. "What about your photographic memory? The eidetic thing."

"It's not like people think. I can recall images, yes, but usually not for as long as I could when I was little. I remember a lot of information, more than most people, and my memories are usually right. But I'm not a computer."

She flapped the codicil and note against her palm. The answer was locked in her mind, and she had no clue of the key. "He's reminding me of something I know, something he believes I've tucked away in my brain. Like you and the bed." Her fist glanced with frustration off the railing. "But I don't remember."

Jared saw the fatigue and strain in her wide, frustrated eyes. He faced her, placing his hands gently on her shoulders. "We'll find it . . . we'll figure it out. But I don't think we'll get any more information here. The answers are in DC."

"I know." Avery saw kindness in his eyes, and she felt her body relax for a moment under the comforting touch of his hands. "Thank you, Jared."

She put the envelopes and letters in her bag, and they descended the stairs. Jared shoved the broken door into place, then went out to the back porch to find some tools. He hammered the doorjamb back into the frame. Not a perfect job, but it would last until he could hire someone to fix it up.

Together, they walked through the house and into the kitchen. Jared ushered Avery out and twisted the lock. "You sure you've got everything?"

"All set."

He pulled the door shut with a satisfying jerk. Behind the cabin, a small dock jutted out into the wide rush of water that hurried past on its way to Blue Ridge Lake.

"I'll see if we can book an earlier flight," Avery said quietly. "Unless you want to hang around for a while longer?"

"Thanks, but no. I'm ready to get back home. Too much nostalgia and fresh air."

"Speaking of fresh air, mind if I walk down the dock first? I'll be quick." She wanted a second to clear her head.

"Sure." He watched as she stepped across the overgrown grass and out onto the rotting wood. "Be careful. Watch your step." His mother's constant warning to him, and, in an instant, images of the three of them fishing off the end flashed bright and solid. His father patiently teaching him to cast. His mother laughing, a sound as pretty as the trickle of water on rock. A younger, happier Jared, secure in the permanence of family. He shut his eyes against the memories.

"Is that your—" Avery turned back and saw a man round the corner of the cabin, a black balaclava hiding his face. "Jared, look out!"

Avery's scream sent Jared into a low crouch on the porch, moments before a bullet whistled past his head and lodged into the wood frame of the cabin. He lunged forward and rammed into the assailant. A grunt spit out overhead, and a second shot fired. With a swift twist, the man tossed Jared over his head.

Avery scrambled over the porch railing, scooping up a discarded canoe paddle. The gunman turned toward her, the gun leveling for a new shot. Before she could react, Jared burst up and tackled him. The bodies twisted, the gun a dark shadow as the assailant tried to gain purchase. With a grunt, Jared shoved at the gunman's hand, forcing the weapon away from Avery. A fist clocked Jared's temple and he sagged, giving the man precious seconds to heave him up and over in a hard throw. Winded, Jared struck out with his legs, catching the man in the kidneys and forcing him back down.

"Run, Avery!" Jared launched himself at the gunman, who roared with frustration and reared up as Jared grabbed his neck. They stumbled together toward the dock, and the gunman rammed an elbow into Jared's sternum.

Jared saw the dull black metal of the weapon rise toward him, but suddenly Avery was swinging the canoe paddle at the masked face. It connected with a loud thunk, and the man fell sideways into the cold water.

Jared gave an instant's thought to following him in, but remembered the gun in the fallen man's hand. Instead, he reached for Avery and jerked her forward on the slippery, splintered wood. He had to keep her safe. He pushed her ahead of him and shouted, "Go!"

They raced to the SUV, and he shoved the key into the ignition. Another gunshot shattered the windshield. Jared jerked the truck into a tight circle, and the wheels dug into the gravel-pitted road and the vehicle lurched down the lane. The lane eventually merged into a county road, gravel ceding to pavement.

"I don't see anyone following us," Avery said, her eyes trained anxiously on the road behind them.

"Doesn't matter." The engine revved as Jared picked up more speed. "They knew how to find us at the cabin. Whoever it is, they'll track us again."

THIRTY-TWO

Betty Papaleo huddled in her office, her vision glazed and blurry from lack of sleep. As she scrolled through the data, she discovered layers and layers of false trails and dodgy leads. Holding companies and wire transfers that appeared and disappeared at will.

But she was nothing if not persistent—and this anomaly was as intriguing as anything she'd come across in her twelve years on the job.

Weary fingers tapped the computer keyboard to call up the data she'd culled from Treasury. Thousands of entries flashed by, and she swigged from a cup of stale coffee. Then she saw it. A name that jarred her attention. *Hygeia.*

Where had she seen that name before? Betty pulled up another screen and flipped through the various approved foreign vendors allowed to receive wire transfers from the feds. The name of the company appeared, vetted by a division of the FDA. Oddly, though, the authorization memo had been sealed and classified.

"That's not standard procedure at all," she murmured to her empty office. "Why would the FDA have a document with military security clearance?" She typed in her codes, trying every entry port she could think of. But the memo remained stubbornly out of reach.

Betty stood up and stretched limbs cramped from hours of hunching. After a career in government, she understood that secrets were hard to keep. The best way to keep information from the public was not to hide it, which broke laws and attracted attention.

No, the best way to hide information was to publish it in one of the millions of reports disseminated annually under Congress's direction.

Politicians routinely answered a crisis by demanding another audit or report or audited report. Minions and political appointees gathered in cloistered rooms for weeks, parsing out opprobrium about the agency that had failed in its impossible task of perfection. Then they published a report of their findings—that bureaucrats were fallible humans and the laws made the simple infinitely complicated. The report got published under a blue or red cover with a gold seal. Reams of paper to be shoveled into landfills after the apathetic populace ignored the dramatic truth.

However, every report found a home somewhere. She simply had to find this one's. Reaching for her phone, she summoned her assistant.

"Boss?" he said, poking his head in the door. "You look like crap. Sleep here last night?"

"As a matter of fact," Betty grumbled. "Mike, who is the biggest nerd in DHS? The one who'd be at a Trekkie convention if there was one in town."

Mike laughed. "Seriously? In this place? It's easier to name the ones who wouldn't be." He propped his shoulder against the doorjamb. "What are you looking for?"

"A government-employed conspiracy theorist who actually keeps copies of the reports they send over here."

His grin split his face. "Oh, that's easy. Me."

Betty frowned. "You?"

"I'm a male secretary who used to work at the Defense Department. I happen to know they are watching us, and I liked having ammunition." He sauntered inside. "What are you looking for?"

"Any report that mentions biogenetic research in India or China. Preferably in the last three years. Got anything like that?"

"What you're looking for is the Dooley Commission Report on the Potential Threat of Bioweapons in Asia."

Betty's mouth fell open. "Are you serious?"

"Pat Dooley, congresswoman from Alabama, had a sub-subcommittee a couple of years ago, and she appointed a task force. My friend over in the House got assigned to do research. Found some crazy stuff, I'll tell you."

"Can I see it?"

"Sure." He left her doorway and returned several minutes later bearing a bound report. "Called in a favor from my friend. He's emailing me his research notes too."

"Did you tell him who was asking?"

Mike looked annoyed. "No."

"Sorry," she apologized with a smile. "I'm on edge."

He walked over and set the stack on her desk. "Then this stuff will give you nightmares."

Two hours later, Betty agreed. The more she read, though, the more nervous she became. Hygeia, it seemed, did more than search for ways to monetize the human genome. They'd taken on the lucrative side project of military research as well. According to the report, they'd begun testing the accuracy of genetic therapies on groups based on haplogroups.

Betty leaned her elbow on the desk, fingers worrying lips chewed free of lipstick. Her training in chemistry gave her the ability to sift through scientific data, but genetics was out of her league. What she needed was a third party. Someone who'd know about chromosomal research and could take a look at the data.

"Okay. If I can't get government information from the government, I'll try the next best thing," she mused aloud. Government databases were designed to take information in, not share it. The Internet was far superior for actual research, if you didn't mind the crazies and whack jobs you stumbled over on your way to the truth.

Smirking to herself, she switched windows and opened a web browser. The familiar search box appeared. The first query yielded only cursory information. Hygeia was a small genetics company in Mumbai, India, run by a wunderkind trained in America's own intellectual laboratories. He'd returned to his native India and founded the biotech, whose venture capital–funded purpose was the exploration of how to monetize the human genome.

The brief corporate bio, accompanied by hundreds of articles, told the same press-released story again and again. Pages listed as cached led to broken links and missing websites. After working her way through nearly a hundred deleted mentions, she hit upon a business magazine announcing Hygeia's acquisition by Advar.

She tracked the article, but nothing popped. Deciding to take a different tack, she typed in the words *Hygeia* and *Advar* and *Haplogroups* and hit enter.

Her computer screen went black.

"What the hell?" She wiggled her mouse, to no avail. Even the cursor had disappeared.

Grumbling, she rebooted the machine and waited for it to whir to life. After running for nearly two days straight, she supposed, a shutdown was inevitable. When the system finally returned to functional, she scanned her desktop as she moved to open the browser. Her finger paused over the mouse.

An unfamiliar icon had appeared on her desktop. The icon was shaped like a question mark, but it had eyes that seemed to dance.

Betty thought about every computer seminar that senior management in DHS had been forced to sit through. Protocols about breaches, viruses, and worms had been emblazoned into her memory. But the genial question mark implored her to ignore that training and go with instinct.

She clicked.

In the Atlanta airport, Jared hunched over his laptop, scanning every few minutes for signs of trouble. Avery sat in the seat beside him, tense, pretending to read. Their narrow escape had bought them time, and no one had followed them to the airport. When the chirp sounded on his monitor, he glanced over to the corner of the screen. And froze.

Someone had tripped his Internet alarm and gone hunting for their search terms. "Avery?"

She glanced up from her book. "What's up?"

"Someone has gone fishing. In a famous river," Jared said cryptically.

Avery struggled to keep her pleasant expression in place. Someone had taken Jared's bait, and someone had tried to kill them. The question was who—and if they were one and the same. "Did they send you the location?"

"Yes." He shifted his computer to give her a better view. A chat box had opened, and the cursor flashed imperiously. "Want to respond?"

"Sure." Avery accepted the laptop, her pulse racing. Tentatively at first, her fingers hovered over the keyboard. Finally, she began to type.

HELLO?

WHO ARE YOU?

Avery cast about for an alias. CASSANDRA. YOU?

In her office, Betty thought about all the nicknames from her childhood. Smiling to herself, she typed, WILMA.

HI WILMA. WHAT ARE YOU LOOKING FOR?

ANSWERS.

WHAT ARE YOUR QUESTIONS?

JUST CURIOUS ABOUT BIOGENETICS AND HAPLOGROUPS.

THEN WE SHOULD TALK.

AREN'T WE ALREADY? No reason, Betty thought, to let on that she had no idea what the hell was going on. NIFTY TRICK WITH THE COMPUTER.

MAGIC. I'M TRYING TO FIND MY FRIEND. CAN YOU HELP?

ANY CONNECTION TO THE FDA?

NO. WHY?

HAVE SECURITY CLEARANCE?

Avery tilted the screen for Jared to see. He silently motioned for her to keep asking questions. In another corner of the screen, red lights turned green as a program traced Wilma's IP address. A few more minutes, and they'd know who had launched his hidden key and triggered the instant messaging service he'd set up last night.

But anyone looking for the computer Avery was writing from would find only a false address traveling through multiple virtual tunnels and pinging against users who'd accessed his security services. A handy skill taught by the Navy that he'd improved over time.

He whispered to Avery, "Keep her online. Nearly got her."

She nodded, then responded, IS THAT NECESSARY?

IF YOU WANT ME TO TALK TO YOU.

WAIT. HAPLOGROUPS AND HYGEIA AND ADVAR. INTERESTING COMBINATION. YOU WORK FOR THEM?

MAYBE. WHAT DO YOU KNOW?

Avery decided to show one of her cards. ANI IS GONE. DO YOU KNOW WHERE HE WENT?

Betty picked up one of the bio sheets on Hygeia. Ani Ramji had been their top scientist, but none of the articles mentioned what had happened to him in the acquisition. Not unusual in itself, but it made Betty scribble a note beside his name.

WE JUST SPOKE.

REALLY? WHERE?

INDIA.

YOU DON'T KNOW WHERE HE IS, DO YOU? Avery smiled at the feint. Wilma didn't trust her, and she didn't trust Wilma. They were pushing pieces around the board, feeling each other out and avoiding engagement. A stalemate. She tried a new tack. DO YOU LIKE SCIENCE?

IT'S MY PASSION. YOU?

NOT A SCIENTIST, BUT DEFINITELY WANT TO LEARN MORE.

ABOUT WHAT?

ABOUT BIOGENETIC RESEARCH IN INDIA. PLANNING TO TAKE A TRIP AND LOOK FOR A JOB. HOPED TO MEET ANI.

SCREWING WITH MY COMPUTER IS A STRANGE WAY OF JOB HUNTING.

I'M VERY, VERY INTERESTED. Avery held her breath and decided to take a chance. WHAT DO YOU KNOW ABOUT HAPLOGROUPS?

WHY?

BECAUSE ANI THOUGHT THEY WERE BEING USED TO HURT PEOPLE. I WANT TO KNOW HOW.

WHO ARE YOU?

A CONCERNED CITIZEN.

WHAT DO YOU KNOW ABOUT HAPLOGROUPS?

I KNOW THEY ARE GENETIC MARKERS. DANGEROUS IN THE WRONG MINDS.

AND THE WRONG HANDS.

WEAPONS?

In her office, Betty stopped typing. On the corner of her desk was one of the handful of reports she'd managed to unearth related to the chromosomal research grants. Among the recognized goals of the S&T grants was investigation into uses of Y haplogroup research. The report had been redacted down to a handful of lines. Pages she'd never be allowed to read.

Nerves returned in force. She was breaking a dozen federal laws by using her government computer to chat with a stranger. So far, she hadn't revealed any classified information, but her gut was starting to clench, a sure sign of trouble. One compounded by a dangerous icon that started a chat with someone who knew more than she did. Someone who knew about Y haplogroups and biogenetic research and weapons. The Science and Technology Directorate.

WHO ARE YOU? Betty typed.

AN INTERESTED PARTY, LIKE YOU. LOOKING FOR TIGRISLOST. HARD TO FIND.

I CAN'T HELP YOU. MUST GO.

Realizing she was about to lose her only lead, Avery tapped the screen where the trace continued. Jared held up three fingers, signaling he needed only a few more seconds.

I KNOW ABOUT HYGEIA. ABOUT THE RESEARCH.

The cursor flashed emptily. Avery took a wild stab in the dark. I KNOW ABOUT ADVAR AND THE COURT.

WHAT ARE YOU TALKING ABOUT?

GENWORKS AND ADVAR AND HYGEIA. JUSTICE WYNN. THEY ARE CONNECTED. I CAN EXPLAIN.

Avery waited, to see if Wilma would take the bait.

TOMORROW. LINCOLN MEMORIAL MUSEUM. BLUE COLUMNS. NINE A.M. RED SCARF. COME ALONE.

The computer dinged as the chat abruptly ended. Avery looked up anxiously at Jared, who nodded. "Got her."

Relieved, she passed the computer back to him and sighed. She'd meet Wilma at the Lincoln Memorial. She wasn't sure which of them should wear the scarf, but she'd take the chance that it should be her.

While Avery watched silently, Jared called up his tracer program. The IP address had been encrypted, the encryption matrix one of the most sophisticated he'd ever encountered. But the sheer level of complexity ruled out all but a few sources, and a telltale protocol eliminated the rest of his suspects. Doing data security in DC, he'd learned to spot the fingerprints of government bodies. They were talented but predictable.

Jared leaned over to Avery, his mouth against her ear. "She is inside a government building. Based on the geotag, it's the Department of Homeland Security."

The idea of a meet suddenly held less appeal. Her swallow was nearly audible. "Major Vance?"

"Or someone in his organization."

"Someone who apparently is looking where she shouldn't be." Avery mulled over the implications. This could be a trap, one too dangerous to walk into blind. "If I wanted to, could I reach out again?"

"Yes," he said. "I captured the computer's address, and I've got a Trojan that will let us get to her again."

Ten feet away from them, a man sitting in an airport chair took note of their whispers and stood up, moving toward their positions. Jared immediately spotted him, and he casually draped his arm across Avery's shoulders and leaned his head against hers. "We're being watched," he said softly.

The agent stopped but kept furtive watch. He glanced at another agent, who sat with a newspaper twenty feet away. Satisfied, Jared murmured, "Yes, you can contact Wilma again, but if DHS is like the rest of the intelligence agencies, they clean their systems regularly. We have to reach out soon."

Avery leaned closer to him, turning her lips to his ear. "It would be better if we could figure out who Wilma really is before I meet with her."

"How?"

"The power of the Court." Avery reached for the computer again, and Jared handed it over. She opened her personal email account and wrote a quick message to one of the few people still talking to her inside the Court.

"Gary, I need your help. I need a roster of employees at the Science and Technology Directorate for DHS." Justice Wynn's FOIA request nudged her to add, "Preferably for the finance or audit division. It's urgent and important. Please."

She hit send and sighed. "What next?"

Jared glanced over at the agents. "We wait."

In her office, Betty Papaleo wondered if she should pack her bags now or later. Surely one of the super-techs in DHS would be knocking on her door soon, demanding her credentials. The only question was whether she'd be in Leavenworth today or next week.

On her desk sat the beginnings of a conspiracy theory that would make Watergate look like high school gossip. She stared at the icon on her screen, the dancing eyes that seemed to know what she was thinking.

Even she didn't.

She did understand the government. Knowledge was more powerful than money, and if she controlled it, she might be safe. Which meant that she needed to know what she knew before her impromptu meeting tomorrow. She had to write down the thoughts writhing through her mind like scattered eels.

But not in her office on a computer that had been compromised. The dancing icon warned her of how insecure her sanctuary had become. Betty stood, gathered up her notes, and headed downstairs to the dead files room and the ancient computer stored there. It had no access to the Internet. Basically, the nineties-era machine was a very large calculator with a simple word processing program.

It was forgotten and perfect.

Betty began typing, her simple memo growing into a treatise. Fingers flew over the keyboard, stopping only when she needed to reference reports to cross-check dates. The more she typed, the queasier her stomach grew. She'd stumbled onto more than a conspiracy.

What she'd found was mortal sin. She'd never imagined herself to be a tattletale—or, in government-speak, a whistleblower. You didn't reach her level of security clearance and access without learning to weigh the difference between sloppy and dangerous, between bad and evil. But the sludge-like sensation that had taken up residence in her gut had only gotten worse. Because the only thing worse than a tattletale was a person too afraid to tell the truth.

Wearily, she reread her work. She didn't bother trying to save the document. The floppy disk drive had grown inoperable years before. Instead, Betty typed in the commands to print. As the pages whirred through the aged printer, she trudged over to the copy machine and duplicated the hundreds of pages Mike had given her. With copies made, she added her manifesto to the stack.

Betty searched the racks of abandoned office supplies. Her fingers closed upon a box suitable for containment. Suddenly aware of what she intended, Betty fumbled a bit as she stacked the pages inside.

To send this information out of the building was illegal and possibly treasonous.

The question was, who to ship it to?

Betty had never considered herself very political. She voted, but party didn't matter. Her job was her politics, and as a career employee, she understood that having no affiliation was the best job security. Still, what sat in front of her was possible proof that this government had committed acts worse than anyone could have suspected. And if what she'd written was true, then God help America.

Now, though, she needed an ally to ship the report and her memo to as backup. Tomorrow, she'd deliver it to her superiors, but she hadn't lasted for more than a decade in government without learning some truths. Laws might protect a whistleblower, but the ones who escaped with their reputations intact had insurance policies. In this case, she needed a person outside Homeland Security with the resources to evade the wrath of the president. Someone who would understand what she'd discovered and present her evidence without fear of reprisal.

With a migraine forming behind her eyes, she scrambled to figure out who might fit the bill. Someone almost as powerful and with a reason to share her findings. And she'd met the perfect candidate at the genetic frontiers conference this past fall, the last stretch of free time she'd enjoyed in many months. October in the Research Triangle of North Carolina was lovely, she'd thought then. Almost as attractive as the keynote speaker.

She'd get the address upstairs before she metered it and added it to the outgoing post. Using a marker she filched from a desk, she wrote the name of her Galahad in all caps across the box.

ATTENTION: NIGEL COOPER
GENWORKS, INC.

THIRTY-THREE

Vance sat alone in his office, scowling as he viewed the mirror image of Betty Papaleo's computer on his screen. He swiftly punched numbers into his phone.

A cell phone rang inside the Atlanta airport. Castillo answered on the first ring.

"Yes?"

"Are you with them?"

Castillo glanced across the gate area from behind a pillar to the line of chairs near the boarding gate. "Full detail," he reported in a low tone. "Six o'clock flight. We board in forty-five minutes."

"Is Keene on a computer?"

"Affirmative. She and Jared Wynn are huddled together."

The curse was short and effective. "Can you terminate access?"

Castillo scanned the crowded gate area. "Yes. I have some equipment with me."

"Do it." Too many ends were flying loose or unraveling too quickly to be snipped off. He shoved free of his desk, grabbed his briefcase, and jerked open the office door. Downstairs, the darkened subterranean parking structure fit his mood perfectly. He slammed his way into his car and revved the engine. Against his hip, his weapon lay heavy, and his fingers itched for action. Too many mistakes had been made, too much remained undone.

It wasn't his way.

He drove down the first level, snaking through the labyrinthine design. As he rounded a corner, it was only by luck that he recognized the woman from the file on his desk. At the southwest corner of the garage, Betty Papaleo hurried across the concrete, arms filled with files. Files he'd bet his pension contained information on Hygeia.

The tiny turn of luck pleased him. For once, the operation was running on his schedule. He left the garage first and waited for her to come out of the structure. She merged into the late-afternoon traffic, where cars were already beginning to slow. Closing in two cars behind her, he kept sight of the ancient Volvo easily. Betty, he learned, obeyed all traffic laws, including the caution to slow as she approached yellow. The vehicles between them honked in annoyance as she eased her car into neutral rather than snaking below an amber warning light.

His field kit rested in the trunk of his car. Because his decision was spur-of-the-moment, he'd have to improvise. But the slow pulsing of excitement felt good in his veins. Control was what he needed. It had vanished the instant Jamie Lewis had placed her errant call. Soon, he'd hold the reins again.

Unaware of her tail, Betty plodded through traffic and across the freeway to one of the ubiquitous condo complexes dotting the Arlington/DC boundary. She paused outside a security gate to scan her pass, and Vance continued along the thoroughfare. A row of adjacent storefronts provided handy cover, and he pulled his car into one of the dimly lit spaces between buildings.

Before he left the unremarkable sedan with its government plates, Vance quickly surveyed the walls for video cameras. In the days after 9/11, amateur surveillance proliferated, capturing the unsuspecting in service of the mundane.

However, the owners of the liquor store and the sandwich shop next door had dismissed their merchandise as likely targets for high-end criminals. Vance popped the trunk and removed his field kit. In one motion he shrugged out of his coat and laid it inside the open trunk. Next came his pristine white shirt, tie, and cuff links, leaving him in a white undershirt. He tugged a maroon sweatshirt over his head.

The field kit contained glass bottles and the implements he'd require for completing his task. He removed a couple of items, then stuffed the remaining items into a black backpack, which he settled firmly across his shoulders. After jerking a baseball cap low over his forehead and shoving on wraparound glasses to fully obscure his face, he snapped latex gloves onto his hands. He put a thin piece of wire with metal bars on the ends into one pocket of the sweatshirt and a wad of material into the other. The trunk closed with a quiet click, and Vance eased out of the alley, head down.

He walked at a quick pace toward the garage entrance he'd seen Betty pull into, and he spotted her. A curious woman who could bring down a president, and the man who'd sworn to prevent his downfall. A cautious scan revealed that they were the only two occupants on this level of the structure. She had a corner spot bordered by a massive column used to stabilize the structure.

Oblivious to his advance, Betty leaned into the passenger door of her car, then stood up and set a stack of files on the roof. She rummaged in her oversized purse for her house keys. The clanging gave her some direction, and she dug them out.

As she loaded the copies of the Hygeia files into her arms, keys in hand, Betty mentally rehearsed her explanation to Undersecretary McLean for tomorrow. He would be her first stop after she returned from the Lincoln Memorial.

She turned toward the elevator and used her hip to bump the car door closed. The folders were unstable, and she silently chided herself for not putting them in a box at the office. Readjusting, she shrugged her purse strap higher; one of the folders started to slip.

"Oh, God!" she gasped, her hand flying to her throat. A man had appeared in the shadowed area of her parking space. On edge, she laughed at her fright. "I didn't see anyone else down here. My goodness, you scared me."

"Sorry to startle you, ma'am." He motioned to her armful of folders as he shifted between the car door and the concrete stanchion. "Can I help?"

The low, raspy voice sounded vaguely familiar, but Betty knew she'd had a crazy day. Jumping at shadows and helpful strangers. She shifted the folders for better control. "Thank you, but that's not necessary." Taking a step forward, she frowned as the man didn't move. "Excuse me."

Instead of backing up, he took a menacing step forward.

"Sir, please get out of my way."

"No." He took another step closer, and Betty scuttled back, her body wedged now between car and concrete, her heart suddenly in her throat. She tried a smile that wobbled as she spoke: "We've got excellent security here. Cameras everywhere."

"Won't help, Betty."

At the sound of her name, she recognized the voice. Trapped, she screamed and tried to ram him out of the way. But Major Vance was immovable.

Instead of moving, Vance caught her right arm, cranked it into a figure four behind her back, and shoved her head against the stanchion. Stunned, she stumbled and the folders fell. He kept her upright and quickly caught her other arm and manacled it to the first one. Betty felt blood and pain, and for a moment, she felt his grip relax as he shifted to hold her arms in one hand. She started to scream again, but he shoved her head against the post a second time. When she struggled, kicking back at him, he trapped her legs with his and pushed something inside her mouth with his free hand.

He pushed her deep into the shadows of the corner, his bulk blocking her from view, any screams muffled. A thin wire loop whipped down around her neck, biting into soft, pale flesh.

The garrote crushed her larynx, and within a few minutes she sagged in death. With easy motions, he removed the keys from the still-warm fingers and unlocked the sedan. He lifted her crumpled body and stashed her across the rear seats of her car. Changing his mind, he pushed her body down to the car's floor.

Vance scooped up her fallen purse and tossed it inside, then picked up the files and placed them on the console next to the driver's seat. He slid behind the wheel and backed the unmarked car out of the spot.

Vance drove at a normal pace down the ramp and out of the complex, merging into traffic as he headed for his first stop. The abandoned construction site near the airport was perfect. Rebar and dirt crunched beneath the car's tires as he wove toward an unfinished structure. He parked between mounds of abandoned rubble and reached for the files. Swiftly, he read through her findings, his eyes narrowing.

Perhaps she'd died taking solace in the fact that she alone knew the truth.

Shrouded by looming concrete, he shoved Betty from the rear of the vehicle and onto the ground littered with debris. He tucked the files tightly against her body. With familiar motions, he removed three bottles. Their deadly chemicals were a perk of his time with CBIRF and the scientists who spent their lives creating new ways to deliver death.

The first bottle's cap unsealed the nearly odorless contents. He doused the body that had once been Betty Papaleo, as well as the files of secrets she'd uncovered. Carefully, he recapped the bottle and stowed it, then added the accelerant and the contents of the third, a desiccant. The chemical combination worked as it always had, shredding through tissue into bone. The open air dispersed the stench of disintegrating flesh. Paper vanished into dust.

No dental records, no fingerprints. DNA might help eventually. For the time after they found her, if they did, there would be only speculation and conjecture.

He returned to the car and headed for the airport. Vance turned into an off-site parking garage that warehoused the cars of travelers. Unlike in the airport parking lot, security here would be lax. He tugged the cap lower and kept his head down as he punched the green button for a ticket. Inside, he drove to a spot in gathered shadows far away from any car that showed recent use.

The car hidden, he emerged from the garage and caught the van carrying passengers to the airport. A quick transfer to a cab, and soon he was mere blocks from his own vehicle. He paid the driver and, after waiting until the car departed, hiked down to the alley. Satisfied, he drove out of the alleyway and merged into traffic.

By voice, he activated the car phone. "Phillips."

"Yes?"

"Purchase a ticket to Mexico for Betty Papaleo. Backdate the purchase two weeks ago and add a second passenger: male—husband—Darren Papaleo. Departing tonight. Find Mr. Papaleo, and make sure he doesn't catch his flight."

THIRTY-FOUR

Friday, June 23

The next morning, a loud pounding rousted Avery, and she tumbled out of bed, her legs twisted in the sheets. "I'm coming," she shouted hoarsely. She kicked free of the tangled covers, tugged her T-shirt down over her shorts.

In the living room, Jared stirred, and she motioned him back to sleep. At the door, she raked back disheveled hair and peered through the keyhole. Noah stood on the other side, holding a newspaper, a stern new agent glaring at his back. Avery fumbled the locks free and opened the door.

"Mr. Noah Fox," the agent said, reading from Noah's confiscated license. "Agent Lee said no visitors."

"He's my attorney," Avery hastily explained. "He's safe." To forestall an argument, she drew him inside. "Agent Lee will approve."

"I'll check," warned the new agent, a stocky, middle-aged woman with a cap of short black curls who introduced herself as Eliza Leighton. When Noah turned and reached for his license, she slipped it into her pocket and patted it once. "I'll check," she repeated.

Noah followed Avery into the kitchen and cast a telling look at Jared.

"We had a slumber party," she explained.

Noah watched as she prepped her coffeemaker, and he laid the folded newspaper on the counter. "Looks like fun."

The percolating began, and Avery reached into the cupboards for mugs. The clock on the microwave revealed that it was not yet five thirty. "Why do you insist on coming here in the wee hours of the morning?"

He leaned against the counter and shifted to block her view of the newspaper. "I've already been to the gym and the office. You're my third stop of the day."

"Third? It's barely past dawn."

"I'm an early riser," he explained slowly. "Thought you might want to talk."

Suspicion had her turning to fully face him. "About?"

"Your phone's going to start ringing soon."

"Why?"

"This." Reaching for the paper, he cautioned, "I know it looks bad, but we just have to figure out our story, okay?"

"Let me see," she demanded. Without waiting for him to act, she unfolded the newspaper and froze. "Oh, God."

"What's wrong?" Jared got to his feet and crossed to the counter. Before Avery or Noah answered, he turned the paper toward him. "Shit. Avery?"

When she refused to respond, Jared circled the counter and stood close to her. "He shouldn't have pulled you into this." He watched with growing concern as she stared at the paper, her eyes unmoving. "Avery, say something."

Ling quickly joined them in the kitchen, where Avery stood. One look at the front page of the newspaper told Ling what had caused the reaction. "God, Avery. Honey, I'm so sorry."

On the front page of the *Washington Gazette,* three photos sat cheek by jowl. The grainy image of Avery and Jared snapped outside her apartment building, a second of Avery half dragging her mother at a Metro stop—a different one than the night she'd run into Justice Wynn—and a third one of Rita, a close-up of her semiconscious face while she was propped against what looked like a dumpster.

Below the images, the sky-high headline read: JUSTICE'S MISTRESS, SON'S GIRLFRIEND, JUNKIE'S DAUGHTER—WHO IS AVERY KEENE?

"Noah, I can make you some coffee," Avery said calmly as she pushed away from the counter. "I thought I'd cook omelets for breakfast."

"Avery, honey, we need to talk about this," Ling ventured softly.

Jared took the paper and skimmed the story. "Son of a bitch. We'll call the *Gazette*. Make them print a retraction."

"Why? If one paper has the story, it'll be all over the airwaves by drive time. The druggie and her daughter." Her fingers curled under the shelf of the bar and scraped along the particleboard. She stretched them long, grappling to steady herself in a world suddenly listing. "The Chief won't believe me this time."

"I'm already drafting a libel suit," Noah announced. "This is out of bounds. It's a slanderous lie designed to discredit you. I'll have our private investigators figure out who this woman is, and we'll—"

Avery's head came up. The smile she offered was brittle. "The woman in the photo is my mother. She's a drug addict living on the streets of DC." She carefully splayed her fingers beneath the counter, her voice as careful. Too loud, and she'd shatter, she was certain. "That center photo is from a Metro camera at Gallery Place, I think. She was crashing, and I was taking her to a motel to sleep it off."

A nub bumped against her right index finger. Shifting her hand, she flicked the tip against the knot. "Her name is Rita Keene. The secretaries for the Chief will confirm her identity, given that she went to visit the Supreme Court on Tuesday."

"How did they get a photo of her passed out in an alleyway?" Ling asked of anyone in the room. "How in the world would they know where to find her?"

"It doesn't matter. They found her." Avery toyed with the bump beneath the counter, her voice listless. "They'll offer her money to tell her story, and she'll take it. A junkie's dream. News at eleven."

"Avery."

She shook her head. "Ling, don't. You know better." Beneath the counter, she pushed at the nub, surprised when it gave beneath the pressure. The object fell to the ground, and Avery knelt.

Afraid she'd gotten ill, Jared moved quickly to support her. He came around the counter and saw her kneeling. As he shifted to help her stand, he saw the black, blinking dot in her hand.

"It'll be fine," he muttered beneath his breath as recognition narrowed his eyes.

Jared covered her hand with his, palming the device. He stood quickly, dragging Avery up with him. He took the device and deftly slid it beneath the rim of a plate on the counter, out of sight, then pulled Avery several steps back. "We need to make a list of the ways they could have gotten these photos." Into her ear, he whispered, "Don't react. Place is bugged. Audio, possibly visual." He hugged her forehead soothingly, then held her away from him.

She leaned back into him, her arms tight around his waist. "Let them hear," she instructed.

She shifted away and said, "I'm okay. As for Rita, they might have followed her from here on Monday." Avery broke off her hold of Jared and hugged Ling. "Place is bugged," she whispered. "Find a way to tell Noah."

Disengaging, she tugged at Jared's hand and led him toward the living room. She motioned them closer to the television. "Let's see if anything has made it onto the news."

Ling put a companionable arm through Noah's, leaned in, and quickly passed the message. Together, they joined Avery and Jared in front of the TV, where every news channel was plastered with the *Gazette* headline.

Noah was the first to speak: "Loyalty has its limits." He pointed to the screen. "This is the tip of a malevolent iceberg, Avery. On Monday, you'll have to stand in open court and defend yourself and your mother in front of the probate judge, Diana McAdoo." He smacked the pages of the paper he'd scooped up against the coffee table. "I'm Justice Wynn's attorney; I don't think this was ever his intent. He couldn't have meant to expose you to this."

"Justice Wynn couldn't have given a damn about what this would cost me," Avery corrected him. "He had a goal, and he needed a weapon. That's me. A blind, stupid, loyal weapon that would stay on course until I hit my target."

"He asked the impossible of you," Jared ground out, leaning in close.

"I'm not quitting." She snatched the paper from Noah. "And I won't be distracted by this tripe."

Jared jabbed a finger into the page. "Read it, Avery. Read the story and tell me my father is worth this."

She focused on the page, the black ink blurring for an instant. The story continued for another column and fell below the fold. Unable to tear her eyes away, Avery continued on to the smaller story tucked into the sparest real estate of the front page.

Jamie Lewis, a Maryland nurse, was found shot to death in her apartment in Tacoma Park, the victim of an apparent home invasion earlier this week. The Tacoma Park police have not released any information on suspects. Her husband, Thomas Lewis, has posted a $15,000 reward for any information that leads to the arrest of the culprits.

The story was wholly inaccurate, but the reminder was more than sufficient. A woman had already lost her life protecting Howard Wynn.

Avery reached for the remote and killed the sound on the television. Whoever was listening in, she wanted them to hear this.

To hear her.

"I'm not going to give up custody of Justice Wynn. Not now, and certainly not because of an article in the newspaper. He left me clues that will lead me to the truth. There's a line that connects all of it." Her hands balled into fists. "They've killed to stop me, but it won't work. I'm going to finish it."

"She's tough." Phillips sat on the opposite side of Vance's desk, watching Keene on the screen. "We should take her out now."

Vance thought the same as he took off his headphones. Slammed with bad press and a brush with death, she plowed on. In another life, he'd admire her, but her tenacity was beginning to piss him off.

Phillips left the office, and Vance reclined in his chair. No one else would begin arriving for at least another hour. Which would give him time to initiate phase two. He jabbed in the extension. On the other line, a woman's firm tones answered, "Special Agent Robert Lee's office. How may I assist you?"

"This is Major Vance at DHS. Liaison for the president."

"Right away, sir."

Muzak piped through the phone for the seconds it took the operator to locate the proper transmission lines. Soon Vance heard a click, and then a voice. "Special Agent Lee."

"Robert. It's Will Vance at DHS. I'm working on this Justice Wynn debacle, and I keep hitting a brick wall."

"The stubbornness of Avery Keene?"

Vance gave the expected chuckle. "Something like that."

"What can I do for you?"

"I assume you've seen the morning paper."

The pages lay open on Lee's cluttered desk, the key passages highlighted in yellow. "Can't miss the headline."

"The president is concerned about how this will affect her judgment as Justice Wynn's guardian."

"Understood. What are you looking for?"

"I've heard about the attempt on her life in Georgia yesterday."

Agent Lee cocked a brow. "News travels fast."

"Bullets travel faster," he replied flatly. "And as long as she's out there on her own, she's exposed."

"What do you suggest?"

"Protective custody. We have shaky grounds to touch her, but the FBI has already established a relationship and jurisdiction. As long as she's out and roaming around, there's no telling who's got their sights on her."

The same thought had occurred to Lee, but he doubted that Avery Keene would agree to his protection. Protective custody, however, had a good angle. Still, he chafed at a suggestion coming from DHS. Turf wars weren't his thing, but Major Vance didn't give him the warm fuzzies. "So you want me to arrest her for her own good?"

"I want a key asset protected. If you can't, I will."

"I'll take it under advisement." Agent Lee pushed back lightly. "I'm on my way to see Ms. Keene now. If I'm not satisfied, I'll give you a call. Let you know if I'm going to bring her in."

"We're responsible for her," Vance reminded him. "We've got to keep her safe." *And silent.*

Agent Lee gathered his binder and stood at his desk. "I'll be in touch."

THIRTY-FIVE

After her cell shrilled through the apartment for the sixth time in less than five minutes, Jared stalked over to where she'd spread out the newspaper on the worktable.

"Why don't you let me answer that? Or, if you won't let me answer the phone, turn it off."

"I can't." Avery spun the phone in a dizzying circle on the table's surface. "The hospital could call."

"Caller ID." Jared leaned in and picked up the phone to flip off the ringer. When she glared at him, his eyes and tone were equally sober. "I'm worried about you."

Her lips curved. "Why? Because I didn't break into hysterics this morning?"

"For starters."

"After twenty-six years, I've learned to handle bad news. The first time I bailed Rita out of jail, I was thirteen. Had to pawn her wedding ring. At some point, I bought and sold most of the appliances in our house." She gave a careless shrug. "Obviously, your father finally noticed a worthwhile talent in me."

"Why didn't you tell me about your mother?" he asked kindly.

"It wasn't relevant. . . . Rita is a fact of life. Usually, she stays away until she crashes. We've worked out a routine."

"What about your father?"

"Dead." When he simply stared, she continued reluctantly: "He was the love of her life. They met in college and railed against apartheid and nuclear energy and environmental racism. They were in a bus crash when I was six. He died. She didn't."

"Is that when she started using?"

"She had some lingering injuries after the crash—she was prescribed painkillers, and it went from there. But she could still feel." Avery twisted her fingers together but kept her voice even. "By the time I was in fifth grade, she'd graduated to the hard-core, and we started moving."

Jared inched the newspaper toward them. "When did you see her last?"

"The day I met you." She traced the grainy photograph. "Rita had a bender that weekend, and she needed cash to soften the landing. But that's not when this photo was taken. She had on a different dress."

"Why do you still take care of her?"

"She's my mother." A threatening harridan one day and a fragile champion the next. Such was life with Rita Keene. What would she be today? Avery wondered, staring at the photo. A wasted harlot willing to service a dealer for a fix? Or, maybe, she'd call the *Gazette* to yell at them for abusing her daughter.

She stood so abruptly, her chair toppled behind her. "I've got to go," she hissed out as her breath hitched in realization. "They know where she is. I've got to find her. Before they hurt her."

Jared rose too. "Where would we look?"

She pressed the heels of her hands against her brows. "Earlier this week, she was in Adams Morgan. But I don't know how to find her." Turning, she took a step toward Jared and gripped a fistful of his T-shirt. "If they could take pictures of her, they can hurt her."

Jared wrapped an arm around Avery and pulled her against him. She let him. "We'll go look for her. Get your things, and I'll clear it with the agent."

Avery nodded and raced into her bedroom. Jared yanked open the front door, only to find a new man standing on the threshold, his hand lifted to knock.

"Mr. Wynn, I'm Special Agent Robert Lee." He nodded to the agent on duty, and the woman headed for the stairwell. "I'm here to talk to you, Ms. Keene, and Dr. Yin."

"Avery and I have to run an errand," Jared said, blocking his entry. He braced his forearms on the doorjamb to reinforce the do-not-enter message. Glaring down at the agent, he explained, "She'll be free to answer your questions in a couple of hours."

Though Jared Wynn had him by at least four inches, Agent Lee held his ground, not bothering to finger the gun that would guarantee him passage. He recognized the attempt at chivalry and respected Jared for the bravado. But time was slipping away. "This isn't a request, Mr. Wynn. You and Ms. Keene are material witnesses to at least one crime I am aware of. I'll talk to you both now."

Jared widened his stance. "Are we under arrest?"

"Not yet, but I can arrange that if you'd like," Agent Lee offered reasonably. "We both want to protect her, Jared. Let me do my job."

Torn, Jared checked over his shoulder, but Avery had not reappeared. He lowered his voice and his chin to Agent Lee. "Did you see the paper this morning?"

"I saw the paper, heard the news reports, and got an earful from the vultures camped outside."

"Avery is worried about her mother. She's afraid whoever tried to kill us might harm her."

Agent Lee nodded. "I understand. I've already dispatched an agent and some DC narcotics officers to find and secure Mrs. Keene." He glanced over Jared's shoulder, saw Avery approach. "Ms. Keene, we're looking for your mother, but I must speak with you both. Now."

"I know what she's like—I'll be able to find her."

"You try to find her, and a reporter or something worse will be with you when you do." Agent Lee shook his head once. "Let me handle this. We'll find her. I promise."

Avery gave Jared a short nod, and he stepped back.

She watched as Lee examined the modest apartment. "Oh, this is just my work apartment," Avery quipped as she shut the door. "The penthouse is under renovation. Marble floors and gold-plated doorknobs."

"I guess you're still raw about the other day."

"About being accused of theft and murder?" She settled onto the futon. "Another day, another slander, Agent Lee."

"You've had a rough week."

"Masterful observation."

He met her look squarely. "I want to help you."

Cognizant of the surveillance, she lied without compunction: "I've told you everything I know."

"I doubt that." Before she could protest, he jerked his chin at Ling, who hovered in the kitchen. "Why don't you join us, Dr. Yin? You're in the thick of this now too." He nodded at Noah. "You too, Mr. Fox."

Ling and Noah entered the main room, eyes equally wary. "Good morning," Ling offered.

"That's a matter of opinion," he said dryly. Four stubborn faces stared blankly at him, and Agent Lee gave an audible sigh. Earning trust was the toughest part of the job, especially once he'd inserted both feet squarely into his mouth. Aiming for the only military man in the room, he asked, "You know why I joined the FBI, Jared?"

"To harass the weak?"

He shifted his elbows to his knees and linked his fingers loosely. "I like puzzles. I like having bits and pieces of information and filling in the blanks." The sharp gaze shifted to Avery. "I'm guessing that's part of the reason you and Noah became lawyers, and why Dr. Yin chose medicine."

Unimpressed, Avery returned his look without reaction. "Your point?"

"Well, my favorite puzzles weren't the ones where you had a picture you had to remake. I always thought that was cheating. I preferred the ones where you had to unlock the code to understand the riddle." He held her eyes with his. "Avery, I think you're the key to unlocking the code. I think Justice Wynn figured out something very big. He hid the answers, and you're the cipher."

"What's the question?" Noah asked.

"I'm not exactly sure," Agent Lee admitted. "But you found something in his house that sent you to Georgia."

"We looked. But we found nothing worth reporting."

"I know you're hiding something, Avery. I want to help you." When she just stared at him, he lifted his hands in surrender. "Look, we got off on the wrong foot."

"Multiple times," she reminded him. "I know what you think of me. An opinion that will now be shared by most of Washington, DC."

"You know nothing of my opinions. I deal in facts. So, if you're not going to clue me in, let's see what we know." He slipped a notebook from his pocket. "One fact: you and Mr. Wynn took a short trip to Georgia yesterday. Who knew you were going?"

Protesting seemed futile, so Avery answered: "Everyone in this room except for you." Including whoever had planted listening devices in her apartment, which could very well have been Lee, Avery reminded herself.

"Anyone else?" When she shook her head, he prompted, "Anyone at all? Doesn't matter how they knew, I need names."

"I booked the tickets online," Avery explained. "I don't have a job anymore, so there's no one at work who could know."

"Did you learn anything new on your trip?"

Avery kept her eyes on the agent and prayed Jared would do the same. If she told him about the attack at the cabin, her detail would increase and she'd never make her appointment with Wilma. She groused, "One more dead end, courtesy of Justice Wynn."

"Jared?"

"Like Avery said, it was a wild-goose chase."

"I see." Agent Lee grilled them for another few minutes, then set the notebook aside. "Someone is working awfully hard to shut you down."

"Ruin my reputation, at least."

"I don't think that knock on the head you got was about your reputation," he corrected. Before she could argue, he held up a hand. "I got a call this morning from Major Vance at DHS. He wants me to put you in protective custody."

Stiffening, she asked, "Is that why you're here?"

"It's worth considering. The midday news will make sure everyone can find you. Besides, this building has no visible security other than a coded door any pizza delivery guy could get through. You're not safe on your own."

"I'm sure Major Vance would be only too happy to have me arrested."

"Not arrested. Protective custody. He's just doing his job." Agent Lee hesitated. "Terrorists use a variety of methods to undermine our national security. Anticipating those threats is Major Vance's job."

"A bit of a stretch. He's in the science department."

Because he didn't disagree, Agent Lee bent in to close the distance between them. "Regardless of Homeland Security's interest, I'm clear on mine. I'm here to see if you're ready to tell me what Justice Wynn wants from you before whoever killed Jamie Lewis makes good on his next attempt."

Avery stood then, well aware that the killers were likely listening in. In solidarity, Noah, Ling, and Jared rose too. "Agent Lee, I appreciate your help yesterday, and I wish I could tell you more. But I've told you all I know."

The agent reluctantly got to his feet, his dismissal clear. "I don't think you have, Ms. Keene." He flicked a look at Jared. "She's putting herself in harm's way for your father. Can't say I'd let a woman put herself in danger for me too."

Jared failed to react. "Avery knows her own mind, Agent Lee."

"Any chance you'll take me up on protective custody?" he asked without much hope. He intended to keep a couple of agents on her regardless, but hiding her would be an easier task. "I'd strongly advise you to consider it."

"I will," Avery told the agent as she led him to the door. His concern was genuine, as was his suspicion. She'd need to leverage one without triggering the other.

"I assume these agents are a permanent fixture?"

"I'd like to keep someone on you, yes. If you protest loudly enough, I'll have to pull them back, but they aren't going anywhere."

Avery blew out a breath. "Well, then can they give us a lift to Lowry Kihneman? I've got a custody hearing on Monday to get prepped for, and I'd rather not take the Metro today."

"We can do that."

Minutes later, they used the service elevator and exited the apartment building directly into an Explorer idling in the alley. Avery sat on the rear bench with Jared. After a brief, tense discussion, Ling and Noah headed for Noah's car, where an agent got into the front seat. Agent Lee took the SUV's passenger side and gave instructions to the agent driving.

As the Explorer pulled away, no one noticed the scruffy fortysomething man peering down from the roof of the adjacent building, his telephoto lens trained on the activity below, most of the images already in his memory drive. The photographer sank down onto a concrete protrusion on the roof, a grin rippling across his face. He pulled out his phone and sent a text to Scott Curlee: "Got your pics—perfect headline for noon broadcast: *Avery Keene Detained by FBI*."

.   .   .

Inside the SUV, Avery turned to Agent Lee. "Want me to trust you? Did you decide to be helpful and get what I asked for?"

"The LUDs on Justice Wynn's house?"

"Yes."

"As a sign of good faith, yes, I did." Smirking at her look of disbelief, he reached into his breast pocket. The folded sheets peeked out, but he didn't offer them. "The man didn't make or receive many calls, and his cell phone had even less use."

"But?" She could hear the hesitation.

"On a whim, I went back a year—longer than the six months you requested. Over a span of three months, he racked up quite a few international calls."

Avery struggled not to seem excited, but her hand reached out for the pages. "Do you have the numbers?"

"Will you accept protective custody?"

"No. Can I have the numbers?"

Lee let out what sounded like a half chuckle. Reluctantly, he handed over the folded sheets. "None of these are working numbers any longer. I've already checked." He cocked his head to study her. "You're not surprised. I don't suppose you'll tell me who he was trying to reach in India?"

"A ghost." Avery plucked the pages free and gave Jared an inclination of her head. "We're still trying to figure it out ourselves."

"That's my job, which I'm pretty good at. So now that we're in the car, why don't you tell me what you were afraid to say in your apartment?"

Avery looked up at him, surprised. Lee gave a thin smile. "I'm guessing your apartment is bugged. Video and audio."

Avery glanced at Jared, who nodded. "The equipment is high-grade. Very," he said.

"We can clean it out now, while you're out," Agent Lee responded, frowning thoughtfully. "When did you know?"

"I found one of the devices this morning, but we've been careful," Avery told him. She squared her shoulders, prepared for the argument. "I'd like to keep them in place."

Agent Lee scowled. "I don't like using civilians as bait, Ms. Keene." Still, the idea had merit. More importantly, it would give him time to secure his own warrant for surveillance. "You sure? You keep those bugs in place, and you're asking for trouble."

Avery flashed him a dry smile. "I'd say I'm already there, Agent Lee."

THIRTY-SIX

The SUV pulled to the curb in front of the Lowry Kihneman building, and Agent Leighton rode the elevator up with Avery and Jared. Ling and Noah met them upstairs with their detail, and together they moved into the conference room where Avery had first learned the details of Justice Wynn's plans. A long credenza loaded with soft drinks, coffee carafes, and water was arrayed against the far wall. As soon as Leighton left the room, closing the door behind herself, Avery looked at the group and put her hands flat on the polished table. "Okay, let's talk."

An hour later, Agent Lee knocked on the conference room door. When he entered, everyone stiffened, except Avery. He sat heavily, studying each of the occupants. The matching looks of feigned innocence made him edgy. "What's the matter?"

Avery asked, "Agent Lee, what's the background on Major Vance?"

"Like everything else at DHS, I think that's classified." Gossip about a fellow officer didn't sit well with him, but the girl deserved some information about the men hounding her. Besides, nothing he'd tell her couldn't be secured from a Freedom of Information Act request. Or his personnel file, which he'd reviewed that morning after Vance's call. "Major Vance is the official liaison from Homeland Security to the president."

"Which means what, exactly?"

"I don't draw the org charts, Ms. Keene. What I know is that Major Vance was formerly Secret Service, and before that, he was in the military. After President Stokes's election as vice president, he shifted from the Secret Service to S&T, with a direct assignment to coordinate with the president on certain Homeland Security matters."

"Is he a scientist by training?"

"Has a BS in biochemistry and a master's in biologics," Agent Lee offered. He'd pulled the man's service record and had been impressed despite himself. "Major Vance went through the Naval Academy, received a commission in the Marine Corps. Attained the rank of major before receiving an honorable discharge. Came stateside and joined the Secret Service."

"Where was he stationed in the Marines?"

"Classified," he answered, then clicked his teeth shut. The sensation of interrogation was jarring to a man used to the other side of the conversation. He stroked his chin where beard growth had started. "Why the twenty questions? I know you two didn't exactly click, but I'd be offended if you grilled him this way about me."

"I appreciate your help, Agent Lee. Are you going to babysit us all day?"

"No. Leighton's got this one." He shoved away from the table and stood. "Let her know when you're ready to move."

After Agent Lee exited the room, he and Leighton moved away to talk, and Jared spoke quickly: "I accessed some files at the Pentagon. Major Vance was assigned to FORECON and CBIRF during his service."

"CBIRF?" Avery asked.

"Chemical Biological Incident Response Force." He rose and paced to the opposite end of the room, his voice pitched low. "CBIRF is a strategic unit of the Marines designed to manage the consequence of chemical and biological threats to national security."

"Where was he stationed?"

"Like Agent Lee said, it's classified, but most of CBIRF's postings in the last twenty years have focused on the Greater Middle East, where various despots have threatened to use chemical weapons."

Avery considered the implications. Major Vance, a high-ranking Marine from an elite unit dedicated to chemical and biological weapons research—tasked by President Stokes to serve as his liaison from the virtually unknown Science and Technology Directorate at the impenetrable DHS. Assigned to a region roiled by ethnic tensions. *Hygeia. The Middle East. Chromosomal research. Biological weapons.*

Look to the river.

She turned to Noah. "What's going on with the case?"

"I think we're ready for the custody hearing on Monday, but I can ask Judge McAdoo to postpone again."

"Would she? I don't know much about the bench at the probate court."

"I've appeared before her several times. She's pretty fair-minded, but not a pushover. The higher your profile goes, the easier it is for Celeste to argue fitness." He lifted his shoulders in a speculative shrug. "Postponement may buy us a few days to rebut the *Gazette*'s story. Maybe offer the *Post* an exclusive with you as counterprogramming."

"And she'll still have Rita to hold over my head. The drug abuse and rehabs. They could insinuate that I may be like her."

"Guardianship is a judgment call, in the strictest sense. If Judge McAdoo doubts your ability to make good choices for Justice Wynn, she's well within her rights to strip you of guardianship. If we had more proof of his intent—"

"We do." Bending, Avery snatched up her bag and rummaged inside. "I didn't have a chance to tell you what we found in Georgia. I think this is the codicil."

"You found it?!"

"Yes." She placed the pages on the table and pushed them across to him. "Like you said, it was instructions in case of a catastrophic event. He left an advance health directive. This should help, right? Proves he wanted me in charge and not Celeste, unless I refused to follow his directions."

Noah reached for the papers. He read them over once, then again. After a third pass, he lifted his head to the expectant eyes watching him. "It's an excellent start, except that he tells you he wants to die by the end of term. What the devil does he expect me to do with that?"

"I don't know," Avery muttered. Noticing a frown from Ling, who was reading something on her tablet, Avery asked, "Is it Rita?"

"No," Ling soothed, "but it's not good. Scott Curlee cites an unnamed source reporting that you've been suspended from the Supreme Court pending an investigation into drug use." She shifted to include Noah in her field of vision. "The story speculates that Justice Wynn's coma isn't because of Boursin's. They're saying he OD'd."

Noah scoffed, "How did they get that? They're just making things up now."

"They know a tox screen was run on his blood." Ling slid the tablet to Avery. "It's probably a leak from the lab. Unfortunately, his doctors cannot rebut the story without violating doctor-patient privilege."

"Should I put out a statement?" Avery asked, exhaustion deadening her voice. "There's no guardian-ward privilege. Besides, we should have the results back by tomorrow."

"I should check with the senior partners and our PR guy," Noah said. "How about you contact the press secretary at the Court? See what he advises."

Avery checked the time on her phone and whispered, "Guys, I have to make it to the Memorial by nine. It's already eight thirty."

"I really don't like the thought of you going alone," Jared warned. "We can reconnect and reschedule."

"No." Bending over her purse, she slipped her wallet out and into her pocket. "She's already skittish. We reschedule, and I might not get another shot. If this isn't Betty Papaleo, then we're looking for a needle in a really big pile of needles. Ling, can I borrow your phone?"

"Hold on," Jared reminded her. "There's an agent on the door, one near the elevator, and one downstairs. I could distract one, but not all three."

"What about the stairwell?" offered Ling. "We're twelve stories up, but you're young and it's all downhill from here."

"Ha-ha. Noah, I assume the doors are key-coded but not the stairwell doors for fire safety," Avery clarified.

"Correct, but you'll need a key card to get out at the bottom floor. Lock deactivates in an emergency, but otherwise, you still need permission."

"Can you get me one?"

"Of course," Noah said, rising and heading for the door. "One key card and expensive press advice coming up."

"Ling, I need to know as much as you can find on the haplogroup research—even the weird rumors. If companies researched this, there had to be experiments or at least discussions. Backtrack all the scientists, and cross-reference their research and their employers."

"Sure thing, Columbo."

Fighting a smile, she instructed Jared, "The FOIA request from Justice Wynn. Can you find a quicker way to locate what he was asking for? A routine request from any one of us will take too long."

"I'm still not sold on you going out there alone."

"If Betty or Wilma is really a threat, I'll be in the open. But unless someone has a better plan, I'm going. Now."

Agent Leighton frowned as Avery entered the corridor. "Ms. Keene, I just spoke to Mr. Fox about leaving. I'd prefer you all stay together," she insisted.

"I'm just going down the hall to his office," Avery replied, pointing to the door that stood ajar a few yards away. "I have a question for Noah, and I'd like some privacy."

After considering the request, Agent Leighton inclined her head. The attorney's office was also in her line of vision. "Quickly, please."

"Deal." Before the woman could change her mind, Avery firmly shut the conference room door. She headed down the hall and entered his office, where he'd settled behind the desk. "Noah, key card, please."

"Sure." He reached for his pocket to retrieve the disk of plastic.

"One more question about the stairwell. Is it monitored?"

"Not that they've told us lowly associates."

"Can you help distract Agent Leighton?" she asked. "I'll be back by ten thirty at the latest."

"On it. The key card will let you out into the lobby. The coffee shop on the ground floor has a doorway to the alley, where folks like to smoke. You can duck through there and avoid the agents."

"Thanks."

They walked into the hallway and up to Agent Leighton. Noah motioned through the soundproof glass to Jared, who came out to join them. "I'm going to put Avery in a guest office to do some research and talk to the hospital."

"Where is the office?"

"Just down the hall." Noah pointed to the far end of the corridor. "Office space is in short supply, and the hearing is Monday."

"Wait and I'll summon another guard." Agent Leighton lifted her wrist to her mouth.

Noah began to protest, but Avery gave a short shake of her head. "Thanks, Agent Leighton. I appreciate you pulling another agent in from the field."

"No, I'm redeploying one of the three assigned to this detail."

Jared asked, "So the lobby will be unprotected?"

"Not at all. I'll move the agent at the elevator down to Ms. Keene's position."

"But from my experience, the elevator is a blind spot, isn't it?" Jared countered dramatically. "If there's a danger zone, it's the elevator."

Slightly annoyed, Agent Leighton exhaled and decided to retake control of her post. "I have a clear sight line to the office down the hall. Mr. Fox will escort Ms. Keene there and return to his office. No one will be reassigned."

Avery and Noah headed to the empty office, and Agent Leighton stared down the hall at Avery's position. Noah angled himself to block a clear view. "Let me know if you need anything."

Timing her movement, Avery waited until Noah had nearly closed the office door, then darted out and around the corner, into the firm's library. Per Noah's instructions, she located the exit door on the other side of the space, and she hurried into the stairwell.

She hoofed down the first five flights with ease, but by the tenth, she was grateful for her choice of jeans and sneakers. The door opened near the coffee shop, as Noah had described. Avery eased into the crowd of morning customers and moved toward the alley with her head down. A block away from the building, she hailed a cab. "The Lincoln Memorial, please."

The driver plowed through traffic, and Avery dialed Gary Stewart's office. "Gary, it's Avery."

"New phone?" His morning coffee unusually alcohol-free, Gary gulped down the hot brew. "Smart move. I see you've been a busy girl."

"I'm not—"

"I know," he interrupted. "So does the Chief. We talked after your mother's visit. Figured this would be the next salvo."

"What should I do?" Avery slumped in the backseat. "They know I was suspended."

"Which is why Matt Brewer has been terminated." The note of satisfaction was difficult to hide. "Apparently, he got a nice advance from a rag to do a tell-all interview. Parts leaked out to PoliticsNOW."

"What? How did you find out it was him?"

"I've been in this game a long time," he reminded her balefully. "Brewer's out, but you should be worried about Scott Curlee."

"I am. The custody hearing is Monday, Gary. I was thinking of putting out my own statement. Maybe doing an interview to set the record straight."

Gary had mulled over the same idea. Already, his desk was littered with interview requests. "Best bet is damage control, Avery. Your lawyer ask for another postponement?"

"He'll try, but I'm not sure if it will work," she said. "Judge McAdoo is probably being pressured by Celeste's attorneys to move quickly."

"I might have an ex-boyfriend over there who owes me a favor," he hedged. "Let me make a call."

"Thank you . . ."

"Let me call, Avery—don't thank me yet."

THIRTY-SEVEN

Avery stepped out of the cab a block from the Lincoln Memorial. Quickly, she made her way through the summer morning crowd and down to the exhibit. Entering the space, she scanned the milling visitors for a red scarf and a blue column. Avery located the columns first. A check of her watch said 8:59. *Right on time.* She reached into her pocket and pulled out the square of red cloth. Draping the kerchief around her throat, she pretended to read the panels inside the glass cases. And waited.

Ten minutes later, Avery remained alone.

At 9:30, she was antsy. By 9:45, impatience had transmuted into worry. Realizing she'd already pushed her luck with the FBI, Avery turned to leave. She bumped into a man strolling around the other side of the pillars and nearly lost her balance. His hands closed on her arms to steady her.

"Very sorry," she muttered in apology, and she rushed away, wondering what had happened to Betty Papaleo, a.k.a. Wilma.

Ling and Jared looked up as Avery came inside. Aware of Agent Leighton's attention, Ling asked, "Finish what you were working on?"

"Couldn't find what I was looking for." She took a seat and dialed Agent Lee.

He answered on the first ring. "Ms. Yin?"

"No, it's Avery."

"Good. I was about to come and visit you."

"Good news?"

"Nope." From the blocked-off corridor, Agent Lee signaled to his team to fall back from the apartment. "We did an external sweep so as not to alert your videographer, but Mr. Wynn was correct. Your place is wired like a Christmas tree."

"When did they get inside?"

"No way to tell."

"Any way to track who 'they' are?" Avery asked.

"Perhaps." His team had canvassed the building, hunting for a transmitter. Nothing inside the building or nearby carried the bandwidth of the surveillance devices in her apartment. According to his tech team, the devices were top-grade and, if he wasn't mistaken, in common use by the more secretive levels of the federal government. The expensive hypertech of the professional spy, not the sort of equipment they gave to the FBI—but probably handed out like candy to Homeland Security. "It may take a few days."

"Agent Lee, can you find somebody for me?"

"I promise we're still looking for your mother, Avery. You know it's not easy to locate someone who's hiding from the law."

"Yes, I know you're looking, but I'd also like to find someone else. Dr. Betty Papaleo, in the Science and Technology Directorate at Homeland."

There was a pause on the line. "Why do you need to find her?"

With a look across the table at Jared, she explained, "I have reason to believe she agreed to meet me this morning."

"Meet you at the law firm?"

"No. The Lincoln Memorial."

"You left the firm?"

Not wanting to burn Agent Leighton, she prevaricated: "Against your orders? I wouldn't risk it. But I don't want to lose a potential contact."

"Contact about what?"

"She's a possible thread, Agent Lee. I'm trying to gather information. She agreed to meet me before the latest scandal broke. Just to answer some questions."

"Questions you don't want to ask Major Vance? Or questions about him?"

"The former. Will you help me?"

Agent Lee savored the request, one of the few Avery had put in the form of a question. "If you'd told me your plans, I could have brought her in to see you. Calling her didn't work?"

"No, I haven't been able to reach her. It's critical that I speak with her today."

"I'll need to know about what." Agent Lee could hear the note of urgency and, if he wasn't mistaken, fear. "Why are you meeting with one of Major Vance's employees?"

"Because when we connected, she asked me to," Avery replied. "It's important."

A call from the FBI to a DHS employee would yield faster results than a request from a disgraced attorney. She was using him, but if he found Dr. Papaleo, Lee would be the first to learn why Papaleo wanted to meet. "I'll do you one better. I'll go and pick her up myself. Bring her to the law firm."

Avery stiffened. If Betty explained how they'd met, Agent Lee's cooperation would probably vanish in an instant, leaving her with less than she had now. Tripping an alert on the Web as a way of connecting with a government employee wasn't illegal, but Agent Lee struck her as inflexible on matters of security. So she hedged: "Please do, but can you try not to scare her? I can tell you from experience, having the FBI come and pick you up does little to encourage friendliness."

"I'll be a gentleman, Ms. Keene."

Vance listened to the latest report from Phillips and his team. So far, the deaths of Betty Papaleo and her husband had gone unnoticed by the police or the press. The police had yet to turn up the abandoned Volvo, and their ersatz vacation would keep questions at bay for at least a week.

Castillo had tracked Keene to the Lincoln Memorial, where she had found nothing. The rest of her movements were restricted by the heavy cloak of the FBI—a temporary solution, but progress, nonetheless. If Curlee kept the public pressure on, Celeste would win custody Monday morning and be a wealthy widow by the middle of the week.

One last loose end. "Where is Rita Keene?"

"She's been stoned all day."

"Where is she now?"

"Sleeping it off at a flophouse down on Wisconsin."

"The FBI has a team out searching for her. Stay on her and send me any good material. Sex for drugs would be perfect, if you can pull it off."

Since the lady wasn't half bad to look at, Phillips shrugged again. "I'll see what I can do."

Phillips left, and Vance punched in Agent Lee's number.

"Special Agent Lee."

"This is Vance."

"Calling to check in on our girl?"

"She's been very popular today. Can't turn on a television without seeing those photos." He'd have fresh ones to pass along if Phillips did his job. "Did Ms. Keene agree to protective custody?"

"Not yet."

"Has she provided any further information on Justice Wynn?"

"No more than we heard on Tuesday."

"The photos? She give any explanation?"

"Didn't ask. We both knew about her mother, Vance. Nothing in that story today was news."

"Public awareness changes the dynamic." Vance flattened his palm against the desk when frustration would have balled it into a fist. He needed Lee's help, and truculence wouldn't work. "We agreed that due to her mother's predilections and her own past habits, she poses a security risk. I'd hoped you might be able to revisit the idea of her voluntarily relinquishing custody."

"No can do. She's in full defense mode now. Determined to prove Justice Wynn didn't make a mistake with her."

"How does she plan to accomplish that?"

"I don't know. We're not friends, but I can read the signs. She's got an idea. She'll let us know when she's ready."

Vance's splayed fingers curled against his will. Agent Lee knew more than he was telling, and, from the tone, Lee relished the imbalance. A curse bubbled in his throat, along with the urge to shout at Lee about how far above his pay grade he was playing.

But Lee had obviously staked out a position in favor of the enemy. *So be it.* He wouldn't be the first to be seduced by the appearance of innocence. Somehow, he'd find nobility in Avery's efforts. Perhaps try to intercede.

Adding a federal agent to his list of potential loose ends, Vance felt a twinge of remorse. Though they both worked in the same shadows, Agent Lee struck him as a man who would not understand nuance or the absolutes of national security. Lee was a domestic soldier, whereas Vance had no such luxury. The commander in chief had given him orders. Nothing meant more.

"I hope you'll keep me apprised," he asked Lee. "We're all playing blind here."

"Of course. As soon as I hear something worth repeating, you'll know it."

THIRTY-EIGHT

J ustice Wynn's blood sample that you secured finally arrived," Indira said into her phone. She flipped the covers aside and swung her legs over the side of the bed. The constant pain she'd learned to overlook spurted with vicious force throughout her body. She walked haltingly to the desk, where samples had been packed and sealed. "I'll expedite testing today to determine the unknown substance from his hospital testing."

"How long will it take?" Nigel asked impatiently.

"We should have initial results in a few hours." Except she would not be revealing the origin of the compound. A scan of the notes Nigel had also pilfered from the hospital had already revealed what she'd suspected. Justice Wynn had ingested a pharmaceutical created by Advar and discontinued due to poor test results. Dr. Ani Ramji had access to the formulary and the side effects. They'd nicknamed it the Sleeping Beauty drug. Irreversible coma but stabilized vital signs. Forcing her voice to sound matter-of-fact, she told Nigel, "As soon as I have anything, you'll be the first to know."

"What about loose ends on your side?"

"There are none," Indira temporized.

"There are always loose ends," Nigel warned. "Trick is to find them first. Do you have any documents I haven't seen? Anything damning?"

"I told you, we're clean."

"I don't believe you," Nigel retorted flatly. "What are you holding back?"

"I suppose you've been completely forthcoming about the beds Gen-Works has slept in?" Indira challenged instead of answering.

"I'm not trying to burn you."

"What happened with Hygeia before we bought it is not the issue, Nigel. We've discussed this." She'd filled him in on many of the details when Stokes made his first move. Still, she'd trust only so far. "I haven't questioned all you've done on your side of the ledger sheet."

Nigel rocked slowly. "The president wasn't pleased with my press conference. I'm booked on *Colbert* for tonight's broadcast."

"Don't overdo it, Nigel," Indira cautioned. "We want Stokes on the defensive, not the warpath."

"I know what I'm doing." He'd take the fight to Stokes and score points in the bargain. "Oh, and Indira?"

"Yes?"

"You should consider a visit. Soon."

"I will."

Nigel hung up the phone, vaguely disturbed. Indira was holding out on him. About what, he wasn't sure, but he knew her too well. What was he missing?

"Mr. Cooper?"

Nigel glanced up at his assistant and away from the streaming headlines on the screen. Images of the woman he'd hoped would be his salvation flashed on the screen, accompanied by still shots of a bedraggled creature identified as her mother. Avery Keene's tenuous hold on Justice Wynn's life got shakier by the day. Frustration swept through him, and he growled, "What?"

"A package arrived for you," his assistant explained tentatively. "I would have opened it, but it's from the Department of Homeland Security." She entered the room, carrying a brown box swathed in tape and red stamps. "The instructions say it's for the recipient only."

Nigel stood and reached over the desk. "Thanks, Merian." He fairly snatched the box away, eager for her to leave the room. As soon as his door shut behind her, he strode over to the reclaimed antique oak table in the corner of his spacious office. Papers sat in tidy stacks, which he ignored in favor of this newest prize.

He set the box down carefully and returned briefly to his desk for a letter opener. Swiftly, he slit through the tape and safety seal. The box opened with gratifying ease, and he pulled back the flaps.

A letter lay on top, the words scrawled by hand rather than by machine.

Dear Mr. Cooper,

The information contained in this box may impact your pending litigation against President Stokes. What I am doing today may be tantamount to treason, but I don't see any other recourse. I pray to God I'm wrong.

Betty Papaleo

Beneath the letter, a memo had been typed out and, from his quick skim, numbered nearly ten pages in cramped, determined lines. Reports with yellow and blue covers and long, officious names were stacked beneath the memo.

The enclosed memo had Nigel dropping into a padded chair, his eyes devouring its contents. More than an hour passed before he broke away from the table. At his desk, he punched in her number a second time, unconcerned about the time difference.

"Someone knows," he declared as soon as the connection was made.

Indira had grown used to the abrupt announcements. She waved associates from her office before replying, "About what exactly?"

"Everything. Hygeia, the president, Tigris, the funds. They've connected the dots."

Her stomach pitched slowly. "Completely?"

"Just about." He raked a hand through his hair. "A scientist at Homeland Security wrote a memo explaining what happened with the funds and Hygeia. We've got to contain this."

"How do you know?"

"She sent it to me, and God knows who else might have a copy. Fuck."

Indira didn't speak for long seconds. Then she sighed. "Tell her."

"Tell who what?"

"Your pet attorney. Use her to reveal the truth."

"Are you insane? Tell her Hygeia attempted to manufacture a genetic virus to kill Muslims—with research *illegally funded by the U.S. government*—and the successor corporation now wants to take over my company? You don't think this might damage our fucking merger?"

Indira shut her eyes, tempted to respond. But she'd kept that one secret too close to share it, even now. The time had come for damage control. The rest would remain buried. She exhaled lightly, soundlessly. "What have we to lose, Nigel? Either Ms. Keene will use what you tell her to stop Stokes, or Stokes will simply win without a fight."

"This is a major risk. The Court might rule in our favor without this."

"Wishful thinking." Indira rubbed idly at her leg, and she stretched the muscles without relief. "If you have this information, someone else does. We've lost, Nigel. Justice Wynn was our last hope. Now we simply need to destroy our enemy."

"I'm no suicide bomber."

"You are today." Indira stared out from the glass and chrome of her office. If she focused their attention on the elephant in the room, perhaps no one would notice the mouse stealing through the cracks. "I'll be in North Carolina tomorrow."

THIRTY-NINE

Agent Leighton returned them to the apartment that evening, and she relinquished the detail to an Agent Foster. The taciturn man ushered them inside and warned them not to leave for the evening. Despite the cramped quarters, no one was willing to go home. Avery and Jared kept the conversation light, and Ling and Noah got the message. No explanations until they could be sure of privacy.

The television blared as they ate pizza. Around ten p.m., Avery's cell phone rang. She checked the phone warily and noted that the number was blocked. NO CALLER ID in her world usually indicated a government line. She hoped it might be Betty Papaleo. "Hello?"

"I saw your messages."

It was a male voice. Avery froze. Jared subtly gestured to the bathroom, and she gave a slight nod in understanding. "Hold on, please." She raced into the bathroom and twisted the shower to on. The pounding of the water would muffle her conversation, and she had to hope that the surveillance did not include the bathroom.

She flipped down the toilet cover and sat hunched over the phone. "Hello?"

"Good evening."

"Who is this?"

The lightly accented voice on the other end responded, "I would like to meet."

"Who is this?"

"One of the bishops. And I would like to meet *in the square*."

"Is this Dr. Ramji?" Silence stretched across the phone. Realizing he wouldn't answer, she consented. "Where? When?"

"In the square."

"What square? Online? I don't understand."

"Ah. That is why . . ." He paused, then said, "No matter. Per his instructions, join me where the other scion of justice is known but not seen. Where the world meets."

"Can you tell me anything more?"

"Only that we must meet in person if you are to finish this."

Eager to learn as much as she could, Avery pressed, "I don't understand. Where are you?"

"You will find me in the square." He sighed heavily with obvious frustration. "He told me that you would understand. In the square. I will be in position from Queen's Rook White to the Bird's Opening. You have two days until I resign my position."

The call terminated. So she had forty-eight hours to figure out where to go. She hunched over, still seated on the commode, and translated his instructions. Picturing a chessboard, she traced the air. *Queen's Rook White to the Bird's Opening.* Queen's Rook White occupied the a1 position on the algebraic board. And the Bird's Opening, one of the more popular opening attacks, moved a pawn to f4.

Dropping the letters, that left one p.m. and four p.m., as she'd assumed he meant in the afternoon. But knowing when meant nothing if she didn't know where she was going. *Where the other scion of justice is known but not seen.* Where the hell was that?

Avery turned off the water and left the bathroom. When she returned to her seat on the sofa, Jared, beside her, tapped instructions into his computer, then dialed his cell phone. "Check your phones. Let me know if you have a signal."

No one did. At Avery's look, he explained. "I'm jamming all signals. Depending on their equipment, they may still be able to view us, but no audio. We've got maybe five minutes or they'll know it's not natural interference. Ling, try to look disgusted." He slid the pizza box toward Avery. "What did your friend want?"

"It was Ani. I'm supposed to meet him in the square in two days. But I don't know where that is." She repeated his instructions.

"You figured out the time from that gibberish?" Noah asked incredulously.

"I like chess. Apparently, works great for cryptic clues."

"Before the jammer fails, any other reports?"

Avery reached for her bag and laid Justice Wynn's letter on the table. She unfolded the sheets and pointed to a single sentence, her eyes meeting Ling's. "We have to get ahead of this. Next week is the end of term, and then my time is up." She jabbed her finger at the page. "Ling, this line here. Do you know what it means?"

"About smallpox. It sounds vaguely familiar. I think it's a reference from the eighteenth century," Ling explained thoughtfully, quietly. "During the outbreaks in Europe, physicians learned of a practice in China, Turkey, and Africa to transfer active cultures from smallpox wounds to healthy children to inoculate them. The doctors initially rejected the idea as insane, but once the Prince and Princess of Wales allowed their own children to be treated, it moved into greater favor."

"But what does that have to do with the judge?" Jared demanded in a low rumble of exasperation. "I've already been diagnosed with Boursin's. There's nothing he could have done to inoculate me against his genes."

"Except guarantee that the research necessary to protect you continues," Avery corrected. Disappointed, she rubbed at the small of her back where a new knot of tension had formed. "I'm running out of clues."

Noah asked the next question, aware their signal block would disappear soon: "What is the Court going to do if you don't solve this?"

"Deadlock," Avery responded wearily. Discarding the last of her ethics about keeping Court secrets secret, she explained, "Rumor has it that Roseborough, Hodgson, Gardner, and Lawrence-Hardy are already in favor of permitting the merger. But Lindenbaum, Newell, and Estrada are ideologues. They staunchly oppose interfering with the power of the executive to make decisions about national security. Seth Bringman is an isolationist—he sees the decision as a referendum on the resilience of the American marketplace. An Indian firm will be the surviving company, which rubs him the wrong way. If there's a tie, the merger will be blocked. Any research they've produced will probably vanish with them."

Jared slammed his fist against the coffee table, and the pizza carton jumped. "He's nearly gotten you killed twice, when he had to know you couldn't help him. You can't save him, and if this evil experiment is true, I don't want you to save me."

"There's some kind of massive cover-up going on here, Jared. We know that," Avery blurted, her stomach clutching. "Your father knew about Hygeia and their experiments. Telling the truth meant the end of the merger because he'd have to recuse himself, especially if what he'd figured out was proven to be true. But attempted genocide would not only scuttle the merger but probably destroy both companies. No cure for you. Although, with the Court in limbo, he apparently believes there are moves left. Sacrificing both bishops wasn't the endgame. It set up Lasker to trap Bauer into making futile attempts to escape the inevitable."

"This isn't a chess game, Avery. And either way, he's wrong," Jared shot back. "A possible cure is not as important as your life."

Avery shifted to the edge of her seat now, her jaw set tight. "I would do this, but I don't know how he expects it to happen. How in the world am I supposed to manipulate the Supreme Court? I have no standing to push for new oral arguments, and I don't have enough real evidence to create a good press witch hunt that doesn't rebound on me." Her voice was heavy with emotion. "Everything I touch disappears, and I can't make this kind of accusation without proof!"

She sprang to her feet and snatched open the door, only to find an agent standing guard. "I need some air right now."

"You're to remain in the apartment."

"I'm going out for a walk," she declared, shoving past him.

The agent caught her arm, and, smartly, shifted as her fist came around in an automatic swing for his nose. He captured her hand and forced it to her side. "Ms. Keene, no one is allowed outside the apartment until morning. Agent Lee's orders."

Avery struggled in his grip, as Jared, Noah, and Ling rushed to the doorway. "Let her go!" Ling insisted.

Jared stepped out of the apartment and circled behind Avery, settling his hands on her shoulders. He glared at the agent, asking, "How about the stairwell? If she stays inside the building, can she go into the stairwell?"

"I don't—" He noticed the sheen of frustrated tears in the wide green eyes and relented. He'd swept the stairs on his way up for his shift. With the door open, it should be safe. "Okay, ten minutes. Then I need you all back inside the apartment for the night."

Avery wrestled with the urge to run, to hide on the humid streets of the city. To shuck off Justice Wynn's expectations—to flee. But the feel of Jared's hands on her shoulders stiffened her spine and her resolve. She gave a short nod and moved to the shadowed stairwell.

Jared followed her. They stood silent in the cloistered dark for nearly five minutes. Then, as though her legs could no longer hold, Avery sank down onto a step. Jared followed her down, sitting a step above her. He leaned down, lightly gripped her shoulders, and turned her toward him. Her eyes glimmered with moisture in the dim overhead light. "You've had a rough week."

A morbid laugh sputtered out. "Yes." She covered his hand, releasing a long, low breath. "But your father is dying. You haven't had a much better time of it."

"I barely know my father, Avery. And the more I learn, I can't say I'm growing fonder." When she started to protest, he simply shook his head. "It's the truth. But if he had to pick a champion, he chose the right one."

"I haven't figured anything out."

"You knew that VGC meant something. You got the corporate names to Ling, and I'm certain you've got a plan for tomorrow."

A sob caught in her throat, but Avery swallowed it down. Yet, when she went to speak, her voice broke. "Thank you, Jared. I don't know—"

"That's bullshit. Whatever you are about to say is bullshit." With his thumb, he swiped at an errant tear. "You know just about everything, Avery. Algebraic tables for chess. How to decode an old man's Don Quixote fantasies. How to make sure his estranged son has a reason to stick around."

"Maybe tilting at windmills is a family trait," she whispered.

"Perhaps. But you're the real deal. You're smart, and you care. That's more than he has the right to ask." He lifted a hand to her chin, stroking the stubborn curve and the plane of her cheek. "Ready to go inside?"

Avery smiled slightly. "I'd like to sit here for a few more minutes."

Jared nodded, shifting down a step to drape his arm around her. She resisted for an instant, then allowed her head to fall onto his shoulder. They sat that way until a knock sounded at the metal door.

"Time's up," Jared said as he stood. He helped her stand and reached for the door. The agent stood at attention on the other side.

"I'm sorry about before. It's been a long day." She gave a half-hearted attempt at a grin. "I won't be any more trouble tonight."

The agent nodded and took a step away. "No problem, Ms. Keene."

Jared opened the apartment door, where Ling hovered near the breakfast bar. Her troubled gaze locked with his. Jared gave a short shake of his head over Avery's head. Beneath his hold on Avery, he'd felt the tremble of nerves.

In silence, he cursed his father and himself. Then he quietly shut the door.

FORTY

Saturday, June 24

The lights were low, despite the morning sun. Bars shared that trait with casinos. The constant illusion of night aided the passage of sour whiskey and the acid burn of rum. Rita Keene swayed on a stool, fingers gripping the glass of vodka with an expert hold. She might fall, but her drink wouldn't.

Above her head, a news anchor droned through the stories of the day. Her free hand dropped onto the sticky wood, bracing for the inevitable. The unflattering image of her bent over a table popped up with numbing regularity. The asshole who'd taken the picture had caught her in a weak moment, her arms flexed for solace.

Bet the judgmental reporters had never lost a husband, she thought in the twisted dimness of righteous indignation. A pain she'd clung to for decades, nursing its bite. Honing the bitterest edges for the cuts she required to justify her choices.

Now she was being publicly humiliated because her daughter had to go and piss off the wrong people. Treated like trash, all because of Avery.

She'd always surfaced when her baby needed her, hadn't she? She'd kept the girl fed, got her into and out of school. Laid on her back to earn bread for the ungrateful brat's mouth, hadn't she? Memories conveniently expiated of detours from the grocery store to a shadowed corner for a tiny bundle of forgetfulness.

Now, because of that bitch, she had to watch herself on a fucking screen, being laughed at by the high and the mighty and the scum of the earth. Like they understood what she'd gone through. What she'd lost.

She tossed off the glass's remnants. The vodka lacked the punch of coke, or the speedy amnesia of heroin, but it was all she could afford. Her sniveling, stingy bitch of a daughter hadn't been home when she'd stopped by. Only cops who refused to let her pass when no one answered the phone.

"Hey!"

The bartender, a tight-assed prick who recognized her from the picture, pretended not to hear. Rita pounded her glass, to no avail. Figures, she thought hazily. She was thirsty and too aware of the world and running low on the cash necessary for oblivion.

So, when a tall, broad-shouldered, square-jawed man joined her at the bar, she hopefully angled her meager cleavage in his direction. Rita smiled, a wobbly curve of a mouth cracked from dehydration and meth. "Hey, handsome. Wanna buy a lady a drink?"

Hazel eyes met hers, and he tapped the bar. When the bartender stopped pretending not to notice, he held up two fingers and pointed at Rita's glass.

The bartender sized up the cut of the new guy's suit and fished out the bottle. He refilled Rita's glass and served up one to the man. The man placed a note on the bar and waved him off.

Saying nothing, the bartender scooped up the cash. The fifty in his hand easily covered Rita's tab and the tip he'd decided on for himself. Surprised, he checked Rita out, squinting. Up close, he could see how she might have been beautiful once, but the skinny whore look did nothing for him. Takes all kinds, he decided, as he returned to ignoring his customers.

Unaware of the bartender's summation, Rita trailed red-tipped fingers along the man's jacket, fumbled for his tie in a gesture that felt sexy. "You like to party, honey?"

"Sure."

Rita smelled no cologne, just a clean scent most of the bar's patrons lacked. She tipped the vodka down her throat in a cleansing rush. "Let's get out of here, then."

Phillips swung his arm around her, guiding her staggering path to the door. "Your place or mine?"

In a voice that carried to the unswept corners, Rita giggled and answered, "Yours, honey. Take me anywhere you want."

Clear of a kidnapping charge, Phillips nodded gallantly. "Yes, ma'am."

Across town, huddled in the conference room at Noah's firm, Avery plowed through the research they'd collected, including the grants from Justice Wynn's FOIA request. The more she read, the more her stomach knotted into tighter bundles.

What exactly are they hiding?

Noah sat down the hall in his office, prepping for Monday's court hearing. Ling pored over documents about smallpox that a friend at the hospital had couriered over. Bent over his computer, Jared had been working to backtrace the surveillance in her apartment, despite knowing the FBI was on the case. Or, as Avery had learned from their brief acquaintance, because of it.

By her elbow, her cell phone rang. The now-familiar NO CALLER ID showed on her screen, and she quickly answered.

"Yes?"

"Hello, Avery. This is your friend."

The voice was synthesized, just as it had been on both previous calls.

"I told you to leave me alone," she replied.

"Remember your mythology, Avery? When Persephone ate the pomegranate seeds, she became indebted to Hades. You've spent some of my money. I thought it was time to call."

"What do you want?"

"You've eaten the seeds. Now I require payment."

"Who are you working with? Why are you disguising your voice?"

"Don't ask irrelevant questions. Just listen." Nigel thumbed through the memo from Betty, then continued to speak into the burner cell. "You know, governments are good at cleaning up messes. If I were you, I'd find out all I could about a company called Hygeia. I'd follow the money."

"Follow the money? That's all you've got for me?" Avery goaded. "I know about Hygeia and GenWorks and Advar. About the research. The money trick was nice, but if that's all you can do, stop calling me."

"You're a cynic, Avery. Good idea to be suspicious, especially of anyone claiming to wear white hats."

"So you're not a white hat?"

"God, no. I'm not the self-sacrificing type. But there's one bureaucrat you can talk to. Try Dr. Elizabeth Papaleo at the Science and Technology Directorate in the Department of Homeland Security. She can verify what I'm telling you."

"Papaleo?" The sneer became a frown. "How do you know her?"

"Follow the money," he repeated. "It's always excellent advice, Avery."

"I've been in touch with Betty, but she's vanished," she told him. "What does she know?"

"Betty's missing?"

"The FBI is looking for her. Tell me what she has."

"You should check out your new email account tomorrow at ten."

"I have a new email account?"

"You will. How about NancyDrew@ariesworld.com? The password will be—" He stopped. "Let's make the password *Nixon,* just to stay with our theme of unreliable public servants. Don't disappoint me."

Avery hung up the phone and sent a quick text to Noah. When he joined them in the conference room, she explained the call. "Whoever this is, he knows about Betty, but he wouldn't say much."

Looking up from his screen, Jared asked, "Have you heard anything more from Agent Lee about her?"

"Not yet. Let me try him now." Avery dialed the agent's number, and he answered on the second ring.

"Everything okay, Ms. Keene?"

"Yes, sir," Avery replied. "I wanted to see if you'd found out anything more about Dr. Papaleo."

In his office, Agent Lee's brow furrowed. "I sent a couple of agents to do a wellness check, but no response. She hasn't been in touch with her coworkers, and there are plane tickets in their names for a trip to Mexico. Passengers recall a couple boarding the plane, but no one can recall what they looked like. Their passports scanned, but surveillance at Dulles and in Puerto Vallarta have no images of either person that matches facial rec."

"How is that possible?"

"It's pretty sophisticated. A lot of trouble to go through for a mid-level bureaucrat." Agent Lee waited a beat, wanting to be sure he was understood. "But if she had some knowledge from Homeland Security that would make her a target for foul play, now's the time to tell me, Avery. I can help."

"If there's something to tell, Agent Lee, I promise, you'll be the first to know."

FORTY-ONE

Sunday, June 25

Avery drummed her fingers on the conference table that had become her new office.

"I have to call the hospital," she announced, getting to her feet. "Agent Leighton, I'd like to use the office down the hall."

At the woman's assent, Avery strode down the hall to the office she'd used as a decoy before. This time, she settled behind the desk and booted up the computer. She used the office phone to dial Dr. Toca. "Doctor, it's Avery Keene."

"Yes, Ms. Keene." The chill carried clearly across the phone. "How can I help you?"

"I wanted an update on Justice Wynn's condition. And you should have received the toxicology report by now."

"His condition is unchanged."

"And the toxicology report?"

"I'm not at liberty to discuss that."

"Is there a problem, Dr. Toca?"

"Mr. Mumford has advised that we limit contact with you until this situation has sorted itself out," he admitted.

"This situation is irrelevant until a court rules that I am no longer his guardian. If Mr. Mumford would like to discuss that with me, he is free to call."

"I will let him know. Is that all?"

"No, sir. I want an answer. Did the hospital determine the drug combination he ingested?"

Dr. Toca did not respond, and Avery demanded, "I am Supreme Court Justice Wynn's legal guardian—you and the hospital will be breaking the law by failing to disclose his test results to me immediately. I can also come and request the information in person, Doctor. I'm sure Mr. Mumford would love to host the media circus following me into the hospital."

With a sigh that sounded like relief, he said, "The labs confirmed what I theorized to you when we last spoke. The compound they found in his blood is not registered by any pharmaceutical company licensed to distribute in the United States. As best we can determine, the drug induces a coma that mimics the effects of an aneurysm, but the body's organs are unharmed. None of our toxicologists have seen anything like it."

"So you don't know if the coma is reversible?"

"No. We know nothing about the drug."

Avery thought of her upcoming meeting with Ani. He would know. It was even more crucial now to figure out the location of their meeting. "Dr. Toca, I need you to call FBI Special Agent Robert Lee. Tell him what you've told me. Do it now."

"Excuse me?"

"Please. Call him and tell him that you've spoken to me. He'll know what to do." Hanging up, she went to the ariesworld.com site and logged in as NancyDrew. Two messages sat in the otherwise empty in-box.

BE CAREFUL, NANCY. THE NATIVES ARE GETTING DESPERATE AND YOU'RE THEIR LAST BARRIER. PROTECT YOURSELF. HERE'S THE NUCLEAR WARHEAD. IT'S UP TO YOU TO FIRE FIRST. DUCK AND COVER! I'LL CHECK ON YOUR PROGRESS.

The second message had several attachments. She clicked on the one titled "Memo" and hit print, then began to read. The memo had been authored by Betty Papaleo, her missing contact. According to her analysis of several reports, the scientist turned budget guru had discovered a connection between the grants from her shop and research happening halfway around the world. In a code that Avery was learning to break, Dr. Papaleo wrote of CRGs that paid for exactly what Ling had surmised—targeting "lineage" for "dissemination of customized genetic information."

She shifted from the memo to the pages of financial records Mr.

Money had uploaded. As they printed, she skimmed the lines that had been highlighted for her. Grants totaling hundreds of millions sent to a small tech company in India. To Hygeia, Ltd.

He had added in financial records from the company. Lasering in, she noted records of funds funneled into chromosomal research from a string of investors, in a variety of tranches.

Not unusual, Avery conceded silently. She wasn't an accountant, but she'd reviewed more than her share of lawsuits that hinged on income statements and financial ledgers. According to the banking records attached, each wire had an American origination. For a young company, funding would likely come from a variety of sources—and Americans had a penchant for foreign investment.

She laid the bank records down, moving to a sheet emblazoned with the Federal Reserve's emblem. The report indicated that the transfers came from a federal account. The next page, as official-looking, traced the origins to the Department of Homeland Security. The Science and Technology Directorate.

Proof, she realized, that the U.S. government had made hundreds of millions in payments to Hygeia, Ltd. She shuffled back to the memo. The payments from the directorate had never been duly authorized, and they'd ceased abruptly. Soon thereafter, so did financial statements for Hygeia.

Chromosomal research conducted in secret and disavowed by TigrisLost.

The weaponization of genetic research to target lineage.

Hundreds of millions in funding from the U.S. Treasury to Hygeia— without authorization.

Major Will Vance, biochemist assigned to CBIRF.

Afghanistan. India. The world's largest Muslim populations within easy reach.

A missing scientist. A missing budget analyst. A dead nurse. An attempted murder.

A Supreme Court justice desperate to save his only son.

The scientists at Hygeia had used American dollars to engage in research that violated every national or international treaty she could imagine, let alone the basic tenets of morality.

The glaring question was simple. Did the president of the United States know what had been done under his watch?

Avery cleared the web browser cache and powered off the computer. She returned to the conference room and summoned Noah to join them. "I got the download from Mr. Money. This is what he sent me."

She dropped the papers on the conference table. Jared read first, then passed pages to Ling as he finished, and she passed them over to Noah. Unable to sit, Avery prowled the room, the quiet punctuated by the inevitable gasps and sharp inhalations that traditionally marked discoveries.

"I know what we imagined, but this is proof," Ling exclaimed. "This is Josef Mengele territory."

"The funding ended before the merger," Jared pointed out, looking up from a balance sheet. "When Ani Ramji started leaking information about the program."

Avery had already come to the same conclusion. "According to the timeline I've charted," she said as she opened a notebook onto the table, "Hygeia started to draw attention from the Indian government. When the CEO of Hygeia realized they were on his trail, he turned to Advar for rescue. Moved the research under their umbrella. Homeland Security had to abort the project and cut off funds."

"Then Advar attempts to merge with GenWorks. If the merger succeeds, the president's archenemy, Nigel Cooper, will have access to data proving his administration sanctioned research into biogenetic genocide."

"More than research," Ling corrected with alarm in her voice. "According to Papaleo's memo, Hygeia did more than theorize. They perfected the technology—a biogenetic virus that can kill anyone with the wrong chromosomal mutation."

Noah asked the question first: "Do we think President Stokes was complicit, or did Major Vance act alone?"

"The person who can tell us is Ani. He's the one who blew the whistle and tipped off Justice Wynn," Avery said. She thought of the video of Wynn's commencement speech, which she had rewatched the night before in her apartment. "If the justice's speech at the commencement is to be believed, he clearly thought President Stokes was a part of the conspiracy."

"Which Ani can confirm, if you can figure out where he is."

Avery had been replaying Ani's riddle in her mind, but to no avail. *Where the other scion of justice is known but not seen. Where the world meets.* Over and over, Justice Wynn and Ani had met online in a virtual world of battle, signaling to each other using the phrase "in the square." Like the constellations in Jared's room at the cabin, the clue had to be more obvious than she realized. Justice Wynn believed she would figure it out.

Ling asked, "Is there any place that is like a chess game? An amusement park or something."

Jared shook his head. "I thought about Bangkok, where they set that musical. We could try it, but I don't know where we'd start. Besides, I can't imagine the judge being a fan of theater."

"No, he would make sure I could connect the dots. A place where we could meet with Ani, and one that we could get to quickly. I doubt he'd send us to Thailand, or India, for that matter. It has to be more domestic. A square that we'd be able to find." Then, like a final move, she understood. *"A nation of favor and folly. Where justice is known but rarely seen,"* she murmured.

"What?"

"Something he said to me the day he had me sign something in his office." Another mystery she hadn't solved yet. Turning her thoughts back, she explained, "He said that America was a nation of favor and folly. Where justice is known but rarely seen. What if he was being literal?"

Looking around for confirmation of their mutual confusion, Ling asked, "What are you talking about?"

"Folly. A nation of folly. Seward Square," Avery explained, growing more excited. "Let me borrow your laptop, Jared." Bemused, he slid the computer to her, and all three watched as she typed. Pages sprang up, and she quickly scanned the contents. She exhaled and leaned back in her chair. "I knew it."

Jared asked, "Care to let us in on the revelation?"

Avery turned to him with a satisfied grin. "Your father loves history and his own name. As you pointed out with the game handle, he compares himself to William Howard Taft. And he sees himself as a child of justice—a scion of justice. Put that together with his comment about folly, and there's only one place he could mean. The only square in Washington, DC, that is also named for a man named William.

William Seward." She swiveled the screen to show an online article. "Farragut, McPherson, Mount Vernon, Lafayette, and Seward. That's where Ani is."

"That's a stretch, Avery," Noah said doubtfully. "You got all that from his cryptic clue?"

"*In the square. Known but not seen.* Seward's statue is not in Seward Square. They've never put one up. He's also a 'scion of justice' because Seward and his wife were abolitionists who hid escaped slaves in their home. And he was an excellent lawyer who might have been president, but he lost to Abraham Lincoln." Growing more certain, she added, "Ani Ramji is in hiding, but he had to get out of India. All his colleagues were being murdered. He and Justice Wynn found a way to bring him here and hide him. If he's waiting for me to find him, he's here in DC."

Jared glanced at the others before he gently asked, "Are you sure?"

Avery gave a soft laugh, aware of the incredulity of her friends. "I have to be. We're almost out of time."

Vance replayed the surveillance of Avery's apartment. The ringing of a telephone shrilled through at 10:43 p.m., but no sound other than the shower running and muffled conversation.

He stabbed the intercom. "Camille, where are the phone records I ordered?"

His assistant walked into the office at her usually efficient clip. "Took a minute to pull from the cell phone provider." She laid the report on the desk and indicated a section she'd highlighted. "I've been trying to narrow down the callers who had masked numbers."

"How many?"

"Two calls came in from untraceable cells. I have them working on it."

"I want an answer in an hour," he said without looking up. Camille took her cue and left him alone. Vance gritted his teeth and continued to study the logs.

Whoever was trying to reach Avery, he had to find them.

Now.

FORTY-TWO

In a coffee shop in Southeast DC, Dr. Ani Ramji sat in an Internet café off the main thoroughfare; college students and vagrants hunched over terminals, oblivious to those around them. He glanced over his shoulder as he typed, not sure of the face he sought. One last fail-safe. A file to be transmitted to his remaining ally, should any harm befall him.

Ani's eyes fluttered in exhaustion, and he drifted into waking sleep, knowing what was to come. The dreams came every time he let his mind wander from a task, the images a nightmare of his own making.

Screams of piercing agony. Bodies writhing on a cold slate floor. Pale walls to reflect the light, to illuminate and sterilize. Weeping and bleeding and prayers for death, the embodiment of a modern Hieronymus Bosch painting. *Destruction perfected.*

He snapped alert, and a couple of deep breaths brought him back. The Internet café was number seven on his rotation. He never returned to the same café in a fourteen-day span, the average time the various owners took to erase their surveillance. But as a faithful man, he believed in the permanence of knowledge, though he might have to help it along. In America, he'd found a friend and ally and a safe haven, one whose devotion to revealing the truth rivaled his own. It was for him that he dared this last meeting.

At the appointed hour, he stood and headed across the road to the park. The layout of the park had been etched into his memory. For weeks, he'd hidden in the forgotten areas of Southeast DC, unseen by those who pursued him. The place known as Seward Square sat at the intersection of Pennsylvania Avenue and North Carolina Avenue in the Capitol Hill neighborhood. Justice Wynn had recommended the location, with its four miniature parks carved out by the intersecting streets.

Taking a seat on the bench nearest the center fountain, he set his satchel on the ground beside him. Grass would stain the leather, but it was of no matter. Although he had not dared to contact Avery again, he was certain she would figure out the location. He had come here each day, and he would for one more, but he had decided he would have to abandon Howard Wynn after that. The fear that rode him daily had come close to overtaking his guilt. If she did not arrive by tomorrow, he would vanish.

He'd found it impossible to relax in the city, even thousands of miles from his home. After they met, he would travel to Canada and then to Turkey and the Tigris region. Perhaps the land of his victims would offer no more protection from the men who hunted him, but he could imagine no true haven from his demons.

Staring up at the cloudless sky, he thought of his role in the master plan. So convoluted, but what choice did either of them have? His partner now lay dying and unaware of whether his sacrifice would mete out justice or leave them all victims of hubris and greed.

"Dr. Ramji?"

Slowly, Ani turned his head to face their anointed champion. Recognizing the voice and the photos from the papers, he said, "Ms. Keene. Were you followed?"

"No, sir." Avery lowered herself to the bench beside him. "This is Jared Wynn. He specialized in reconnaissance and stealth maneuvers in another life. We were able to evade our shadows, but we do not have long."

"Ah, the Navy analyst." Ani nodded to himself. "You lost your dream because of Boursin's. And now you risk much for your father. He was not certain you would."

"Neither was I."

"Why do you?"

"Now is not the time for our confessions, Dr. Ramji." Jared spoke quickly, his voice low. "We've come to hear your story."

"My confession, yes." Ani hunched his shoulders. "I have much to atone for."

Avery watched him as his eyes darted toward the park entrance, then toward her. "What do you want, Dr. Ramji?"

"To give you the keys to Jared's survival." He reached into his pocket and removed a USB drive. "What we did—what I did at Hygeia—was monstrous. Ungodly. But with this, perhaps some good will come."

"Then it's true?" Avery asked. "You conceptualized a genetic weapon to kill Muslims?"

"Religion is an imprecise scientific tool, but yes. Those who shared the genetic markers of the targeted haplogroup would die from the virus we developed. India has made great strides, but our leaders continue to fear that a partition between Hindu and Muslim is insufficient. They wanted a—a fail-safe, I think you'd call it. A way to act should conflict arise and threaten our existence."

"How far did the research go?"

"How far?" Ani repeated, his brow furrowing. "What do you mean?"

Ling had told her what to ask for. "Is this information on the genetic structure of the weapon? A genomic map of the proposed virus? Theoretical models?" Avery pushed: "What did you give us?"

"I thought you knew." Ani's forehead cleared, and his eyes darkened. "We perfected the weapon. Tested it."

"Tested?"

"What I have given you is a video of the experiments, as well as other information. The virus works almost perfectly. Three hundred subjects tested. A twenty-four percent survival rate."

Avery and Jared were silent as the shock set in.

"You infected people . . . and a majority died?" Avery whispered.

"Yes. That is why I am here," Ani replied.

"There are people you infected who are still alive?" Jared demanded.

"No, there are not. Eventually, all test subjects were terminated for the sake of secrecy." Ani lifted his chin. "The evidence you will need to prove what happened is here. We recorded our findings, for later review and examination. And for protection. We had a liaison in America, and he was kept apprised of our work. When we ran our tests, he was present."

"Who?"

"I do not know his name. But my colleagues and I thought it best to have proof that we were operating under governmental direction, hired by the Americans to work in partnership." Ani knew their actions were indefensible, but penance required confession. "If it means anything, we used prisoners. Offered them extraordinary sums for their families if they agreed to participate."

"Did they know what was going to happen?"

"No. No one knew except us."

Jared shifted and scanned the perimeter. "Who else has this information?"

"No one. After we were told to terminate the survivors, I could not continue. I joined the project out of patriotism and scientific curiosity. To understand the power of the genome. To play God. But we were not gods, and patriotism cannot justify our sins. When our team tried to tell the Indian government that we would not continue, they shut down the lab, and my colleagues began to die. I have managed to hide, but they will find me soon if I remain here much longer. I offered the recording to Howard, but he refused to take it. He said it would not be safe with him. Only with you two."

Looking at the drive in his hand, Jared asked, "What is Avery supposed to do with this?"

"Show it to the world. Save your life and others. Do not let those men and women die in vain." Abruptly, he turned to Avery and grabbed her hands. "I believed initially this research would have a patriotic purpose. Even ethical, if the jihadists are to be believed. I was wrong. And my weakness pulled me too deeply into the horrors. Justice Wynn was a good man who faced a terrible choice. He knew you would figure out how to stop them from winning. But if you reveal what has been done, they will try to kill you and everyone you love."

"What about your family?"

His face turned ashen. "Slaughtered for my sins."

In the silence that followed, Ani clenched his fingers tighter around hers. "Good can come of this, Avery, but it cannot be either buried or revealed. Do you understand?"

"No," Avery admitted, turning her hands beneath his. "Come with us. You can tell the FBI what's happened. You can help me finish this."

"I cannot go with you."

Refusing to accept his rejection, Avery argued, "I have a friend who will help you. He'll put you in protective custody. I need your help."

"They will kill me."

"Like you killed Justice Wynn?"

"What?" he sputtered.

"I know you gave him the compound. You put him in the coma."

Ani squinted, then his face cleared. "Ah, the Sleeping Beauty drug. In the proper dosage, they could keep him alive for years. I developed the formulary for Hygeia in another line of genetic experiments, before Tigris. Advar took over the company before I discovered a way to reverse the coma, but I believe it is possible."

"Is that why he took it?" she asked. "To put himself in a coma indefinitely?"

"If the research is reinitialized, his coma may be ended, and he could wake up. But he does not expect to survive. He simply wanted to determine when he would lose control of his body. This was a compromise between us."

Jared asked, "But it is possible to wake him up?"

"I cannot, but my earlier experimental results are also on the drive."

Ani stood, and Avery also rose. He stared at her in silence, then added, "Howard was willing to die to stop them. I am not as brave. Once I leave, I will not return." He bent down to pick up his bag. With jerky motions, he tossed the leather strap over his shoulder.

At the mention of Justice Wynn, Avery said, "One more question. Do you know what this means? *If I had accepted absurdity and given smallpox to my child, I would not be mourning him today and the atrocities would not have been.*"

"I am sorry, no. We did not discuss smallpox."

"You can't just walk away," Jared ordered. "You deserve to be in prison for what you've done."

Ani took a step back. "I long ago abandoned my Hindu faith, but if our gods exist, Yama will mete out his own punishment. My actions have killed my family, my friends, and possibly your father. There is no prison greater than the hell I live in every day, but your nation will not be my judge. Not when they have been complicit in my crimes." With a terse nod to Jared, he faced Avery. "Use the information I have given you. Save him."

He turned and jogged across the park. Jared reached for his phone, and Avery grabbed his hand. "What are you doing?"

"Calling Agent Lee. That man is a mass murderer. I don't care why he did it, he should answer for his crimes."

"Yes, he should. But think about it. He's managed to evade DHS for months. By the time the FBI gets here, do you really think they'll find him? More likely, we'll be taken into custody, have to explain what he's done, show them information we haven't seen yet, and hope for the best."

Knowing she was right, Jared tightened his fingers around the phone. "That's assuming Major Vance doesn't have us detained and transported under an extraordinary rendition order." He shook his head in disgust. "Avery, we have to expose them. All of them."

"I know. If what we have proves that President Stokes and Major Vance were part of this, we will. I promise."

Jared took her hand and began to lead her across the park to the Metro station. "I believe you. Let's get back before they figure out we're gone."

FORTY-THREE

Avery and Jared returned to the law firm and, using a signal they'd prearranged with Noah and Ling, made their way to the conference room without alerting their security detail. An hour later, Agent Lee arrived at the firm. Through the glass, they watched him as he spoke to one of the agents on duty.

She felt the flash drive tucked ominously in her pocket. As she had all weekend, she swung wildly between wanting to tell Agent Lee everything and wanting to keep the documents a secret until she solved Justice Wynn's final riddle. But Nurse Lewis was dead. Betty Papaleo was missing. She and Jared had been attacked. Ani Ramji was on the run, and Justice Wynn lay in a self-induced coma. As long as she tried to fix this herself, she was risking her friends' lives and her own. Yet if she told the FBI agent the truth, there was no way to predict how he'd react. Or who he'd tell. Her mind circled with the conundrum, but no new answer emerged.

She decided to stick with what she knew. Who she trusted. Pulling out the flash drive, she announced, "Jared, we need to review the drive."

With a nod, he reached out his hand for the slim casing, and Avery placed it in his palm. In short order, files began to open on his screen. Jared had taken extra precautions. No eavesdropper or hacker would be able to access what they read, the data immediately encrypted.

In silence, the team huddled around the screen and read the data, absorbing the information that confirmed their own research. Ling homed in on the images of DNA strands and scientific formulas, her occasional gasps signaling both wonder and horror.

A video file was next on the directory.

"Hold on," Noah said. He opened the door and spoke to their guard. "I know you like to keep an eye on us, but we need to watch a few videos. We'll need to use the blackout screens and the projector."

"Understood."

Noah came back and, using the audiovisual controls, darkened the room and dropped the screen. Jared connected his laptop and started the video.

They watched as a large room appeared. Bunk beds had been lined up across the far wall, five in the row, stacked two deep. Off camera, a soft alarm sounded, rousing the occupants from sleep. One by one, they woke from their slumber. A few young men, in their early twenties by their looks, climbed down from the bunks. Others moved more slowly, particularly the elderly men who had bunked side by side on the lower level. A nurse entered the room from the left, her peach scrubs identical to the ones worn by the occupants, except theirs were either blue or green.

As she moved among them, she offered each a bottle of water and a tablet from her rolling cart. To a person, they accepted the pill and quickly swallowed it down, as though this was a set routine. She waited while each person finished their bottles, then she carefully retrieved each bottle with gloved hands, swiftly labeling them before storage. No one spoke—not to the nurse, not to one another.

The room, a pale yellow, had a set of four seating areas, with five chairs at each grouping. The camera angle changed, revealing a small sink and a mirror, which reflected the row of beds. One by one, the men approached the sink. Avery noted the range of ages, from teenager to septuagenarian. A quick brush of teeth confirmed the video time stamp of 7:18 a.m. Off camera, a faint sound of flushing could be heard.

Once the occupants had completed their ablutions, they sorted themselves into the five arranged seating groups. Various games stood in arrested states of play. The teams began their activities, again without words.

"Why is no one talking?" Noah wondered aloud.

"I've got the volume up as high as it'll go," Jared responded. "You can hear the background noise. They're just not talking." He glanced at Avery. "Want me to fast-forward?"

"Not yet."

They watched the silent room for another eight minutes before a figure entered the frame. He wore a white lab coat and a surgical mask, and he carried a clipboard. "Tigris test gamma one twenty-nine," he announced.

"That sounds like Ani," Jared said. "Can't be sure because of the mask."

"I think you're right."

He moved from table to table, placing an oximeter on a silently proffered finger. With the completion of each blood oxygen test, he recorded the results before moving to the next. His rounds completed, he stared up into the camera and gave a short nod. Then he turned back to the group. "Hygeia appreciates your service. We are nearing the end of this phase of the trial. I will ask that you continue your assignments, and that you remain in your stations. Thank you again for your participation."

Ani exited the room, and the test subjects continued to play their games, solve their puzzles. Suddenly, a hiss of air disrupted the silence. The susurration was followed by staccato bursts of air. The occupants paused in their games to look around and at one another. When a second round of bursts followed, one of the younger men got up and moved to the side of the room where the beds were located. He stared up at the narrow vents that ran along the ceiling, then moved to the catty-corner wall and stared up again. A third volley of air bursts could be heard, and the young man climbed up to the top bunk and examined the vents, running his finger along the metal base.

One of the older men approached the bed and grabbed at the bottom of his pants leg. He tugged once, hard, but the younger man waved him off. He yanked again and pointed imperiously at the door. With an angry gesture, he instructed him to come down, pointing in the direction of the camera. Reluctantly, the young man clambered down, frowning.

The video continued for another five minutes, but nothing new happened. "Fast-forward," said Avery.

Jared increased the film speed by 1x and then by 4x, rushing forward by nearly six hours. Like marionettes, the figures changed tables, ate lunch, then dinner. Jared reduced it to normal speed when white-coated figures entered the room, but the actions in the room rarely varied. No one left or broke the routine except to go into what they assumed was the bathroom. Jared sped up the video again as the test subjects slept through the night.

Suddenly, while the morning routine was repeating itself, Ling urged, "Stop. Play right here." She got up and walked closer to the screen and tapped on the image of the young man who had climbed up to the vent. "Look."

Seated at a table with an incomplete puzzle, he reached up to his face and thumbed away a nosebleed. As Ling watched, the young man used the sleeve of his scrubs to wipe at his nose again as the drip became a steady stream. One of his companions rose and hurried over to the bathroom, returning with paper towels. While he tried to stem the now-constant flow, a voice cried out, "What is wrong, Harjit?"

The older man who had intervened yesterday had his head in his hands, moaning, "What is this? What is this?" He lifted his head, and crimson streaked down his wizened cheeks as his eyes bled. "I cannot see!"

Soon, the once-silent room erupted into a cacophony of screams and cries. Another young man doubled over, vomiting, clutching his stomach. Another elderly man moved toward his screaming friend, only to collapse near his chair, convulsing, blood vessels bursting across his skin. A middle-aged man, who appeared unaffected, beat at the door, demanding to be released. More occupants joined him, alternately pulling on the handle and banging on the metal door. To no avail.

"My God," Ling whispered to the room.

Avery turned to her. "Do you know what's happening?"

"I hope not." Ling told Jared to speed up the video, skipping through the horrific images at blur. When play resumed, the pale yellow room contained twenty bodies collapsed across beds, furniture, and the floor. Blood streaked the walls and the exit door, where a tangle of limbs spoke of their final desperate minutes.

From a concealed panel, three people outfitted in masks entered the room. They methodically checked each body, and when they found one person alive, they took a blood sample, checked his blood oxygen level, and swabbed his cheek. Then a second attendant injected the prisoner with a needle. Over the intercom, Ani's voice sounded: "Test Tau one twenty-nine completed. Fourteen dead. Six survivors. All subjects terminated."

The video ended, stilled on the final image of the bunks. "What the living hell just happened?" Noah demanded. "How did they do that?"

"Based on the symptoms, I'm guessing those men were dosed with a bioengineered viral vector that targets haplotypes and edits genes to limit clotting factors," Ling answered hoarsely. "With a side of hemorrhagic fever, like some supercharged version of Ebola or Marburg. But they went from exposure to death in less than thirty-six hours. That's insane."

"How long would it usually take?"

"When the transmission is aerosolized? Maybe up to five days for initial symptoms. I've never seen anything like this."

Shaken, Avery swallowed hard. "See if there's another video, Jared. Please." She and the others waited as he scrolled through the directory.

"There are sixteen more videos," Jared warned. "Labeled Tau one thirty through one forty-five."

Avery clasped her hands, pressing them to her forehead. Ani had told them the truth. More than three hundred people murdered in the name of a perverted science that weaponized their religious heritage. Bile strangled her as she stared at the screen. "You all can go, but I need to watch these. All of them."

No one moved.

They made their way through the horrific videos, until, at Tau 142, an American soldier entered the laboratory and stooped next to a body, his mask firmly in place. A scientist joined him, and he waited silently for the American to speak.

"Control groups?"

"Genetic testing is not foolproof. We have found crossovers in our experimental groups and our controls. However, in nontargeted haplogroups, the incidence rates for the infection are below eight percent. The survival rate among our targets is twenty-four percent."

"And it looks like an aggressive form of Ebola or dengue fever?"

"Exactly."

"Am I at any risk?"

"Not unless you have been lied to about your heritage." The scientist pointed to the concealed panel. "We can continue discussion in the clean room while the attendants see to the test subjects."

In the clean room, both men removed their masks and disrobed. The tall, slim Indian man was a new face. But the American was absolutely familiar.

"My God, that's Vance," Avery said quietly. "That's him. Let's see what else Ani gave us."

Nearly an hour later, Avery's mind was reeling.

They had pored over the files on the drive and handed out assignments for one another. She now had proof of a massive scheme to murder millions, but she couldn't reveal what they'd learned until she figured out what else Justice Wynn had left for her.

They had proof of the crimes against humanity and concrete evidence that the United States had outsourced the project. They had chromosomal grants, the videos, and carefully detailed records saved by Ani. She could prove what Justice Wynn suspected, but the damned man expected even more from her. Until all the riddles were solved, she wasn't finished.

Even if she published Dr. Papaleo's memo and the financial information and showed the video from Dr. Ramji, who was to say anyone would believe what they read and saw? Accusations against governments sprouted like kudzu on the Internet, the lifeblood of conspiracy theorists. Deep fakes had become de rigueur, and gory videos could be produced by anyone. What they had could take years to validate. In the meantime, she would be dismissed as simply one more lunatic media whore who had been discredited and wanted redemption.

"Avery?"

She looked up and saw Noah frowning. "What?"

"I asked, what are we going to tell Agent Lee?"

Wearily, Avery responded, "I don't know yet."

"The information on this drive corroborates the files you received, so we have to give it to Agent Lee," Noah stated flatly. "You're an officer of the Court."

"For God's sake, President Stokes has committed treason," Ling said. "Genocide. We have to tell someone."

"We can't prove that," Avery countered. "We can't really prove anything. All we can show is that Vance is in a video, but without authentication from the authors, no court will accept it. We don't know if this goes anywhere above Vance. Again, based on documents we cannot authenticate, the only thing we can confirm is that the money and direction were from Homeland Security and that Vance is involved, based—again—on a video that could be faked. And not one shred of evidence implicates the president yet."

She had most of the pieces—the pawns, the rooks, the bishops. But she couldn't quite maneuver around the strongest pieces left on the board. Vance was protecting the king. She had reached a stalemate.

"Until we have a plan that lets us use what we've found, we can't move."

"Agreed," Jared said. "But we know we're right. My contact at the Pentagon came through and confirmed it—prior to joining the Secret Service, Major Vance served in the CBIRF." He named the unit in a tight, hard voice. "He's a highly skilled specialist whose bread and butter in the military was figuring out ways to anticipate the next anthrax or sarin gas attack."

Ling asked, "What happened?"

"Apparently, while stationed in Afghanistan, he met a group of scientists working on a special project for a company in India. They'd posited that biogenetic weapons could be developed to target religious groups based on common ancestry. Vance brought it to his superiors; and six weeks later, he was stateside with a military pension and an honorable discharge."

"Is that how he ended up in the Secret Service?" asked Avery.

"Seems so. The Service assigned him to the detail of an old friend—a young U.S. senator running on the ticket as vice president, who previously served a tour with him in the Gulf."

"Stokes and Vance. Like minds."

"Exactly. He links up with then-senator Stokes and, once they take the White House, Vance gets assigned to the Science and Technology Directorate at DHS, which has the authority to disburse funds to foreign entities for research, including chromosomal projects. Then President Cadres dies, and Stokes becomes president."

"President Stokes. Major Vance. The full weight of Homeland Security and the White House," Avery muttered. "All I've got are some documents written by a missing employee who may have stolen government materials, which were likely emailed to me by the man who stands to benefit if his company joins forces with Hygeia's successor. Authenticated by a renegade scientist who has vanished again."

Ling looked at her best friend. "That's some desk job you have, Avery. What do you want to do?"

"We wait. If we don't, under the best-case scenario, you three find yourselves living under armed guard for a few months until there's a trial, while I'm held in custody in a federal detention center. It won't matter that you don't know where the information came from or what happened. You'll be material witnesses.

"After weeks and weeks, they might strike you from a witness list, but President Stokes and his lawyers and DHS will have your names. They'll know you spoke with the FBI and with DOJ. Which means your lives as you live them are over. No more medicine for Ling. No more security firm for Jared. No more corporate law firm for Noah. You'll find yourselves mysteriously blackballed, assuming you don't spend three to five years of your lives unraveling mistakes on your licenses and fending off lawsuits. Or worse.

"And Jared." She leaned in, facing him closely. "They'll kill your father. Just like they killed Jamie Lewis."

"I don't understand why we can't trust Agent Lee," Noah offered quietly. "We're out of our league here. He seems to be on our side."

"I like him, Noah. I do. But anyone who works for the federal government has to be suspect. We just saw Major Vance blithely check on the murder of hundreds of Muslims, and he has access to everything I say or do. I'm not just worried about Agent Lee for our sakes; I'm afraid for him."

Jared nodded in agreement. "Noah, I know why you suggested giving this evidence to Agent Lee, but I agree it's a mistake. He's an FBI agent, not a miracle worker. Nothing this big can be kept hidden by the FBI. They might be able to offer witness protection, but there's nowhere we can hide that DHS can't find us."

Jared turned to Avery. "You're in an impossible spot—but you'll figure out what to do. My father trusted you for a reason. Look at how much you've figured out already."

"Look at how many people have died." She dipped her head, her voice low. "Okay, we keep gathering evidence. And we're not telling the FBI or anyone else. Not yet. Agreed."

Ling nodded, as did Noah.

"Let's get back to work."

The team spent the next hour focused on their assignments. Jared had outfitted each of them with laptops that encrypted their data and searches, and he'd established an autonomous VPN to keep their activities hidden from anyone hunting for digital fingerprints.

Avery finally closed her computer. "I've got to clear my head, and I need to visit Justice Wynn at the hospital. Maybe while I'm there, I'll figure out what his letter is trying to tell me." She'd just stood up, ready to ask the protective agent outside to arrange for a ride, when her phone rang. Avery wanted to ignore the summons and didn't recognize the number, but she answered out of caution.

A man's scratchy voice said, "I want to talk to Avery Keene."

"This is she." Unable to place him, she asked, "Who is this?"

"I'm the person who has your mother. Say hello, Rita."

"Baby? Oh, God, I'm sorry. So sorry." Her voice was small.

A strangled cry reached Avery's ears. "Momma?"

"Don't do it, Avery," Rita cried. "Whatever they want—"

The crack of a hand against flesh carried as clearly as a voice. "That's not what I told you to say, Rita."

"What do you want?" Avery demanded as her hand clenched the phone. Ling steadied her while Noah rushed to the door to get Agent Leighton.

Jared stopped him with a hand on his arm. "Wait."

"You have a simple choice, Ms. Keene. By tomorrow at five p.m., either Howard Wynn dies or your mother does."

FORTY-FOUR

The phone fell from Avery's nerveless fingers. *What have I done?* A single, devastating answer reverberated through her taut body. She'd protected everyone except the woman who gave her life. Because of her, Rita would die unless she killed the man she'd just fought to save.

She stared blindly at the carpet and marveled that her knees held her upright still. As if waiting for the cue, they gave way beneath her. Blackness encroached as she went down hard, her limp body doing nothing to stop the fall.

"Jared!" Ling caught and half dragged a trembling Avery to the sofa. Her light brown skin had gone chalky. Ling shifted to track her friend's pulse. Way too fast, just like the stuttering breaths coming from lungs that sounded desperate for air. Plucking up Avery's hand, Ling found the skin clammy, and the fingers moved restively in her hold. Ling diagnosed the basic symptoms of shock in a woman whose stoicism was rivaled by no one she'd ever known.

Jared knelt beside her, brushing her forehead with his fingers. "Who was on the phone, Avery?"

"He's got her." The admission escaped on a strangled whisper. She shuddered once, her throat a desert choked with sand. "He said they'll kill her."

He braced a hand at her shoulder, as much for stability as comfort. The fragments of the call came together. "Someone has taken your mother?"

"He said he had Rita. She was crying." Avery could hear the crack of his hand against Rita's cheek, and her eyes squeezed closed as she remembered the horror. "He hit her when she told me not to do it."

Ling caught Jared's look. "Not to do what, Avery?"

"Kill your father." *Didn't I tell them already?* The thought was distant, remote. Murder Justice Wynn to save Rita. Her entire body had gone numb, but not her mind. Her thoughts spun like a crazed pinwheel, retracing every step, every decision. *Every mistake.*

Why hadn't she seen this coming and demanded more protection for Rita? When the FBI had failed to find her, she'd thought nothing of it. Nothing of her missing mother while she hunted for killers and protected a dead man.

"My fault. This is my fault."

"Avery, focus."

All Avery could hear were internal accusations, loud and damning. She'd sent her mother away the last time. Outside her apartment, when all Rita wanted was money. She'd sent her away and let them take her.

"Avery." Jared framed her face to hold her attention. "You're whispering. I can't understand you. What exactly did they say to you?"

"They want me to kill him." Stricken, she gripped his wrist in a vise. "If I don't take Justice Wynn off life support by five p.m. tomorrow, they'll kill her. Vance will kill my mother."

Jared's curse punctured the air as he sprang up from the sofa. A couple of strides carried him to the door. "Stay with her," he told Ling. "I'll call Agent Lee."

"No!" Avery lunged from the couch, her eyes wild. "No FBI."

"You can't be serious." Ling stood as well. "I know you're terrified, Avery, but this isn't the time for us to go it alone."

"This is my mother's life, Ling!"

The quiet, bald statement had Jared lifting his hand from the doorknob. "And my father's. What are you going to do?"

Avery headed for the window that overlooked the cars streaming by on the interstate. Somewhere out there, beyond the twists of asphalt, men were holding her mother for a life's ransom. Again, Rita's sobs ripped through her, and she laid her forehead against the cool glass. "I don't know."

"We'll get her back, Avery," Jared said.

She lifted her gaze to meet Jared's. Fresh guilt twisted. His father for her mother. "How?"

"I don't know yet."

Her brain swirled with recrimination and fear, doubling and redoubling on itself. She was missing something. She, who had made her way by always being able to outthink the others. Didn't matter who. But now, when her mother's life was at stake, she couldn't hold a steady thought. Rita would die because of it. But Rita couldn't die. She wouldn't lose them both—Rita and Justice Wynn. *Save them.*

Then, suddenly, the solution dawned on her. She took another breath, this one steadying and determined. "I do know." Her lips drew down into a flat, menacing line. Justice Wynn had picked her for a reason: because she was more than book-smart; she had street smarts. And she didn't scare easy. Shoving aside the panic that still threatened to strangle her, Avery murmured, "I've got the documents. Leverage."

Jared rejected the idea. "Even if you return the documents, there's nothing to stop you from implicating Stokes later. They need my father off the bench so Stokes can name his replacement. Hold the Court hostage until he gets the votes he needs."

"Which is why I know that killing Justice Wynn won't get my mother back." She spoke the truth aloud, acknowledging what had already occurred to Jared. "If they know I have proof, their only recourse is to finish all of us."

Noah spoke for the first time: "The Chief as much as admitted that the Court wouldn't move without you taking action. The president and Vance are desperate. They've got no choice but to come after us."

"To tie up loose ends." Jared added, "They'll probably set a meetup for Avery. Lure her in and take both her and Rita out. The three of us will be next."

Ling's gasp was matched by Noah's imprecation. "What in the hell can we do? Either way, we're dead. We're out of options."

"No, we're not." Avery moved past Jared and made her way to the door. "Agent Leighton?"

"Yes?"

"We need to go out. Now."

The agent reached for her communicator. "Where to?"

"Bethesda Naval Hospital."

.　　.　　.

Ling and Noah sat in the waiting room, joined by Agent Leighton. Down the hall, Avery and Jared entered Justice Wynn's hospital room. The muted whirring of respirator and monitors provided the only sound.

"He looks so frail," Jared murmured. This was his first time seeing Justice Wynn in the hospital. His image of his father, a vibrant force of a man, had been winnowed away, replaced by the sickly, wiry body prostrate on a bed that looked too large for him. "Like a different man."

A cue tripped in Avery's brain, but she couldn't quite access the message. She murmured the lines from the letter: "*If I had accepted absurdity and given smallpox to my child, I would not be mourning him today.* It's not quite right."

"We've searched for the phrases, Avery. No one said it."

She raked her hand through her hair. "Smallpox refers to you, to Boursin's. He blames himself for passing it on to you. The atrocity is the research conducted by Hygeia. But he had no connection to them."

"No connection? He knew what our government did, but he still kept his mouth shut and never told anyone what he'd found." Jared added grimly, "None of this would be happening if he'd recused himself and revealed the truth. No one should have died."

"He had an answer, Jared. All I have to do is find it."

"There's nowhere else to look."

"There must be." She'd dissected the letter and every bit of information she'd collected. The riddle, she thought, had been too clever. Perhaps more clever than she was. "I don't know where else to look, but there's an answer. He would tell me that we're in the endgame now. The most important pieces are in play, and I've got only a few moves left."

"What are they? Because I'm not seeing many."

Avery hesitated. "Your father taught me more than any professor about the law and reasoning. This puzzle is like a ruling. Usually, we get the case and we let the record and the questions guide the answer. But when he has a long-standing posture on an issue, it's up to his clerks to find the evidence to support the outcome."

"How would you do that?"

"Research." What she'd done nonstop since the day she learned her new role. "I've read case law and journal articles and unpublished rulings on every aspect of this issue. I don't know where else to look."

Jared returned his gaze to his father. "Maybe you're going too deep."

"In what way?"

He thought quietly for a moment. "When we used to go to the cabin, I'd beg him to take us out in a boat. Then, after we got a ways from the dock, I'd pester him to go even farther out. So far we could barely see the cabin."

"And he wouldn't?"

"Nope. I remember one time, I threw a fit and threatened to jump out of the boat and swim to the center of the lake."

"I can only imagine his reaction."

Jared smiled fondly. "He didn't tell me no. But he warned me that I might not be ready for what would happen. That while I was a strong swimmer, sometimes the question wasn't what a person could do. It was what waited in the unknown. The judge said that the wisest minds understand not simply the depths and the surface, but everything in between."

"The space in between."

"Yes, the space in between." A rueful grin quirked his lips. "I always thought it meant he was too lazy to row that far or too stingy to buy a motorboat."

Her mind returned to the strange conversation in his office all those months ago. *The space in between. Eighteenth-century physicians. Just quit and suffer the consequences. French literature.* "God, I know where it is."

"Where what is?"

"The clue. The last clue. It's at his house." Avery leaned past Jared to stroke the immobile arm that lay on the sheet. "Justice Wynn, I've got it."

The alarm trilled as Avery punched in the code. Jared followed her inside, trailed by Noah and Ling. They looked at Jared as they entered the house.

"Do we know what she's looking for?" Noah asked Jared.

"She does." At least, he assumed she did. She'd been mostly silent on the ride over, only asking that he call the others, and he could fairly hear her mind working. They entered the library, and she headed for the far wall of books. He joined her, staying a few paces away. "Can we help you look?"

"No. I've got it." She walked along the shelves, tracing titles as she went. Midway across, she stopped. Slowly, she inched out a volume. The cover was dusky rose, embossed with gold lettering. "Voltaire."

"Why are you looking for a French philosopher?" Jared came alongside her. "How will he help us figure out what the judge wanted?"

"It's not Voltaire," Avery explained as she opened the book. The spine creaked slightly as she opened it. The book fell open to reveal a hollowed-out segment. "It's not Voltaire. It's the space in between." With a murmur of triumph, she identified the contents—an envelope addressed to Ms. Avery Keene and a plastic bag.

"How did you know where to look?" Jared asked, amazed.

"François-Marie Arouet, better known as the French philosopher Voltaire. He wrote thousands of works, including essays on scientific experiments in the eighteenth century during the Enlightenment period." As she spoke, she moved to the desk in the library. She set the volume on the desktop and rummaged for a letter opener, aware of the three pairs of eyes that followed her. "When Justice Wynn called me into his office in January, he asked me about my studies in college."

"Which one?" Ling teased. "You had a dozen majors."

"Six. Including, for one semester at Oberlin, a major in French. In his office, he asked me my favorite French writer."

"Voltaire?" Noah joined her at the desk. "But how did you leap from that to this?"

Avery located an opener and slit through the envelope. "Ling told us about European physicians and their disdain for inoculation. Voltaire once wrote an essay on the women of Circassia who also performed primitive inoculations on their children. He'd also written about infamy, and how those in power convinced the rest of us to ignore their violence and accept it as good. I'd forgotten about it, but my memory hadn't. Justice Wynn knew I'd remember it eventually."

The bag contained a pill bottle, with the word *FINGERPRINTS* written across the bag in black marker. She ignored the bottle and instead slit open the envelope, removing a single sheet of paper. Her attention immediately focused on the signature scrawled at the bottom. "This is what he had me sign in his office. What he had me witness," she explained as she skimmed the contents. As she suspected, Justice Wynn had anticipated this final act. "This is what Ani sent him. He couldn't quit without atoning first."

She handed the letter to Jared. "This is how we're going to save my mother and your father. And bring down the president."

FORTY-FIVE

At Avery's apartment, Agent Leighton punched the button on the newly secured elevator and radioed their position down to the idling Expedition. The doors slid open, and she led them down the short hall, her charges buffered by additional men brought in for the occasion. Following Lee's protocol, she used Avery's key to get inside, motioning for them to stay on the threshold while she checked out the interior.

"All clear." Agent Leighton emerged from the bathroom. "We'll be outside, Ms. Keene."

"Thank you." Avery found her apartment in pristine condition. Even the dishes she'd left in the washer had been put through their cycles. "Home sweet home."

"Are you sure it's safe to be here?" Ling asked the prearranged question, but the note of fear was real.

Avery walked into the kitchen and filled a glass with water. "Agent Lee said we'd be fine." She took a gulp, readying for her act. "Do you think I made a mistake?"

"By not telling the FBI about your mom?" Jared asked on cue. "No, you have no choice. We have no idea who has her and what the kidnappers would do if the feds got involved."

"I know you're right, but maybe he could help me figure out who has her. Maybe I could negotiate."

"With what?" Noah asked. "You've got no leverage, Avery."

With the listening devices transmitting every word, Avery replied, "I could resign him from the Court. As his guardian, I can take any actions I deem necessary for his protection. I can't imagine President Stokes refusing to accept his resignation. Then whoever wants him off the Court will have what they want."

"Would that really work?" The question came from Ling. "Can she resign a Supreme Court justice from his position, Noah?"

"I don't see why not," he answered thoughtfully. "Legal guardians have pretty broad powers. As long as she can demonstrate that resigning is in his best interests, she's on solid ground. Besides, who'd protest it? Celeste wanted him dead."

"And I don't want to lose him to save your mother." Jared had been assigned the trigger line. "All of this is a moot issue, though, if we can't get in touch with the men who have your mom. The five-o'clock deadline is only twenty-four hours away."

"I can't kill him." Avery made the plea to the hidden microphones, her voice cracking slightly. "They have to call."

"How's Mrs. Keene?" Vance entered the warehouse. The rank odor from the river seeped into every board and crevice.

Phillips sat on an overturned crate and reassembled his firearm. "She won't shut up."

In the corner, Rita whimpered steadily. "Please," she begged of the new voice in the darkened space. Her blindfold shut out time and reality, but her hearing told her she had another opportunity to make her plea. Turning her head blindly toward the footfalls, she pleaded, "Don't do this to Avery. She's a good girl. Don't make her kill that man for me."

"I may not have to." Vance crouched next to Rita. "Your daughter is a fine attorney. Brilliant. She came up with one solution none of us thought of."

Phillips turned to his boss. "You think it will work?"

"It should. All we want is Justice Wynn off the Court now. The vote will remain split, Congress will have to go on recess, and President Stokes will make an appointment in August. Our man will caucus with the other four, and GenWorks will be dead."

Phillips scowled. "What about the others? They know too much."

"I imagine there will be a tragic fire in her apartment while they are visiting. Old buildings catch fire often in the early summer. We can dump our guest's body there, for effect."

In her corner, Rita's whimpers faded to the occasional sob. Vance heard the shift to utter despair. "You'll die with your daughter, Mrs. Keene. Family should stay together."

Less than a minute before midnight, Avery answered her cell phone. "Avery Keene."

"I have a proposal for you." Vance had engaged the voice modulator. On his wrist, he set a timer. Any trace on the cell line would ping a number of towers, which gave him sufficient time for his task. "At seven in the morning, you will call the White House at this number." He rattled off digits that rang directly to the Oval Office. "Request a meeting with President Brandon Stokes."

Avery scoffed. "The president won't take my call."

"He'll take this one if you tell his assistant that you wish to resign Justice Howard Wynn from the U.S. Supreme Court."

"What? How did you know about that?" The tremors in her voice didn't have to be faked.

"Do you want your mother alive, or do you want to haggle over your right to privacy?"

"If I offer his resignation and the president accepts, you'll let Rita go?"

"You have my word."

Unable to resist, Avery inquired, "The word of honor of a kidnapper? Please."

"Don't question my word of honor, Ms. Keene. I uphold my pledges."

"I apologize." Avery spoke quickly, afraid she'd overplayed. "I'm just scared for my mother. I'm sorry."

"Be very careful. Seven a.m., or I return to my original demand."

"I'll contact the president," Avery swore. "And then I get my mother?"

"Fair trade." The alarm buzzed. "Tomorrow."

The phone disconnected and Avery leaned forward, elbows propped on her knees, head in hands. A firm hand closed over her hunched shoulders. Ten minutes later, she sat up, her eyes clear. "Status?"

"I've almost got it," Jared told her, pointing to the laptop he'd rigged to track the call to her phone. In his hand, he held the jammer that would block all surveillance equipment for the next thirty seconds, sending the listener ambient noises and fuzzing the signal from the cameras. "According to the signal, the call bounced around a number of cell towers, but I'm fairly certain Rita is near."

Avery released a shaky breath. "God, forgive me."

"For what?" Jared sat beside her on the bed. "For saving two lives?"

"For not letting the FBI go and rescue her now."

"Do what you must," he forced himself to say.

Avery knew better, knew his father's life rested in her hands. "She'll be safe until tomorrow," she reminded herself. She was in a Philidor position, where she'd run out of moves for a victory. Instead, outmatched, she had to play for a draw. In the endgame, there were only two real options: win or stay alive. For now, staying alive had to be paramount for all of them. "If the FBI storms the location now, the rest of the plan falls apart. We have to wait."

FORTY-SIX

Monday, June 26

R eady." In all her imaginings, Avery had never expected to be
huddled on her sofa over a phone, waiting for an audience with
the president of the United States. Noah and Ling hovered at
her shoulder. Jared leaned in the doorway to the bathroom, his impatience fairly palpable.

At precisely seven a.m., she dialed the number from Vance. Soon, a
polite, well-trained voice greeted her. In seconds, she hopscotched over
layers of protocol to reach the Oval Office. If worry for her mother
hadn't occupied every corner of her mind not concerned with the failure
of her plan, she might have been impressed with herself.

As it was, a permanent case of nausea jitterbugged with nerve-searing
apprehension. Which metastasized into unadulterated panic when President Stokes greeted her.

"Ms. Avery Keene. You're almost as famous as I am."

Pundits raptured at President Stokes's capacity to infuse the recita-
tion of a name with an intimacy that left the listener certain of her
unique place in his world. That ability translated itself into devoted vol-
unteers and throngs of voters who failed to heed the clarion calls from a
bewildered press dutifully chronicling his misdeeds. Under Stokes, the
common touch had supplanted common sense in droves, driven by a
mellifluous gift of charm.

This pleased him immensely. "How can I help you, Avery?"

Avery discovered that she was not immune. Her skin warmed, and she took a deep breath that sputtered out when she spoke. "President Stokes. Thank you for taking the time to talk with me this morning."

"I can't say I expected to hear from you." A statement belied by Vance's skulking presence in his office, his ear pressed to an extension. "However, given your newfound responsibilities—and your access to a rather private number—I thought I should take your call. How can I help?"

"This is an awkward conversation, Mr. President." The wobble of her voice required no pretense as she explained, "My mother is in trouble, and I think you can help me. I hope."

"Let's take it one step at a time. What's happened?"

"Yesterday, a man contacted me. He told me my mother was being held hostage. In exchange for her life, he told me I'd have to commit an unconscionable act."

Relishing his role, President Stokes flipped through the dossier Vance had provided for the morning's exchange. Press clippings and rehab reports told a nasty, pathetic tale. "I hate to be indelicate, but your mother is a drug addict, isn't she? Could this have been an attempt to extort some money she owed to dealers? She interacts with a vicious lot, I'd imagine. I hope you've learned from her mistakes. I'd hate to have the Court sullied at this vulnerable time."

The flush dissipated. Her tone was icy as she reminded him, "My mother has her faults, sir, but no one deserves to be used this way. Not even an addict."

"Certainly not," he permitted graciously. "But one must be wary of the company you keep. As my grandfather told me more than once, you lay down with dogs, you get up with fleas."

Explains why my skin is crawling, Avery thought acidly. "The man who has my mother isn't interested in money, Mr. President. He has a very specific goal, and he directed me to do something heinous in exchange for her life."

" 'Heinous'?" The word galled him, and he ground his perfectly straight teeth in offense. *Heinous* was a word for terrorists and madmen. Not for a man willing to sacrifice his political future to protect his country. Vance caught his eye, and he restrained himself, with effort. "What does he want, Avery?"

"He insisted I use my guardianship of Justice Wynn to terminate life support."

"That seems rather sophisticated for drug dealers." Stokes prided himself on the twin notes of shock and disgust. Outrage came next, a bluster of sound that covered his internal laughter. He'd have what he wanted soon. A matter of hours. "I blame these left-wing ideologues! Imagine, extorting you to use euthanasia to advance their agenda." A fist pounded on the desk for effect.

Vance had warned him to play up his astonishment and to lay false leads where possible. According to the agent, blogs across the Internet already carried incendiary messages ordering the death of Justice Wynn. Should Avery decide to turn to the FBI for aid, no trails would lead anywhere near the White House, except for his coming act of chivalry. "I'll double the protection on him at the hospital. Bring you in to speak with Homeland Security and the FBI. My liaison, Major Vance, will be in touch with you this morning."

"Thank you, sir." She'd spoken to Will Vance more than enough to suit her. The next time she saw him, she planned for it to be a perp walk out of DHS. "I appreciate the extra protection for Justice Wynn, but I proposed an alternative to the kidnapper last night, and he seemed amenable." She let her voice drift into uncertainty. "I spoke with a friend of mine, who is also an attorney. We think that if I resign on Justice Wynn's behalf, and you accept it, they'll get what they want."

"Justice Wynn off the bench."

"Yes, sir." *You son of a bitch,* she thought. She'd been certain before, but the smug note of satisfaction sealed it. "Would you be willing to do that, sir? If I tender his resignation, will you publicly accept it today?"

"Well, now, I'll need to run this past White House counsel. We want to do this right." Which is why he'd keep the Justice Department in the dark for now. His busybody of an attorney general had grown increasingly shrill about legal matters, and Vance had warned him to keep this away from any of the folks in the Hoover Building. "It'll take a couple of hours, most likely."

"I understand, sir. So you'll do it?"

A heavy pause followed, then, "Yes, Avery. With a heavy heart and deep regret, I will accept his letter of resignation."

"Thank you so much, sir. Should I bring the letter myself?"

"I'll make sure they know to let you right in." Sighing deeply, he added, "Keep sending up those prayers, Avery. Your mother will be safe."

Though the words nearly strangled her, she repeated, "Thank you, sir."

President Stokes disconnected the call and rocked triumphantly in his chair. A weight lifted, he spun around to Vance, barely containing his glee. Already, he could see the coverage on the evening news. "We should hold a press conference. A formal announcement on the South Lawn. The Keene girl is quite lovely. I'm sure she'll look bereft, which is excellent for camera feeds."

"Sir."

Busy planning, the president bounded to his feet and folded his hands behind himself. "I want the Speaker and the majority leader here for the press conference. Rub my triumph in their faces. My conservative base will be delighted, and the liberals will just have to suck it up. Their lion has been neutered. Again. I'll get my appointee on the Court this summer and be reelected by fall. I will have Bible-thumping, strict constructionists who believe that *Miranda* coddles criminals. The Right Reverend Donaldson can brush off his law degree."

"Sir," Vance tried again. "A press conference would be ill-advised."

Stokes glowered across the room. "Why? Because I thought of it?"

"It is a brilliant suggestion were we not trying to keep the spotlight off you," Vance corrected smoothly. The resignation solution, which had seemed inspired last night, had begun to worry him. He'd prefer a hand-off in the privacy of the Oval Office, not a media spectacle that provided B-roll for the news cameras to play later. Couching his opposition as strategy, he explained, "Hold a press conference, and you give the girl a chance to plead for her mother's safe return or some heartstring crap that will undercut your message."

Stokes wasn't impressed. Flicking a hand, he instructed, "Then you'll call and tell her not to breathe a word until she gets her crack whore safely in her arms again."

Avery dressed carefully for the press conference. Word had come minutes past noon. Bring the letter of resignation, witnessed and notarized, to the White House at three p.m. Noah's assistant had come over to stamp and seal the simple five-line statement.

They'd continued their performance the entire time, speaking in hushed tones of grief and dismay at the end of an era. Avery smoothed the slim black skirt, dusted on powder at her cheeks. Performing, like hustling, was one of Rita's tools, but Avery had learned well.

Ready for Act II, she exited the bathroom and motioned to Jared. He jammed the frequency, and she made a new call.

"Nigel Cooper."

"Avery Keene."

"Ah, the famous woman herself." In North Carolina, Nigel motioned to Indira, who crossed to his desk. He engaged the speaker on his phone. "To what do I owe the honor?"

"I need to speak with you."

"Why?"

"To give you what you want."

"We want our merger to succeed. Can you deliver that?"

"Come to DC, and I'll tell you how." Avery waited a beat, then added, "I'll require Dr. Srinivasan as well."

He didn't ask how she knew Indira's role, but Avery had proven herself quite adept at unraveling mysteries. "By when?"

"Tomorrow morning."

"That's impossible," Nigel hedged. "She's in India."

"You're rich. Figure it out."

Nigel read Indira's look of refusal. "I can't do that," he said. "We can't risk that kind of exposure until the Court rules."

"I'm not negotiating. I'll expect to see you and Dr. Srinivasan in DC tomorrow. The St. Regis hotel. I'll meet you at seven a.m."

"And if we don't comply?"

"Watch the news today, Mr. Cooper. I'll see you in the morning."

Avery ended the call, and Jared prepped his tracking program. The jammer cycled off, and when he nodded, she said, "Noah, I'm having second thoughts. How do we know he'll deliver my mother like he promised? Once I turn over the letter, that's it. We're screwed."

"You don't have a choice. Without this resignation, they'll kill her. You've done everything you can."

"I can't do it." She let her voice rise, the pitch thready and sharp. "I can't trade them both without knowing for sure. Call the White House. Tell them I'm having second thoughts. I'll get Agent Lee and tell him everything. Maybe he can help us find Rita."

"Avery—"

The jangle of her phone came instantly. "Avery Keene."

"Ms. Keene, this is the man who has your mother."

The voice modulator engaged, Phillips wiped at his brow, the sultry heat of the early summer heightened by the confines of the warehouse. At Vance's orders, he'd been cooped up inside all day with the whimpering, jonesing Rita. Nothing, he decided, was worse than a terrified junkie going through the DTs. He'd amused himself by monitoring the chatter inside the Keene apartment, lucky for Vance. Hearing Avery's threat to call the FBI had propelled him into action. "We wanted to make sure you were going to keep your promise about today."

Avery cut a look to Jared, who rolled his finger in a loop, cautioning her to draw out the conversation. On the screen, she could see a red dot and thin red circles fluttering in a pattern. A perimeter for the location of the call. With their earlier data and his military-grade equipment, Jared had targeted signals coming from southern DC. All he needed was another minute, and he'd have a location.

"I spoke with the president," Avery told the man, whose cadence sounded slightly off. This wasn't Vance. "But I have to know how I'll get Rita back. When will you release her?"

"As soon as President Stokes announces that Justice Wynn no longer sits on the Court, we'll release her."

"That's not good enough," Avery protested. "She'll be sick. Disoriented."

"Excuse me?"

"Unless you've been supplying her, she's coming down hard." If the past was any guide, the combination of anxiety and forced sobriety would cripple Rita. "I want to come and get her."

"Out of the question. This isn't a negotiation, miss. When you've delivered on your end of the deal, we'll put your mother back where we found her."

"Where was that?" She sliced a look to Jared, who warned her that he needed ten more seconds. "Where did you find her?"

"A dive bar in the gutter, Ms. Keene. She's your mom. You find her."

Phillips checked over his shoulder; Rita had curled into a ball. Sweat matted the skimpy T-shirt, the frazzled hair. "Keep your appointment, or she won't see the light of day again." The call disconnected.

Avery spun toward Jared as the red dot began to flash in triumph.

Typing on the screen, he wrote, "We've found her. She's in a warehouse on the Southwest Waterfront."

"Thank God," she whispered; then the jammer went dim. "I don't know what to do," she pitched.

"Do what the man says." Ling began to gather up their bags. "You should head over to the White House. I'll go with you."

"I'm not coming," Jared said briskly. "I understand why you have to do this, but I can't watch you give away my father's legacy."

"Noah?"

"Protecting Justice Wynn's final wishes is my job. I can't help you do this, Avery."

Perfect performances. Avery opened the door, where Agent Leighton stood at attention. "Agent, I'll need to go to the White House. Now."

Ling and Avery followed Agent Leighton, with Noah and Jared close behind. Downstairs, in the service alley, they all climbed into the SUV. Safely away from microphones, Avery used the burner phone and punched in Agent Lee's cell phone number.

"This is Special Agent Lee."

"It's Avery. I'm on my way to the White House."

"What the devil for?"

"To tender Justice Wynn's resignation to President Stokes. There's a press conference in thirty minutes."

"What game are you playing, Avery?"

"I'm saving my mother's life. Here's how you can help."

FORTY-SEVEN

Faithfully tended flowers bloomed in an organized profusion of crimson and purple around the soft ripples of the fountain, spurred by jets of spray arcing in symphony. Majestic trees, planted by gardeners long since passed, towered over the stretch of manicured green. The quickly assembled press corps jockeyed for angles and scanned the wisps of clouds overhead for unexpected but not unusual late June showers.

Brandon Stokes loved the South Lawn. He loved jogging across the grass to climb into Marine One, his private helicopter. He loved to host fawning children at Easter, watching their parents try to disguise their awe at hunting for candy eggs at the president's house. He loved striding up to the pewter lectern, clasping the sides, and commanding the attention of a nation.

No way in hell a fucking law clerk was going to cost him all of that. The thought seared through him as he gallantly led Avery and her friend down to the lectern. Flashbulbs popped like firecrackers, their progeny in digital no match for the trusted Speed Graphic camera.

His press secretary arrayed the young women to his right, his good side; his congressional foes stiffly flanked him on the left. President Stokes stepped up to the twin blue microphones stretching above the Great Seal. His notes had been laid out for him, but he'd rehearsed his delivery and had the language down cold. A hush greeted him.

"Good afternoon. Early last week, a tragedy struck America. Supreme Court justice Howard Wynn was discovered unconscious, and he was rushed to Bethesda Naval Hospital. Despite the efforts of the nation's top medical teams, Justice Wynn lapsed into a persistent coma, a side effect of the degenerative disorder known as Boursin's syndrome. Prior to falling ill, Justice Wynn appointed his trusted law clerk, Ms. Avery Keene, to serve as his legal guardian. She has diligently met that obligation, and her sincere devotion to her duty brings us here today."

He paused, letting attention shift from him to the surprisingly stoic young woman standing in black a pace behind him. Her expression was oddly serene, a blend of acceptance and anticipation. After waiting another beat, he continued: "The Supreme Court has been paralyzed by Justice Wynn's absence, and the gears of justice have ground to a halt. As you know, Article Three of the U.S. Constitution does not acknowledge the potential for a sitting justice to be brought low by an illness that does not also take his life. Nothing in the Framers' experience contemplated the medical miracles we enjoy today.

"Justice Wynn will remain on life support, and his life expectancy could stretch over decades. While we pray that medical science will use that time to cure this great man, the work of the Court must continue. And so, it is with a heavy heart that I accepted this afternoon Justice Wynn's resignation from the Supreme Court, proffered by his legal guardian. This resignation is effective immediately."

"Mr. President!"

The shouted title buffeted the trio at the lectern. Used to the barrage, President Stokes pointed into the crowd. "Ashley, you have a question?"

"Thank you, Mr. President. Under what legal precedent can Ms. Keene resign for Justice Wynn?"

"According to the White House counsel's research, Ms. Keene's action is supported by the generally broad powers of guardianship. She has the obligation to act in Justice Wynn's best interest."

"Excuse me, sir, but how is this in his best interest? It appears to serve your interests more."

President Stokes froze for a moment, then gave a deprecating smile. "Justice Wynn and I certainly did not agree on many of his positions, but I respect the man's commitment to the law. Ms. Keene does not believe he would want to stand in the way of the Court's operations, especially so close to the end of a critical term. Several opinions remain to be issued, and without his participation, justice may be delayed. I think he'd feel—as Ms. Keene does—that to do so is contrary to his oath as an officer of the law." Pivoting away from her, he indicated another reporter. "Ben?"

"Mr. President, as you just pointed out, the Supreme Court only has four days remaining in term, then it and the Congress go on recess. Without Justice Wynn, the Court will sit at eight members, and we know that he was the swing vote on a number of issues. What exactly will this resignation accomplish?"

"It will provide clarity for the Court and permit the immediate search for a worthy successor to Justice Wynn."

"You believe Congress will confirm a successor that quickly?"

President Stokes inclined his head at the majority leader. "I think Congress will do what's in the best interest of the nation. Look, the Supreme Court can extend its term if it chooses. The June term is tradition, but if they wish to go longer, they can. With the critical issue of an empty seat, I'm certain Congress will act swiftly in the interest of justice." Let the reporters figure out that he could simply make the appointment while the legislature enjoyed the Fourth of July. His very own Oliver Wendell Holmes. He nodded to a friendly face. "Sophie?"

"Mr. President, have you already developed a short list for the spot?"

"I have not. Last question. Casey?"

"Thank you, sir. Is Ms. Keene denying rumors of drug use and"—he checked his notebook—"allegations that she was detained by the FBI over the weekend to prevent her from exercising undue influence over Justice Wynn? And isn't the White House concerned about the DC probate court's decision to recognize her guardianship instead of his wife, Celeste Turner-Wynn, who is a friend of your family?"

"Judge McAdoo found no cause to remove Ms. Keene as guardian, and that is the end of the matter, as far as the White House is concerned. This resignation will accomplish a fitting resolution for all involved. Those cases hanging in limbo will have their final answers, which is the job of the Court."

"Including the challenge to your presidential authority by Nigel Cooper?"

President Stokes gave a thin smile. "The Court will undoubtedly rule on the role of the president in discerning national security. This isn't a schoolyard fight. It is a matter of protecting this nation. But yes, I believe the Court will recognize that a ruling would be most prudent."

"Ms. Keene, will you respond to allegations about your relationship with Justice Wynn?"

Before the president could stop her, Avery stepped forward and touched his arm. Nonplussed, he glared at her.

"If I may?" she asked sotto voce.

Prepared to make her first and last statement to the press, she waited while President Stokes reluctantly yielded the lectern. She cleared her throat once, then a second time. "Justice Howard Wynn has been my mentor and my employer. Nothing more. Any rumors to the contrary besmirch the reputation of a man who has spent his life in service of this nation. For printing those lies, you should be ashamed—except that Justice Wynn would support the right of a free press to print any opprobrium, especially about him, as long as it used a good adjective or nice turn of phrase."

An appreciative laugh came from a reporter in the front row, and others joined for a few seconds. Then Avery continued: "He despised the willingness of the powerful to prey upon the weak. He found the use of authority in the pursuit of illegal acts to be contemptible. In an age of terrorism, he held fast to the notion of freedom, refusing to permit desperation to rob us of our humanity."

Her eyes hardened, as did her tone. "His core belief held that the pursuit of right should not end at the courthouse steps but must prevail when all other avenues have been blocked. He celebrated the nuance of law, its supple ability to cure impossible ailments. Even as we mourn his illness, we must cheer his dedication to service. What I do here today will provide a clear path to his most sacred principle—justice."

She turned away as questions pelted her. An irate and upstaged President Stokes flicked a pissed look to the press secretary, who came to the lectern. "A statement will be available in the pressroom. Thank you all for coming."

The press secretary ushered them inside, and soon Avery stood with Ling and the president alone. "You have the letter, President Stokes."

Behind her, Ling quietly asked, "It's done?"

President Stokes lifted the letter from his desk. "Legal counsel says he's off the bench."

"Now what?"

The question came from Ling, but Avery had the same thought. Her cell phone rested in her suit pocket, set to vibrate when the call came through. They should have heard the signal, should be closing in.

"I have taken the liberty of asking for Homeland Security's assistance with the matter of your mother, Avery," President Stokes said. He depressed a button on his desk, and the anteroom door swung open to admit Major Vance. "I believe you know my liaison to the White House."

"Ms. Keene." Vance crossed to where Avery and Ling stood near the center of the room. "I understand your mother is in some distress."

What is he doing here? Her pulse began to gallop, and Avery summoned every ounce of theatrics she'd ever learned. Jared and Agent Lee were en route to the warehouse, poised to free her mother and capture Major Vance and his henchmen in the act. But the first domino stood in the Oval Office. "Major Vance," she greeted him stiffly. "Domestic kidnappings are the province of the FBI. Why would Homeland Security be involved?"

"Major Vance has special military training," the president explained firmly. "More importantly, DHS has broad authority to act in certain matters, and with an alacrity the FBI lacks. He can get your mother for you. Of that, I'm certain."

The irony of the president's reassurance shook Avery's composure. "Major Vance has shown little interest in assisting me," she argued. "I'd prefer to deal with someone else."

"Time is of the essence," Major Vance told her coldly. "If you care to retrieve your mother, you'll let me handle this."

"What about the FBI?" she stubbornly argued. "They have the top hostage negotiators. How will you find her faster than they can?"

"Tell me what you know, and we'll have her home to you by dinner."

Agent Lee drove with deadly speed along the waterfront. In the seat beside him, Agent Leighton radioed instructions to other units: "Establish a six-block perimeter and hold radio silence until my mark."

Once she coded off, he resumed his diatribe: "Goddamn it, Jared. I'd expect this kind of stunt from Avery, but you're a freaking military officer."

"Former."

Agent Lee whipped around a parked semi unloading freight. He throttled down the speed, but his hands clenched tighter on the wheel. "Baiting a man who is holding her mother hostage? She might be too green to understand the danger, but you're not! Rita Keene dies, and it's on all your heads!"

They'd been in motion for nearly ten minutes, car stereo tuned in to C-SPAN's satellite coverage of the White House. Agent Lee had been stunned to hear the president's announcement and Avery's statement.

Jared scanned the buildings for the one beeping on his handheld GPS. "Avery has a plan. We're doing this her way."

"Her way? A law clerk orchestrating a search and rescue? What the hell is wrong with you? And you!" he shouted at Noah, catching him in the rearview mirror. "If she's already traded Justice Wynn's job for her mother, why in the hell are you still helping her?" he demanded as the SUV approached the address Jared provided.

"Believe me, she's thought of that too," Noah said, placating the FBI man. "She brought you in, Agent Lee, despite having every reason to do this alone."

"She's got no right to operate outside the law."

"Which she hasn't done." Noah scooted forward, bracing his arms on the back of Agent Leighton's seat. Haranguing his way into the SUV had taken all his persuasive skills. But with Avery and Ling at the White House, he wasn't going to sit at home twiddling his thumbs. Avery's plan had to work—and he'd be along for the ride. He slanted a look at Agent Lee through the rearview mirror. "Justice Wynn knew what she was capable of. Soon, so will the people who kidnapped Rita."

Jared gave a brief shake of his head, and Noah subsided. He raised the GPS. "The warehouse is up ahead. We should go in on foot from here. The building is in the second row."

Agent Lee started hunting for a place to stop, but he continued his rant. "You two will stay in the car."

"No way." Jared reached behind his back to the piece he'd retrieved from his apartment before they'd gone into hiding. "I've got a special military permit, and I'm an excellent shot."

"This isn't a discussion." Agent Lee jammed the truck into a space and killed the engine. "I don't take civilians on retrieval operations."

"You do if you can't get the coordinates any other way." Jared cut power to the unit. "Rita Keene is being held hostage, and her only bargaining chip has just been publicly traded away by her daughter."

Cursing, Agent Lee gave a sharp nod. "But the lawyer stays in the vehicle."

Noah raised his hands to show no resistance. "Fine with me. Just remember to Mirandize the son of a bitch."

The agents and Jared emerged from the SUV and met up with several more agents yards away. "Coordinates."

"Building 73179," Jared answered in a terse whisper. Training, now encoded in his blood, shifted him into position as they moved in silence toward the building.

The faded green metal-and-wood structure had been marked for demolition, a casualty of the city's waterfront revitalization plan. Slats high on the walls provided minimal ventilation, and the doors had been welded with no care for covert entry. Agent Lee held up three fingers, sending a team around to the rear. Jared clung like a burr to Lee's position, determined to go in with the entry team.

A grimy window offered the lone source of light, and Jared tapped Agent Leighton's shoulder. She nodded in understanding and shifted so he could boost her up to peer inside. She tapped his shoulder, and he lowered her to the ground. Two fingers came up, then shifted into a mockery of a gun.

Rita and her kidnapper were inside, a gun at the ready. Jared felt the surge of adrenaline, but the weapon in his hand felt cool and steady. His job was to save Avery's mom, while she did her best to save his father. He wouldn't let her down.

"On my mark," Lee instructed in a harsh whisper. "Go!"

The battering ram broke through the door, and FBI agents swarmed inside the shadowed cavern of space. Footsteps pounded concrete, and Phillips spun around, his hand already drawing his weapon. Agent Lee came in low, Jared on his left flank. Orders snapped out like bullets, bouncing off the walls.

"On the ground! On the ground! Now! Now!"

Blue jackets emblazoned with yellow filled the warehouse. Surrounded, Phillips still refused to comply. Vance had anticipated almost every result, including discovery, and Phillips had his orders. Moving quickly, he leaped and slid over the console table, landing near Rita's position. His arm vised around her neck and clamped against her airway. "Come any closer and I'll kill her!"

Rita's blind cry filled the warehouse, and the cavern amplified the sound into a piercing wail. "Shut up," he demanded as he shoved the barrel to her temple. Death was imminent, he realized, but he had one last task to accomplish. Focusing on the lead agent, he instructed tersely, "Fall back. All of you. Far corner."

Agent Lee gave the signal and began to shuffle against the concrete, and his agents followed suit, weapons trained on Phillips's position. He recognized the firm, wide stance, the grip of the Walther. This man had seen combat in the field. Leveling his tone, he asked, "What's your name, soldier?"

"Phillips."

"What branch?"

"Marine Corps." The information was easily found, Phillips decided. No reason to lie. "Chief warrant officer."

"Well, Chief, I'm going to be honest with you. You've got no way out of here," he told him bluntly. "Give us Mrs. Keene and tell us who hired you. Then I'll talk to the U.S. attorney about leniency."

Adrenaline burst like bubbles in Phillips's veins, but he'd been taught how to channel the rush. How to hold the mission in his sight lines, regardless of distractions. But he also knew how to feint. He barked across the room, "How tight is your perimeter?"

"What do you mean?"

The shriek of pain from Rita came as answer, as the gun dug into bruised flesh. "Your perimeter?"

"Six blocks. We've surrounded the waterfront. Unless you plan to swim out to the Potomac and drift down to Virginia, there's no way you escape. Cooperate, and we'll work out a deal."

Phillips calmed his breathing and hunted his memory for any escape hatch, but there were none. He'd been sent in to guard, and to die if necessary. The finality of his situation barely disturbed him. He'd made it up to chief in the Corps, but his bent had never been toward leadership. He was a soldier, and Vance's instructions had not included the possibility of capture.

But the mission was clear. Protect the commander in chief.

The Walther in his hand shifted for a split second, but Agent Lee read the signs. In a single whip of motion, Phillips twisted toward the computer setup and pumped ammunition into the casing. Smoke billowed as he swung the weapon in a tight, deadly arc.

In the time it took for Phillips's arm to complete its motion, the report from his gun ripped through the building as Lee's shot buried itself in Phillips's chest, and a second round collapsed his lung.

"Hold your fire!" Agent Lee bellowed to the rest of the team.

Rita felt the grip on her arm loosen and dropped to the concrete like a stone.

"He's down! He's down!" Agent Lee and his team surged forward to secure Phillips and Rita.

Jared reached her first. Rheumy green eyes lifted to meet his. The resemblance, though pallid and haggard, was still visible. He knelt on the ground and extended his hand. "My name is Jared Wynn. Your daughter, Avery, sent us."

Rita squeezed the hands in a grip palsied with aftershocks and withdrawal. "She's okay? Avery?"

"Yes, ma'am. She's fine." Jared thought of his father, the machines pushing air into lungs that had forgotten how to breathe. "She sent me to look out for you. But I'm just returning a favor."

FORTY-EIGHT

I could bring all of you up on charges."

Avery nodded, her arms wrapped around the wiry, vibrating form of her mother. Rita cowered against the lumpy green couch that stretched along Agent Lee's office wall. She'd refused a trip to the hospital, clinging first to Jared and then to Avery.

The thin blanket unearthed from an emergency kit carried a musty odor, but Avery was oblivious. Her mother was safe and unharmed, her bloodshot eyes the result of terror and detox rather than an overnight stupor.

"This was my idea," Avery told the livid agent, who hadn't stopped ranting since they'd reached his office. "Jared and the others were only trying to help."

"Obstruction of justice. Conspiracy. Evidence tampering." The list was punctuated by smacks against Agent Lee's palm. "Not to mention perjury."

"Actually, we never lied under oath," Noah interjected, only to receive a swift kick to his shins from Ling.

"If I hadn't taken down the kidnapper, who the hell knows what would have happened?"

Rita shuddered in Avery's arms, and Avery shot Agent Lee a quelling look. "We screwed up, I get it. But now we've got proof."

"Proof? You mean the busted-to-hell computers Phillips pumped lead into before he died?" He didn't mention that he already had teams working on reconstruction. "He could have had grenades in there. Anything."

The fresh shudder from Rita had Avery bundling her to her feet. She half carried her to the door. "Agent Lee, is there a quieter room where my mother can lie down while you relive her trauma?"

Agent Lee rubbed at his face in chagrin, then approached Rita with hesitant steps. "Well, crap. I'm so sorry, Mrs. Keene." He shoved his fists into his pockets and barely fought off the impulse to scuff his heel against the carpet. He knew better than to subject a kidnapping victim to the harsh sound of anger. Swallowing remorse, he jerked open the door. "Agent Madison!"

The field agent who'd tended to Rita on-site appeared in his doorway. "Sir?"

"Please take Mrs. Keene down to your office, if she still refuses to go to the hospital." At Rita's spastic nod, he relented. "Your office for now. Make her comfortable and see if she needs anything."

Avery turned to hand her off to the woman, but Rita clung, nails biting into skin. "No, no. I'm okay. I want to stay here. With you." The piteous voice pleaded, "Don't make me go."

Tucking her mother's head into the curve of her shoulder, she rocked her lightly, whispering, "I'll walk down there with you, Momma. Then I'll be just down the hall, for a few minutes. I promise."

With Agent Madison behind her, she helped Rita to the agent's cubbyhole of a space. She settled her into the lone chair and wrapped the police blanket more securely beneath her chin. Crouching low, she stroked the fading streak of a bruise that mottled the gaunt cheek. "Are you hungry? Do you want anything? Coffee? Water?"

Rita darted a look up at the agent and leaned in to Avery. "I need—I need—"

Avery braced for the request, her stomach plummeting. "What is it, Rita?"

"Can I have a candy bar? Something sweet? I need a chocolate bar." The tremulous smile she gave her daughter accompanied a soft pat to her cheek. "Chocolate will take the edge off."

"You've come to the right place." Agent Madison circled her desk and rummaged through the drawers. "I keep a secret stash in here. Snickers. Hershey's. I've even got a Zero in here, I think." Candy bars piled on the cluttered desktop and spilled over into an untidy selection. "I'll get you a Coke or some water to wash it down."

The agent went to retrieve the drinks, leaving them alone for the first time. Rita curled her fingers against Avery's shoulder. "In that last place you put me, they told us that sugar and caffeine have the same effect as, well, you know. Almost."

The gallows humor twisted at her heart, and Avery broke. "Momma, I'm so sorry. So sorry they did this to you." Her head hung low, eyes shut in misery. "I should have brought you home with me."

"Why? So I could rob you and still get taken?" Rita tilted her chin up, gave a husky laugh. "I don't blame you, baby. Cheapest rehab yet. Maybe this time, they scared me straight."

Avery flinched. "Don't joke."

Pushing aside the panic that spurted still, Rita traced a line along her daughter's chin. The stubborn jut she'd gotten from her father. Through her shock, she'd heard enough of the FBI's yelling to understand that Avery had done something stupid and courageous. Something for her. "I'm sorry, baby."

"Momma, I was so scared for you."

"He banged me up some, but nothing that won't heal." Then, because it had to be said, she added, "I'm the same woman I was last week, Avery. You did the right thing sending me away, and this isn't your fault."

"If he'd shot you—" She cut herself off, the guilt a vicious bite.

"If you hadn't found me," Rita countered, "I'd be dead. So you go down to that angry man's office and finish whatever this is you've got going. Oh, and make sure they keep men watching your building. One of the men said they planned to torch your apartment. Make it look like I set it on fire with a crack pipe or something."

"They won't have a chance to do anything else, Momma. It's almost over, I promise."

"I believe you." She pressed a kiss to Avery's forehead, inhaled the scent of her only child. "You go on now. I'll be good down here."

"You sure?"

Rita smiled. "I've got a stack of candy bars to hold me. Go on."

Aware of the timing of the next part, Avery let herself be urged out. She rose, bending to hug her mother tight. "Ten minutes tops, then I'll be back down here, and we'll get you home."

"Ten minutes," Rita dutifully repeated. She squeezed Avery once more. "I'm okay."

Avery slowly left the room and headed down the hall to Agent Lee's office. A long, cold shudder racked through her, and she stumbled. Breath backed up in lungs too tight to expand, and Avery crouched low, gasping. Her hand flexed against a wall of cabinets lining the hallway.

She'd nearly killed Rita. The realization slammed into her and wrenched a sob from her closing throat. If Agent Lee hadn't agreed to ferry them to the warehouse. If he hadn't made his shot. *If. If. If.*

The word tumbled around, careening off doubt and guilt and panic. She'd nearly killed her mother to save another man, and she still might fail.

"Ms. Keene?" Agent Madison stood a pace away, her eyes soft with concern. "It will pass."

"What?"

"The adrenaline. From fear. Now that you've gotten her back, it's flooding through you. It'll pass."

Avery started to argue—to tell the well-intentioned woman that her trials still had a third act. But instead, she gained her feet, her knees wobbly. "Thank you. I'd appreciate it if you'd stay with my mother. She's detoxing. It can be—difficult. I'd like to get her into a treatment bed as soon as possible. Can you help?"

"I've got her, and I'm sure the Bureau can make the arrangements."

Avery nodded gratefully and continued down the hall to Agent Lee's office.

Inside, Agent Lee had managed to find a semblance of calm. He'd also received a sheet on Chief Warrant Officer Marcus Phillips, of late, attaché to Major Will Vance of the S&T Directorate. When Avery entered the room, he passed her the file. She scanned the contents without comment.

"I notice you're not surprised."

She wasn't. Though having a name for the dead man was news, his former employer was not. Avery handed the file to Jared and folded her arms. She decided to stand, assuming it would be easier to take the agent's anger on her feet. "I didn't have proof," she acknowledged. "But based on what I've learned, I had good reason to believe Major Vance was involved."

"Any chance you'd like to tell me what you've learned?" Agent Lee propped a hip on his desk. "If you don't mind, of course."

"I do." When his brows winged northward, she apologized: "I'm not finished yet."

"Finished with what?" Before she could respond, he shook his head. "Never mind. Let's do the easy question first. How did you know Major Vance had your mother?"

"I guessed." Avery hated to be difficult, but until she'd played her final hand, she couldn't be honest with him. Real remorse filled her voice. "You've been very good to me, Agent Lee. However, if I tell you what I know, you'll get shut down. Because there's not enough evidence for you to act."

"But you can stop the president's adviser on your own?" The derision was palpable. "Avery, you've saved your mother and Justice Wynn by pulling him off the bench. Now it's time to turn this over to the FBI and let us do our jobs."

"With what I can prove, you can't guarantee a conviction against Major Vance." Avery stepped forward and held his eyes with a solemn look. She'd given him a glimpse, but now he had to let her finish her course. She reached into her purse and removed the plastic bag from Justice Wynn's study. "Test this pill bottle for prints and let me know what you find. In forty-eight hours, I promise you the bust of your career."

"I don't haggle, Ms. Keene. I gave you twenty-four hours, and the clock's just about run on that."

Jared intervened: "Then you can go and question Vance about his attaché. He'll tell you Phillips was freelancing, and you'll have nothing to contradict him. I'm sure Vance has manufactured evidence of a right-wing group that Phillips will be conveniently aligned with."

Knowing he was correct did nothing to sweeten Agent Lee's temper. "I'll make something work."

"You'll lose him." She clasped her hands behind herself. "DHS versus the FBI. National security threat or war hero?"

"I'm not getting into a pissing match with you or Vance. I'm doing my job."

"Which will be easier if you let me do mine."

"What exactly do you think your job is, Avery?"

"I'm Justice Wynn's guardian. Let me stand up for him." She faced Agent Lee fully, stubbornly insistent. "Forty-eight more hours, and then they're all yours."

FORTY-NINE

Tuesday, June 27

At seven the next morning, Avery and Jared arrived at the St. Regis hotel. Indira Srinivasan opened the door and welcomed them inside. A bodyguard began to frisk Jared, who stood patiently. After patting down Avery and wanding them both, the guard stepped away. "They're clean."

"Good morning," Nigel offered, rising. He extended a hand to Jared. "Mr. Wynn."

"Mr. Cooper." Jared took a seat on the opposite sofa, and Avery sat beside him. "Dr. Srinivasan."

"Indira and Nigel." Nigel settled beside Indira, who opted to perch on the arm of the sofa. He stroked her hand absently. "Titles seem so formal when we're about to go bankrupt."

"I don't want to destroy your companies," Avery corrected. "Jared needs the work you'll do together."

"What work?"

"Tigris and all the rest. I know all about it."

"And yet you let them win by tendering Wynn's resignation, Avery." Nigel lifted a glass of Perrier to his lips. "I expected a better return on investment."

Before Avery could respond, Indira interjected: "Nigel gave you sufficient information to unmask your president and his henchman." She waved a hand at the papers on the low table, identical to the ones emailed to Avery. "Why do you require our presence?"

"The information that Nigel sent to me requires authentication."

"Then have Dr. Papaleo do so," Indira stubbornly argued. "Or get a subpoena for our records."

"We believe Dr. Papaleo is dead. And getting the Indian government to compel you to comply with a warrant will take years."

"Perhaps."

"Absolutely, and you know it. By then, President Stokes will have hidden himself in a country with no extradition treaty. GenWorks will have missed its chance to share technology with Advar, and you both will be out billions. Assuming, of course, your companies don't go under after a string of congressional hearings, FDA inquiries, and charges from the International Criminal Court."

"Then what do you suggest?" Indira stood, and Avery rose to face her. "Publicity didn't work. Supplying you with the documents didn't either. What else can we do?"

"Before I tell you, I have one more question."

"Yes?"

"Did you know how far Hygeia went?" Avery took a step closer. "That the Tigris Project didn't stop at theory?"

"What?" Nigel shot to his feet, alarmed. "That's impossible. Neither Indira nor I would sanction the actual production of the Tigris technology. That would be barbaric."

"But that's exactly what happened, isn't it?" Avery focused on Indira, who gave no reaction. "Ani Ramji likely died because he did more than theorize about how to weaponize the human genome. He proved it." Her eyes boring into Indira's, Avery said accusingly, "He tested his technology, and it worked. When you bought out Hygeia, you didn't stop the research. You tried to replicate it, expand its potential, but Ani refused to help you."

"Didn't happen," Nigel refuted. "The technology has promise, but they never had time for human trials, right, Indira?"

Avery nodded to Jared, who dropped a folder onto the glass-topped table. "There's proof." Stark images downloaded from Ani's flash drive spilled across in graphic detail. Mangled bodies captured in cold, sterile light.

Indira turned away.

"Indira?"

She stared out at the grand specter of the White House. "The chairman of Advar funded my dream of a company. When he called about Hygeia, I could not say no."

"To what?"

"The prime minister had learned of a dangerous, promising project funded by his ministry and funds from overseas. A consortium of scientists and governments who wanted to stop terrorism." She clasped the window frame, her back to the room. "You Americans recall 9/11 as a singular event. But in India, to be Hindu is to be hated by the Muslims. Bali, Mumbai, London. All over, they explode themselves as living sacrifice."

"So why not make them experiments?" Jared finished harshly. "Is that how they justified it?"

Indira whirled around. "I only found out about Tigris long after the human trials. After we took over the company, I found records of hundreds of prisoners enticed from the Brahmaputra Valley and from Kashmir and targeted by Tigris. As the new president, I conducted a thorough investigation and evaluated the technology to determine if it had other uses."

"Like purging Muslims?" Avery asked quietly.

"I am a scientist. Editing genes is our mission, and Dr. Ramji's team had discovered a way to use viruses in ways I had not imagined." She paused, her expression stoic. "Later, Dr. Ramji wanted to atone, so he began to publish the truth. Neither government could afford the potential scrutiny, nor could our company. We had only inherited his work. It was a bilateral decision to target Dr. Ramji and his colleagues. I was not in charge, but I was kept apprised."

"And you said nothing," Avery reminded her.

"I cannot contradict heads of state, Ms. Keene. Instead, I focused my attention where it could be effective. I convinced my board to let me assimilate the Hygeia technology. Their efforts were horrific, but the implications are astounding. We can cure diseases like Boursin's and Parkinson's in less than a decade. Using viral vectors to edit gene sequences."

"So the technology already exists. Once we merge, you simply require our pharmaceuticals." Nigel backed away. "President Stokes knows about all of this, doesn't he?"

"Of course. He authorized American funding of the project when he was vice president," Indira replied derisively. "When Tigris was about to be discovered, he issued the Exon-Florio decision. That's when our chairman learned that U.S. intelligence was terminating the scientists who participated. I contacted Major Vance to call them off, but it was too late. Only Dr. Ramji remained."

"That's not all of it, is it?" Avery asked.

"No." Indira squared her shoulders in defiance. "Dr. Ramji's findings were unique, but not irreplaceable. Qian Ku has similar technology, similar research, but they are only a few years behind. I will not let them beat me. This can be used for good."

"And what happened to Dr. Ramji?" Jared asked.

"I don't know." Indira lifted her hands defensively. "I truly don't know. Not until Nigel told me about your father's research did I realize Ani might have managed to share his information. My investigators tracked him to Chennai, and I notified Major Vance. I assume—"

Nigel sputtered, "You had him killed?"

"I don't know." Indira returned to the tableau where the trio stood frozen. "The Tigris incident cannot be allowed to stop this technology from moving forward. It will save an incalculable number of lives."

"And cure you, too?" Avery asked.

Indira gave a slight shrug. "If I benefit from our creations, then I will have more time to devote to saving others. I see no harm in my salvaging a measure of personal privilege from this debacle. I did not create Tigris, and I did not murder its subjects."

"You are a criminal, Dr. Srinivasan," Jared said starkly. "Whether you ordered their deaths or not, you are complicit."

"Prove it. I will deny this conversation took place. You will be unlikely to find confirmation among the Research and Analysis Wing—India's CIA." She motioned dismissively to Nigel. "He may be appalled, but right now, he's calculating the share price of our stock once we are able to announce that we've developed a biogenetic technology to cure Alzheimer's and arthritis and cancer."

"We'll agree to provide affidavits to the Court confirming the documents from Dr. Papaleo on our side," Nigel offered solemnly. "Indira will locate sufficient information to support your theory without admitting any wrongdoing by Hygeia, beyond the heinous research that preceded her tenure." He gestured to the photos with a shudder. "These pictures disappear."

"And you escape unscathed?" Avery retorted, incredulous.

Reaching down to the table, Indira lifted a china cup next to the images of the dead. With a delicate sip of tea, she suggested, "You must choose your poison, Ms. Keene. But as a sweetener, I will also reauthorize research into the antidote to Sleeping Beauty."

"What's Sleeping Beauty?" Nigel demanded.

Indira patted his arm soothingly. "The compound that put Justice Wynn into a coma. Developed by Advar. In a few months, GenWorks and Advar will debut a wonder drug that can put humans into lifesaving comas and bring them out, with minimal side effects." She turned to Avery. "My understanding is that he maintains minimal brain activity, which is what the drug causes. Think of it as low-grade cryogenics. His condition may be reversed, in time."

Jared demanded, "You barter for his life?"

"Yes. Do we have a deal?"

Jared squeezed Avery's hand, and, unwilling to demand such a sacrifice of him, she gave a stiff nod. "Yes."

She'd protected Ani with the rumor that he'd been killed, and now she had to make her final moves.

Indira rose gracefully and summoned several associates from a nearby room. When the documents had been finished and the notary exited, she limped over to the wide bay windows of the suite. "I inherited evil, but I didn't create it."

Avery bent to lift the notarized statements. "You didn't stop it either."

Jared walked Avery to the door, then gave Nigel a pitying look. "I'd be careful of your partners, Mr. Cooper. Very careful."

FIFTY

Noah dropped off the complaint at nine a.m.

Judge Kenneth Stapleton was a bluff oak tree of a man, from the dark brown complexion down to the tree trunk limbs. Before taking up law, he'd been on the short list for the Heisman Trophy. Less than a month later, a car accident had ruined his football career, and he'd spent his recovery time studying for the LSAT. His conservative leanings and his stellar career as prosecutor for the state of Virginia had secured him a spot on the District Court of the District of Columbia, courtesy of the first round of appointments by President Brandon Stokes.

In two years, though, his affinity with his benefactor had weakened. To his mind, President Stokes had systematically shredded the Constitution, a document Stapleton held as sacred as the Bible. Both of them sat on his nightstand at home and his desk in the DC District Court.

Lifetime appointment stood as the finest of the perks of federal judgeships. Unless the judge committed an act of hubris that landed him in an impeachment hearing, he couldn't lose his job. But if he failed to uphold the standards of the party that had brought him to the dance, he wouldn't move any higher up the ladder.

At fifty-two, Judge Stapleton hadn't quite decided whether he intended to stay put on the DC court or strive for an appeals court post. But the complaint lying on his desk seemed determined to make the choice for him.

Frivolous complaints landed on his desk every day. Pleas from federal prisoners, immigrants facing deportation, and generally annoyed citizens, intent on leveraging the remarkable accessibility of the federal courts, crowded into the hoppers on his clerks' desks. Few, however, arrived with his political future attached as an exhibit.

By eleven thirty, he'd memorized the sparely written pages and their arguments. He could act as his gut said he should, summoning the courage that had gotten him through eight months of rehab. Or he could punt, recalling the best advice his old coach ever gave him: "Don't stand there holding the ball if a freight train's headed for you. Can't play in the second quarter if you're dead."

With Coach's words ringing in his ears, Judge Kenneth Stapleton rejected the complaint on the grounds that Civil Action 2012-1058 had been improperly filed in his office. But, aware of the client of the young attorney who awaited his decision, he immediately kicked it up to the United States Circuit Court of Appeals for the District of Columbia. Signing the paperwork, he glanced bemusedly at the heading, his own head shaking in disbelief.

HOWARD JEFFERSON WYNN,
Associate Justice of the Supreme Court of the United States
Petitioner,

v.

THE UNITED STATES OF AMERICA,
Respondent.

Among the judges sitting en banc on Tuesday at the DC Circuit Court, none had played college football. In the three legal minds, though, the varying metaphors resolved themselves into a singular notion of a ticking time bomb and a fatal explosion. Wrestling their collective cowardice into action, they did as anyone would when faced with the ability to pass the grenade.

They concurred with the lower court and chucked Civil Action 2012-1058 off to the very folks who'd benefit or burn from the blast. With a unanimous vote, the complaint to invalidate the stunning resignation of Associate Justice Howard Wynn, by the very legal guardian who'd submitted the same only the afternoon before, went flying down Constitution Avenue to the United States Supreme Court, the court of original jurisdiction in a dispute between a citizen and his country.

And into the lap of Chief Justice Teresa Roseborough.

FIFTY-ONE

During the previous September, days before the start of the new term, Justice Howard Wynn had administered the oaths of admission to his law clerks. He'd found it asinine, he told them, to have judicial assistants not permitted to appear before the bench they aided. Thus, Avery Keene had standing to argue before the United States Supreme Court.

The Chief's injunction against her had been lifted to allow Avery a few moments of privacy in her old office. The entire suite was empty—the secretaries had been idle for the past week, and with today's highly unusual hearing, they'd been relieved of their daily duties and permitted to view the proceedings.

Avery entered the chambers slowly, her eyes running over the familiar furniture. Behind her, Jared waited in the doorway. Ling and Noah had already gone down to the main level to await the hearing. But she'd wanted Jared to see where his father had done his work for the nation.

"He was always here before even the secretaries," she murmured as she reached for the closed door to his office. "Justice Wynn read every brief and every case cited by an attorney. Even the citations' citations." She motioned for Jared to follow her into Justice Wynn's carpeted office. Books lined every free surface. Brown volumes with red piping and others in blue and black contained the case law of every federal court in the country.

A number of them were scattered across his worktable, their pages untouched in his absence. Tabs and pens marked pages, and yellow legal pads bore his familiar green scrawl. A scholarly clutter of newspapers and journals leaned drunkenly against shelves and rose in haphazard towers from the carpet. "No one was allowed to clean his office," she explained with a soft smile.

"Ever?"

"Rumor has it that a secretary attempted to do a cleaning after session several decades ago. He had her transferred to the Commerce Department."

Jared had a hazy memory of his mother scolding the judge for the state of his office at home. "Mom wouldn't let him get away with it," he remembered. "She told him he could be as messy as he wanted to at work, but home was her domain." He thought of the orderly study they'd searched. "I guess he never forgot."

They stood side by side in the quiet chambers, and Avery reached out and squeezed Jared's hand. "Justice Wynn is a hard man, but he was always good. Not kind, no. But good."

"I suppose that's something."

She thought of her mother, lying in a treatment ward in a posh Maryland hospital. "Sometimes, it's everything."

Annoyed with himself, Jared exhaled and turned to Avery. "I appreciate you bringing me here, Avery. Showing me something of him." He studied her, his eyes tracing the fine texture of her skin, the shadow of exhaustion beneath the green eyes. "He made the right choice, turning to you."

"It's not done yet."

"Maybe not, but you've done more than he had any right to expect. You've brought this full circle. Whatever happens in there, you've been his champion. I just want to say thank you."

She smiled at him, and Jared leaned toward her slowly, giving her time to escape. But Avery held herself still and ready. When his mouth covered hers, she lifted her hands to his shoulders, holding on to the solid strength of him. The kiss stretched beyond time, beyond promise.

Too soon, she let her eyes flutter open, and the pair quietly broke apart. She swallowed once. "Well, that's something I never expected to happen in this room. . . ."

Jared grinned, and Avery laughed. "I guess it's showtime," she said.

The U.S. Supreme Court chamber boasted a forty-four-foot ceiling and twenty-four columns of Siena marble from Liguria, Italy. Avery sat alone at a glossy mahogany table, her foot tapping restlessly on the carpeted floor. Before her stretched the bench, and to the left sat the clerk of court. The marshal of the Court kept time from a desk on the right, flashing white and red lights to hasten the closure of oral argument.

A bronze railing ran the length behind her. Red benches arrayed against the left side of the courtroom were crowded with reporters primed for an unusual sight. Across the room, red benches held guests of the justices, including invitations for Jared, Noah, and Ling, courtesy of the Chief. Black chairs in front of those benches held an assemblage of unusual guests, men and women who spent lifetimes avoiding the entry of a courthouse. The Speaker slouched in one chair, his shoulder nudging the majority leader of the Senate.

"Must hurt," DuBose whispered.

"Hmm?" Ken cocked his head to listen to the low tone. "What does?"

"Having some girl hand you your wet dream and then snatch it back in public." The Speaker spiked a finger toward the solitary young woman seated at the respondent's table. "Son of a bitch almost had an open seat during recess."

The majority leader nodded vigorously. "Had senators camped outside my door yesterday. Everybody screaming about recess appointments and right-wing judges. No one wanted to be on a plane Tuesday, and no one could afford to stay. Primaries are coming up fast, and everybody has to hit the money trail." As the leader of the Senate, he scrupulously hoarded an immense war chest, but he'd stayed in power by taking nothing for granted. Especially the desperate acts of fools. What he didn't know was what could happen today. "You went to law school. Does she have a shot?"

"How the hell should I know?" DuBose muttered. "Never heard of anything like this in ten years as a DA. Complaint zipped through district court and the appeals court like it had grease. Or an STD. My guess is, none of the judges wanted to be on either side of a bad ruling. Legal counsel says what's happened is technically legal, but don't quote her on it."

"Think the law clerk will win? Knock Stokes on his ass?"

"Against the solicitor general?" The Speaker examined Avery Keene, who was hunched over a stack of papers. She scribbled notes on a legal pad, then paused to slash through what she'd written. He gave a chuckle. "The solicitor general will eat her for lunch."

"Better hope he gets indigestion, or we'll have a packed court unless we permanently cancel recess. In an election year, that's impossible."

"Sly son of a bitch." Cracking his knuckles, DuBose cursed, "Damned if you do, defeated if you don't."

Behind them, a stir trickled through the crowd, and both men angled to see the latest development. A phalanx glided into the courtroom, and the Speaker cursed. President Brandon Stokes, attended by the U.S. solicitor general and a cadre of Secret Service personnel and assistants, threaded through the aisle.

Avery watched too, and the nerves that had been coursing now scraped with jagged spikes. President Stokes had not come alone. Major Vance walked a pace behind. Her eyes glued to their progress, she saw the president take his seat beside the Speaker and the majority leader. Armed men fanned out to cover exits and vulnerable points.

David Ralston, the solicitor general, strode over to Avery's table, and she hastily stood.

"Ms. Keene," he greeted her, his hand extended. She placed hers inside, and he gave the slender hand a perfunctory pump. "I understand from my staff that you've been very busy this week. A resignation one day and a complaint to invalidate it the next. I can't for the life of me understand what we're doing here, though."

"Sir?"

"I've reviewed the tapes and your brief." The smile he gave her gleamed with condescension. "You didn't seem all that distressed when you relinquished Justice Wynn's seat, Ms. Keene. No evidence of coercion."

Avery bristled. "I'm a good actress."

"But, my dear, this is a court, not a theater. You'd do well to understand the difference. I don't take a lawsuit against my nation lightly." He spun on his heel and took his place at his table.

Avery sank into her seat and returned to her notes, staring blankly. She hadn't expected the president to actually come to the Court. To her knowledge, no sitting president had come to watch an oral argument. With him sitting next to the congressional leaders, the physical separation of powers had fully collapsed.

When she felt her internal chuckle edging toward hysteria, she dragged in a calming breath. Coming to the Supreme Court had been a gamble—a huge one. As the court of original jurisdiction, the Supreme Court had no obligation to follow the rules of civil procedure. However, in this court, there were no sympathetic juries or surprise witnesses.

She was winging it.

Hope rested in the gravity of the accusation and the vigilance of women and men obliged to seek justice. Behind her, in the gallery, Indira and Nigel sat still as statues. Their fates rested with hers.

They were all doomed.

Then the watch at her wrist ticked off ten a.m. Like everyone in the courtroom, including President Stokes, she rose to her feet as the eight justices filed onto the bench. The rostrum, a winged bend of mahogany, held seats for each one. She'd witnessed the spectacle dozens of times, first as a law student and then as a clerk. Never, though, she thought, as a petitioner.

Never with the ninth chair empty.

Chief Roseborough called proceedings to order at 10:03 a.m. "We'll hear argument now on *Associate Justice Howard Jefferson Wynn versus the United States of America.*" The kindly brown eyes held no favor as they focused on Avery. "Ms. Keene, traditionally you would begin; however, we have received a special request from the solicitor general to make prefatory comments. Given the singular nature of this proceeding, we have agreed to permit him to address this body. Mr. Ralston."

With carefully practiced gravitas, Solicitor General David Ralston rose and stood solemnly before the eight justices.

"Madam Justice and may it please the Court, I have requested this opportunity to state the categorical objection of the United States to this proceeding. In *Marbury v. Madison,* Chief Justice John Marshall decided that the Supreme Court's original jurisdiction did not extend over U.S. federal government officials. President Stokes accepted the tendered resignation of Justice Howard Wynn, not the United States. Under that precedent alone, this case should not be before this court. Moreover, no motion to void a resignation exists within the canons of law or as a federal question. Ms. Keene cannot legally achieve her objective, which is to unring a bell. I challenge her standing and the ability of this Court to entertain her cause célèbre."

Avery stirred at her seat, ready to object, but the Chief spoke: "We received your brief, Mr. Ralston, and while this Court agrees with your concerns about this action, we have determined to hear oral arguments. Your objection, and that of your client, is duly noted."

"Thank you, Madam Chief Justice." A visibly hostile Ralston returned to his table and sat heavily.

"Ms. Keene."

Avery moved to the lectern and waited for the white light to flare. Apprehension shivered over her, but she forced her voice to project a confidence she prayed she'd feel. "Madam Chief Justice and may it please the Court. Today is an unusual plea for remedy from this body. On Monday, June 26, I submitted a letter of resignation for Justice Howard Wynn, acting as his legal guardian. Subsequent to that action, I filed the complaint before you, the intent of which is to void the letter of resignation. I do so on the grounds that the resignation was not tendered in the best interest of Justice Wynn and instead was the result of coercion."

Justice Bringman, whose vitriol against liberals found its most consistent target in Justice Wynn, opened with the first volley: "While my colleagues have opted to hear this petition on what I find to be spurious legal grounds, I have been democratically outvoted. But for my peace of mind, Ms. Keene, can you tell me how this is a valid case against the United States? Would it not be more accurate to file against the president, as the person who accepted the resignation?"

Avery flashed to moot court, the rite of passage for law students who wanted to litigate. While most TV lawyer shows focused on the fight between the prosecution and the defense, law students and grown-up attorneys knew that the real agony came from judicial grilling. Being forced to defend your every thought in front of hostile judges who faced no limits to what they could ask and how deeply they could insult you. Bracing herself, Avery answered almost steadily, "I stand by the accuracy of this filing, as the president stands in the stead of all American citizens. Therefore, the United States is the only actor with the ability to accept the resignation of Justice Wynn or to vitiate it."

Surely, she told herself, no one could hear the thumping beat of her heart. "A Supreme Court justice is nominated by the president, confirmed by the United States Senate, and seated by the Supreme Court. The act of becoming a Supreme Court justice requires the participation of all three branches of the federal government. By extension, any action related to Justice Wynn must involve the entire government too—the United States of America."

Bringman went silent, and Justice Lindenbaum interjected, "Are you certain this is a question subject to judicial review?"

Before Avery could respond, Bringman recovered. "More importantly, is a resignation a question subject to this Court's review? Why shouldn't this matter be in front of a probate judge?"

The barrage of questions from Bringman met with appreciative nods from two others on the bench. Two more votes she wouldn't get. The shiver of apprehension morphed into a cloaked shudder. "The probate courts are ill-equipped to address the complexity of this issue, Justice Bringman. The lower courts agreed and promptly transmitted the complaint to this body."

"Maybe they sped it through because they understood the weakness of your contention. And the paucity of your evidence." He thumbed through a ream of pages. "Special Agent Robert Lee of the Federal Bureau of Investigation states that your mother was held hostage and rescued on Monday."

"Correct."

"This is your proof of coercion?"

"Yes, Justice Bringman."

"Do you have evidence that President Stokes somehow participated in the abduction of your mother or in her incarceration?"

Of course she didn't, but she couldn't say that so plainly. "The appropriate standard is not who coerced me, but whether I was indeed coerced. Agent Lee's affidavit clearly states that the man holding my mother hostage was an employee of Major Will Vance, liaison to the president."

"Which proves," chimed in Justice Newell, "only that Major Vance should improve his hiring practices. Can you demonstrate active involvement by President Stokes? Yes or no?"

Avery hesitated, but found no alternative. "No. I cannot demonstrate active involvement by President Stokes. However—"

"I fail to see why his acceptance of the resignation should be voided. He did not act against the public's interest or Justice Wynn's interest. You did."

"I had no choice."

"Did I understand you to say you had direct communications with an agent of the FBI?" The query shot out from Justice Hodgson, whose stern demeanor spoke volumes. "If he knew where to find your mother, I fail to comprehend why you couldn't simply delay tendering the resignation. An element of coercion is the well-founded belief that your actions are required to avoid the threatened consequence."

"I believed my mother was in danger. I believed I had to attend that press conference." Avery met the justice's dubious gaze. Anxiously, she clutched at the lectern, wondering if she'd made the wrong call. "Agent Lee promised to do his best. I did mine."

Apparently mollified, Justice Hodgson subsided, and Justice Gardner moved in to grill her: "Let's set aside the coercion for a moment. I am more interested in your assertion that the submission of resignation winds its way to a constitutional question. Assuming, arguendo, that this Court has original jurisdiction to act."

Several rounds of arguments with Noah had prepared her for this one. Her thudding pulse slowed, and Avery answered, "The question at hand is the constitutionality of removing a Supreme Court justice absent his consent. Jurisdiction for all cases in law and equity arise under the Constitution."

Warming up, she said, "Moreover, the Twenty-Fifth Amendment addresses the issue of how to handle succession in office in the event of incapacitation of a president. However, the Constitution remains silent on the incapacitation of any other constitutional officer, including those who hold lifetime appointments. The Constitution does not contemplate the ability of a third party to unilaterally decide the issue of removing a Supreme Court justice from his seat. To the contrary, the country chose to have the Constitution remain mute on the issue."

"But the Framers could not have anticipated the medical machinery of the twenty-first century in 1787," Justice Gardner retorted.

"The voters in 1967 could have. The Twenty-Fifth Amendment goes into great detail to identify how to treat the incapacity of the president. Not his or her death, but simply the long-term inability to perform the duties of the job that lasts only four years at a time, let alone a lifetime appointment."

"So you're asserting that even absent coercion, your resignation is invalid."

"Yes, Justice Gardner. I am." Her argument was exactly the opposite of the one she'd have made a week ago, but that was before she discovered the president was a terrorist. "I lack the ability to arbitrarily participate in the removal of a Supreme Court justice from his seat. The president's action merely continues my unconstitutional act and, therefore, should be nullified. If I never could resign him without his consent, then there cannot be an open seat to fill."

Her assertion opened the floodgates, and the inquisition took on a new fervor. Except from the Chief. She sat quietly, her silence uncustomary and noted by the regular Supreme Court reporters. No inquiries about political questions or standing or coercion or guardianship rights. Not a word until Avery wound down a riposte to Justice Lawrence-Hardy.

Then the Chief spoke.

"So, Ms. Keene, under no circumstances, in your view of the world, could a legal guardian resign on behalf of a person holding a lifetime appointment? We'll simply have to expand the Court each time one of my colleagues falls ill without signing a resignation letter first?"

Avery had waited for the pitch, and she took a mental step back. And swung. "I wrote that letter of resignation. My argument is that for the resignation to be valid, it would have to be consistent with wishes expressed by the holder of office before the illness." She locked eyes with the Chief. "Otherwise, the resignation is meaningless if it is not affirmatively in the person's best interest. I think I should reserve the balance of my time for rebuttal."

"Thank you, Ms. Keene." Avery shifted away from the lectern as the Chief said, "Mr. Ralston, we'll hear from you."

He thanked the Court and launched his first salvo: "I'd like to begin by addressing Justice Bringman's initial query. There is no jurisdiction here. Try as Ms. Keene might to link her motion to the Twenty-Fifth Amendment, the chain is too short. As Ms. Keene's attorney argued so eloquently in his brief before the probate court of the District of Columbia, she alone is charged with acting in Justice Wynn's best interest. While that case is still pending, the immediate actions taken by Ms. Keene are consistent with his assertion. It is her responsibility to assess whether Justice Wynn's wishes are served by hamstringing the activities of this Court by leaving him inert to its operations but occupying its ninth seat."

As he intended, all eyes swung to the empty chair. "It seems to us that the remedy available to Ms. Keene is that of acceptance. She made a choice, horrible as it was, and it achieved her purposes. Mrs. Keene is safe. Justice Wynn is safe. The Supreme Court is now free to accept a functioning member of the body, and President Stokes stands at the ready to act."

He fixed the bench with a steely gaze. "In less legal terms, what's done is done."

FIFTY-TWO

For the next fifteen minutes, the solicitor general earned his place in history. He thrust and parried with four justices certain that their own seats might be next. With careful, precise answers, he eviscerated Avery's constitutional argument, laying bare the glaring problem of her petition.

"The law is made by the Congress, acting for the people. Ms. Keene failed to highlight any statute or operation of law that accords her the right to come to this body for remedy. She acted in concert with her assessment of Justice Wynn's best interest, and she now seeks to repent that act. This is not the proper forum. A house of worship is."

The Chief leaned in a degree. "Is that a point of law, Mr. Ralston?"

The solicitor general cleared his throat. "Hyperbole, Madam Chief Justice. What I am saying is that this is not a federal matter. It is not a question for this Court or for any other. The right of a guardian to act on behalf of a ward is settled law. The prerogative of the president to accept resignations is also settled law, opined upon by the subject of this proceeding, Justice Howard Wynn. This unusual circumstance does not pose a nexus where the Court should intervene." The red light flickered, precisely on time.

The Chief spoke: "Thank you, Mr. Ralston. Ms. Keene, you have five minutes remaining."

"Thank you, Madam Chief Justice." She paused, vibrantly aware of the passage of time, and the rules she was about to break. The empty seat studied her in turn, demanding that she act. For him.

"With his incapacity imminent, Justice Wynn searched for a cure that would preserve the life of his estranged son, who had inherited

Boursin's syndrome from his father. Then Justice Wynn took great pains to express his wishes to me. He entrusted his conferring of his power of attorney to Chief Justice Roseborough. He hid away his living will beneath the childhood bed of that estranged son, an estrangement he broke to ensure that I would find his testament. He updated his final will and testament with codicils anticipating what might occur should he not be available to explain what he had learned.

"In the process of preparing for his own demise, Justice Wynn discovered a secret. A dire, epic secret: that our government had committed atrocities in the name of national security. He found allies who had proof of our nation's complicity in grisly experiments an ocean away. When he realized that his life was in jeopardy, he attempted to pass me a message, through his nurse, Mrs. Jamie Lewis. Within hours of delivering this message, Nurse Lewis was shot to death in her home."

Avery paused.

"After I received guardianship, I was physically attacked, beaten, and shot at, first at Justice Wynn's home and then near his cabin in Georgia. An employee of the Department of Homeland Security, Dr. Betty Papaleo of the Science and Technology Directorate, who uncovered proof of covert financial transactions between DHS and the laboratory they hired, attempted to meet with me, and yet she went missing, along with her husband. As did the lead scientist on what became known as the Tigris Project. Marcus Phillips, the man who kidnapped my mother, died trying to destroy evidence of this secret.

"The common link between these acts is information I could not submit in probate court. Information that ties Major Will Vance, who sits in this courtroom now, to U.S. government funds used to support illegal research into biogenetic weapons that will target and kill Muslims, including a video recording of his witness to these experiments."

Avery paused again, making eye contact with each of the eight justices. It was now or never. "Major Vance received his orders directly from the president of the United States."

The ripple of gasps crashed around her, but Avery refused to stop. The white light switched abruptly to red, and the microphone lost power. So she pitched her voice louder to reach every section of the room: "I have memos and financial records proving the United States conspired to conduct research not allowed by American law. I also have sworn affidavits attesting to the authenticity of these documents from Dr. Indira Srinivasan and Mr. Nigel Cooper. Lastly, I have documentary evidence of the experiments performed."

The acoustics carried her accusations to the rafters of the vaulted ceiling. The clerk and a dozen reporters would record every word, even the ones later stricken. Above demands from the solicitor general and furious threats from Justice Estrada, she persevered. "This president should not be allowed to threaten any citizen into action to hide his crimes. If he can pervert his power to threaten Justice Wynn, what is to stop him from doing the same to you?"

For the first time since leaving the district court, Chief Roseborough reached for the ceremonial gavel at her elbow. "Order!"

Avery's red light blinked furiously, and members of the Secret Service began moving toward the lectern. At the Chief's signal, a U.S. marshal blocked their passage. The thud of the gavel finally penetrated the din.

The Chief gave Avery a long, narrow look, one captured for posterity by a sketch artist employed by the *Post.* Later, a close observer would note the distant glimmer of pride. "Ms. Keene, you are out of order. Your time has elapsed. Please be seated." She turned to the clerk. "The case is submitted. President Stokes, Mr. Ralston, Ms. Keene, I will see you in my chambers. Dr. Srinivasan and Mr. Cooper, you come along as well. Marshal, I no longer see Major Vance in the Court. Please locate him immediately."

"This hearing is a farce," President Stokes exploded as soon as the door shut behind them. He'd been summoned to the principal's office—a president of the United States. This would not stand. But even as he sputtered, enraged, he understood the gravity of Ms. Keene's play. Whether the accusations were believed or not, his dreams of reelection had been shattered. Lasker-Bauer, indeed. The canny devil Wynn had tricked him. Wynn was one of the bishops that would die.

But he would not be denied his revenge. "I call your judgment into question, Roseborough. Permitting this tripe in the U.S. Supreme Court. The Senate will certainly be investigating your fitness to serve."

"That is your prerogative, Mr. President," she responded disinterestedly. "Are you denying Ms. Keene's accusations?"

"I won't dignify them with a response." He inclined his head imperiously. The training from too many lawyers had taught him the drill.

The solicitor general stepped forward, astonishment shifting into damage control. Whatever the son of a bitch had done, exposing his crimes in open court had to break some law, even if he could not name it offhand. "If I may, Madam Chief, we should have the Secret Service and the FBI in here now. Ms. Keene should be detained until we have reviewed this information. And I recommend an investigation into her reckless conduct. If she has participated in obstruction of justice, action should be taken."

"I agree." Chief Roseborough depressed the button that summoned the Court police, ignoring Avery's intake of breath.

Avery brandished the authenticated documents and the drive. "Chief, I have proof."

"Which you should have turned over to the proper authorities." Chief Roseborough gave her a steady look. "If what you say is true, you should know better, Avery. The Court isn't a playground."

Before Avery could protest, the door opened behind her. The occupants of the chamber turned as five burly men entered, gunmetal glinting dully at their hips. Agent Lee waited behind them with more agents at the ready.

The Speaker and the majority leader had squeezed behind them, nearly out of sight. On his phone, the majority leader hastily typed out a message to his chief of staff. Senate hearings into the Tigris Project and the possible impeachment of President Brandon Stokes would commence tomorrow. Subpoenas would be drafted and start circulating within hours.

His press conference announcing the extraordinary event would convene on the steps of Capitol Hill in forty-five minutes, which would allow sound trucks time to set up and secure satellite feeds. A camera would be positioned behind him, showing his vantage point of a fallen White House. Thoughts of a late entry into the race for president fleetingly crossed his mind until he realized that a scandal this salacious would earn him a supermajority and nearly unfettered power. LBJ's legacy as master of the Senate would become a footnote if he played his cards right.

His companion, the Speaker of the House, not to be outdone, had already convened the Democratic members of the House Committee on Intelligence for a meeting in his office in thirty minutes. Congressional aides had been instructed to locate their members and have them in a caucus meeting in an hour and a half. By the close of business, his members would be scattered across the major networks and hurried into recording studios to tape the commercials that would simultaneously scare the bejesus out of every American citizen and secure the millions to fill the DCCC coffers for the coming elections.

Because he understood the vagaries of the human condition, he also scheduled a clandestine meeting with the investigator he'd hired to do opposition research on the minority leader of the House. The likely surrogate for a fallen Stokes, the telegenic young woman who had breached her party's power structure and taken on the mantle, would be a formidable opponent in the autumn elections. Representative Carolyn Hall had been a pilot in the Air Force and had faced court-martial for revealing misconduct in her squadron. She'd emerged a folk hero, and if she played her cards right, she could parlay this moment into her political triumph and challenge Stokes for the presidency.

Filling the sudden silence, President Stokes pointed at an FBI agent and ordered, "Place Ms. Keene under arrest."

One of the armed men asked, "Sir?"

"I am the commander in chief. Arrest her!" He pointed at Avery and wished, for the first time, that he had gone to law school.

Agent Lee shouldered his way forward to the chief justice's desk. "Chief Roseborough, I've just spoken with the director. We've been instructed to detain Ms. Keene. And President Stokes, I also have a warrant for your arrest."

"On what grounds?" Stokes growled.

"We received evidence that you attempted to kill Justice Wynn. A pill bottle containing trace amounts of an unknown chemical was turned over to my office. This chemical was matched to the only other sample we've seen in this country—Justice Wynn's blood tests. On my orders, the FBI crime lab ran the prints on the bottle, and there are two sets.

His and yours. I don't know how you managed it, but right now, you are under arrest for attempted murder."

"I did not touch him or any pill bottle!" In a flash, the strange moment with Howard Wynn at the graduation replayed in Stokes's mind. Wynn had shaken his hand awkwardly and grinned, then leaned toward him and whispered, "Checkmate, Stokes." *Goddamn it.*

Across the room, an officer approached Avery and clasped her elbow. "Please come with me," he said politely.

She stared at him but said nothing. All of this, and she was being perp-walked out of the Chief's chambers.

He escorted her toward the door, past where another pair of agents negotiated in muffled tones with the president. Avery stopped, paces away from the president, where Agent Lee had joined him.

"A second, please," she asked quietly.

Agent Lee nodded and signaled for the agents to step back. When only Lee and Stokes could hear her, she asked, "Where's Dr. Ramji? Dr. Papaleo?"

"I don't know." A bitter smile showcased the president's perfect teeth, and he looked at Agent Lee, who remained within earshot. "A moment alone with Ms. Keene, if you will?"

Agent Lee gave Avery a warning look. At her nod, he shifted away. When they were by themselves, President Stokes said, "You hurt America today, young lady. Destroyed our chance to save lives."

"You're a murderer," Avery said unflinchingly. "I know it, and so will everyone else."

"I am a patriot. Other presidents have tried and failed because their vision got clouded by rules. They refused to leverage the power of command. I didn't." He gave her another grating smile. "But we both know I will not serve a day in prison. Despite your sleuthing and Wynn's cheap trick with the pill bottle, what you've done here today is no more than judiciary theater. You have no proof."

"Whose idea was it to target DNA?" Avery came closer until less than a step separated them. "Who thought about using biogenetics?"

"If there is any truth to your accusations, I deny any knowledge," Stokes said. He linked his fingers behind himself, as he did when preparing a speech. Calculating. He hadn't gone to law school, but Brandon Stokes understood the fine art of setting the stage. Before lawyers and judges got involved, before anyone left this room and headed for microphones or clandestine meetings, he would dictate the narrative for this next stage. Wynn wasn't the only one who understood chess strategy. Stokes had been checkmated in the first game, but a new one had started. A traditionalist, he appreciated the classics.

Agent Lee appeared again by Avery's side.

Stokes squared his shoulders but allowed his eyes to show a glimmer of fear. "As for Ms. Keene's accusations, I had no knowledge of this Tigris Project until very recently. Major Vance created this gruesome endeavor on his own. Based on his years of military service and our close friendship, I thought it was proper to allow him to serve as my liaison, and I trusted him. To advise me on the ways we could defend our country against the constant threat of terrorism."

"He did this without your knowledge?" Agent Lee asked disbelievingly. "I saw the transfers, sir. You had to have known."

"Congress should have," President Stokes countered, glaring at the vultures staring at him in doubt. "But Congress is afraid to ask about DHS funding. Billions of dollars allocated to acronyms they'll never decipher. As long as we come begging and give them treats to share with their constituents. When I discovered his activity, I tried to force him out, but he used the lives of several innocent Americans as leverage— including Justice Wynn. Knowing that, knowing what he had done and what he was capable of, I didn't dare expose him. I was in the process of executing a plan to stop him."

"You were afraid of Vance?"

"No one is impervious to harm. He threatened to tie me to the conspiracy."

Avery shook her head. "You're lying. You knew exactly what he was doing. Both of you did this. Hundreds died because of you. And millions more remain at risk because of what the United States funded—a weapon of genocide against Muslims."

The blood rose in Stokes's face, and his hard-fought control showed signs of cracking. "I didn't kill anyone," he growled. "Vance did. And from what I was told, they were disposable. Terrorists. Prisoners." He locked eyes with her. "Like drug addicts, Ms. Keene, no one would care if they lived or died."

The sharp crack of her knuckles against his nose echoed throughout the chamber. Avery stood her ground, ready for reprisal. "I'll see you in prison."

Hours later, the FBI brought her back to the Court, her hand wrapped, her evidence in custody, and her statement recorded for posterity. Jared, Ling, and Noah had each taken their turns, separated from one another on Agent Lee's orders.

Awaiting her fate, she turned on the television. Scott Curlee had become the lead anchor for PoliticsNOW, his unceasing coverage bolstered by tidbits of information no other reporter had managed to capture. Curlee was in the middle of breaking down the GenWorks story. According to his sources, Indira and Nigel would be guests of the federal government for the foreseeable future, and the Indian government was speculating about the nationalization of Advar. The closing bell on Wall Street apparently did not mind the potential, as the stock price of GenWorks soared on rumors of biotechnology that could cure a host of genetic maladies.

Speculation about the weaponization of gene therapy had added a lift, and defense contractors were salivating. Indira looked unfazed in the images of her exiting the Supreme Court, with a suitably somber yet eerily pleased Nigel Cooper gallantly clasping her elbow. Curlee had it on good information that nothing short of a court mandate would stop the merger of GenWorks and Advar now.

Unable to stomach his voice any longer, Avery channel-surfed and found the falsely moderate station, whose anchor reported on whispers that President Stokes's personal attorney had already begun to negotiate with the attorney general for a deal. The colorful graphics on the screen competed for viewers' attention: *Downfall of President . . . Genocide in the White House . . .*

Whether the claims stuck, the reporter explained, would be irrelevant. Impeachment hearings would begin in less than a week, and the live telecast would be carried, uninterrupted, on every media feed.

Avery listened as the floating heads on the conservative network debated whether she would lose her license to practice law and be disbarred. An international manhunt had been declared for Major Will

Vance, who, sources reported, was the real architect of the debacle. One commentator brazenly offered a tentative defense of the Tigris Project, warning that until all the evidence was out, America should withhold judgment. A slightly appalled counterpart tried to change the subject, musing that it would be decades before Stokes or Vance came to justice.

Avery slumped over her desk in Justice Wynn's chambers, her head cradled in her arms. When she'd asked about Major Vance, the agent on duty had told her that by the time he'd gotten word to the Secret Service to detain him, the ex-soldier had slipped out of the courtroom and vanished.

Ling had offered to check on Rita at the treatment center, while Jared and Noah trekked over to the Hoover Building to fill in more of the blanks for Agent Lee. In the Justices' Conference Room, with its blue leather seats and paneled walls, the justices deliberated on her complaint and the fate of their comrade.

The dimly lit office matched Avery's mood. She'd toppled a president, but her mentor still lay inert to the world.

"You shouldn't be alone."

Avery's head shot up, her throat working toward a scream. One that died when she saw the gun in Major Vance's grip. "Are you going to kill me?"

Vance contemplated the shadowed eyes, the tousled hair. He set a duffel bag on a small table just inside the office. "You set me up."

"You murdered innocent people."

He came inside and gently shut the door. "How long had you known about the bugs in your apartment?"

"Awhile."

"And who told you about Hygeia?"

"Betty." She inched her hand along the desk toward the phone. Willing her voice to stay level, she continued, "Before you killed her." Her fingers slid farther along the desk.

"Touch the phone, and I will kill you immediately, Ms. Keene." He waved the gun at her, rummaged through the bag, and threw a zip tie onto the desk. "Bind your right hand to the chair, please." When she complied, he crossed to her and secured the other to the desk's center compartment.

Terrified, tied, yet oddly calm, Avery waited until he moved back to the door. "Why are you here? Everyone thinks you escaped after oral arguments."

"Unfinished business. And it's easier to hide in plain sight. Basic rule of warfare and covert operations." He leaned against a bookcase near the door. "I understand the president is laying the responsibility for this squarely on my shoulders."

"He says you blackmailed him about Hygeia and ran the project without his knowledge."

"What do you think?"

"That it was your idea, and he loved it."

He was silent for a moment. "You and I both know that Stokes had nothing to do with Justice Wynn's coma. How did you do that?"

"I did nothing. But the president should be careful who he shakes hands with. Especially in public."

"The graduation?"

Avery shrugged, but Vance gave an appreciative nod. "Crafty bastard. He had something on his hand to transfer the prints to the bottle. Unexpected. And impressive. But Stokes will find a way to wriggle out of it."

"By claiming Justice Wynn set him up?"

"He'll try."

"He'll fail. Justice Wynn is a brilliant man—and you and President Stokes underestimated him."

"Which is why I owe you an apology."

"For kidnapping my mother?"

"For that too, then." He inclined his head, his gaze thoughtful. "You protected Wynn."

"Of course."

"I initially assumed that he picked you because you were sleeping with him."

"I wouldn't do that."

"I know. You're loyal, Ms. Keene. A rare trait." He listened for noises beyond the door. "Stokes likes to fashion himself a patriot."

"He's not." Feeling brave, Avery added, "And neither are you. You're monsters."

"It was a noble joint operation." The sigh was almost too low to reach her ears. "Human life is a casualty of war, Ms. Keene. And make no mistake, we are at war."

"Not with prisoners from India or a nurse for an old man," she argued before she could stop herself. "Don't delude yourself, Major Vance. Killing Nurse Lewis and Dr. Papaleo and diverting taxpayer dollars to a proxy to prepare for genocide are not acts of war. They are acts of cowardice."

"Tigris is a weapon, and we have enemies who will not hesitate to use it. They must be destroyed."

"You can't believe that. What happened to you?"

"Don't be naïve," he snapped. "I did what patriots do. I served my country. And when it was necessary, I protected her against all enemies, foreign and domestic."

"None of those people you killed were your enemies. Besides, it doesn't matter why you did it. It's over now."

He slipped his free hand into his pocket. "Surely you're not that innocent, Avery. Technology like Tigris has more than one source. More than one progenitor. And we would not have trusted a sole source contractor."

"I know there are others." She thought about the portfolio of companies. "Who else? I already know about Qian Ku."

"I assume Dr. Ramji told you about the others when he gave you his research."

"No, he didn't." She thought of Ani's confession and his refusal to turn himself in to the authorities. "Dr. Ramji tried to stop you."

"Perhaps. You should know that Dr. Ramji consulted with colleagues who also received funding." Vance moved toward the desk. "His virus is one approach. One of many if genes are your target. His innovation was the use of viral vectors. Pathogens are another track we were eager to explore." He did not blink or shift his eyes from her, the message clear. "You have no idea what we're facing as a nation. I do."

"Are you saying there are other scientists doing similar work?"

"I am suggesting that scientific curiosity may get the better of humanity yet again. As it always has. Oppenheimer wasn't a pioneer. He was just another scientist afraid to stop thinking." He considered her for a long, silent moment. Took in the steady green eyes trying admirably to hide their terror. The wide, mobile mouth that trembled despite the effort to hold still. "However, as for your accusations in court, you are correct. I broke domestic laws. That's unforgivable."

"Will you turn yourself in?"

"Not yet." He dropped a thumb drive onto the desk. "But I dislike being betrayed. I will help you hold Stokes accountable for at least one of his deeds. I recorded then–vice president Stokes injecting President Cadres with an air embolism. . . . It was the moment he seized power."

Aghast, Avery took a minute to speak. "He murdered President Cadres?"

Vance maintained eye contact, nodding.

"And you recorded him?"

"I worked for Homeland Security, Avery. We watch everything. Usually, though, no one watches us." He moved suddenly and placed a hand on the back of her chair, caging her. But the muzzle of the gun never wavered. "Dr. Papaleo's remains are in a construction site near the airport. You won't find much of her. Her husband's body is in the trunk of his car at an abandoned lot on Wisconsin."

She simply stared at him.

Vance placed the gun on the far corner of the desk and reached into his bag. He uncapped a small bottle and poured several clear drops of liquid onto a gauze pad.

"What are you doing?" Avery asked, straining at the zip ties on her wrists.

"I'd prefer not to hit you again. But I can't be careless."

"I won't scream."

"You won't be able to." With blinding speed he moved behind Avery and cupped her head. The gauze came down forcefully over her nose and mouth.

"I'll be sure someone looks for you by morning. Goodbye, Ms. Keene."

FIFTY-THREE

Avery, wake up."

The insistent tone penetrated the fog of her brain. "Major Vance?"

"Avery, look at me."

With effort, Avery blinked away the haze and found herself staring at the Chief. "Ma'am?"

"What happened to you?" The petite woman squatted next to her. "I came to your office looking for you, and your door was closed. I'd thought you'd gone, but the light was still on."

"Major Vance," Avery repeated groggily, and her hand automatically closed over the thumb drive. "He was here."

"In this office?" The Chief popped up and reached for the phone. "How long ago?"

Rubbing at her pounding temples, she replied, "What time is it?"

"A little after six. Conference ran rather long. What did Vance do to you?"

Avery's head began to clear. "He put something over my face, and I blacked out."

"Are you feeling okay? Should I call for a paramedic?"

"I'm fine," she said, shaking her head.

Frowning, the Chief hesitated, then relented. "Come with me—I'll make you comfortable in my office. There are people waiting to see you."

She hooked Avery's elbow and guided the shaky younger woman to her feet. "Good news, by the way. We granted your motion to void the letter of resignation."

"Really?"

"Yes." She checked the corridor. "There's another one, isn't there?"

"A real one, yes." Avery stopped. "How did you know?"

"I've read Howard's opinions too. I assume he has a real, authentic one hidden somewhere?"

"I have it, and I'll use it when the time is right."

"When will that be?"

"If his coma truly is irreversible. Dr. Ramji and Dr. Srinivasan hinted that we may be able to wake him, but it's too soon to know if the research is promising."

"I'm so glad to hear there's hope," the Chief said.

Avery made her way mincingly through the corridors, with the Chief's hand steadying her at her elbow. Gary Stewart waited inside, along with Jared, Noah, and Ling. Her mother sat on the sofa. Agent Lee stood in the corner he'd occupied at their first meeting.

"Momma? What are you doing here?" She shot a worried look at Ling. "She's supposed to be in treatment."

"Special dispensation. I'm taking her back in a little while," Ling explained. Seeing the foggy look in Avery's eyes, she quickly crossed over to her. "What happened to you?"

"Major Vance paid me a visit," she grumbled. "Then he knocked me out. Again."

Seeing Agent Lee, she took out the drive Vance had given her and dropped it into his hand. "He said to tell you there's evidence of Stokes killing President Cadres on this. More than enough to defeat any plea bargain."

Lee's eyes went wide, and he secured the drive in his hand. He guided Avery to one of the upholstered wing chairs and eased her down to sit. "I'll give it to the attorney general."

"You told her about the stay?" Gary inquired from the leather sofa. "I'm doing a press release in the morning. By seven a.m. tomorrow, you'll be one of the youngest attorneys to successfully argue before the Court. Oughta get yourself a good PR agent."

"For what?" She looked at the lovely appointments in the Chief's private chambers and realized her time at the Court had reached its end. "I don't have a job."

"I doubt that will be a problem," Noah smirked from beside her mother. "Lawyers are shallow creatures. I'm sure my firm will hire you for celebrity alone. Add the fact that you actually know a little law, and you'll have the firms beating down your door—"

The Chief interrupted: "Unless you'd rather come back to the Court to serve as my head clerk—before you embark upon your luminous career, Ms. Keene."

Avery smiled at the Chief. "I guess first I should apologize for making a mockery of your court."

"Howard would be proud." The Chief nodded to Agent Lee. "I assume you'll provide security for them all until Vance is found."

"He won't be." Avery spoke with absolute certainty. For an instant, she thought of telling them about what he'd told her, but caution held her tongue. She needed time to process and figure out what to do. But her next step was crystal clear. "I just want to go home."

"I concur," announced the Chief. "Agent Lee, you're up."

The motley band all got to their feet, the fatigue and climax of the week rushing in on waves of exhaustion. They headed for the door, Rita reaching out to catch her daughter's hand. "I'm proud of you, Avery."

"Thanks, Momma," she said softly, and soon found herself wrapped in a tight embrace. One that did not smell of liquor. "Keep taking care of yourself."

"I'll try, baby." Neither of them expected more. Rita stepped through the doorway, followed by Noah.

Avery reached out and caught Noah's hand. "You're a fantastic lawyer. Thank you for representing me."

"You're the most exciting client I've ever had." Noah leaned in and hugged her. "Congratulations, Avery. It's been my honor."

As Noah stepped out, he gallantly offered his arm to Rita, earning a coy smile. Ling laughed at the gesture and wrapped Avery in a long hug. "I was so proud of you today. . . . I didn't realize how enormous that brain of yours really is."

Avery chuckled, resting her forehead against Ling's. "Without you, I wouldn't have had a chance. I'm glad you're my best friend."

"Ditto." She squeezed her once more. "Speaking of which, let me catch up with Noah. I've got to get your mother back to the hospital."

Agent Lee made his way past. "I'll debrief you further tomorrow, okay?" He gave Avery a gentle chuck on the chin. "Nice moves,
counselor."

"Thank you, sir. For everything."

Agent Lee nodded and exited the office.

"Avery. Jared." The Chief stood behind her desk. "A moment, if you
will."

Jared reached for Avery and took her hand in his. They approached
the Chief and stopped at the desk's edge. "Yes?"

The Chief slid open a drawer and removed a folder. "This information is embargoed until we release it, understood?" She laid the folder
on the surface and walked to the door. "Justice Bringman is truly a
libertarian. Read quickly."

With trembling fingers, Avery flipped open the manila cover and
read the key opening lines of the opinion.

Avery stood with Jared at Justice Wynn's bedside. Machines hissed out
air and beeped with the steady progress of deterioration. She clasped the
justice's still, pale hand as she recited the decision from memory.

"Chief Justice Roseborough delivered the opinion of the Court. Petitioner's claim that the respondent unfairly applied the Exon-Florio Act
to the proposed merger of GenWorks, Incorporated, and Advar, Ltd.,
an Indian corporation, which shall be the surviving entity. Specifically,
the petitioners allege that the respondent's claim of a national threat is
spurious and does not meet a threshold test for applicability. Respondent denies, asserting that presidential use of the Act should be given
virtually unfettered latitude. The Court of Appeals rejected the petitioner's claim, and we granted certiorari to review its holding that the
Exon-Florio Act could be rejected."

Her eyes fell to his inert form, and tears welled as she whispered aloud:
"We deny the lower court's ruling and rule in favor of the petitioner.

"You did it, Justice Wynn. You won."

She thought of the true resignation hidden in her apartment. She
and Jared had discussed it, and they'd decided that it would hold for a
few more months. At least until after the political conventions and the

elections. Until after she'd found a job. A deadlocked court wasn't the worst calamity to befall America.

Maybe GenWorks and Advar would be in need of in-house counsel once the SEC, FDA, and Homeland Security finished scouring their deal sometime in the next millennium. Yet Avery had little doubt that a new company would find its way into existence in no time at all.

"I would not be mourning him today." Repeating the phrase from Voltaire, Jared put his arm around Avery and pulled her close. "You gave him this. Gave me him."

"Your father wanted to save his family and save his country. I think he's always been torn, sacrificing his family for his version of patriotism. For once, he found a way to do it all. To expose the corruption, preserve the science, save you, and protect America. Convoluted and complicated strategy, just like Justice Wynn, but ultimately, it worked."

"It wouldn't have if you didn't share just a little bit of his mad genius."

"Hmm. The Court made the decision, and he put it all in motion," she demurred, wiping at the damp at her cheeks. She reminded Jared wryly, "I'm just a law clerk."

ACKNOWLEDGMENTS

While Justice Sleeps began with a conversation with the brilliant jurist Teresa Wynn Roseborough. So indebted am I that two of the key characters bear her name. As a lawyer, I am pretty good at research, but no amount of reading can substitute for lived experience. Thus, I owe a debt to the real legal mastermind of the family, my sister and constant editor, Judge Leslie Abrams Gardner, who helped me understand the life of a clerk and hew as closely to reality as fiction allows. The role of science in this novel also demanded a keen eye and a fair approximation of the possible. For that, I made up what I could and then leveraged the epidemiological cleverness of my sister Dr. Jeanine Abrams McLean, to scare and amaze. For pacing, plausibility, and sheer readability, I owe gratitude to my brothers, Richard Abrams and Walter Abrams, who pored over drafts, nixed scenes, and asked the right questions to keep the story going. My sister Dr. Andrea Abrams stayed alert for gut checks and tangled threads. And my parents, the Reverends Robert and Carolyn Abrams, who raised us to do whatever we could imagine (and saved me a fortune in research assistance).

Once the novel had form, I turned to friends as my second readers, ones who liked me enough to tell me the truth. Deepest gratitude to Brandon Evans, Rebecca DeHart, Camille Johnson, Wanda Mosley, and Mirtha Estrada Oliveros for reading the earliest drafts and helping me refine the narrative and not press delete when no one bought it.

The journey from completion to publication is often tortured, so I must acknowledge my first agent, Marc Gerald, and his assistant, Sarah Stephens, who helped me shape the next round of revisions. My team at UTA, who heard me describe the novel in passing and demanded I give it more than short shrift. I am truly grateful to Kellen Alberstone, Alyssa Lanz, Lucinda Moorhead, Albert Lee, and Jason Richman for their encouragement, and effusive gratitude to Darnell Strom, who patiently waited for me to see more for my future.

While Justice Sleeps would not be out in the world without the talents of my agent and friend, Linda Loewenthal, who has represented not only my interests but my dreams. And without Jason Kaufman of Doubleday, who polished, questioned, scribbled perfect notes, and delighted in the margins, I would not be so proud of the final story that inhabits these pages. My thanks also to the copyeditors, graphic designers, art editors, marketing team, and countless others who played a role.

This is an incomplete list of those who brought this twelve-year journey to its critical arc—a novel that I really had fun conceiving, writing, rewriting, and reading. For anyone who expected to see their name here, please assume you are written in using Justice Wynn's disappearing script. To all, I hope you've enjoyed Avery's debut and those who helped her discover the truth and a little bit more.

ABOUT THE AUTHOR

Stacey Abrams is the two-time *New York Times* bestselling author of *Our Time Is Now* and *Lead from the Outside*. She served eleven years in the Georgia House of Representatives, seven as Minority Leader, and became the 2018 Democratic nominee for governor of Georgia, where she won more votes than any other Democrat in the state's history. She is the founder of Fair Fight, Fair Count, and the Southern Economic Advancement Project—organizations devoted to voting rights and tackling social issues at the state, national, and international levels. Her work played a pivotal role in the 2020 elections for the U.S. presidency and control of the U.S. Senate.